P9-CQS-808

Joshua Colter—He was ten years old when he survived a bloody Indian massacre—and set off on a journey of survival in a wild land.

Alphus Colter—He came to North Carolina to build a home, until wanderlust drove him to the land over the mountains, where he met a wild boy named Joshua whom he raised as his own.

John Hawk—A son of the Overhill Cherokees, John Hawk guarded his friendship with Joshua Colter—until the spirit of war split them apart.

Christiana Cox—She was a strong pioneer woman, a survivor of massacre and degradation. To Joshua she gave the fierce love of a second mother, and a skill which would serve him as well as those of hunter and trader.

Jack Byrum—Joshua's natural father made his livelihood cheating the Indians in trade, and cut a bloody trail from Charles Town to the hills of Tennessee.

Gabriel Colter—He was more suited to a soft city life than the ways of a fighting man. Unable to accept Joshua as his brother, he made him into his bitterest enemy.

The Little Carpenter—The Cherokee leader had the respect of his own people and the British. But the peace he made could not hold up to a storm of treachery and anger.

Israel Coffman—A man of God who found a deeper faith on the frontier, he stood against the forces of greed and injustice.

Tilly Hampton—She survived a senseless act of frontier violence, but it was her own private demons that tore her from Joshua Colter's side.

Darcy Fiske—Caught between two feuding brothers, she chose her own path. And when the Cherokees attacked Fort Caswell, she was on her own.

Peter Haverly—This ambitious empire-builder founded an outpost on the new frontier, and then entered in a treacherous pact with the British.

Hester Byrum—A woman fragile in body and spirit, Joshua's mother's life was slowly drained from her by a wild land and a harsh husband. Yet in death she brought forth a life to which Joshua would be bound with ties of love and honor.

THE

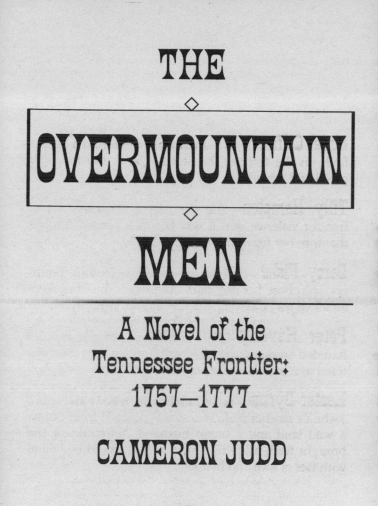

OVERMOUNTAIN

MEN

A Novel of the Tennessee Frontier: 1757–1777

CAMERON JUDD

DOMAIN™

BANTAM BOOKS
NEW YORK · TORONTO · LONDON · SYDNEY · AUCKLAND

THE OVERMOUNTAIN MEN
A Bantam Domain Book / August 1991

*DOMAIN and the portrayal of a boxed "d" are trademarks of
Bantam Books, a division of Bantam Doubleday Dell
Publishing Group, Inc.*

*All rights reserved.
Copyright © 1991 by Cameron Judd.
Cover art copyright © 1991 by Len Laager.*

*No part of this book may be reproduced or transmitted in any
form or by any means, electronic or mechanical, including
photocopying, recording, or by any information storage and
retrieval system, without permission in writing from the
publisher.
For information address: Bantam Books.*

ISBN 0-553-29081-9

Published simultaneously in the United States and Canada

*Bantam Books are published by Bantam Books, a division of
Bantam Doubleday Dell Publishing Group, Inc. Its trademark,
consisting of the words "Bantam Books" and the portrayal of a
rooster, is Registered in U.S. Patent and Trademark Office and
in other countries. Marca Registrada. Bantam Books, 666 Fifth
Avenue, New York, New York 10103.*

PRINTED IN THE UNITED STATES OF AMERICA

OPM   0 9 8 7 6 5 4 3 2 1

To Rhonda,
who became my wife
"way down yonder in
the Cumberland Gap"

THE

OVERMOUNTAIN

MEN

PROLOGUE

Joshua Byrum knelt where slanting rays of morning sun, piercing through the open cabin door, touched the dirt floor of the house of Awahili of Tikwalitsi. Before him lay a naked, sweat-drenched Cherokee boy swaddled in trade blankets, and in the boy's left hand was a wing feather of a hawk.

In Awahili's house this breezy Sunday morning, October, 19, 1760, the smell of illness was almost as strong as that of the heavy woodsmoke rising toward the roof-hole from the dying central fire. Joshua had wrinkled his nose at the sickly stench the moment he ducked inside the door. Now he looked around the cabin, letting his eyes recover from the brilliant autumn sun and adjust to the dimmer interior light. He squeezed the crude rawhide grip of his flint knife tightly, swallowed with a sandy throat, and wondered if he would have either the opportunity or the courage to do what he had come to do.

1

At the moment, all was relatively quiet in the Cherokee village of Tikwalitsi. The pervading stillness was broken only by barking dogs, windborne voices, rustling trees, and the steady, distant thump of a squaw's wood pestle in a corn mortar hollowed from a hickory log. Ten-year-old Joshua had sneaked through the town's mix of log summer houses, earth-covered winter hothouses, corn-cribs, food shelters, and gardens filled with dead vines and brown stalks, and settled in a hidden place to watch the house of Awahili, known to the white men as the Bloody Eagle of Tikwalitsi. Only when he saw the warrior's wife leave to gather firewood by the river did he go to the cabin and enter.

No one had seen him, and he had not expected that anyone would. Joshua was proudly aware of his inborn ability to travel silently and unseen, and on this, his chosen day of vengeance, the skill had served him well.

But now he was bewildered. He had heard talk of sickness in the house of Bloody Eagle, and it had been his understanding that it was the warrior himself who was ill. Apparently that was not true, for Bloody Eagle was not here. Joshua wondered if the warrior might be in his winter house, trying to sweat away his illness, but a glance outside revealed no smoke rising from the conical winter house. Obviously it was this boy, not Bloody Eagle himself, who was ill, and Joshua had simply misunderstood.

Joshua looked closely at the sleeping Indian's face. The youth's thick hair and smooth brow were sodden. Despite his dark, almost olive skin, the Cherokee looked wan and wasted, and each breath obviously required effort. He trembled slightly as he slept, the tremors evident in the shaking of the hawk's feather held against his chest. Joshua wondered if the feather had medical or spiritual significance, for he knew the Cherokees' respect for the great Tlanuwas. Those mighty hawks of legend, the storytellers said, had destroyed the serpentine water-dwelling Uktena, a fearsome creature in which even the white traders firmly believed. Maybe the feather made reference to them for some reason—or maybe it had simply blown in the door, and the sick boy had picked it up idly or unconsciously in his writhings.

Joshua felt an unexpected surge of pity and was displeased. Over these past many weeks he had striven to erase such soft feelings. If he yielded to them, he feared, they would render him unable to do the grim task he felt his duty, the task he had come here to do. But Joshua's pity for the boy, whom he now recognized as the orphaned nephew of Bloody Eagle, the only son of the pox-scarred warrior's sister, would not subside. Joshua grew angry with himself.

That a kinsman of Bloody Eagle, of all men, should so affect him was intolerable. Joshua had much cause to hate Bloody Eagle. That warrior, in conjunction with the great chief Oconostota, had been a main instigator of the recent long siege of Fort Loudoun. Because of that siege, Joshua had suffered much and lost much, and he would not forget or forgive it.

Joshua turned to see the familiar scalp lock that hung on a post outside Bloody Eagle's door and let the dried and painted clump of flesh and windblown hair restir his hatred. He looked down at the knife he had secretly chipped out over the past month from a long shard of flint and mentally repeated the vow he had made a few weeks before on a bloody field as a jubilant Bloody Eagle tauntingly slapped in his face that same gruesome scalp that now stirred in the wind outside. He had sworn that he would slay and scalp Bloody Eagle, even at the cost of his own life. Since then, he had repeated the vow to himself until he lost all doubt he could fulfill it.

Now, though, Joshua was not so confident. Bloody Eagle's unexpected absence threw matters out of balance. If I'm wise, Joshua thought, I will leave and await another opportunity. The idea seemed temptingly sensible, yet Joshua was reluctant to follow it. It had taken too long to build up his courage to make even this attempt; he doubted he would be able to do so again.

Then a new possibility suddenly came to mind. He could achieve his vengeance, even with Bloody Eagle absent. After all, would not the best revenge be to slay the son of the warrior's sister, the youth who under Cherokee practice was the responsibility chiefly of Bloody Eagle, as maternal uncle? The thought made Joshua's heart race. Fighting away his lingering sense of pity, he lifted the stone blade high, holding it in both hands. For several moments he was gripped by a strange paralysis and could not move or breathe, but with a great forcing of his will, he finally brought down the knife.

At the last second, he faltered, averting the blade to the side. The flint blade stuck into the dirt floor and snapped at the center. At the same time, the long-strained wall shoring up Joshua's emotions also broke, and against his will he began to cry. Now he did not feel like the brave and vengeful man he had wanted to be but like the frightened captive child he truly was. The idea of more revenge and violence no longer held any appeal. He had seen more than enough of both these past months.

Ashamed of his crying, Joshua quickly dried his tears on the sleeve of his homespun shirt. Picking up the pieces of his knife, he tucked them inside the pocket formed by the shirt where it draped over the cloth sash around his thin waist. When he looked again at the Indian boy, he was surprised to see the sunken eyes tremble open and the face turn toward him. The Cherokee initially stared listlessly at Joshua, then looked afraid as he realized this was a stranger, and a white one at that.

For many moments, the two boys looked at each other in silence, each fearing the other. Finally Joshua lifted his head haughtily and tried to sound gruff and manly when he spoke. "I am Ayunini, the Swimmer," he said, slapping his right hand across his chest. "I am very brave and strong."

Joshua was proud of the Cherokee name by which Attakullakulla, whom the whites called Little Carpenter, had called him. Using it made Joshua feel more courageous, more a part of the world in which he was now forced to live.

Though his status as a prisoner in the Cherokees' world was new to him, that world itself was not. He had lived among the Overhill Cherokee for three years, since he and his mother had accompanied his father and Henry Dorey across the mountains as they delivered cannon from Fort Prince George to Fort Loudoun. Life had brought many traumatic changes since that time. Fort Loudoun had fallen, and most of its officers had been killed; the cannon had been seized and taken to the Cherokee sacred city of Chota; and Joshua and the other surviving Fort Loudoun refugees had been imprisoned in various Cherokee towns, facing the rescue by ransom, a netherworld existence as Cherokee slaves, or death.

The Indian boy's lips moved. His voice was a feverish whisper as he haltingly tried to voice his name. "Tsan . . . Tsanta . . ." He got no further.

That the young Cherokee was sick nearly to the point of death seemed evident to Joshua. Another unwanted surge of pity arose, threatening to bring the tears out of his eyes again. He could not understand his emotions or what had aroused them.

Joshua's next action was pure impulse, surprising even himself. Reaching back beneath his loose-fitting shirt, over his head he pulled a deerhide thong that had encircled his neck. On the thong hung an ancient coin with strange words engraved: *Antonius Augustus Pius, Princeps Pontifex Tertio Consule*. Of the words on the other side, only two were legible: *Aurelius Caesar*.

The coin was one of the few things that Jack Byrum had ever given his son. The trader had obtained the trinket years ago through barter with the recently deceased Cherokee leader Connecorte called Old Hop by the whites. The ancient Indian had told Byrum that the coin had been found, with others like it, beside a river to the west. Byrum had given the coin to his son in a moment of affection, and because such gestures from Byrum were rare indeed, Joshua had guarded the coin closely, finding an inexplicable reassurance and comfort in feeling its cool face lying against his chest. But now he held it up for the Cherokee boy to see, then reached across and placed it in his hands.

"For you," Joshua said in a slightly choked voice. "To

help you live." He was surprised at himself as soon as he
had done it, amazed he cared what happened to the sick
boy. But care he did.

The Cherokee clutched the coin and breathed loudly,
his eyes closing again. Joshua rose, wiped his face again
on his sleeve, and turned to go, thinking the Indian was
asleep once more. He wondered if the boy, whose mumbled name he had interpreted as Tsani, would ever remember where the coin had come from—if he lived to
consider the matter at all.

Joshua had reached the door when the boy made a
guttural sound. Looking back, Joshua saw the Indian was
trying to give him a gift in return. It was the hawk
feather, held loosely in his uplifted hand. Joshua knelt
again and accepted it. The Cherokee had presented him
the only thing he had to give, and to the already emotional Joshua, the gesture was deeply touching. "I accept
your gift," he said, trying to hide his emotions by talking
the haughty style he had heard his father use in barter-
ing with the Cherokees. "And because it is the feather of
a hawk, to me you will be Tsani Tlanuwa—John Hawk."

The Indian did not respond. His eyes closed again. For
a frightful moment, Joshua thought John Hawk had died,
but then the troubled breathing started anew. Joshua
rose again and slipped out of the cabin. Outside the door,
he paused and looked up at the scalp lock, and felt
ashamed.

Jack Byrum would surely have scorned his son for this
failure. The trader had always believed in calculated
revenge, believed in it even more strongly, if that was
possible, than the Cherokees he served and cheated.
Joshua had been raised to believe that every blow deserved one in turn. Today he had been untrue to that
belief.

He was sure that what he had done was not right. By
rights, he should have killed Bloody Eagle's sick nephew
instead of giving him a gift and name. No kinsman of
Bloody Eagle's deserved mercy. Awahili of Tikwalitsi certainly knew nothing of mercy; he was reputed to be a
heartless and cruel killer. In the Cherokee towns and

even in Fort Loudoun, Joshua had heard many tales of the pockmarked warrior's brutality toward the white race that had brought smallpox to the Ani-Yunwiya, as the Cherokees called themselves, leaving him and many others scarred for life. The Fort Loudoun soldiers had even claimed that the blood-red forehead birthmark that had given Bloody Eagle his designation among the whites was the personal mark of the devils he served. Joshua had never been sure what to make of that tale, for he had known many men, his own father included, who seemed faithful enough servants of the devil, without any physical marks to identify them.

Somewhere on the other side of Tikwalitsi, the corn mortar continued its thumping and grinding. Beyond a line of brilliantly leaved maple trees, the Tellico River splashed. Joshua set off across the town again, and as he concentrated on stealth, the October wind snatched the hawk feather from his hand and sent it flying through the air with an east-moving shower of golden and crimson leaves. He paused long enough to watch it twist out of sight, then went on.

I

THE
OVERHILL
TOWNS

1

Three years and seven months before Joshua Byrum gave the Roman coin to John Hawk, his life was still being lived far from the land of the Overhill Cherokees, and of their ways he had known nothing but what his father told him on his periodic visits home. And little enough that was; Jackson Bartholomew Byrum had no real affection for the Indians from whom he gouged his livelihood and talked only briefly of them.

Byrum's homecomings to the little clapboard house outside Charles Town, South Carolina, inevitably brought a mixture of blessing and tension to Joshua and his mother, Hester Byrum. For Hester in particular they were stressful times, for Byrum's habit was to get drunk and then make up for months without access to his wife's physical charms. Hester endured his rough, loveless molestations patiently and silently, even though she knew it was likely that Byrum was an unfaithful husband. He probably kept company with a Cherokee woman back across the mountains, the habit of many traders. She never asked him about it and would not as long as he came home with money in hand, for on that money and

11

what food she could raise she and Joshua depended for life. As long as Jack Byrum provided sustenance, Hester would ask no more of him.

And her husband's visits, though trying, were after all brief enough to be endurable. After only a few weeks, sometimes just a few days, Byrum would be gone, heading back to the wilderness beyond the mountains, trailing behind him another string of packhorses laden with cheap trade rifles, beads, blankets, ammunition, knives, cloth, mirrors, kettles, and vermilion paint. Hester would watch him go, then kneel and kiss her son. "We have money and all is well," she would say. "We are together again, alone, and that is as it should be."

But one morning Jack Byrum rode home again, and matters were different from then on.

Joshua was the first to see him return. At age seven, the boy was already showing clear evidence of a special affinity for life outdoors. From dawn until Hester called him in after dark, Joshua spent most of his time outside the clapboard cabin, exploring the creek, the fields behind the farmstead, the weed-grown picket-fencerows, and the little cave out of which the spring bubbled. From time to time when he thought of it, he would lift his eyes toward the place where the road emerged between two low hills west of the farmstead and look for the approaching form of his father. Byrum's homecomings followed no obvious schedule and could come as often as three times or as few as one time a year.

Usually Joshua saw nothing but empty road between those hills, or some local rider, wagoner, or pedestrian. On this morning of Thursday, March 19, 1757, however, Joshua saw an approaching horseman that he recognized at once, despite the distance, and a second rider as well. For a full minute he stared, then turned and ran into the house. "He's coming, Mother! And there's another man with him!"

Hester put down the smock she was stitching and without a word followed her son outside. There was no need to ask to whom "he" referred. She stood in the front yard, her arm over Joshua's shoulder, and silently watched as Byrum rode through the crumbling picket gate. Her eyes trailed up and down the hefty length of her husband, then shifted suspiciously to the hulking slump-shouldered man with him.

Byrum nodded at his wife before he dismounted. "Hester," he said. Glancing down to Joshua, he said, "Hello, boy. Getting bigger all the time."

"I know how to set a rabbit snare," Joshua said, unveiling his latest accomplishment in hopes of praise.

Byrum did not listen. Dismounting, he waved back toward the big man with him. The latter had a full black beard, the bottom of which dusted his broad chest, the top growing out of his cheeks halfway up to his eyes, making him appear masked. "This is Henry Dorcy, from North Carolina," Byrum said. "Him and me is partners together on a special job, and I've come from Fort Prince George to get you and Joshua. Henry, he came along with me for company."

"Get us? Why?" Hester asked.

Byrum led his horse to a rainwater rivulet, still filled from a dawn downpour. "I'm taking you and Joshua back with me," he said. "From now on, we'll be together. That's good, eh?"

Hester said nothing. Joshua, not sure whether to be excited or horrified by what he had just heard, looked up to his mother for guidance. She did not look back at him but stared wordlessly across at the western horizon. Henry Dorey was only now dismounting.

"It looks like another rain will blow in," she said at last. "Joshua, you help your father and Mr. Dorey see to their horses." She turned and walked back inside the house, having not yet kissed or even touched her husband.

Jack Byrum put on an expression Joshua could not read and watched her depart, then reached down distractedly to tousle his son's thick nut-brown hair. "You big enough to lead this horse into the barn, boy? Good . . . water it some more and feed it some. I'm going to go in and talk to your mother."

Joshua felt proud to have been given an important job but a little frightened to be left alone, even for a few

moments, with the stranger Henry Dorey. He watched
the big North Carolinian from the corner of his eye.
Dorey looked down at him, and the black beard parted
along the line of his mouth as he grinned. Dorey's teeth
were yellow and crooked, worn down like those of an
ancient dog.

"Think you'll like living among the bloody Cherokee,
boy?" He dropped the reins of his horse and let the
animal wander away from him to a patch of new grass
that it immediately began to crop.

Joshua mumbled a meaningless answer and led the
horse across the dirt lot toward the barn while Dorey
filled and lit a long clay pipe he had pulled from beneath
the matchcoat that draped his shoulders. When Joshua
came out of the barn, he was shocked to see that Dorey
was emptying his bladder against the side of the house.
He turned and grinned at Joshua as he did so, sending
smoke out between his ripe-corn teeth. Joshua felt a
great burst of disgust but didn't let it show. He had
learned long ago to hide his feelings when his father was
home.

"That makes a man feel better," Dorey said. "Put up
my horse too, won't you, boy?" Rehitching his French fly
trousers, Dorey walked around the front of the house.
Joshua heard him stomp the mud from his feet onto the
porch, then swing open and slam the door. Adult voices
murmured inside; Dorey laughed at something Byrum
said.

Joshua took Dorey's horse to the barn and did not come
out again for a long time, even after he had finished
tending the animal. Instead he walked to the open west
door of the barn and looked out, staring at the horizon as
his mother had, wondering what lay beyond it as he
fingered the Roman coin hanging on the cord around his
neck.

Jack Byrum took a long swallow of buttermilk and
wiped the remainders of it from his beard onto a sleeve
already thick with the residue of prior swipes. A tallow
lamp sent pale, weak light across the slab table, which

was spread with the remnants of a salt pork and hominy supper. Byrum resumed talking as Hester and Joshua listened silently and Henry Dorey picked scraps of meat from between his teeth. He had hardly spoken at all throughout the evening, but he had stared openly at Hester in a way that made Joshua feel defensive toward his mother.

"They're building a big diamond-shaped stockade and calling it Fort Loudoun, after the earl of Loudoun," Byrum said. "He's the new commander of all the British soldiers in the colonies, or some such. The Cherokees, they're happy as dogs in horsemeat to finally have a real fort there among them, and real soldiers. I'm happy about it too. Some of those red sods have been talking to the French on the sneak, trying to set up trade with them. We let that happen, and we're finished. The fort will go a long way to keep us and the Cherokees doing good friendly business.

"You'll like it there, Hester, don't you worry. The place is crawling with folks besides the Cherokees—South Carolina provincials doing most of the building and the British regulars keeping it all supervised. Unakas, the Cherokees call the white folk. A lot of the soldiers are bringing their families in, so there's other white women, plus all the Cherokee womenfolk.

"The man in charge is named Demere, Captain Raymond Demere. Regular British and a soldier all the way. He put up with a lot from the man who designed the fort—a German, name of DeBrahm. Demere called him a madman to his face one time, and he's right. Demere and him argued all the time—it got so bad that DeBrahm moved out to one of the Cherokee towns and give out his orders from there. But things are better now. DeBrahm is gone. He run off this past Christmas. The big chief Old Hop took to calling him Warrior Who Ran Away in the Night."

Joshua asked, "Is it DeBrahm who hired you to bring the cannon to the fort?"

"No, that's Demere. Hell, DeBrahm didn't even want cannon in the place! But Demere's ready to pay me and

Henry good wages to haul several in from Fort Prince George, though I don't believe he thinks we can really do it. And it's going to be a devil of a job, that's God's truth. The damned things weigh three hundred pounds and upward apiece, and there's no way to get a wagon through those mountains. But Henry and me and a string of good packhorses could move them mountains themselves if the money was good enough."

Hester spoke for the first time in an hour. "Why must you take me and Joshua with you? Why can't we stay where we are?"

Byrum's expression made it clear the question was not well taken. "You don't think a family should be together, Hester?"

"You've never thought so before now."

Byrum's face flushed so that it was evident, even in the feeble lamplight. "This is naught that we should be talking about before a guest, Hester. I'll charge you to keep your mouth shut about such matters."

Hester looked down at her plate. Joshua felt vaguely sick to his stomach.

Byrum smiled at his son, seeking to relieve the tense atmosphere. "You think you'd like to be raised among the redskins, boy?"

Joshua glanced at his mother, then nodded, fearing to do anything else. But there was more than forced agreement in his answer. The truth was that the idea of traveling across the distant mountains and away from this port-city area he had always known did have much appeal. Joshua knew little about Indians except that they were reputed to be the finest of woodsmen and hunters, and that was exactly what he hoped to be someday. To live among the Overhill Cherokees would mean exposure to their knowledge and skills, and probably, when he was older, access to their rich hunting grounds.

"See there, Hester? Joshua wants to go," Byrum said, and Hester nodded compliantly.

That night, before retiring to the barn—for he had given up his bed to Henry Dorey—Joshua found his mother alone behind the house. He crept up to her so silently that she was startled when he touched her arm.

"Jack, please—can't you allow me even a moment's peace?" She looked surprised, pleasantly, when she saw it was Joshua.

Joshua said, "Don't worry about going over the mountains, Mother. I'll be with you."

"Aye, and that's the one comfort to me," she said. "You're God's blessing in a life that's had few of them." She knelt so her face was level with Joshua's and smiled at him. "Only seven years old and already so much a little man, ready to go into the wilderness. What a brave son I have!"

"Why don't you want to go, Mother? Haven't you ever wondered what might be there?"

"I know what's there—wilderness and heathens who strip the hair from those they murder. The land across the mountains will be the death of me, if I go."

Joshua was chilled. "Don't talk so, Mother!"

Tears pooled in her eyes. "Forgive me for it, but I can talk no other way. The wilderness is a fearful place for me. I should never have married a man as drawn to it as Jack Byrum is." She stood, drying her tears, and took a deep breath. "But marry Jack Byrum I did, and go with him I shall, though I know as well as I know my own name that I shall not return. Now, be off to bed. The morning will come early."

That night Joshua lay awake a long time, thrilled at the thought of the adventure before him but afraid because of the grim way his mother had spoken. At last he went to sleep, nestling down in his blankets in the barn loft, listening to mice scampering in the straw.

After that night, Joshua seldom saw his mother shed tears about the change that had come sweeping into their lives. She became ever more resigned and quiet. Even when Jack Byrum went into Charles Town and sold the farmstead, Hester kept her emotions masked. When the family, along with Henry Dorey, rode away from their

South Carolina home for the last time, Hester did not even look back.

The journey across to Fort Prince George, built four years earlier as South Carolina's westernmost outpost, was uneventful and finally dull, despite Joshua's initial eagerness. The negative impression made upon Joshua by Henry Dorey did not mellow with time, and the boy stayed close to his mother, feeling instinctively that the ever-staring Dorey was a threat.

Arrival at Fort Prince George itself was a time of excitement and welcome respite from long and uninterrupted travel. Even Hester seemed revitalized. But Byrum and Dorey grew more somber and intense after reaching the fort, for here their real job began, and they knew far better than Hester or Joshua how difficult it would be.

Soon enough it was clear to all. Joshua found the journey to Fort Loudoun heartbreaking, for he had inherited his mother's concern for animals, and the method Byrum and Dorey contrived to carry the cannon proved brutal to the packhorses they purchased. The two traders placed the cannon atop individual packsaddles and lashed them tight with belts around the straining animals' midsections. Then they drove the horses as hard as they could along the hundred and fifty miles of narrow mountain trails that led to Fort Loudoun.

The trails were often almost impossible for the cannon-laden horses to maneuver, and on several occasions a horse would fall, its back snapping with a sickening *pop* as the heavy cannons shifted. Joshua would cry when that occurred, and Hester would comfort him as his father or Dorey shot the hopelessly injured animal and shifted the cannon to a spare horse. Then they would proceed, leaving the carcass to the carrion birds. So went the grueling six-miles-a-day journey from its beginning until its welcome end, weeks later.

Arrival at Fort Loudoun, a large palisaded enclosure that stood on an elevation south of the Little Tanisi River where it met the Tellico River, so overwhelmed Joshua that he almost forgot the rigors of the journey. The fort itself was far more elaborate than Fort Prince George, and Captain Raymond Demere, in his officer's uniform, greatly impressed Joshua. Demere enthusiastically welcomed Byrum, Dorey, and their artillery. It was one of the few moments in his life when Joshua was truly proud of his father, despite the horror he still felt at Byrum and Dorey's brutality to the horses.

The cannon had been nailed up with steel spikes and were placed that evening into a large fire to soften the spikes for drilling out. Joshua, watched by his silent mother, danced in his excitement by the fire in the center of the fort, as lively as the sparks the flames spat skyward.

Everywhere Joshua looked he saw amazing things and intriguing people. The British soldiers looked dashing in their Prussian-style uniforms of red coats marked with the facings of the Forty-second Regiment. They wore tricorn hats, pipe-clayed white breeches, and gaiters. Scores of them circled in the light of the fire, some leaning on their eleven-pound Brown Bess muskets and watching the blacksmith tend to the heating of the cannon. Others were seated or reclining on the ground, smoking or picking their teeth with twigs. But soldiers Joshua had seen earlier at Fort Prince George. The Cherokees, who came into the fort from the nearby Overhill towns, were the people who truly fascinated him.

The younger Cherokees, those Joshua's age and even several years older, were brown-skinned from head to toe and wore no clothing at all. The men wore breechcloths, some with tasseled sashes that hung down their thighs. Most also wore leggins and had chests decorated with intricate gunpowder tattoos impressed into their skin, symbolizing valor and wartime achievements. A few men wore moccasins, but most were barefoot. Several of the oldest men had ornaments of silver hanging from their earlobes, which had been stretched and cut ornamentally.

The hair of the warriors was generally absent, except for one long braid at the crown of the scalp. This was greased heavily with bear oil. "They pluck out the rest by the roots," Byrum told Joshua when he asked. "And they flinch not a bit, those sods. Pain means nothing to them."

The Cherokee women for the most part had long braids of hair rolled into wreathlike piles atop their heads, held in place with silver brooches. Many wore colored ribbons or strips of cloth plaited into their hair or streaming from it past their shoulders. They wore knee-length skirts made of softened deerskin. A few wore short calico waist-coats, apparently obtained through British trade, and some wore nothing above the waist. The younger girls were entirely without clothing, like the boys. At first Joshua stared openly at the Indians' nakedness, for he was unaccustomed to it, until Hester scolded him in a whisper and made him ashamed.

Many of the Cherokee women and older girls kept close company with soldiers, and Joshua soon realized, to the extent he was able to understand such things, that these had been taken by the soldiers as mates or concu-bines. But there were also several white women and their children about, the recently arrived families of some of the soldiers. White and Indian mixed freely within the fort's boundaries. All in all, there was a spirit of unity between the Cherokees and the soldiers palpable enough even for young Joshua to detect.

He went to his mother's side and into her ear whis-pered, "I'm glad we've come here, Mother."

Hester Byrum smiled and patted his shoulder. As the red light of the fire smoothed away the creases around Hester's eyes and mouth and erased the eternal dark circles beneath her eyes, Joshua thought that his mother was the most beautiful woman he ever had seen.

Joshua and Hester spent the first night within the fort itself, sleeping on their blankets near a rocky promontory that jutted out of the ground between the parade ground and the officers' barracks near the north palisade. The scent of the dying bonfire lay heavily within the fort, mixing with the organic stench of the trench latrine. Where Jack Byrum was neither Hester nor Joshua knew; he had vanished earlier in the evening and had not returned for them. "Be patient," Hester said. "Your father is not a man to be rushed or told what to do. When he is ready, he will come for us." Joshua knew as well as his mother that Byrum was probably passed out over a jug of rum somewhere.

Drumbeats of reveille awakened Joshua the next morning. He rose, rolled up his blanket, and climbed atop the ledge, from where he watched the colors raised over the Prince of Wales Bastion on the northeastern corner of the irregularly shaped fortification. Afterward, he and his mother shared a silent breakfast of beef jerky and parched corn left over from the journey across the mountains and watched the soldiers drill on the parade grounds.

Joshua and Hester slowly explored the fort and surrounding grounds together for more than half of the day, staying out of the way of the red-coated regulars who drilled, practiced with bayonets, stood guard at the big gates of the fort, and did the other duties of military routine. But the soldiers accounted for only a portion of the bustling activity inside Fort Loudoun. Children played near the barracks west of the parade ground, and soldiers' wives sat in the shade of the various log and clapboard structures within the fort walls and talked as they sewed, churned, and in some cases nursed infants hidden beneath discreetly placed shawls.

In early afternoon Joshua left his mother in the company of a plump, talkative soldier's wife named Christiana Cox and left for further exploration on his own.

The cannon were being emplaced atop high platforms at the fort's bastions. Joshua watched as one of the guns was rolled into place at the Duke of Cumberland Bastion on the southwest corner and looked for his father among the mix of regulars, South Carolina provincials, civilians, and Cherokees watching the work. He did not see him but did spot Captain Demere, who in the morning light looked more haggard than he had the day before. Joshua would later learn that Demere's health had declined under the strain of seeing to Fort Loudoun's completion, his only respite being that the cantankerous engineer DeBrahm was long gone.

Despite his eccentricities, DeBrahm had designed a
fort that was sound if overly ornate. With Demere's more
practical alterations, it was now an impressive fortification. Fort Loudoun's walls consisted of an ample palisade
of logs sharpened at the top and angled slightly outward
over a sloping earthwork. Loopholes for muskets were
drilled through the palisade at regular intervals.

Such features were designed to make besieging the
wall difficult and scaling it all but impossible. Even
reaching the walls would be difficult. Outside the line of
pales and beyond the earthwork was an encircling moat
about ten feet wide and four feet deep, filled with honey
locusts that formed an impenetrable barrier. The moat
was bridged to allow access to the fort's big gate.

The soldiers' barracks stood along the west palisade.
At the northwest-facing King George Bastion was a powder magazine, and nearby, an area sufficiently large to
graze livestock for food in time of siege. The much-used
parade ground was a rectangular area in the center of
the fort. The guardhouse stood near the east gate, between the Prince of Wales Bastion and the blacksmith
shop. Nearby was the well and garden area, and the
fourth bastion, called the Queen Bastion.

The blacksmith shop was bustling at the moment.
Joshua approached it. A group of Cherokees had brought
in three trade muskets for repairs; one of the Indians was
arguing forcibly with someone. Joshua moved around to
see more clearly and realized the Cherokee—who was a
full head taller than his fellows, very scarred, and marked
from long-ago smallpox—was raging at none other than
Jack Byrum. The sight frightened Joshua. The Indian
had a tomahawk on his hip. What if he became angry
enough to use it? Joshua knew little of Indians but had
heard they were violent people.

The Indian and Byrum were arguing in a mix of
English and Cherokee. Though he could not understand
much of it, Joshua made out that the dispute was over
one of the muskets, which the Indian apparently claimed
was defective. Byrum, obviously the trader who had sold
the gun in the first place, was just as vigorously alleging

that any problem was the result of carelessness or abuse by the warrior himself, whom Byrum referred to as Bloody Eagle.

The fort blacksmith stood close by, listening to the argument with a growing look of alarm. At last he stepped forward, pulled Byrum aside, and spoke to him out of earshot of the Indians. Joshua, however, was close enough to hear what was said. "Byrum, you keep your head! If Bloody Eagle takes a dislike to you, he'll make you suffer for it, and the rest of us besides, no doubt. Tell him you are his friend, that you respect him, and that I'll see his musket repaired at your expense, or I'll wrap my hammer around your head. Do you understand me?"

Byrum snorted and grew red. "I'll not pay to repair the musket of that red sod! Go to Satan's blazes, the both of you!" With that, he turned on his heel and walked away, almost knocking Joshua over in the process, yet not even noticing him. A strong rum smell trailed after Byrum.

The blacksmith returned to Bloody Eagle, who stood very straight, arms crossed over his chest, looking down a long crooked nose at the smith. "You are as powerful in persuasion as you are in war, Awahili," the blacksmith said. "The gun shall be repaired as you wish. I am proud to repair the musket of the great Bloody Eagle . . . a gift from me to you."

The warrior's expression never changed, but Joshua read satisfaction in the dark narrow eyes. Bloody Eagle and the other Cherokees turned and walked away with great dignity.

The smith watched them go, shook his head, and turned to Joshua, who had come nearer. "If ever there's one to be careful about, it's the Bloody Eagle," he said. "He'd be glad to hang the scalp of any of us unakas from his pole any day—and I'll not lose my hair because Jack Byrum is so rummy a fool. I plan to keep my thatch. How about you, young gentleman?"

"Yes, sir." Joshua wheeled and took off at a trot after Byrum, who was walking with an uneven drunken gait across the parade yard.

At that moment a loud boom echoed across the stockade from the direction of the King George Bastion. As the blast echoed away, Joshua heard a babble of voices, some sending up distinctly British cheers, others Cherokee war cries.

The first of the cannon Jack Byrum had brought across the mountains had been tested, and the results, it seemed, had been pleasing. Joshua smiled but then looked at his father and was shocked.

Jack Byrum had fallen to his knees in the middle of the parade ground, his hands flat on the top of his head. Joshua's smile faded; he ran forward. "Father! What's wrong?"

Byrum, startled by his son, looked up sharply. Suddenly he seemed embarrassed. "Nothing's wrong, boy," he said. "It's just that for a second, when them Cherokees yelled, as clear as day I could see that Bloody Eagle coming up behind me and . . ." He didn't finish, but shuddered and rose. "Where's your mother?" he asked. "It's time I took you home."

Joshua was crestfallen. "Home? Back to Charles Town?"

Byrum cast up his eyes. "Don't be a fool, boy. Your home ain't Charles Town no more. It's Tuskegee. You're going to live among the Indians, boy. You like that notion, eh?"

"Yes," Joshua said. "I like that."

But Byrum hadn't waited to hear the answer. He had seen Hester across the stockade yard, still talking to Christiana Cox, and had already headed toward her. Joshua followed.

For the next month Joshua Byrum's life was a blur of change. Greater even than he had imagined was the transition from South Carolina yard child to Overhill Cherokee trader's assistant, which was, in effect, what he became. His usefulness to his father was limited at best, but what jobs he could handle—cleaning trade muskets, folding hides, polishing hatchets, stacking boxes and kegs—he did with enthusiasm at the little complex of three log huts that composed Jack Byrum's

trading center in the little town of Tuskegee, close by
Fort Loudoun.

Hester, Joshua was pleased to see, adapted to her new
life more readily than he had thought she would. Though
his sensitivities were limited by his age, Joshua nevertheless was a good reader of his mother's mind and heart;
when she was happy or when she hurt, he sensed it.

Such sensitivities Joshua certainly had not inherited
from his father. Jack Byrum went through life virtually
oblivious to his wife's feelings and needs. To him she was
handy for preparing a good meal, warming his bed on
cold nights, fulfilling his physical desires. Only one thing
seemed to make him aware of his wife as a woman worthy
of attention and protection, and that was the increasingly
obvious efforts of Henry Dorey to steal her from him.

Dorey, whose trade store was in Tikwalitsi, Bloody
Eagle's village, was not particularly focused in his amo-
rous endeavors. He already had on his string at least two
Cherokee women, one expatriated Creek girl, and the
wife of one of the provincial soldiers, but he seemed
particularly determined to steal Hester away from Byrum.
Byrum at first ignored Dorey's lechery, for he had seen
the man striving just as hard to woo the plump and
religious Christiana Cox from her red-haired soldier husband—but after a time, and several warnings that Dorey
ignored, Byrum lost his patience. Though not prone to
give much affection of his own to his wife, he was even
less prone to let somebody else try to fill the gap. Joshua
watched the growing conflict from the perspective of a
child but as he usually did, understood far more than the
adults around him suspected.

On August 18, 1757, the day before Captain Raymond
Demere was to turn over command of Fort Loudoun to
his newly arrived brother, Captain Paul Demere, and
leave the wilderness for reasons of health, the conflict
between Byrum and Dorey came to blows, then to blades.
Dorey was left bleeding on the ground beside Byrum's
store, a shallow but painful gash across his chest. Sol-

diers came at the behest of the Cherokees and hauled both victim and wounder to Fort Loudoun, where they were detained in the guardhouse until morning. Joshua managed to slip inside the fort in the confusion and spent the night on the soft ground at the edge of one of the gardens near the southern palisades.

2

Morning light streaming into Fort Loudoun found Joshua Byrum already awake. He thought briefly of his mother and wondered if she was worried by his absence from their cabin in Tuskegee, then put aside the concern, knowing that by now she surely was accustomed to his wandering ways. A natural-born son of the frontier, Joshua had even at his age spent nights away from home, sleeping at the houses of Cherokee friends or even in the forests around Tuskegee.

Standing and shaking the sleep from his brain, Joshua brushed off his clothing. A commotion at the gate drew his attention. When the guards threw open the gate, Joshua's eyes widened as a small but notable Indian processional entered.

At its head was an Indian man of remarkably small stature and thin frame. At first glance, Joshua could almost have taken him for a boy, but that would have been a judgment from size alone, for the man's face, even from this distance, gave a clear impression of age. Joshua guessed him to be of middle age or older. Glinting in the morning sunlight were beaded silver ornaments hanging from the cut lobes of his ears, and on his cheeks

27

were large scars of the sort worn by Cherokees of distinction. Accompanying him was a small group of warriors, seemingly serving as bodyguards and escorts.

Joshua knew immediately that he was seeing the famous Cherokee leader and diplomat Attakullakulla, called Little Carpenter because of his craftsmanlike skill in piecing together treaties and diplomatic accords. Joshua was impressed to be seeing such a celebrated Indian. He had heard that Little Carpenter, in the days when he was still a young man, had journeyed all the way to Loudoun and been given an audience with King George II in Windsor Castle.

Little Carpenter had the respect of both the Cherokees and the British. He was probably the most famous and influential of the Overhill leaders at present, his power rivaling that even of the "emperor" Old Hop, his uncle, and it was largely through his diplomatic efforts that Fort Loudoun had come to be built. Likely, Little Carpenter was at the fort today to greet the new commander. Joshua watched as Little Carpenter and his delegation were welcomed by Raymond Demere outside the officer's quarters, then ushered inside.

Joshua's thoughts turned to his father. In the somnolent morning atmosphere hanging like a haze over the fort, Joshua quietly crossed over to the guardhouse in hopes of seeing Byrum. No one stopped him. The sentries were busy at the gate, bringing in the big guard dogs that were put outside the walls each night.

"Whoa there, Joshua! Where goes my young friend?" The voice was familiar and came from behind. Joshua wheeled and faced Nathan Cox, husband of his mother's friend Christiana. Cox's hair was almost as red as his coat. "Where are you going, son?" Cox looked him up and down. "From the look of you, I'd guess you spent the night on damp ground."

"I did, over yonder. I came in when they brought in Father."

Cox looked serious. "Aye. I heard about what happened. A sorry thing to occur in the captain's last hours here."

"What will happen to Father?"

Cox shook his head. "That I don't know. But if I had my guesses, it's more likely that the worst of it will go to Dorey. I won't be false with you, Joshua—there are plenty enough complaints received here from the Indians about both Henry Dorey and Jack Byrum. Bloody Eagle in particular seems to dislike your father. But Dorey is the worse by far, and Captain Demere knows that. Likely this will result in Dorey leaving our midst, and for that we can all be glad."

"I want to speak with Father."

Cox shook his head. "That will not be possible. You'll see him later, I'm sure. Now be off with you—we've got important visitors in the fort this morning."

"Little Carpenter?"

"Indeed. Coming laden with white beads to give the new Captain Demere. For my part, I hate to see the old Captain Demere go. He's a fine officer, and knows how to deal with the Cherokees. If the new one does not, we'll all feel the results. You repeat none of this, by the way."

Joshua looked toward the officers' quarters. "I wish I could meet Little Carpenter."

Nathan Cox laughed. "Perhaps you shall, before all is done. Now be gone before someone skins you for poking about where you don't belong."

As it turned out, Joshua did meet Little Carpenter, shortly after noon that day. With his father in the stockade, there was no work to be done, so Joshua went down to the river to skip stones across the water, aiming the missiles at floating sticks that he pretended were French vessels. So wrapped up in his game he became that he did not hear the approach of a man behind him. Turning to search for a new flat stone, he saw the figure all at once, yelled in surprise, and staggered back into the water where he fell into a pool in the midst of a jumble of eroded boulders.

Joshua thrashed and kicked, then thrashed back to the bank. The man who had startled him walked down and extended his hand. Joshua was awed to realize it was

Little Carpenter himself. The bumps that rose on his skin were not entirely caused by the cold water.

Little Carpenter spoke in the dialect of the Overhill Cherokees among whom he had spent his life. "Come up, young friend. You need not fear me."

Joshua, once out of the water, stood staring at the Cherokee leader, who apparently had wandered down to the river alone. Though the day was hot, the boy shivered as the wind wrapped itself around him.

"I am Attakullakulla," the Indian said. "I am sorry I frightened you."

"I am Joshua Byrum," Joshua responded haltingly, for he was still learning the Cherokee language. "I was not frightened. I just wanted to swim."

Little Carpenter did not laugh aloud, but his dark eyes sparkled with mirth. "Then I hope your swim was pleasant. Good day to you, Swimmer."

When Little Carpenter was gone, Joshua ran back to Tuskegee and into his father's cabin, wanting to tell Hester what had just happened. He was startled to find Jack Byrum already there and stopped on his heels.

"You're wet, boy."

"I fell in the river."

Byrum laughed; he seemed unusually happy. "Fell in the river! That's about what I'd expect of you." He returned his attention to Hester. "I think they'd been looking for a reason to send Dorey on his way, in any case," he said. "There's not a soul about, red or white, who likes him. He won't worry me or you or nobody else anymore."

"Is everything all right again?" Joshua asked.

"Aye, it is, boy," Byrum said. He went to the back of the cabin and picked up a crockery jug. Pulling the stopper, he took a long swallow of rum and wiped his mouth with the back of his hand.

"I met Little Carpenter," Joshua said.

"That's good, dear," Hester responded in a distracted tone. Byrum said nothing; he was busy with another celebratorial mouthful of rum.

"And he called me Ayunini," Joshua continued.

"Good name for a boy who falls into rivers," Byrum said.

Joshua left the cabin to let the sun finish drying his clothing.

Byrum took a third swallow of rum, closed the jug, and sat it on the table. He laughed aloud. "Good riddance to Henry Dorey, and may he go to damnation," he said as he closed the cabin door. In the darkened cabin he wiped his mouth once more, gave his wife a look that filled her with a familiar dread, and came toward her.

Captain Raymond Demere left Fort Loudoun that same day, leaving the command in the hands of his brother. Raymond Demere would never return to the fort, and though he did not yet know it, neither would he see his brother again, for grim changes were in the wind both for Fort Loudoun and for the British and Cherokees in general.

Henry Dorey also left the Overhill towns, as ordered. Byrum's business increased thereafter, but so did his abuses of his trade. As months passed, Joshua sensed a growing coolness on the part of the Cherokees who dealt with his father. That concerned him, but not nearly as much as the increasing sadness he sensed in his mother.

Hester kept more to herself these days and cried often. Joshua caught her in tears several times, but when he asked her what was wrong, she would not answer him beyond saying she missed her home at Charles Town. Joshua remembered her prediction that she would never return home if she crossed the mountains and felt a great dread he could not shake off.

Joshua saw Little Carpenter many times over the next three years. The chief visited the fort frequently, conferring with Captain Paul Demere, who proved to be a more ineffective dealer with the Cherokees than his brother before him. Paul Demere, the troops grumbled privately, antagonized the Cherokees with patronizations and disrespect. The level of unhappiness at the fort grew, and as time passed, a sense of tension began to develop

between the Overhill Cherokees and the approximately
three hundred British colonials in and about Fort Loudoun.

Joshua remained friendly with the Cherokees, despite
their growing dislike for his father and his exhorbitant
credit rates and weighted trade scales. Still, Byrum's
business flourished, and in his store he kept a ready
stock of cloth, matchcoats, powder, balls, knives, rum,
blankets, axes, paints, and jewelry. The trade muskets
that he sold—short guns of high caliber, low price (about
ten shillings), and poor workmanship—kept the Fort
Loudoun blacksmith continually busy making repairs for
the Cherokees, who openly fretted about the low quality
of goods Byrum sold them. Byrum's most vocal critic was
Bloody Eagle, from the village of Tikwalitsi.

On several occasions Joshua saw the pox-scarred warrior, who sometimes brought to the fort his nephew of
about Joshua's age. Joshua stayed clear of Bloody Eagle,
for he had heard the Indian was cruel and evil, and ate
the roasted livers of white boys. Joshua didn't really
believe the latter but saw no reason to take chances.
Besides, Bloody Eagle obviously knew that Joshua was
Byrum's son and disliked him for it. Twice, before Joshua
had started keeping his distance, Bloody Eagle had
abruptly jumped toward Joshua, growling, "Byrum!" and
laughed as Joshua scrambled away.

Byrum made occasional trips back to Charles Town for
resupply but never took Joshua or Hester with him,
though Hester often pleaded to go. Byrum's indifference
to Hester angered Joshua, but there was nothing he could
do to counter it. He sadly watched his mother's spirits
steadily darken. The only things that seemed to brighten
them were Joshua himself, the friendship of some of the
Cherokee women, and the gentle and ever-talkative
Christiana Cox.

The fort itself expanded under Paul Demere's command. By the end of 1757 he had constructed two corn
houses within the fort, along with a permanent double-
chimneyed guardroom. Early in 1758 he had constructed
a house for himself and was talking of building a large

observation tower of a sort the engineer DeBrahm had proposed but never constructed.

Life at the fort was for the soldiers usually a drudgery. The barracks were wet when it rained, hot in the dry midsummer, and bitter cold in the winter. The trench latrine in the fort stank terribly and kept the enclosure swarming with flies during warm weather. Pay was low, and unless the Cherokees helped out through barter and trade, the soldiers faced continual low supplies of food and other goods.

Corn was raised at the fort, but most of the vegetables came from the Cherokee fields. Livestock was also raised in and about the fort, and the two butchers stationed there were kept continually at work. The vast piles of bones and offal they produced combined a sickly sweet rotting smell with the musky stench of the latrines. Nathan Cox complained constantly about the conditions and his fear of the Cherokees, who he believed disliked him for some reason and wished him harm.

Captain John Stuart, according to Cox, was a particular favorite of Little Carpenter and had proven himself the best diplomat in the fort. Through his contact with the Cherokees, the supply problems were controlled if not overcome. Meanwhile, Stuart, Demere, and other officers continued in their efforts to keep the Cherokees allied with Britain against the French, and many times from Byrum's store Joshua heard the boom of the fort's cannon heralding war parties coming home with French scalps and the occasional severed French head, swinging from poles.

On the surface, the British-Cherokee alliance appeared strong. Little Carpenter himself kept busy on behalf of the British cause. In September of 1757 he left Fort Loudoun, the cannon firing in his honor, and went out with a war party to battle the French. He and his men killed several French soldiers near Fort de L'Assumption at the confluence of the Tennessee and Ohio rivers, took prisoners, and came home victorious in January of 1758. In the spring of that year Little Carpenter was given the

honor of traveling to Charles Town to report personally
on his military successes.

When Hester heard of it, she told her son: "Even a
heathen chief is privileged to do that which I am kept
from," and closed herself up in the house to brood.

When Little Carpenter returned the next January,
telling of his reception in Carolina, even Jack Byrum was
impressed. Upon arrival in Charles Town, the chief had
been met by two companies of the Highland Regiment,
greeted at the town hall by a company of salute-firing
grenadiers, and then taken to meet with Governor William Henry Lyttleton. It was treatment worthy of royalty,
and Little Carpenter relished the gifts and attention.

But as usual, the English colonials wanted a gift of
their own—in this case, a pledge—and Little Carpenter
gave it, though with some reluctance, to both South
Carolina's Lyttleton and Virginia's Colonel William Byrd:
The Overhill Cherokees, Little Carpenter agreed, would
provide direct aid to Virginia's war efforts, even though
Little Carpenter had long been displeased with Cherokee
relations with Virginia.

He had sufficient cause for displeasure. As early as
1756, some Cherokees already in the service of that
colony had been killed and their scalps presented fraud-
ulently as those of French-supporting Indians for the
sake of the bounty upon such, creating a crisis in British-
Indian relations. Further, Virginia had always been slow
or unwilling to respond to requests from the Cherokees.
For example, sometime before Fort Loudoun was built,
Virginia had placed a fort in the Overhill country, then
neglected to garrison it.

Little Carpenter was good to his word, and by June of
1758, a large war party was ready to leave Chota to help
the Virginians. Then came a delay that infuriated the
British. A Cherokee conjurer detected signs that war
efforts for Virginia would be met with death and illness
if undertaken immediately. The mission was therefore
delayed by decision of the Cherokee council, for warriors
could by no means take on an effort doomed from the
beginning.

Though the British were furious at the delay—partly because gifts and ammunition had already been given to the warriors—the Indians would not be swayed. Byrum laughed about the officers' plight over his supper table and derided both the superstitious Indians and the chagrined British military leaders.

The following month, Little Carpenter abruptly announced the delay was over. He now would lead warriors on Virginia's behalf, as promised. He and a contingent of sixty Cherokee and Catawba warriors joined General John Forbes as he prepared to march against the northern French outpost of Fort Duquesne.

Word trickled back to Fort Loudoun of the troubles that beset Little Carpenter. Forbes had taken an immediate dislike to the Indian, who demanded many presents from Forbes's already dwindling store of supplies. Forbes considered Little Carpenter a "rascal" and complained of his "stupid speeches." Nevertheless, he gave in to Little Carpenter's demands, though from then on he treated the Indians poorly.

A dispatch from Virginia's Governor Dinwiddie was to interrupt Little Carpenter's war plans yet again and forewarn of coming troubles that would disrupt the lives of the people of Fort Loudoun. Strife had again arisen between Virginia frontiersmen and Cherokees; Little Carpenter was needed to negotiate peace. The chief left to answer Dinwiddie's call, despite Forbes's efforts to keep him from it, and Forbes labeled Little Carpenter a deserter. The chief's small party was intercepted and disarmed. Shortly thereafter, Forbes took Fort Duquesne with unexpected ease, for the French had abandoned it.

Little Carpenter defended his "desertion" by telling Governor Lyttleton that he had learned in advance from the Shawnees that the French were going to abandon the fort and thus his services would be unnecessary in any case. He had tried to pass that word on to Forbes, he said, but Forbes just would not listen.

Word of these events, though slow to arrive, generated great interest at Fort Loudoun where life had gone on much as usual despite the atmosphere of growing tension between the Cherokees and British.

In 1758, the fort was visited by two Presbyterian preachers: the Reverend John Martin, who preached to the Indians with little success, and later, the Reverend William Richardson, a younger man who remained until February of 1759. Richardson was at the fort when the cold of winter had settled over the land, and in the Cherokee towns beside the frozen river he found Old Hop, Standing Turkey, and other Cherokee leaders cordial and yet tense as they talked of "the Great Man Above."

Since Joshua had heard none of Martin's talks, Richardson's were the first authentic sermons he had ever heard, and he was impressed by the young preacher's lofty words, spoken in the soft accent of his native Whitehaven, England. Particularly fascinated was Joshua to witness the baptism of two children in the fort. Hester tried to have Joshua baptized as well, but Jack Byrum would not hear of it.

As 1759 progressed, Christiana Cox gave to Joshua a gift that would serve him the rest of his days. Using as her only resources a battered Bible and a stick with which she scratched letters and words in the sand, she taught Joshua to read—not well, but enough to serve him. It was a skill neither his father nor mother possessed, and though Hester was proud of Joshua's literacy and even tried to learn the rudiments of reading herself, Jack Byrum was bitter about it.

"It's no good when a young bugger begins to see himself better than them what raised him," he complained.

But Joshua paid little heed to his father; as he grew older, he was steadily building and strengthening an invisible wall between himself and Jack Byrum, as impenetrable as the moat-circled palisades of Fort Loudoun.

The beginning of the end of Fort Loudoun happened far from its own grounds, along the Catawba and Yadkin rivers in North Carolina. A band of Cherokees killed fifteen settlers in retaliation for the slaying of other Cherokees in Virginia. The North Carolina slayings were too much for the colonial authorities, and the call went out to the Overhill Cherokees to turn over the guilty Indians.

Meanwhile, Little Carpenter went off in 1759 for further fighting against the French in the Illinois country, this despite Paul Demere's request that he remain in the towns of the Overhills to soothe growing local tensions. Old Hop and other prominent Overhill Cherokees were starting to favor a shifting of allegiances to France; it was rumored that Old Hop had visited with French emmisaries in Chota itself.

The Cherokees' law left it up to the kinsmen of those Indians guilty of the North Carolina slayings to decide whether they would heed the demand to turn them over—and the answer was a firm, frustrating no.

"There'll be blood to come of this, just you wait," Jack Byrum predicted to his family. "The time may arrive when we'll find out firsthand whether Fort Loudoun is strong enough to protect us."

Joshua, with three years of maturing and living among the Cherokees behind him, understood the precariousness of the situation, and on the afternoon that an ashen-faced Jack Byrum came into the cabin with news that Lyttleton had embargoed all ammunition for to the Cherokees, he saw at once that matters would certainly worsen. A main complaint of the Cherokees had long been a lack of ammunition, and with their supply completely cut off, they had no good way to maintain the deerskin trade that had become vital to them, to kill game for their own tables with the efficiency to which they had become accustomed, or to defend themselves from enemies. The embargo would only heighten Cherokee resentment of the British, turn the Indians toward the French as an ammunition source, and make raids against border settlements more likely.

By September, the situation had degenerated to the point that many traders fled back over the mountains into South Carolina. Hester pleaded with her husband to do the same, but he refused. "We'll take to the fort," he said. "Maybe this will be a storm that blows over."

It did not, and a series of unfortunate occurrences only stirred it to greater fury. Cherokee war chief Oconostota, along with several other Indians, including Bloody Eagle, traveled to Charles Town to seek an end to the ammunition embargo. When they arrived, they found Lyttleton already set in a posture of war, and the entire Cherokee delegation was taken hostage. Word was sent back to the Overhill towns that the prisoners would be held until the Indians guilty of the fatal border raids were turned over to the British authorities.

In October, a force of seventy provincials arrived at Fort Loudoun, bearing supplies of food and ammunition. A good supply of salted meat was already in the fort, for the influential Cherokee Ostenaco had attempted to steal the Fort Loudoun cattle herd in September. Demere had responded by having the herd driven inside the fort for slaughter, butchering, and salting.

Joshua, like everyone else, was offended by the stenches of the butchering, but he noticed that his mother was made outright sick by it. He asked Christiana Cox about it, and a smile both happy and sad spread the woman's broad face. "Don't you know, Joshua? That's always the way of a woman with a little one in her belly. Your mother is bearing a child—just as I am."

Joshua's eyes widened in surprise. He had not suspected his mother's pregnancy and certainly had not realized Christiana was also with child; the latter had always been plump in any case, and pregnancy made little difference in her shape.

Hope continued for a peaceful resolution of the Cherokee problem, but in the meantime, living conditions for the fort's inhabitants were crowded and unsanitary. The Byrums were forced to make their home in a tent pitched near the soldiers' barracks. All the usual stenches and deprivations of fort life doubled, then tripled. Hester Byrum became chronically depressed and seemed to age a decade within a month.

In December, Lyttleton himself, with his hostages in

tow, arrived at Fort Prince George on the first leg of a planned military campaign against the Cherokees. Little Carpenter, meanwhile, came home from war and found Old Hop openly favoring an alliance with France. When he learned of Lyttleton's hostages, Little Carpenter traveled to Fort Prince George under a British flag and there negotiated the release of Oconostota and Bloody Eagle. Eventually Lyttleton returned to Charles Town, leaving the remaining hostages at Fort Prince George.

In the Cherokee towns, the situation was volatile. Emperor Old Hop died suddenly, and Standing Turkey came to power in his place. Oconostota and Bloody Eagle, meanwhile, stirred war spirit against the British. The year 1759 ended with a bleak situation on the frontier, and in February of 1760, two months before Joshua Byrum's tenth birthday, an event occurred that erased almost all hope of peace.

Oconostota and Bloody Eagle traveled to Fort Prince George, ostensibly to talk to its commander about a diplomatic mission to Charles Town. The commander, believing the Indians to be sincere, left the fort to meet with them and fell, mortally wounded, when more than a score of hidden Indian gunmen opened fire upon Oconostota's signal.

Inside the fort, the enraged soldiers descended upon the twenty-three Cherokee hostages and killed them. Little Carpenter, near Fort Prince George at the time, was appalled by all that had occurred, returned to the Overhill towns, gathered his family, and moved into the forest to live alone as a gesture of noninvolvement.

With the slaying of the hostages the fate of Fort Loudoun was sure. In March, the Cherokees began firing on the crowded fort. For four days, Joshua and Hester huddled together, listening to the relentless hammering of the Indian guns.

"Don't worry, Mother—Father's cannon will keep them out," Joshua said.

And so they did. Because of the great guns, the Indians could not get close enough to fire effectively on the fort. At length, the gunfire subsided, the Cherokees growing weary of wasting their precious ammunition. Hester ventured the hope that the siege was ending, but a grim Jack Byrum shook his head.

Not ending, he said, but just beginning. "The damned red devils are going to starve us out, and once they get us outside them walls, it will be a worse hell than any preacher ever dreamed up."

Nathan Cox, who was sharing a meal with the Byrums when the comment was made, looked up, his face growing white. "Torture?" he asked.

"Aye. And for you soldiers, the worst of it, no doubt."

Cox was silent for half a minute, thinking. "What will come of this siege, Jack? Is there hope for us?"

The trader shrugged and lit his pipe. "If I were a soldier, I'd head for the forest," he said. "I'd never let them get their bloody hands on me."

Cox put down his fork and ate nothing else the rest of the meal.

That night, Hester Byrum held Joshua to her so tightly he could barely breathe and talked fondly of Charles Town as she patted her swelling belly. Meanwhile, on a cot hidden behind a curtain in the soldiers' barracks, Christiana Cox gave birth to a baby girl whom she named Beth.

In the days that followed, Joshua noticed a paradox of time common to prisoners: days passing as slowly as weeks, weeks passing as rapidly as days. Demere tried to keep the fort's routine and daily life as close to normal as possible, but the strain showed on every face and in the never-ending parade-ground military exercises, which now seemed travesties to the people forced to watch them.

In May, Demere finally was able to give news that brought cheer: Colonel Archibald Montgomery was marching toward Fort Prince George with an army of thirteen hundred regular and three hundred fifty provincial troops, their purpose the relief of Fort Loudoun. For the first time in days, Joshua was surrounded by smiles. Hester seemed younger, reminding him of the way she had been before Jack Byrum brought them over the mountains.

Joshua had had much time to observe the sort of siege to which Fort Loudoun was being subjected and found it a peculiar one in several ways. Though the fort was supposed to be cut off by the besieging Cherokees, it nevertheless had abundant visitors, chief among them Little Carpenter, who came almost daily. Other Cherokees came as well, including the Cherokee mates of Fort Loudoun soldiers. Many foodstuffs, even a few live hogs and game birds, were smuggled into the fort by them, though not in quantities great enough to staunch the diminishing of supply levels. In mid-May, Demere announced that rations would be cut to one daily quart of corn per person.

On May 25, the fort's gates opened to two South Carolina traders who brought in several horseloads of relief supplies that they had obtained through trade with sympathetic Cherokees. Demere conferred with them, and by way of Nathan Cox, the Byrum family heard their story: Lieutenant Governor William Bull of South Carolina, now exercising power in the absence of Lyttleton, who had been named governor of Jamaica, had sent the traders with loads of ribbons and paint to barter for supplies for the fort. Along the way, though, the traders had been raided by white bandits in the mountains and had lost three packhorse loads of the goods. The identity of the bandits was unknown, but it was suspected they were traders who hoped to use the stolen goods for their own profit.

Arrival of the goods cheered the fort's haggard residents, but not enough was received to make a substantial difference in the worsening situation. In early June, Little Carpenter informed Demere that his own status among the Cherokees was declining because of his pro-British stand. "My brothers hide everything from me, and call me the friend of the whites," he said. "Only Tomatly town wishes peace; the rest want war."

After June 5, Little Carpenter came no more to Fort Loudoun, nor did any more Cherokee women come bear-

ing food. Little Carpenter was expelled from the Cherokee council and once again took to the woods with his
family to live alone.

Then, in midmonth, word came that threw the fort's
inhabitants into their greatest despair yet. The relief
force under Montgomery had been attacked in a mountain pass near the town of Etchoe. Though only twenty-
five of the huge force were killed and seventy wounded,
Montgomery had declared a retreat. Though he had
ravaged several Cherokee towns, he would not be coming
to the aid of Fort Loudoun after all.

On July 7, the Fort Loudoun occupants consumed the
last of their bread. Rations were cut to four ounces of
horsemeat a day, plus a handful of beans and plums. By
August 1, there were left only eight thin horses to use for
meat, and Demere in despair declared the fort "abandoned and forsaken by God and man."

On the night of August 4, several of Fort Loudoun's
soldiers deserted into the surrounding woods. Christiana
Cox, brave woman that she was, did not publicly shed
even a tear when she learned that her husband was
among them. Nathan Cox, overwhelmed at the prospect
of Indian torture, had left his family abandoned in a fort
on the verge of collapse.

On the night of August 5, Jack Byrum shook Joshua
awake. Byrum's breath stank of rum, for he had been
drinking from a flask he had secreted since entering the
fort.

"Go get help, boy," he said. "Your mother's about to
birth a baby."

3

J oshua wiped the linen cloth across his mother's brow again, and there were faint stains of red on it when it came away. In her strain she was bursting tiny vessels beneath the surface of her skin, mixing her sweat with blood. The sight of it terrified Joshua.

Hester was fighting with stubborn determination to give birth to a child equally determined not to be born. That childbirth was painful Joshua had known; just how wrenchingly painful he had not realized until now.

"It's going to be well, Mother," he said, trying to comfort himself as much as her. "The baby is coming, and when it's done, you will be well."

If Hester heard his reassurances, she did not give evidence of it. Her pain was obviously building again, swelling to an even higher peak. She threw back her head, closed her eyes, and bit her lip until it bled, barely restraining a scream. Tears came to Joshua's eyes, and he looked at Christiana Cox imploringly.

In the corner of the tent, Jack Byrum drained the last of his rum and turned away. He ducked out through the flap door, having seen all he wanted to see; now he wanted to get as far away as he could, smoke his pipe, and try to forget what was happening. Joshua saw his father leave and hated him for it. Again he swiped the cloth across his mother's brow. Her pain was partially subsiding once more, but Joshua knew that in a few moments another agonizing cramp, worse than before, would seize her.

"If only she wasn't so weakened," Christiana said. "So little food she's had, and poor at that—a woman needs her strength for such a time as this, and poor Hester's got none left."

Joshua could barely make himself ask the inescapable question: "Will she die?"

Christiana gave him a reprimanding look. "Hush, boy. Don't let that thought free in this place. Keep your fears to yourself and send your prayers to God. Now, brace yourself—here comes another thrust, and perhaps this time she will—"

Hester could not hold back the scream this time. She cried out in agony and gripped Joshua's wrist so tightly that his hand grew red and he feared she would snap his bones like brittle sticks. Christiana's eyes grew larger, and she began to urge Hester on.

"That's right, Hester, push it out! You're doing it, dear—just keep on, keep on. . . ."

Hester tried hard, but her strength broke. She closed her eyes and became limp. Joshua was truly scared now; he leaned close to his mother's ashen face.

"It's all right, Joshua," Christiana said. "Let her rest. The next time, it will come."

"But she won't be able to survive another one," Joshua said. "I can tell she won't."

"Be quiet, boy! What do you know of women? God never made stronger creatures. Hark! Now we begin again!"

Joshua did not watch this time. He closed his eyes tight and prayed as best he knew how. Christiana made noises of encouragement, then fear . . . and then delight. With his eyes still closed, Joshua heard the slap of a hand on wet flesh, then the weak but fresh cry of an infant.

He opened his eyes and gazed in awe at a tiny clay-colored boy that Christiana held in her hands. He had never seen a child that looked so small and feeble. Yet the baby was crying lustily, its eyes wet wrinkles in a gray face, its mouth wide open and toothless.

"His color—"

"All is as it should be. As he cries, he will fill his lungs with good air and turn pink as a rose. This is a miracle you are seeing, Joshua. Look! Even now, he's searching for a good breast to feed him! It's a small but strong brother you have, Joshua Byrum!"

Joshua wiped away his tears, smiled, and took his mother's hand. "Mother, look what you've done! He's . . ."

Christiana held the baby close to warm it, then wrapped it in its receiving cloth and prepared to give it to its mother. She had not noticed the abruptness with which Joshua had cut off his words.

"Hester, your boy is ready to—"

When Christiana looked up, Joshua's eyes were wet again, his lip trembling. His right hand lay across his mother's brow, and his left gripped a waxen hand that was much too limp. Hester's bosom was not rising and falling with breath, and her eyes were half opened and fixed, staring up into the peak of the tent.

"Oh, Joshua," Christiana whispered.

Joshua's voice was quavering yet sounded fierce as he spat out his words. "It's *his* fault. He killed her."

"Joshua, you must not blame this child. He did not bring himself into being."

"Not the baby! My father! Mother said she would die if she came across the mountains. But he made her come. She never had a choice. And now she's dead—because of him."

Christiana said nothing. She drew the baby to her, then quietly lowered one side of her dress and let it begin to nurse.

"It's up to Jack Byrum to name him, I suppose," she said.

"No," Joshua responded. "I will give him a name."

Christiana looked at him questioningly. "Your father will allow that?"

"Why should he care? He has never cared about anything or anyone else but himself." Joshua went to the baby, reached out and touched its narrow shoulders under the swaddling receiving cloth.

"His name will be Samuel," he said.

"Is that a special name?"

Joshua said, "It's the name I would have chosen for myself."

Christiana smiled down at the baby, who was almost choking in a milk flow too heavy for a newborn. "Samuel Byrum," Christiana said. "It is a good name indeed."

"No. Not Byrum," Joshua said, forcefully.

Christiana was confused. "I don't understand."

"His name," Joshua said, "will be Samuel Cox. My father is not fit to raise him. He is yours . . . if you'll have him."

Christiana did not answer with words, but her smile of assent spoke just as clearly. She hugged the baby closer.

Joshua looked into Hester's pale face, closed her eyes with his fingers, kissed her clammy cooling cheek, and finally drew up the blanket until she was completely covered. After that, he looked at her and touched her no more.

Little Samuel, in a way, proved to be the salvation of both Joshua and Christiana. By smothering the baby with as much love as she gave her own natural child, Christiana soothed her hidden grief over the desertion of her husband. And Joshua devoted himself to the safety and welfare of his brother in a fierce determination not to see Hester's fatal childbirthing efforts come to naught.

As for Jack Byrum, his disinterest was as great as Joshua had predicted. Byrum expressed no concern for his new offspring or any visible grief over the death of his wife. He acted as if nothing mattered any longer, as if fate had some grim inescapable doom awaiting him. He moved about in a way that reminded Joshua of Nathan Cox's manner before his desertion and often talked fearfully of Bloody Eagle, as if the warrior were lying in wait for him just beyond the fort's palisades.

Hester was buried with a minimum of ceremony near the King George Bastion. Her grave was marked with wood rather than stone, for permanence did not seem to matter. The unspoken belief of all the fort's people now was that Fort Loudoun and all in it would soon not exist; the Cherokees would destroy it as soon as Paul Demere accepted the inevitable and opted for surrender.

The troop desertions had diminished not only the fort's manpower but also drained the last remnants of the will to resist by those remaining. Even as Hester Byrum was buried, negotiations with the Cherokees were beginning. Captain John Stuart, rather than Demere, represented the British in the negotiations, for he was as popular with the Cherokees as Paul Demere was unpopular. Joshua saw Demere from time to time on those last days. He looked wasted and pale, and moved in the same kind of cloud of doom that Jack Byrum did. Joshua found himself drawing away from Demere when he passed, for the man was like an incarnation of defeat and death.

On Friday, August 8, Fort Loudoun's remaining troops staged a final parade on the grounds. The civilians and soldiers' dependents stood about, watching in silence as the British colors were lowered. That night Fort Loudoun's people spent in silent musing over what was to come after they passed out of the stockade.

Joshua slept little; he stayed close-by Christiana and Samuel, urging himself to remain brave no matter what. But he could not feel brave. Even though Stuart had announced that the surrender terms included freedom for Fort Loudoun's people, an escorted march to Virginia or South Carolina, and the right to keep such arms as were needed for the journey, Joshua could not convince himself the ordeal really was over. More than anything, he feared for what would happen to Samuel, whose survival had become the most important thing in his life.

The next morning, the remaining hundred and eighty men and threescore women and children of Fort Loudoun passed through the gates for the last time, crossing

the log bridge spanning Gerald DeBrahm's locust-filled
moat. At the head of the march were Demere and Stuart,
the former deliberately erect and soldierly, the latter
more relaxed but grim of expression. When Joshua
passed through the gate, he turned and looked linger-
ingly behind him, for his mother was still inside, her
body buried in soil upon which she had never wanted to
tread. To Joshua, that irony seemed the most tragic and
cruel part of this entire ordeal.

Announcement came back through the lines that the
group would be marched to Fort Prince George. That
heartened Joshua somewhat, for he liked the idea of
returning to South Carolina, but he also dreaded the
prospect of passing through the treacherous mountains.
He remembered the traders who had recently come and
their talk of bandits. Would such lie in wait to raid the
enfeebled refugees in some mountain pass? He feared
for Samuel.

The day dragged on; the people trudged ceaselessly.
Every mile seemed like three, and to Joshua there was no
beauty or joy in the land any longer. Even the sense of
unconfinement, so noticeable to people long penned up,
counted for little. The Cherokees who escorted the refugees wore expressions that frightened Joshua.

Christiana must have noted his fear, for three times
she pulled him close to her and said in a low voice, "You
are mine now as much as Samuel. I will see to your care
as I would my own born flesh."

Jack Byrum did not walk near his offspring but farther
back in the processional, among other women and children. Occasionally Joshua would turn and look for him,
and each time he noted Byrum's look of pure fear. That
did nothing to make Joshua feel better, and eventually he
quit looking at his father at all, telling himself that he did
not care what happened to Jack Byrum in any case. It
was a lie, and he knew it. Even if Jack Byrum was
ultimately responsible for Hester's death, even if he
wasn't a good father, he was still the only father he had
and his only blood link to the life he had known before.
That counted for something, even if he wished it did not.

When the refugees reached a meadow where Cane Creek flowed into the Tellico River, they stopped to make camp. Fort Loudoun was some fifteen miles behind; it would not have been a particularly long journey for a day under normal circumstances, but for the hunger-weakened refugees, the trek had been an ordeal. Joshua wondered how they would make it the full distance to Fort Prince George; at this rate, it would take them a long time to get there.

The weary travelers spread blankets on the soft grasses, gnawed on what meager foodstuffs they had, and tried as best they could to rest. Christiana nursed the babies and strove to look cheerful, but Joshua could see she was as frightened as he was. As darkness descended, only a few windblown campfires illuminated the scene.

When at last the babies lay asleep in blankets on the ground, Joshua curled up nearby and tried to rest. As tired and weakened as he was, he could not fall asleep. When finally he started to drift off, a movement nearby roused him. He sat up.

"Look there, boy," Jack Byrum said. He was kneeling beside Joshua and pointing. A faint red glow from a nearby fire lit his face and revealed an intense expression. Byrum had a Brown Bess musket in his hands, held horizontally across his knee.

Joshua looked. At first, he could make out only the ragged line where trees edged against the meadow. As he peered more closely, however, he detected three Indians, members of the escort group, slipping into the forest. "Where are they going?" Joshua asked.

"They're leaving, boy. Running out in the night. Them's not the first to do it tonight—they're all going off, a few at a time, giving one excuse or another or slipping out when they think they aren't seen. Now why do you think they would do that?"

"I don't know."

"I don't either, but I don't like it. I'm going to get out of here, and if you want to go with me, now's the time to decide."

Joshua looked at tiny Samuel, sleeping on his blanket. The sleeping Christiana's hand trailed over and almost touched the baby. "What about Samuel?" Joshua asked.

"Hell, boy, you can't slip through a woods full of Indians with a squally baby in arms! Leave him here! You can go, you can stay—it's up to you. Me, I'm going, and I can't sit around much longer waiting for you to make up your mind."

Joshua looked at his father and felt a deep repulsion. "Then go," he said. "I won't leave Samuel. I don't run off on people the way you and Nathan Cox do."

Byrum's lips twitched. "You think you're mighty pure and good, don't you! Hell, boy, you're flesh of my flesh, like it or not, and if you don't care much for your old father, you just keep in mind that what I am, you are too, and in the end you'll show it."

"I'll never be like you. I hate you."

Byrum actually looked stung for a moment, then put on an impassive expression. "Maybe you do hate me. Maybe you got a right to. But you got no right to think yourself better than me. I've yet to see a river rise higher than its source, boy. I'm going now. I hope you come through all right. Here—this is for you." He handed Joshua a loaded flintlock pistol, a shot pouch, and a small powder horn. "Maybe that will come in handy."

Byrum moved away, heading out into the dark. In a few moments, Joshua lost sight of him. "Father?" he whispered. "Wait—don't go."

There was no one to hear him. Byrum was gone. Despite the declaration of hate just made, Joshua hoped his father would make it to safety.

Before he lay down again, Joshua took another look around. Not an Indian within his view. He wondered what it meant, if anything. Samuel coughed and stirred nearby. Joshua reached out and stroked the infant with one hand, and held the pistol with the other.

Joshua awakened twice more before morning, both times because of the babies' crying. Christiana rose and nursed, comforted and cleaned them, and put them down again. Each time she patted Joshua soothingly and smiled. Joshua smiled back.

He opened his eyes with the morning light and sat up, feeling an unexplainable sense of alarm. Looking around, he saw others rising and from the expressions on several faces, realized that at least a few of them also felt that something was wrong.

Joshua stood, eyeing the woods at the edge of the meadow. Turning, he saw Paul Demere and several other men a few yards away. Demere seemed disturbed and was looking furtively about. His eyes came to rest on Joshua just as a rifle cracked from the tree line. Demere spasmed and fell to his knees.

From the camp arose a chorus of shouts, which along with the gunshot awakened anyone still sleeping. The babies sent up a double wail just as a volley of rifle fire blazed out from the woods. Joshua saw three men fall, felt a ball breeze a quarter inch above his own head, then dropped, arching his body over the babies to protect them. Christiana stood, screamed, then dropped down beside him, cringing with her hands to her mouth.

A horrid screech resounded from the woods, followed by a new hail of gunfire and swarms of arrows. Screams and angry shouts arose from the Fort Loudoun refugees, and some of them began returning fire. Then the Cherokees appeared. How many of them there were Joshua could not tell, but it seemed thousands; later he would hear the count estimated at about seven hundred. Painted, nearly naked figures emerged from the trees, sending up unnerving war cries, moving into the midst of the people. Women grasped their children, men grasped their women, and a few tried to fight. These were promptly disarmed and in some cases tomahawked. It took only a minute for many of the armed refugees to shout their surrender. To resist such an overwhelming force was pointless.

Joshua, still covering the crying babies with his body, looked wildly around in horror. He remembered the flintlock pistol, but it was out of reach, and he would not move to get it. A warrior swept past, crouched, and picked up the pistol. The Indian whooped in delight at his prize and leapt away over a fallen body. Joshua realized with a feeling of sickness that the body was that of a woman. A soldier, apparently her husband, staggered up and knelt beside her body. After a moment of examination he sent up a terrible despairing cry and lunged toward the nearest warrior, pulling a knife from a belt sheath. The warrior lithely spun, lifted and brought down a tomahawk, and crushed the soldier's skull. Using the soldier's knife, the Indian quickly took his victim's scalp and waved it triumphantly.

Christiana began to pray aloud.

Never had Joshua seen anything like this. He had heard that Indians were brutal fighters and knew of the practice of scalping, but seeing a man killed and scalped close at hand stunned him. He stared at the soldier's scalped body and understood better now why Nathan Cox and the other soldiers had deserted the fort.

A rough hand gripped the back of Joshua's neck and jerked him up and around. He found himself staring up into the face of Bloody Eagle. The warrior's red hairline birthmark was pulsing like a vein.

Bloody Eagle looked at Joshua as if trying to recognize him. "Byrum?" he said tentatively—then firmly, with a dark grin, "Byrum!" With that, he pushed Joshua down and knelt over him. Joshua heard Christiana Cox scream nearby; he wanted to scream himself, but there was no voice in him to do it. He was certain he was about to be scalped.

"Byrum!" the pock-faced warrior shouted again, triumphantly. Then he thrust something foul into Joshua's face, laughing.

It was a scalp lock. Joshua knew at once it was his father's. Jack Byrum had not made good his escape after all. Joshua pulled back, revolted, as the Indian shoved the hideous thing against his nose and mouth.

Christiana let out a screech almost as wildly primitive as the one the Indians had raised as they rushed from the woods. She struck Bloody Eagle with both fists, continuing her high shriek all the while. The Indian bellowed and swung a muscled arm around, knocking Christiana to the ground. Bloody Eagle turned his attention away from Joshua to the woman. Joshua saw a tomahawk in his hand; it went up threateningly.

"No!" he shouted, jumping to his feet and lunging toward Bloody Eagle.

Something came between him and the warrior, bumping hard against him. Joshua fell back on his rump.

What had bumped against him was another Cherokee. Joshua recognized him as Ostenaco, whom he had seen twice before at Byrum's store in Tuskegee. Ostenaco grasped Bloody Eagle's arm and held him back from tomahawking Christiana.

In Cherokee, Ostenaco said, "She is just a woman, Awahili. The one we want is there, and we are about to kill him. Leave the women and children and come with me."

Bloody Eagle's eyes flashed wildly, but he lowered the tomahawk. He looked down at Christiana and turned on his heel.

"Oh!" Christiana suddenly cried out. "Oh, God above!"

"It's all right," Joshua said. "He's not going to hurt you."

But the woman cried out in the same way again, coming to her feet and actually going after Bloody Eagle, who wheeled to again face her, moving the tomahawk threateningly once more. Joshua was amazed at Christiana's action and wondered what had possessed her to behave so dangerously.

When Christiana dropped to her knees and reached out toward the sash around Bloody Eagle's waist, Joshua suddenly understood. There was a second scalp lock hanging there. The hair was a bright orange-red.

"Oh, Nathan! God help me, Nathan!" Christiana cried out. Then she collapsed facedown in a dead faint.

Joshua was sickened. First his father's scalp lock and now Nathan Cox's. Bloody Eagle's scalping knife had been busy. Joshua felt a burst of hatred so intense, it froze him in place and brought tears to his eyes.

Bloody Eagle laughed down at Christiana's prone form,

kicked her roughly, and followed Ostenaco away through the crowd. Joshua watched them go, standing transfixed while all about him rose terrible war cries, pleading and crying voices, prayers, and occasional death screams as the Indians killed soldiers. Within his own immediate area Joshua saw at least seven corpses. Christiana, meanwhile, pushed herself to her feet and staggered over to protect the babies.

Joshua broke out of his stupor and followed Bloody Eagle and Ostenaco. His thoughts fluctuated between the irrational notion that he could somehow kill Bloody Eagle for what he had just done and a morbid curiosity to find out who it was Ostenaco had said was about to be put to death.

The two warriors moved together toward a place where a large group of warriors were gathered—laughing, jeering, and yelling. Joshua also drew closer, and a parting in the group of men let him see something he was utterly unprepared for, which he would never forget.

Captain Demere, wounded and minus his scalp, was dancing. His captors clapped in time with his pitiful flailings. Whenever he would falter or stumble, one or more of the warriors would prod him with a knife or arrow. There was something stuffed in Demere's mouth—dirt, it appeared. In horror, Joshua watched Demere's prancings, which went on a long time. When at last the humiliated soldier fell, the Indians gathered around him. Joshua turned away when they began cutting off Demere's arms and legs, one by one.

When the screaming stopped and Demere was mercifully dead, some of the warriors turned to look for fresh victims. But Ostenaco lifted his arms and said in a loud voice: "Stop! We have got the man we wanted! Let there be no more killing!"

Joshua was trying now to get back to Christiana and the babies, but for some reason his legs would not function as they should. Not only that, the countryside around him was going into a wild spin, like a whirlpool, pulling him down toward the center of the vortex. His legs lost the last of their strength, and he collapsed, sinking into blackness.

Christiana's arm around his shoulder reminded Joshua of the times his mother had comforted him similarly, and the feeling was both pleasing and saddening. In the ten weeks since the massacre, Joshua had come to love Christiana Cox deeply, but right now he longed for his mother. Even the sight of Jack Byrum, miraculously alive and well, would have thrilled him, and he wondered if maybe he had loved his father, at least a little, after all. Hardly a day passed that he did not think of him—in no small part because he was forced daily to see Byrum's scalp lock hanging outside the door of Bloody Eagle's house. The warrior had placed it there so that all could see how he had dealt with the trader he so long had hated.

Joshua stirred beside Christiana, swallowed down the impulse to weep, and reminded himself that for his own sake he could not afford to think much on his parents. They were gone, dead, and would not return. Christiana was his mother now; she had been true to her word and claimed Joshua as her own to the Cherokees. Though most of them knew Joshua to be the son of Byrum the trader, they nevertheless honored Christiana's claim and allowed her to keep both Samuel and Joshua with her. In fact, the Cherokees had treated them well since they had been brought here to Tikwalitsi from the massacre at Cane Creek.

At Cane Creek the Cherokees had slain twenty-nine people—twenty-three soldiers, three officers, and three women. The number was roughly comparable to the number of the Cherokee hostages killed at Fort Prince George, and Joshua knew as well as anyone that the match was no coincidence. He had recently learned that the massacre had been prompted by a faction of the Cherokees displeased with terms of the Fort Loudoun surrender, and he had also heard a rumor that one of those terms—the turning over of all major arms and powder—might have been breached by Demere.

The surviving Fort Loudoun residents had been divided up between the various Overhill towns, and though rumor had it that a few had been tortured to death in some of the other towns, most of the prisoners were apparently being treated relatively well.

Only one officer, Captain John Stuart, had been spared death. He was kept prisoner in Fort Loudoun briefly, then, according to rumor, escorted back to Virginia by none other than Little Carpenter himself. Stuart had long been known to be a favorite of Little Carpenter, so Joshua did not doubt the story was true.

Outside, the sun was beginning to set, sending long shadows across Tikwalitsi. Leaves rustled in an evening wind, their bright colors muted now in dusklight. In the cabin it was darker than it was outside, and cooler.

Samuel was sleeping now, and Joshua looked at him by the light of the fire. Christiana and her charges had been treated particularly well, being put up in a small previously empty house belonging to a recently widowed older Cherokee woman named Kwali. The warrior who had claimed Christiana, Joshua, and the babies as his prisoners was apparently a nephew of Kwali's, and Joshua had developed the suspicion that the four of them had been given to the old woman almost as pets.

Christiana seemed particularly to intrigue Kwali, who sometimes would come in and kneel before her just to stroke her face gently. Joshua secretly wondered if Kwali was sane. Whether she was or not, she provided sufficiently for all of them and treated them all more as guests than prisoners.

"God has blessed us by putting us in Kwali's care," Christiana once told him. "Let us be careful to treat her well and with respect, and perhaps we will be kept in good condition until we can be ransomed."

"Who will ransom us?" Joshua had asked.

"I don't know," Christiana answered. "But I have a sense of assurance that someone will come, and we can return to our own people again. Cling to that hope with me, Joshua, for it is hard for me to cling to it alone."

Beth, Christiana's natural infant, stirred and began to

cry. She was wrapped in a deerskin that Kwali had provided, for it was the Cherokee way to wrap infant girls in the skin of a deer. Kwali had provided the traditional baby boy's cougarskin wrapping for Samuel. Christiana picked Beth up and began to feed her. Joshua stood and walked toward the door of the cabin.

"Where are you going, Joshua?"

"I just want to walk outside a few minutes," he said. "Don't worry—I won't go far."

"Please don't. It's late, and soon we should sleep."

Outside the little house, built of upright logs in the common Cherokee fashion, Joshua walked to a nearby stump, and from a hollow place near its base pulled a long, narrow object wrapped in a scrap of deerhide. Looking about to make sure he was not observed, Joshua unwrapped the object and held it up. It was a flint knife, made by his own hands.

Red light from the waning sun shone on the concave facets of the chipped-out blade. The knife, crude as it was, gave Joshua a feeling of power.

He looked across the little village of Tikwalitsi in the direction of the house of Bloody Eagle. The warrior, he had heard, was ill. That meant Joshua would be able to find him home and do the bloody task he had set for himself.

"Tomorrow, Bloody Eagle," he said beneath his breath. "Tomorrow Ayunini will come and take his vengeance upon you."

Joshua's day of vengeance came and went, leaving him with nothing but a broken knife, confusion, a feeling of failure, and a troubling sense of linkage with the ailing Indian boy he had encountered in Bloody Eagle's house.

Despite his efforts to forget it all, Joshua could not. The boy he had dubbed John Hawk and given the Roman coin stayed on his mind continually. Finally, three days afterward, as casually as possible he asked Kwali about the boy's status, hoping the inquiry would not rouse questions.

The old woman, Tikwalitsi's resident gossip, proved a wealth of information. Tsantawu—for that, not Tsani, was the name John Hawk had tried to voice to Joshua—was no better, Kwali said, and was suffering abdominal pain. Bloody Eagle had called in a Cherokee priest from Chota to see to his nephew's healing. Upon his first examination of John Hawk, the priest had immediately ordered that the boy be secluded in the winter house, cut off from everyone but members of his household. No pregnant or menstruating women were to come near him for fear of possible pollution that could hamper his recov-

ery. John Hawk was to receive no hot or seasoned food—
which, Kwali wryly noted, was an easy enough prohibi-
tion since the boy could keep nothing on his stomach in
any case—and was to be given a rigorous regime of
sweats in steam made from water treated with parsnip
roots. Each sweat was to be followed by a cold river
plunge.

But the priest doubted such standard efforts would
help, Kwali said, for he had through one of his conjura-
tions determined that John Hawk was doomed to die.
Joshua asked how the priest thought he could know such
a thing, and Kwali answered him. The priest had waded
into the river and used a stick to make a small circle
around him, uttering a formula all the while. Into the
circle a leaf had floated—a clear sign that the boy was
not to recover.

But Kwali was not as sure as the priest about the
outcome of the illness. She told Joshua that the sick boy
had also been made to vomit into the river, and the vomit
had floated—evidence he would ultimately be well. The
priest could stake his faith on floating leaves if he wanted;
Kwali had more confidence in floating vomit, for she had
seen that particular sign of coming recovery vindicated
three times in her experience.

Joshua had no faith in either sign, for he did not much
believe in the magic, divinations, and conjuring in which
the Cherokees invested so much confidence. Besides,
while she was teaching him to read back at Fort Loudoun, Christiana Cox had said it wasn't right to stake
one's faith on such things. So he listened with unex-
pressed skepticism as Kwali told of the priest's conclusion
that the sick boy had either a snake or lizard curled up
in his abdomen and described various ceremonial ways
he was seeking to remove it.

Kwali's tone indicated to Joshua that she, like him, did
not hold the priest in particularly high regard, though
clearly her attitude, unlike Joshua's, had nothing to do
with doubts about basic premises. Kwali proudly said she
had devoted a long lifetime to learning much of the
sacred knowledge herself—this at risk of being thought

a witch, especially now that she was old—and felt that she could diagnose the cause and predict the outcome of John Hawk's illness better than the priest.

Her theory was that Bloody Eagle had probably failed to go through the proper rituals on a recent hunt, and had thus invited a vengeful animal spirit into his house. Bloody Eagle's family had a history of laxness in following the sacred formulas, she noted. Had not she herself, while a young woman, warned Bloody Eagle's pregnant mother to watch her diet more carefully while she was carrying a child? The woman had not done so, had eaten a speckled fish. The result was just what Kwali had feared: Bloody Eagle had been born with a birthmark on his hairline.

Joshua rather enjoyed Kwali's chatter, for it provided interesting information, filled time, greatly improved his fluency in the Cherokee language, and took his mind off his situation. Christiana had a harder time with the old woman, however; Kwali was determined that the infants Beth and Samuel should properly be bound, in the old style, on a cradleboard. Christiana would have none of it, leading Kwali to cluck with her tongue and predict that the babies would grow up stooped and weak.

Under the influence of Kwali and his surroundings in general, Joshua began following the Indian habit of taking a plunge in the river first thing every morning. The colder the water, the better the plunge was the Cherokee way of looking at it, and Joshua adopted the same attitude, though not as thoroughly as his Indian captors. Back during the peaceful days in Tuskegee, he had sometimes seen Cherokee men and boys breaking through ice on the river on bitterly cold mornings and taking dips more eagerly than they did in the summer when they often complained that the river was too warm.

On a chilly morning in November, Joshua left Kwali's house, descended to the river for his usual dip, and was surprised when through the surface of the water before him rose the head of John Hawk. The Indian boy shook the water from his eyes, looked up at Joshua on the bank, and nodded in greeting. Rising a bit higher from the water, he pointed to his chest. The Roman coin hung there.

Joshua was pleased that John Hawk had lived, but felt ambivalent about the obvious fact that the young Indian recognized him as giver of the coin. Perhaps John Hawk also remembered Joshua's blubbering emotional display and thought him weak for it.

If so, John Hawk did not show it. He looked warmly at Joshua, touched the coin again. "The power of your gift drove the snake from my belly."

"That is good," Joshua replied. "But perhaps it was the work of the priest that healed you."

"No," John Hawk said. "It was your gift. A dream showed that to me. I think there is magic in this amulet." He rose, splashed out of the river, and came near Joshua. Putting his palm on Joshua's shoulder, he said, "You are my elder brother, Ayunini. John Hawk will not forget you."

Joshua watched the lean young Indian stride away and felt rather amazed. Not only had John Hawk remembered his giving of the coin, but he had also recalled, and obviously accepted, the name Joshua had given him. The water was particularly cold this morning and left Joshua chilled to his marrow. He walked shivering back to Kwali's house and stopped abruptly when he saw a man standing outside it, conversing with Kwali and several Cherokee men, including Kwali's nephew. Nearby stood three packhorses, being eagerly unloaded by several other Cherokees.

Immediately Joshua felt sure that what was happening here had something to do with himself and Christiana. He approached slowly, still wet and shivering. The white man turned and saw him, and Joshua blanched.

It was Henry Dorey.

Christiana wiped her eyes and shook her head. The firelight glimmered in her hair, which Kwali had lovingly slickened earlier in the day with bear oil and plaited with one of the ribbons Henry Dorey had brought in. "It's wrong, I suppose, to agree to marry a man simply so he'll get you out of a bad situation, but I know nothing else to be done for it. If I didn't agree to that, then we might be here forever."

"He's a bad man, Christiana," Joshua said. He had begun calling his surrogate mother by her first name two weeks before, at her insistence, and now it seemed a natural and comfortable title. "You remember when the traders came to Fort Loudoun, talking of bandits? He was one of the bandits, I'd wager. The wares he traded for us were just like those the traders brought in during the siege."

"Aye, the same has already come to my mind, Joshua. But what else can I do? He declares he loves me, and that he has spent these past weeks trying to find what became of me after the fort fell. He knows now that Nathan is dead. He's taken great risk in moving among the Cherokees at such a time. He has traded three packhorses of goods for me, and the Cherokees have already accepted his bargain."

"What will become of Samuel?"

"Why, he will go with me, as my own. And you as well. I've made it clear to Mr. Dorey that I will never agree to his proposal unless he accepts you, Samuel, and Beth along with me. Mercy on me! Would I ever have thought I would be bargaining and trading my own self like a piece of cheese! It's sad to have fallen so low." Christiana smiled sadly. "But, strange to say, it's Kwali for whom I feel saddest. She has come to love us, the babies in particular, and will surely miss us."

Joshua was not listening very well, for his thoughts had suddenly become concentrated on the prospect of life under the thumb of Henry Dorey. Of even greater concern was the future of Samuel under such circumstances. That Dorey would raise the boy as his son seemed preposterous, not to mention undesirable. For all Joshua knew, Dorey might abandon them both, once on the trail; as a trader, he would be used to tossing off unwanted merchandise.

But to remain in Tikwalitsi would mean more weeks, months, even years, in a state of perpetual uncertainty.

Joshua did not really know his status among the Cherokees at the moment. That he and the others were prisoners was clear enough, but whether they were to be ransomed, adopted, enslaved, or finally killed was a murky question. Probably even the Cherokees themselves had not decided. Death by torture or life as a slave, possibly maimed to halt any possibility of running away, were not options Joshua found appealing. Dorey's offer at least meant leaving behind such uncertainties, even if only to accept others.

Where would Dorey take them? South Carolina, Joshua hoped. Perhaps back to Charles Town. Perhaps anywhere where Dorey thought he could make a shilling.

Joshua wondered if Christiana would really marry the trader. At the moment, she seemed resigned to do so, but Joshua couldn't picture it. Once Dorey got Christiana back to civilization, likely she would bolt with little Beth like a cat out of a box. If so, she surely would take Joshua and Samuel with her as well.

With that, Joshua made his decision, if it was ever his to make. He would go along with Dorey and Christiana, and once across the mountains, decide what to do thereafter. For Samuel's sake, he could not remain here. He was determined that his brother would grow up knowing his true heritage, not just the life of the Indians. Joshua owed that much to the memory of his mother.

"When will we leave?" Joshua asked Christiana.

"Tomorrow. Mr. Dorey is eager to get away from here."

"We will go to Charles Town?"

"So I hope." She smiled. "If so, that at least will be something good out of this. I'm so eager to see real streets, real buildings, real dresses and breeches and hats and coats. And I have family there, too. I truly do love Charles Town."

"Mother loved it too," Joshua said. "I wished she were alive to go with us."

"So do I, Joshua," said Christiana.

Henry Dorey eyed Joshua the way he would a lame and useless horse. Joshua, who stood beside Christiana's horse and held its leads, refused to look back at the big trader and wondered if Dorey was the sort to hold against him his old grudge with Jack Byrum.

In cradleboards provided by Kwali the two babies rode, strapped to Christiana's horse. It was ironic that only at the end had Kwali's encouragement of cradleboards prevailed, but that had happened solely because Christiana could conceive of no better way to carry the babies while on horseback.

They set off, plodding slowly out of Tikwalitsi and onto a trail leading northeast. Dorey stared straight ahead as he rode, but Joshua looked around, knowing he might never see Tikwalitsi again. When he passed the edge of town, he saw Bloody Eagle standing haughtily, arms crossed. Beside him was John Hawk. Joshua looked away from both and did not look again until they were far from the Indian town.

Dorey let out a long, slow whistle of relief. "Godamighty, but I didn't know but what I would lose my hair doing this," he said, twisting in the saddle to look at Christiana. "Woman, I hope you know what I've risked for you."

Christiana gave him a sweet smile, which seemed to satisfy him. He turned forward again; Christiana's smile died at once, and she shuddered subtly.

Once away from the Cherokee village, Dorey seemed prone to talk. In that such was unusual for him, Joshua put it down to nervousness. Dorey chattered on about what he had heard of developments since the fall of Fort Loudoun. As rumored, Little Carpenter had successfully spirited John Stuart away to safety, and Virginia had sent back to the Cherokee harsh warnings of reprisal if all Fort Loudoun prisoners were not turned over, the captured cannon given back, and the fort relinquished by the Cherokees for British reoccupation. The British were also demanding that the Cherokees recognize Little Carpenter as the emperor of the whole Cherokee nation, but Dorey doubted that would happen.

In Little Carpenter's absence as he was taking John Stuart to safety, some of the staunchly anti-British Cherokee leaders had stirred war spirits higher and in a gesture of contempt had even plundered Little Carpenter's house. Some of the Fort Loudoun prisoners in other towns had been tortured; hearing of that made Joshua realize how fortunate he, Christiana, and the babies had been in Tikwalitsi.

The fort was likely to be burned down, if it hadn't been already, Dorey said. All in all, it was no time for a free white man to be loitering about the Overhill towns, and Dorey was eager to get away.

They traveled twenty miles the first day, pausing only to eat dried meat and hominy and allow Christiana to tend the babies. That night they camped in a thicket near a spring. Dorey built a small fire, parched corn, and roasted some salted beef for their supper.

"Will we go to Charles Town?" Joshua asked.

Dorey, who seemed offended every time Joshua said anything, glared at the boy as if he were stupid. "Charles Town! Why would I go to Charles Town, you little fool?"

Joshua glanced at Christiana, who looked as surprised as he, and murmured, "I just thought . . ."

"Well, you thought wrong, you little swillhead. Where we're going makes no difference anyway. A man's woman, she goes wherever he says and don't mind it. Ain't that right, dear heart?"

Dorey had only today begun calling Christiana dear heart, and Joshua could see how much she hated it. She did not respond to Dorey's question. Dorey noted her silence, and as Joshua covertly watched him, began stewing in anger. After a couple of minutes, the trader stood and went to one of the packs from which he removed a jug. He unstopped it and tilted it back; the breeze carried the smell of rum.

Joshua went to Christiana's side and pretended to be playing with Beth and Samuel as he whispered quietly to her. "Don't worry, Christiana. You can get away from him and get back to Charles Town soon. I'll help you."

"What are you over there whispering about, you squat pisshead?" Dorey bellowed at Joshua.

Christiana looked deeply offended and angry. "Mr.

Dorey, if you expect to keep company with me, I'm obliged to ask you to keep your language decent."

Dorey snarled and took another swig of rum, after which he muttered to himself. Joshua said nothing else, fearing to speak. Dorey drew near to the fire and settled down, drinking more rum. Finally he stopped the jug, sat it beside him, and lay on his side, turning his back to the fire, gazing into the thicket with his chin in his hand. A few minutes later his hand dropped, his head lolled to the ground, and he began snoring.

Joshua wondered if Christiana felt as hopeless as he. The fire slowly died, and the evening grew colder. Joshua rose and silently added sticks to the blaze. As he did so, a big spark jumped out of the fire and wafted over to settle on Dorey's left ear.

The big man woke up with a yowl and a curse, and leapt to his feet with surprising celerity. He spun and looked furiously at Joshua. "Burn me, will you?" he bellowed. "I'll learn you to burn me, you little swine's arse!"

Dorey reached to the fire and picked up a smoldering brand. The wood glowed angry red. The drunken trader whipped the brand back and down again, striking Joshua on the shoulders. Sparks and pieces of smoldering wood exploded, some of them going down Joshua's back, beneath his shirt. Joshua cried out, and Christiana did the same.

Swearing bitterly, Dorey hit the boy again, and again. Joshua collapsed into a shuddering heap, fearing for his life. Christiana broke into loud wails and pleaded with Dorey to stop. The babies, disturbed by the commotion and noise, fretted with thin choking cries that in the forest sounded as weak as the calls of newly hatched robins.

Only when Christiana ran to Dorey and grabbed his arm did the trader's brutality stop. His shoulders slowly slumped, his lower lip jutted out through his whiskers, and his arms hung apishly at his sides, the glowing brand still in one hand.

Christiana's fear changed to anger. "If ever, ever again

you lift a hand against one of mine, you will never lay that hand on me, Mr. Dorey!" she declared. "You are a beast!"

Dorey's ugly eyes shifted sideways to study her. His outthrust lower lip held a single drop of saliva that refused to let go and fall. "A 'beast' you say? Hell, if I am, I'm the beast who saved your hide from the Indians! You're mine now, woman, paid for with good trade wares, and I'll have respect from you, I will!"

He pointed a thick finger down at Joshua. "Your father was scum, and as far as I'm concerned, you're skimmed off the same pool. For the sake of my woman, I'm allowing you to be here, but if ever you lift a hand to harm me again, I'll scalp you like Bloody Eagle scalped your father. The Cherokees told me about that, they did. Bloody Eagle peeled your pap's nightcap pretty as you please, they say, and it's the best damn thing that red sod ever did." He laughed hoarsely.

Joshua sat up slowly, then like a cat leapt straight at Dorey, trying to hit him at knee level. Dorey sidestepped and kicked, catching Joshua in the side of the head and leaving him stunned on the ground.

After that, Joshua kept away from Dorey, but to his misfortune, Dorey did not keep away from him. As the travelers moved farther northeast, following buffalo and Indian trails and the courses of streams, Dorey became more abusive toward Joshua and more aggressive toward Christiana. It was evident now, even to young Joshua, that Dorey's idea of "marriage" to Christiana did not mean marriage in the usual sense. The trader considered her a bought woman and clearly would not long stand for his perceived carnal rights to be denied. Nevertheless, Christiana had managed so far to keep him at arm's length, usually by pleading for him to show restraint, given Joshua's presence.

That served its purpose for Christiana but also added to Dorey's frustration and his dislike for Joshua. Further, it became evident that Dorey really did see Joshua as the embodiment of Jack Byrum, and often when he beat Joshua he raged about his hatred of Byrum. Christiana continued to come to Joshua's defense, but there was nothing she could do to stop him. Joshua grew increasingly sore and bruised and more than once feared Dorey would beat him to death.

One night, as the trader snored, Christiana crept to Joshua's side. "You must leave," she whispered.

"I mustn't," Joshua replied just as softly. "He might hurt you."

"Bless you, sweet boy, but do you think there is aught you could do to stop him hurting me if that's what he chooses? I know beyond doubt that if he keeps on at you as he has, he'll have you dead. You've got to run."

"Then run away from him with me. Bring the babies. . . ."

"No. He would run us down and kill us all. If you go alone, he'll be glad to let you go, and I can remain to see that the babies are kept safe until I can get away from him myself, once we reach towns and decent people again."

Dorey turned and snorted in his sleep; Joshua waited until he had resettled into a steady snoring sleep before responding to Christiana. "I'm not sure he's going to anyplace where there are towns and people. The traders who came to the fort talked of more than one bandit—he may have partners waiting somewhere ahead, waiting for him to come."

"I've thought of all the same things, Joshua, and feared what it might mean to me, but you mustn't let that stop you. What with the babies, I've no choice but to stay with old Satan yonder. But you can escape, and must."

Joshua shook his head. "I promised myself and Mother, after she died, that I would see to Samuel. I cannot leave him."

"If you stay, it's all the same as leaving him. You'll be leaving him when Dorey kills you. Don't worry about Samuel—I'll keep him safe, and someday we'll be reunited."

"But how? If I leave, I may never see you again."

Christiana smiled sadly. "We must trust to God, my boy. Only he can know how we will be brought together again. Keep your faith strong, and he will see us through."

"I have no food, no gun—"

"Yes, you do. I've been stealing from Dorey's packs without him knowing, and I've taken you a musket this very night. It's a sad enough weapon, the sort the traders sell the Indians, but it will have to do." Christiana reached out to him and framed his face in her hands. They were callused and gritty against his cheeks. "Oh, would that I could know I was doing the right thing to send you off! Yet I know I cannot let you stay to be beaten into your grave by Henry Dorey. I can do nothing but let you go, and trust to God and to your own woodsman's skill to keep you safe. You're more a woodsman even as a boy than that sleeping swine there ever will hope to be, and him full-grown. You're a remarkable lad, Joshua Byrum. I sense unseen hands upon you. You will survive and go on to do greater things than ever your father or mother, God rest them, could have thought of."

"My father told me I was blood of his blood, and could be no better than he was," Joshua said.

"Your father was a fool, Joshua, if you'll forgive me for so speaking. But now we must hush. It is time for you to sleep. Then you will go."

"Tonight?"

"No, but soon. Tomorrow night, if you can. You can go up the great valley into Virginia. The food I have saved will not be enough to keep you long, and you will have to provide for yourself. You will be alone, but not really alone, for I will be with you in my thoughts and prayers, and God will be at your side." She gave Joshua an emotional hug. "Dear little orphaned boy! I'm afraid to send you out, even though I don't doubt you will make it through, somehow. Just beware the Indians as you go."

"I will." Joshua lifted his head and tried to look manly. "If I find Indians, I will kill them and take their scalps."

"You'll hide from them, if you're wise. Now, come here and sleep close to me tonight. Soon enough we'll be seeing each other no more, and it may be a long time indeed before we are together again."

Joshua took his blankets and lay down beside Christiana near the banked fire that Dorey had built before drowning his consciousness once more in his seemingly unending supply of rum. Joshua felt the woman's motherly warmth against him and realized how deeply he loved and admired Christiana Cox. His mother had been much like Christiana, though not as talkative or demonstrative. In Christiana it was as if a little bit of Hester Byrum was living still.

The boy closed his eyes and wondered what it would be like to face the wilderness alone. The prospect was daunting but not really frightening. Joshua felt at home in the forests, and he had learned much about its secrets during his three years among the Overhill Cherokees. Like Christiana, he did not doubt he would survive.

Only one thing nagged at him, making him doubt: leaving Samuel. Was it right to abandon his own baby brother, leaving him accessible to the harm Dorey could inflict? He did not know and tried to reason the question out.

When sleep overtook him, he had still found no answer.

Joshua's impending departure was a secret that hung in the air between the boy and Christiana all the next day. Every mutual glance was heavy with it; every reference to other matters actually referred to it. Christiana stayed closer than usual to Joshua throughout the day's travel, but Dorey did not seem to notice. Twice during the afternoon he found excuses to strike Joshua, bruising an eye the first time and leaving a swollen red welt on his shoulder the next. Joshua now felt sure that Dorey was knowingly or unknowingly trying to kill him.

They camped that night near a small creek that ran out of a limestone crevice in a steep hillside. Joshua lay in his blankets, curled for warmth in his bearskin cloak, and wondered if he really had the will to leave. Rolling over, he felt the pain of the many bruises Dorey had given him and knew he had no choice.

He heard Christiana sniffing faintly from time to time.

She was crying quietly, not sleeping. No doubt she was waiting for him to rise, take the pouch she had secretly packed and concealed behind one of the packsaddles on the ground nearby, and go. For Joshua to leave remained out of the question, however, as long as Dorey was awake, and tonight the brutish man seemed uninclined to rest.

"We're getting close," Dorey said at length, heading for the packs to get another jug. "Two days from now we'll be sleeping under a real roof, together in a real bed, Christiana. Going to be sweet, ain't it, dear heart?" He tilted back the jug, and Joshua heard the gurgle of it from fifteen feet away.

Another hour passed, and finally Dorey lay down. In five minutes he was snoring loudly. Still Joshua did not move. Christiana had risen a little earlier to feed the infants and remained awake. Joshua had already decided that when he left, he wanted to do so without tear-filled eyes watching him. He hoped exhaustion from the day's journey would soon claim Christiana.

The fire was a bed of coals and the sky was pitch dark when Joshua at last rose. Dorey still snored; Christiana breathed evenly and deeply. As silent as the darkness itself, Joshua moved to the packsaddle and picked up the pouch. The short trade musket also lay waiting; he hefted it up, slinging the pouch, powder horn, and shot bag across his shoulder. He hoped Dorey would blame him alone for taking the items, so that Christiana would not suffer for it.

He walked on moccasined feet to the edge of the camp and paused to look back. Christiana remained motionless, breathing regularly as before. Dorey was still snoring. Samuel shifted and cooed in his sleep—and that, more than anything, was what made Joshua feel suddenly choked and sad. Before he had time to lose control of his will, he turned and walked into the dark forest. Tonight he would travel as far away from the camp as the inky blackness would allow and wait until well into the next day to move on.

* * *

He found it ironic that as he traveled through the night, distancing himself from Dorey's camp, he was not much aware of being alone. It was only when the morning sun scoured the forest with light and awakened the weary boy that he sensed his isolation.

It roused some fear in him, but not panic. He was in an element very familiar to him, and his examination of the goods Christiana had packed for him out of Dorey's supplies proved encouraging. She had included flint and steel, plenty of parched corn, boiled corn bread still wrapped in the shucks in which it had been cooked, handfuls of roasted pumpkin seeds, chestnuts, jerked beef, boiled acorns, and round slices of dried pumpkin. He could survive on this fare alone for quite some time.

Still, the supplies would almost certainly not last him for his entire journey, the length of which he was unsure of. His ammunition and powder were limited, and his trade musket was of the lowest quality and poorest accuracy. Danger from Indians would be significant. Survival might be a challenge.

But better this than traveling with Dorey. Joshua ran his hands across his various bruises and winced. Again he worried for Samuel and wondered if he had been right to leave him behind.

After a lean breakfast consisting of a piece of beef and a slice of dried pumpkin, Joshua set out, giving no thought to the fact that his situation was most unusual for a ten-year-old boy and that his adventure, once known, would make his name known and be the subject of conversations by campfires and hearths for many years to come.

He reshifted his pack, checked the lock of his musket once more, and set out across the Tanisi wilderness, heading toward Virginia.

5

On thio day, Thursday, December 6, 1760, an early snow had fallen since noon but had only lightly blanketed the forest. The temperature had hovered just around the freezing point most of the afternoon, causing the snow to melt rather than accumulate. Now the air was becoming colder as the day waned toward dusk. Alphus Colter's moss-stuffed moccasins had grown as moist as the sodden leaves upon which they trod, so he made little sound as he descended the ridge to the creek running along its base, leading his deerskin-laden packhorse behind him, his two dogs sniffing along ahead.

At the water's side he knelt and drank with one hand, holding his long rifle with the other. The wind stirred the bare treetops as he drank, beginning with a distant whispering noise somewhere beyond the ridgetop, and sweeping down toward the creek, growing louder as it approached, then fading. The branches above Alphus swayed, making the shadow patterns on the leafy forest floor a flurry of change, and then grew still again. The rich speckling cast across the ground by the sunlight

73

from the west calmed its frantic dance, and in the nearly
motionless pattern, Alphus was all but invisible.

He stood, letting the horse take its turn at the stream,
and stretched his shoulders, rolling them beneath his
frocklike caped rifleman's coat of dressed fringed deerskin. The coat, which hung to the middle of his thighs,
covered a shirt of similar design, but made of a combination of linen and wool fibers. His flat-brimmed hat was of
dark felt and sat comfortably on his head, just tight
enough around his brow to keep the hat from easily
blowing off. Around his waist was a broad brown sash,
tied in the back, hung with a belt ax and a scabbarded
knife. His rifle bag and powder horn hung at his right
hip, slung over his left shoulder. Alphus's trousers were
of the French fly pattern common on the frontier, made
of heavy wool. His moccasins, each made after the Indian
style from a single piece of deerskin, had large flaplike
tops that were bound around his calves with whang strips
that attached to the moccasins where they narrowed
about the ankles. His clothing, unlike that of some of his
peers, was deliberately unornamented, avoiding the
beads and dyed cloth fringes some favored.

Alphus was, for his era and people, a tall man, a
quarter inch above six feet. He had in his time encountered a few men taller than he, but such were rare on the
frontier. His height and features, which were more well
formed and impressive than outright handsome, had
often drawn attention that embarrassed him, for he was
reticent by nature. Alphus was never comfortable with
eyes exploring him and talk peppering at him. In the
background away from people was where he felt most at
ease. His natural reticence and love of solitude had made
his life as a North Carolina borderer and far-ranging
Tanisi hunter all but inevitable.

He stretched once more and led the horse over the
narrow stream and through the forest, following the
water's course. At length the stream widened in a marshy
area in which tall cane grew. An old buffalo trail cut
through the cane, and Alphus followed it. This land was
familiar to him, for he had hunted here two weeks ago,

traveling in the opposite direction. His eyes scanned the canebrake as he passed through it, and at the end he stopped and examined the forest before and around him prior to going on. With another bale of deerskins on his packsaddle, Alphus felt well heeled and cheerful, though eternally cautious, as a woodsman must be. He traveled quickly, moving toward the predetermined rendezvous as naturally as a snake gliding through summer grass.

The land through which he traveled was to a man of his temperament and interests a virtual paradise, despite the dangers that hid behind the beauty. Rich with game and resources, this region was hunted by a variety of Indians. Even the northern tribes maintained they held rights over it, but the best Indian claim, in Alphus's view, was that of the Cherokees living to the southwest.

Yet even they did not truly own this land in his way of looking at it. Nobody owned it—it was simply there, virtually untouched, filled with deer, turkey, buffalo, bear, otter, beaver, and elk that grazed on the high mountain balds in summer. Alphus had seen pigeon flocks that hung like storm clouds in the sky and took many minutes to pass over, wild turkeys so fat they could scarcely move, and herds of buffalo that tramped out excellent pathways through the valleys, forests, and thickets. Every tree was alive with squirrels, hundreds of varieties of fowl, and occasional egg-hunting black-snakes.

He and Levi Hampton had hunted here for the first time this year. Few hunters had penetrated this far. Alphus, who had the eye of an untrained naturalist, had already made himself familiar with the land and its vegetation. In the river bottoms grew wetland trees: sycamore, river birch, sweet gum, and willow. On the benches above the stream bottoms grew boxelder, white ash, beech, and elm, along with a mix of red and white oak, hickory, walnut, and pecan. The nut-bearing trees had been planted by the streams themselves, which swept the bouyant nuts along and deposited them in times of flooding on the streamside terraces. Thickets of green alder grew in the worst of the flood-ravaged areas and with the willows dominated the sandbanks and gravel bars of the rivers.

The often rocky forest hillsides were covered with oak, maple, hickory, chestnut, poplar, ash, black gum, and black locust, particularly on the north-facing slopes, which were densely shaded, undergrown with dogwood and sourwood and overgrown with ivy and vines, some of the latter extending to the tops of the highest trees and growing as thick as a strong man's leg. The southern and southwest slopes were hotter and drier, and hosted stands of pine, or pine and oak mixed. Here Alphus often saw the signs of periodic fires that kept the undergrowth from becoming too heavy.

The higher northern slopes and the mountain coves were filled with huge chestnut trees that provided feasts in season and also made the forest floor hazardous with foot-piercing burrs. Yellow poplar, red oak, basswood, cherry, maple, oak, and buckeye grew among them. On the south-facing higher slopes were a variety of oak, pine, mountain ash, and spruce.

At the highest levels of the mountains grew spruce and lichen-covered fir, intermixed with balds and thickets of rhododendron on the north slopes and mountain laurel on the south slopes and ridgetops.

With his summers back in North Carolina dominated by the necessary drudgery of farming, Alphus had not had the opportunity to see the Tanisi country in the summer months. A rich land indeed this would be in the warm season. He could picture it easily: fish-filled streams gushing down the mountainsides and watering the valleys, wild strawberries growing thick; old Indian fields and natural fire-created meadows wide and breezy, the massive forests open and parklike in many places, tangled and undergrown in others; ridges rich with great patches of elderberries, huckleberries, and blueberries. Even an inexperienced woodsman would have little excuse for going hungry in such a land in the summer, and an experienced one such as Alphus could live well indeed. Someday he might come back to this country for good. Put in a crop of corn, build a cabin, and settle—if ever the Indian trouble subsided and the land opened.

Exactly when that could happen Alphus could not guess. There was plenty enough reason at the moment for a man to think twice or even three times before venturing long into the wilderness. He had heard from another hunter of the fall of Fort Loudoun many weeks ago. No doubt there would be some sort of reprisal for it come spring. Yet such matters seemed relatively distant to Alphus, whose life since the death of his wife ten years ago had been one of solitude and minding strictly his own affairs.

He had always been drawn to new country, as had his father before him, and even the rugged mountains sepa rating the Tanisi land from his own little creekside farmstead in North Carolina had proven too small a deterrent to check his restlessness. Even now, with half a century's age on him, he could barely endure the summers of farming. The turning of the leaves and the coming of harvest was to Alphus Colter a period of joy, for it heralded the time he could put aside duty for pleasure. In good years the pleasure also brought profit, but even without that motivation, Alphus would have hunted out of pure restlessness. He wondered sometimes if he would ever become settled and feel at home, as a decent man should.

When he had come to North Carolina four years ago at the behest of his merchant brother Thomas, it had been in hopes that in Carolina he would find a place he could feel content to stay, while also giving Gabriel, his son, a chance to learn the merchant's trade from Thomas. For the first year, Alphus thought he had actually found his long-sought haven. The hunting within a few easy miles of his cabin was good, and neighbors were far enough away not to make him feel choked. He had come to know Levi Hampton, the closest of his neighbors, and had found in him a kindred soul. Together the men ventured out on hunts that ranged increasingly far. Alphus often listened as Levi talked longingly about going over the mountains into the land beyond. The more Levi talked, the more Alphus felt the familiar old restlessness.

It all was nothing but talk at the beginning, but this year the pair had actually taken their hunt, almost without conscious plan, deep into the Tanisi country. They had immediately begun gathering deerskins, beaver and otter pelts, and stockpiling them at a crude but sturdy station-camp cabin built on the side of a slope behind a laurel thicket that made the cabin all but invisible until a man was within twenty feet of it. For fear of Indians, they had carefully erased any trails they made to the cabin, and so far they had avoided detection.

Alphus had felt a little reluctant at first to hunt in the Tanisi country with the Indian question still unsettled, but his almost-neighbor Daniel Boone was doing the same, hunting down along a tributary of the Watauga River some miles away. If Boone was willing to risk the Indians, then by Joseph, so were Alphus Colter and Levi Hampton. And so far, to Alphus's pleasure, he and his partner had seen few signs of Indian presence.

Alphus followed the dogs down an ancient buffalo path that was worn six inches deep into the earth through forest undergrowth and emerged on a rocky flat that began a gradual descent into a valley fifty feet beyond. He winced when an unseen chestnut burr stabbed through the thin sole of one of his moccasins, which were almost worn out. Such footwear didn't last long in this country. Limping on more slowly until the pain subsided, he descended the slope to the valley floor and reached another creek.

With his eyes scanning the darkening land around him for signs of human presence, he followed a faintly visible path along the streambank until he came to the base of a familiar limestone cliff marked black with the soot of an earlier fire. He knew before he reached the cliff that Levi had not yet arrived. There had been no marks on the earth and no smell of horses or fresh woodsmoke.

Alphus was glad he had reached the rendezvous as early as he had, for a difference of a few minutes would have meant either traveling in darkness or waiting until morning to finish his trek. As it was, he would have time to gather wood before the sun was fully gone.

After circling the area and satisfying himself there was no danger about, Alphus removed the horse's pack, bale, and saddle, then hobbled the animal in a patch of drying grass. A fat wild turkey that had been tied on the pack he slung on a sapling branch, high enough off the ground to keep it out of reach of the dogs. He began gathering dry wood from beneath the snow-dusted leaves and the dry undersides of deadfalls. The wind was kicking up, colder than before; the coming night bore the prospect of further snowfall.

When he had a good supply of wood close-by, Alphus cleared a spot in front of a deep recess in the cliff base and laid a few dry twigs at hand. Using flint, steel, and punk, he sparked a blaze. Shielding it to regulate the wind that reached it, he allowed the fire to catch well, then began placing slightly larger twigs and sticks in place until at last he had a sizable fire blazing. It cast an orange glow up the face of the cliff above him and a semicircle of light that reached out several feet from the escarpment base. As Alphus worked with the fire, he avoided staring directly into it to minimize loss of vision that such carelessness would create if something in the dark land around him suddenly required his attention.

When the fire was blazing well, he set two stout sticks into the earth on the side of the fire away from the cliff. Angling them out a few degrees, he firmed them, then began stacking sticks of similar size horizontally against them, creating a heat reflector that also served to break the wind, hide the fire somewhat, and create the proper draft to funnel the smoke skyward and away from the recess in the cliff.

When that was done, Alphus retrieved the turkey. As night fell, he plucked the bird, cut off its head, and cleaned the carcass, feeding the offal to the dogs. He stoked the fire again, then carried the turkey to a stream running close-by. There he coated it thickly with mud.

Some distance from the cliff he scooped out a hole,

which he lined with coals from the fire. On these he placed the mud-coated bird. More coals went on top of the turkey, then dirt to bury it entirely. Returning to the fireside, he ate a simple meal of corn and dried meat, then removed his moccasins for drying. Putting on a spare pair of moccasins, he settled back to smoke his pipe and listen to the night-music of the land around him. Occasionally he would rise and walk over to the turkey, slowly roasting beneath the ground.

This would be a good land to live in. The thought went through his mind again, as it had a score of other times today. Alphus relit his pipe and debated the propriety of thinking like that. He had a good home where he was. Gabriel, though lacking a mother, at least had a stout roof over his head and a chance to learn a business that could see him through life. To leave all that behind would be foolish. Besides, this land was Indian land, forbidden for settlement by law. A white man would have no right to settle here—not yet. To do so would invite separation from his topknot. Of course, North Carolina had seen more than its share of Indian troubles, too, what with all the border warfare. The little Hankins Creek settlement where Alphus lived was still abandoned, as it had been for several months, because of endless Indian raids. Alphus had sent Gabriel off with Thomas into Virginia to wait out the hostilities. No doubt, when he finally re-turned to the settlement, he would find his farmstead either damaged or destroyed. No matter; a man could always rebuild, and Alphus had done it before.

The evening waned, the snow increased, as Alphus had expected, and this time it lay. Only the area around the fire, under the cliff recess and about the hump of earth under which the turkey roasted, remained free of a white mantle. Alphus smoked his pipe, kept the fire going, huddled beneath his blankets, and occasionally dozed.

It was about midnight when he became aware of the presence in the nearby forest. He had been dozing again, and his pipe had fallen from his teeth. Picking it up, he shook out the old tobacco, refilled the bowl, and lit it with the glowing end of a stick from the fire. When he had it going, he put more wood on the coals and stirred the fire to full flame again.

"I hope you brought more than an empty gut with you, Levi," he said to the darkness.

"I did. Brought me a powerful thirst as well," Levi Hampton said, stepping into the circle of light. "Knew I was coming, did you?"

"Smelt you about five minutes ago, in my sleep."

"The horse, you mean."

"First you. Then the horse."

Levi laughed, thinking it a joke, but it was true; Alphus had always been able to pick up his partner's scent and had tonight, even before the smell of his horse and dogs had become distinguishable from that of Alphus's animals.

Levi took his bundle and tossed it back into the recess. Alphus rose and helped him load his own bale of deerskins back under the protective overhang. In silence the men saw to Levi's horse, and Levi then settled to warm himself by the fire and dry his moccasins as Alphus had earlier.

"That bird in the ground is starting to smell tempting."

"That it is," Alphus said, "but it's got a long time yet to cook. You'll have to settle for dried meat and corn tonight, I'm afraid."

"I've fared worse."

Levi ate in silence. He was of average height, about five feet five inches, and stockily built. When Levi stood still, Alphus always perceived him as firmly rooted into the ground, like a short but stout oak. One of the best shots in North Carolina and a fierce fighter when he had to be, Levi was nevertheless a gentle man by nature and preferred to avoid conflict. "Live peaceably with all men" he was fond of quoting.

"Find any trouble?" Alphus asked.

"None. No sign of Indians." He picked at his teeth with a fingernail. "You?"

"Same."

"So where to from here?"

"Back to the hill," said Alphus, using the informal name the two hunters had given to their station camp. "Scaffold up what we've got, then head out again."

Levi nodded and took another bite of tough dried meat, then walked to the stream to take several long swallows of water with the gourd drinking cup he always carried on his waist sash, hanging it by the curved wood handle he had carved and fitted for it.

Returning to the fireside, Levi poked the brands and coals with a stick. "Been thinking on Sina quite a bit these days," he said.

"Worrying for her?"

"Not really. Just thinking of her, wanting to be sure all is well."

"By Joseph, Levi, we haven't been gone from her any time at all. I never seen a man so attached to a woman."

Once again there was a time of silence, common between the two hunters, not uncomfortable. "So you're planning to return already?" Alphus asked.

Levi shook his head. "No. There's no need for that. We've just gotten started, as you say."

Alphus retired his pipe yet again; the wind had just blown most of his lighted ashes from the bowl. "I've been thinking some myself, Levi. You can do what you want about this, but it's struck me not to go back at all this next year."

Levi lifted bushy brows. His eyes were deep brown and small, set in a broad face kept meticulously clean-shaven, even in the wilderness. "A full year's hunt?"

"Aye. There's no returning yet to Hankins Creek, and I can't abide the thought of sitting on my thumbs up in Virginia, waiting for the Cherokees to settle. Gabriel is in Thomas's hands, safe enough, and he knew even before I set out that I might wait a second spring before returning."

Levi looked up at the black sky, which was pelting down icy flakes of white more heavily now. "It's a fair thought," he admitted, "but you've got no woman waiting for you. The womenfolk, they don't like a man to be gone too long at a time. It frets them."

"You told Sina you might hunt long this time, did you not?"

"That I did. Still . . ."

"I won't push you on it, Levi. I can stay here alone if need be. But the hunting is better with two, and together we could make enough with an extra year to see our families better off for it."

They slept well that night, but then they almost always slept well. Their daily treks were typically long and if not always strenuous, were tiring in their steadiness. The morning sun, however, found both men already awake an hour and Alphus busy digging up the roasted turkey, which he speared deeply with a sharpened stick and drew up from the hole.

Poking in the stick fractured off about half the baked mud that had protected the turkey from the coals. A delicious aroma drifted across the cliff-base camp, drawing one of Levi's ready smiles. Alphus was less prone to smile than his partner, though not because he was joyless. He tended to show his feelings more in his pale blue eyes, which were large and remarkably soft in appearance for a man of his age and weathering.

The men broke the rest of the mud from the thoroughly roasted bird, gently washing off the remnants with water, then made corn cakes and breakfasted royally, eating most of the turkey between them. Such feasts were rare for them in the wilderness. Only upon occasions such as reuniting after separate hunts, like this, or in times of especially good fortune did they bother with such a meal.

After they had eaten, they relaxed only long enough for a couple of pipefuls of tobacco each, then smothered the fire, packed up, and began traveling toward the station camp. They did not push hard; there was no hurry, and both men enjoyed the slower pace. On the ground was about an inch of snow, but by noon much of that had melted, and the hooves of the packhorses made slogging sounds on the sodden earth.

In early afternoon they reached the Nolichucky River, paused there to eat, then proceeded, winding along buffalo and Indian trails that took them through open forest, tangled thickets, and rich canebrakes. They killed and skinned two deer along the way, field-dressed the hides, which would dry down to about two pounds each, then traveled northeast as the sun slid toward the west.

On the flat mud beside a spring at which they paused to drink, they detected the first sign of other humans either had seen in weeks. A footprint it was, clearly defined despite the crumbling of the edges. Both men knelt and examined it closely.

"Indian moccasins, but small. Too small for a woman," Alphus commented.

"Well, it's a child, then," Levi returned. He rose and carefully studied the ground all around. "Aye—here's more sign, though it appears somebody's tried to cover it, and done a good job of it, too."

"Any other marks?"

"No, and that's hard to figure. Judging from the size, I'd say that's a right small child to be out alone this far from the Overhill towns. There's bound to be others."

Alphus stood, shifting his rifle a little. "If there are others, then they've covered their tracks."

"Aye." Levi eyed the forest, sniffed the air, and listened. No sound did he hear but the north wind through the barren treetops, the chattering of chickadees, titmice, and finches, and the crashing of the river on the other side of the closest hill.

From then on, they kept their travel especially quiet and their senses deliberately attuned. Neither spoke except when necessary—which was not much of a change since both were prone to be taciturn anyway.

They approached their station camp from the north, a different route than they usually took. Each time they came, they took a different way, seeking to minimize wearing any detectable trails. The closer they got, the more careful they became, stepping as much as possible on rocks and walking along deadfalls to break up their path. At length they paused to hobble the horses temporarily and proceed in on foot, the dogs preceding them.

Their route led them in from above the cabin, which

was set on a wide sandy ledge. They reached the crest of the hill and looked down on the dirt-roofed building, which looked wider than it was because it was built so low. Alphus could stand to full height only at the rear of the cabin, and that was possible only because of a natural depression in the dirt floor.

"See anything?" Levi whispered.

"No, but the dogs have caught a scent. See them?"

"Aye."

Silent as the ghosts of dead warriors, the two hunters divided and came around to different sides of the cabin at the same time. There was only one window, and it was small, put there for the sake not only of ventilation but also defense if it came to that. The window was still shuttered.

Levi looked across at Alphus and wrinkled his nose. Alphus nodded, confirming that he too had detected a new scent about the place. Both men had a keen sense of smell, honed all the keener by their time in the wilderness, and Alphus had noted that it was one of the mysteries of life that this sharpened sense tended to dull, the longer he was away from his hunts, only to heighten again shortly after returning to the wilds.

For two minutes the men stood as still as the rocks of the hillside against which the cabin stood. The dogs growled faintly, bristling but not barking, for they were well trained. Finally Alphus reached out, pulled the latchstring, and swung open the door.

Nothing happened. Alphus picked up and tossed in a rock, expecting some reaction, but none came. Cautiously, Alphus swung around and stooped to enter the door, the top of which was two feet too short for him. As he thrust his head inside, a loud blast filled the cabin, and Alphus jerked backward, dropped his rifle, and fell. The dogs sent up a howl. Levi was so surprised, he let out a yell, then spun around, lowering his long rifle at the same time. He stuck it inside the door, and his finger tightened on the trigger.

* * *

Had Levi's finger tightened half a hairsbreadth more, the life of the wild-eyed young Indian before him would have ended. At the last quarter second, something made him halt. Later he would be glad he had halted, for he had observed two things: Alphus Colter was alive, though bleeding slightly from the outside part of his shoulder, and the young Indian was not an Indian at all.

The boy's skin was begrimed and his hair unkempt, but his features and skin were clearly those of no Indian, though his eyes were as fiery and crazed as those of any drunken warrior Levi had ever encountered in reality or nightmare. The boy was holding a short trade musket, still smoking.

Alphus stood as straight as the low roof would allow, picking up his rifle in the process. He looked at his shoulder wound, found it superficial, so ignored it, concentrating on studying the young fellow before him.

"Reckon you would have took my scalp once I was dead," Alphus said at last. "You look savage enough to do it."

"Who are you?" Levi asked.

No answer. Alphus glanced at his partner's face and saw a cold expression slowly warming with the heat of anger. Levi, for all his usual good humor, had a short temper, particularly in tense situations.

"Listen to me, you little—"

Alphus reached out his hand and touched Levi's shoulder. "Let me talk to him," he said.

He stepped forward and began to kneel to be more on the level of the boy, who was crouched against the back wall. But as he did, the boy tried to strike him with the empty musket. Alphus reached out, grabbed the musket, and pulled it away.

"Ain't you the heathen, now!" he declared. "You always try to kill men coming back to their own camp?"

Now Alphus did kneel; he drew closer to the boy. "Listen to me, son—we're white men, and friends. We're sorry we put a scare into you like we did. My name is Alphus Colter, and this here is Levi Hampton. We come from North Carolina. Now, can you tell us your name?"

The dirty face took on the haughty expression of those who are afraid and trying to hide it. "I am Ayunini," the boy said in a strong voice with only a hint of a tremble.

"He's been a Cherokee prisoner, sure as we're living," Levi said to Alphus.

"Is that right, son? You been a prisoner of the Indians?"

A nod, then: "I'm not afraid of you."

"No need to be. I'm your friend. You got a white name?"

"Joshua Byrum. The name Ayunini was given to me by Attakullakulla." Alphus detected pride in the boy's voice.

"That's the Little Carpenter," Levi said, still talking to Alphus as if Joshua could not hear him. "He's been among the Cherokees for certain."

Alphus asked, "Fort Loudoun?"

"Yes."

"You got living kin?"

"No."

"Cherokees killed them?"

"My mother died in the fort. My father was killed and scalped by the Bloody Eagle of Tikwalitsi."

Alphus said, "Sorry to hear that. How did you get away?"

Joshua did not answer at once, and Alphus could see that he was trying to decide what to say. "I escaped" was all he finally came out with.

"Where you from, before Fort Loudoun?"

"Charles Town. My father, he was a trader out of Carolina to the Overhill towns."

Levi's eyes sparked. "Jack Byrum?" It was the first thing he had said directly to Joshua.

"Aye," Joshua responded.

"I've heard of him," Levi said, now talking to Alphus again. "Cherokee trader, and a bloody sorry one, from what I hear."

"Do you have other kin back in Carolina?" Alphus asked.

"No."

"No aunts, uncles, brothers or such anywhere?"

Again Joshua was slow to answer, and at this question seemed a trifle upset. "No," he said softly.

Alphus took a deep breath, forgot where he was, and stood too quickly. He bumped his head on a beam but did not swear; Levi had never heard Alphus swear, even once.

The two hunters withdrew outside, making sure they took all the weaponry with them, for they did not trust the young heathen inside not to try to blow their heads off.

"What are we supposed to do now?" Levi asked.

"Feed him some supper, I reckon."

"Blast and blazes, Alphus, you know what I mean! That boy's an orphan! What are going to do with an orphan out here?"

Alphus dabbed at his bloody shoulder. "Send him out hunting, I'd say. If he can bark a tree limb the way he barked my shoulder, by Joseph, we'll eat some fine squirrel stews."

With that, Alphus turned and reentered the cabin, leaving Levi staring after him. Alphus had strange and irritating ways about him sometimes and could be awfully slow to come to grips with problems. Always wanted to think things out for half an eternity first. Levi shook his head philosophically, then climbed up the hill to the packhorses.

CAROLINA

6

In the year and a half since
he had stumbled upon the hunting camp of Alphus and
Levi, much had happened to Joshua. His boyish form,
though still lean, had become more muscled, and his
hair was now very long. He wore it in a queue at the back
of his neck, tied with a rawhide whang. The clothing he
had worn upon leaving Dorey's party had worn out thoroughly and had been replaced by deerskin hunter's garb,
carefully stitched together by Levi Hampton, who was
good with a needle.

It had taken a few weeks for Joshua to become fully
relaxed in the company of the two hunters. Alphus, who
could tell that Joshua felt drawn to him, had gradually
cajoled the boy into telling him more of his story. He did
not initially understand Joshua's seeming reluctance to
talk about his experiences and finally put it down to the
trauma of having seen people butchered and tortured,
and having been left on his own in the wilderness at
such a young age.

As months passed, however, Alphus had begun to
doubt the latter part of his assessment. He felt increasingly sure that the wilderness had never held many

terrors for Joshua Byrum. Never had he seen a boy so
naturally fitted for life in the forests. Even with the
clumsy trade musket, the youth was a decent and improving shot. Further, he seemed already to know skills
and tricks of the forest that most hunters had to learn
through years of trial and error. That Joshua had picked
up these from his Cherokee associations was evidenced
by such practices as his throwing a tiny piece of meat
from any animal he killed into the fire before eating of it
himself. The Cherokees did that as an offering to sacred
fire; Joshua seemed to do it in natural, perhaps even
unconscious imitation of them.

Alphus and Levi had kept Joshua holed up in the cabin
for the first week after his arrival and ranged only short
distances to hunt, but then that had started cutting into
their take of deerskins. Levi had fretted—he always
tended to fret much more than Alphus did—that trying
to be nursemaids to an orphan boy and effective hunters
at the same time was impossible. Alphus had agreed and
suggested that perhaps a boy who could survive for a
month alone in the Tanisi wilderness might not need
nursemaids. Why not take him along with them on their
hunts?

Levi had been doubtful about that, saying that maybe
he should take Joshua up into Virginia and at the same
time check on the welfare of his and Alphus's families
and try to get an idea of when they might safely be able
to reoccupy their North Carolina farmsteads.

Alphus had puffed his pipe, and thought over the
proposal, and concluded that it might have merit—especially if Levi was going to worry himself to death otherwise. The negative side was that Levi would miss out on
some good hunting and trapping, and both of them would
suffer for the resulting lowered harvest of skins and pelts,
which by agreement they were going to share evenly.
Further, there was the question of who would take
Joshua into care once he reached Virginia.

Eventually they had put the question to Joshua. At first
mention of Virginia, which Alphus had surmised had
been Joshua's original destination, the boy's eyes spar-

kled. Then Alphus presented the alternative of staying to hunt, and the sparkle was replaced by a hungry gleam. The notion of spending months of isolation in the wilderness, hunting deer and trapping beaver and otter with two graying Carolina hunters, obviously was no unappealing prospect to Joshua.

Levi, obviously uncomfortable with the conclusion of the matter, had talked about heading into Virginia on his own, and Alphus had not tried to dissuade him. But Levi never got around to going. When the spring of 1761 came, he had dallied to help Alphus and Joshua plant a small corn crop on the edge of a remote meadow. Then he stayed around to help tend and guard it. The crop flourished, and through the summer the three of them had fared well, living on the abundant game, the natural foods available from the land, and their corn supply. Autumn came, bringing with it the first anniversary of Joshua's appearance in the cabin. By then, Levi had ceased talking about going back to Virginia.

On a snowy day in December of 1761, the three had encountered a lone hunter on the north fork of the Holston River. Since Joshua had come to them, this was only the second human being, save for one small Cherokee hunting party, the hunters had seen. The first had been fellow North Carolinian Daniel Boone, with whom they had shared a meal of venison back at the end of 1760 after Boone had traced their sign and found them camped in a thicket.

This second man was also a hunter, but unlike Boone, not a white man. He was a freed slave from Salisbury by the name of Gillam Smith. Having lost his entire family to the ague in the spring, he had ventured out across the mountains to hunt and console himself in solitude and in the fall had returned briefly to Salisbury before crossing the mountains again.

Eager for information about social and political affairs back home, Alphus and Levi had quizzed Smith closely and were told that some families were already returning to the Carolina border settlements. The Cherokees had suffered several blows since the fall of Fort Loudoun.

Back in May, according to Smith, a force of more than two thousand under the command of Colonel James Grant of South Carolina had arrived at Fort Prince George. They were but one prong of a punitive thrust against the Cherokees being waged by the Carolinas and Virginia. Colonel William Byrd of Virginia had led a force to the Holston headwaters and enforted at Fort Attakullakulla, named for Little Carpenter, still the strongest Cherokee ally the British had. And later in the year yet another force, a band of North Carolinians under Colonel Hugh Waddell, had joined the campaign.

Byrd's efforts against the Cherokees had been only desultory and halfhearted, but Grant's had proven bloody and effective, Smith reported. Grant had attacked the Lower and Middle Cherokee towns, burning cornfields and houses, sending thousands of Indians homeless into the wilderness. Little Carpenter had made overtures for peace, traveling between Grant and his old friend Byrd, but it had taken months of suffering by the Cherokees before a settlement was reached.

Alphus had noticed that Joshua's expression became animated when he heard the name of Little Carpenter and remembered Joshua's claim that the famous Cherokee himself had given him the name Ayunini. Joshua had never told any more of that particular story. Alphus was sure there were other parts of Joshua's experiences not yet expounded.

He had drawn that conclusion by simple observation and good instincts. Joshua, though cheerful and enthusiastic in most situations, at times became pensive and withdrawn. Four times in the past year, Alphus had observed the boy slipping out of his blankets at night and creeping into the woods. On two occasions, Alphus had quietly followed and seen Joshua apparently wiping tears as he sat alone in the darkness. And there were the boy's dreams as well; sometimes Joshua wakened with a yell, and on one such occasion had called the name Samuel. Who Samuel was Alphus did not know, and he didn't ask. He wasn't an intrusive man.

Smith had stayed with the hunters for nearly a week

and sold two packhorses to them. After his departure, Levi and Alphus had determined that in the spring of the following year they would return to North Carolina and resume their agrarian lives at Hankins Creek. Almost certainly they would have much rebuilding to do, many fields to reclear, and relationships to reestablish.

But that would be later. The hunting still was good, and the more skins and pelts they could gather, the better fitted financially they would be to resettle their families.

In March they had loaded their best deerskins on their horses, hiding and protecting what deerskins they could not carry, and headed back toward home. Travel went well, though it had seemed too slow to the eager men until on Tuesday, April 6, 1762, they finally reached the little mountain gap that led down to their settlement.

They found burnt cabins, barns, and corncribs where once there had been thriving farmsteads. Many of the outlying farms remained ravaged and empty, but the closer they came to Hankins Creek, the more resettlement they found. They stopped to talk with neighbors they had not seen for two years, learned of marriages, deaths, and births—and most exciting of all, that Thomas and Gabriel Colter had already returned and reestablished the store at Hankins Creek. Not only that, but they had brought Levi's family back with them. There would be no need to head into Virginia to retrieve their kin; they would be reunited with them this very day.

The hunters trailed their string of packhorses along a dusty road between stands of evergreens, Levi eagerly in the lead, Alphus second, and Joshua lagging behind, the dogs trailing alongside.

At length Alphus told Levi to go on alone. He stopped and turned to Joshua. "Boy, how are you feeling about this?" he asked.

Joshua looked uncomfortable but mumbled that he felt fine.

"There's something I want to tell you before we get there," Alphus said. "I should have done this before, but

I never could quite do it." He paused and cleared his throat. "I plan on keeping you with me permanent, if you'll have it."

Joshua looked away and nodded, masking whatever feelings he had.

"And if you're agreeable to it, I want to give you my name."

Joshua swung a surprised gaze to Alphus, who fidgeted and licked his lips. Neither said anything for a few moments.

Alphus cleared his throat again and though unsure of Joshua's feelings, went on: "It just seems to me that if you're to live as my son, it's best that you have my name."

"You've already got a son," Joshua said.

"I'd like to think I've now got two," Alphus responded. "And there was another son once, after Gabriel. He died the first day of his life . . . the day my Dulcie died giving him birth." The frontiersman's lip quivered in an uncharacteristic show of feeling, and his voice grew tight. "To me, it seems like you were sent to me in his place. I'm usually not much one for such notions, but I can't get this one out of my head. It came to me the very day I saw you, even after you tried to blow my head off my shoulders." He chuckled self-consciously and swiped a hand down across his mouth and beard. "I don't talk so much often, and I reckon I've said too much."

They continued on in silence, Alphus acting quite embarrassed. Up ahead a few minutes later they saw Levi. Hurrying, they caught up with him.

Levi wore a broad grin. "Look yonder, Alphus—the path's already been cleared."

They had reached a narrow road cutting back through the trees. It had recently been cleared of underbrush that now lay in drying piles beside it.

"Thomas or Gabriel, I'll wager, or maybe Sina herself, if she found the time," Levi said. "God above, but I'm glad to be home."

They traveled together down the path, facing into a warming spring breeze that carried the smell of livestock and chickens. In a few moments they reached a clearing.

In it stood a cabin, made of old and new logs. A stack of burnt timbers lay to the side, evidence that the cabin had been partially burnt, apparently months ago, and since repaired. A corncrib east of the cabin had also been burned down and had not yet been replaced, though a stack of cut saplings lay nearby, ready to be built into a new crib. A new woodshed and outhouse stood at the rear of the clearing. Nearby, a turned field obviously awaiting planting.

Levi let out a whoop, abandoned his horses, and ran down the sloping path to the cabin. The dogs set up an excited canine racket and ran with him. The front door opened when he was halfway across the yard, and a dark-haired severe-looking woman emerged. She was as thin and straight as a young poplar. When she saw Levi bounding toward her, her angular face came alight, her arms rose toward the sky, and she ran out into his arms. The stout hunter swept her off the ground and spun her around three times, then planted a kiss on her narrow lips.

"That's Sina Hampton, and you won't see her grin like that often," Alphus said to Joshua. "She's a somber woman, but as fine a one as I've ever known, excepting my Dulcie, God rest her."

As he spoke, Alphus glanced at Joshua and saw that the boy was looking at another figure who had just appeared at the cabin door. It was a young girl about Joshua's age, dressed in a short shift of plain homespun. At her side was a boy of about four, wearing only an oversized hunting shirt that looked to be one of Levi's castoffs.

"That girl there is Matilda, or Tilly, as they call her. She's Levi and Sina's oldest. The little boy is Amos—just a sprout when last I saw him. And that Tilly has grown like a weed. Well, come on—let's go give our respects."

Alphus led Joshua down to the cabin and there received a warm hug from Sina. The woman tossed an uncertain glance at Joshua and nodded in cautious greeting. Tilly and Amos remained back at the cabin until Levi let out another whoop, crouched, and extended his arms. The children came forward, Tilly all but dragging the mystified Amos by one arm. The little boy began to cry when Levi reached for him, pulled away from Tilly, and ran to his mother. Tilly threw her arms around her father, who picked her up as lightly as if she were a sack of pillow feathers.

"Amos is going to have to get to know his father all over again," Sina said, stroking the child's hair. He had buried his face in his mother's skirt. "He was but two years old when Levi set off."

Alphus said, "It won't take Levi long to win him over again. Right now, all this just seems too new to the child." He stepped back and put his hand on Joshua's shoulder. "I've got a new thing or two to reveal myself. Sina Hampton, I want you to meet Joshua."

The introduction made Sina feel free to examine the newcomer with undisguised interest. Joshua gave a rather weak "hello" and fidgeted under her gaze.

"Joshua came to us in the forest. He had been a prisoner of the Cherokees, and escaped," Alphus said.

Sina's eyes widened, then narrowed again. "God's been with you, young man," she said, "if you've been among the heathen and come out alive."

Joshua mumbled a thank-you, not knowing how else to respond to the comment.

"Where's his family?" Sina asked Alphus.

"Dead," Alphus replied. "Joshua was alone in the world until he found Levi and me."

Alphus could tell exactly what Sina was thinking: Joshua was about to be handed to her as a foundling son. Her posture became straighter even than before, and her eyes shifted back and forth between Alphus and the discomfitured Joshua. "What's your family name, boy?" she asked Joshua.

Joshua looked at the ground. "My father's name was Byrum."

"Joshua Byrum. It's a fine-sounding name."

"Yes. But it's not my name anymore."

Alphus gave Joshua an expectant look. Joshua raised his eyes, looked squarely into Sina's face, cleared his throat, and stood as tall as he could. "My name now," he said, "is Colter. Joshua Colter."

Unlike the Hampton cabin, nothing but the foundation stones of Thomas Colter's store had survived the fire set by Cherokee raiders. Even now, the store building was only half restored to its original state, and the business was temporarily operating out of a tent standing beside the half-finished hewn-log structure going up on the original site.

A hatless man in an open shirt was busy near the unfinished building, scoring a log with a felling ax in preparation for hewing. A chisel-edged broadax leaned against a stack of other hewn logs waiting for notching. As Alphus and Joshua approached, the man stood, wiped sweat from his forehead. His well-muscled chest was heaving from exertion and gleamed in the sunlight with sweat. He shaded his eyes for a moment, watching the approaching figures, then tossed down the ax and ran toward them.

"Hello, Thomas," Alphus said, pumping the man's hand. "Good to see you sound and well, by Joseph."

"Aye, and you the same, brother," Thomas Colter said. He was a slightly younger near-image of Alphus Colter, though his hair was thinner and more sandy. He was deeply tanned up to a line on his forehead, where suddenly the skin turned pale, showing that he seldom worked outdoors without a hat. "I've been looking for your return."

Alphus waved toward the store. "I'll be 'round to give you a hand with that as soon as we've settled."

Thomas Colter indicated Joshua. "Is this young man part of the 'we'?"

"Indeed he is, and will be from now on. Joshua, this is my brother, Thomas. Thomas, meet Joshua, formerly of the surname Byrum—" he paused and grinned, "but now of our own."

"No! How came this to be, Alphus?"

"A long story, and I'm too dry in the throat to tell it now. Besides, I want to see Gabriel."

"Father!" The voice came in perfect time with Alphus's comment. Joshua and Alphus turned.

A boy about halfway through his teens stood in the door of the tent. His thick hair was as sandy as Thomas Colter's, but his face was an even more exact youngish duplicate of Alphus's. He walked, limping slightly, out toward the group, extending his arms, and when he reached Alphus, he gave him a massive hug.

Alphus squeezed him in return, then pushed him back to look him over. "As tall as I am you are, Gabriel! By Joseph, but you've changed! I came looking for the sprout I left in Virginia!"

"No more a sprout, but a man, and a finer hand than ever in the store," Thomas Colter said. "Though you may have noticed the limp."

"Aye," Alphus said, looking a bit concerned.

"I broke my foot last year," Gabriel said. "It didn't set well, and I'm half lame."

"It's not so bad as that, Gabriel, though it may seem so to you," Thomas said. "Don't mislead your father. What you've got is a limp and a foot that will likely ache you every winter for the rest of your days, but beyond that, you're sound enough."

"I've missed you, Father," Gabriel said. His voice was touched only slightly with the rough edge of the Carolina frontier, sounding to Alphus even more cultivated than it had the last time he talked to him. "Was the hunting good?"

"So good we had to leave some of our skins hidden," Alphus answered. "Levi and I will go back for them after the planting is done. How soon depends upon how much rebuilding we'll have to do."

"You haven't been home, then, I take it," Thomas said cheerily. "Still standing, every log. The Cherokees must like you, brother, to have taken such pity."

"Praise be!" Alphus exclaimed. "I was ready for the worst, especially after seeing how much of Levi's place had to be restored. Someone's done a good job with that, by the by."

"That would be Gabriel and me, if I may be allowed to

boast," Thomas said. "We've spent as much time rebuilding for Sina as we have tending to our own situation here. It seemed the fitting thing to do, with Levi far away."

Joshua had meandered back some distance from the group, looking out of place. Alphus realized he had almost forgotten Joshua entirely and beckoned him over. Joshua advanced only a step or two.

"Gabriel, I want you to meet someone," Alphus said, hoping he did not sound as nervous as he suddenly felt. "This is Joshua. He came to Levi and me over in Tanisi, after escaping from the Cherokees."

"A Cherokee prisoner!" Thomas exclaimed. "Lord have mercy!"

Alphus's eyes flitted over to Gabriel, searching his son's expression. He was rather dismayed to see a visible coldness in Gabriel's eyes.

"Come ahead, Joshua, don't lag," Alphus urged. "This is my family. And now yours."

Gabriel turned sharply when he heard that, his brows lowering, his face full of question.

Thomas gave a perplexed chuckle. "What do you mean by that, Alphus?"

"This will take a good deal of telling to make clear," Alphus said. "And my throat's still dry. If you've some rum in that store tent of yours, it would make matters easier for me."

"Come inside, then," Thomas said. "Gabriel, fetch that jug from the box."

The natural-born son of Alphus Colter nodded slowly, fired a slow burning gaze up and down Joshua's length, and limped to the tent. All the others but Joshua followed.

Over on the stack of hewn logs, a jaybird alighted and set up a raucous challenge to a squirrel on a hickory branch above it. Joshua picked up a stone and tossed it at the jay, sending it flying, then scuffed the dirt with the toe of his moccasin.

"Joshua," Alphus said from the doorway of the tent, "don't you want to come in with us?"

"Not yet," Joshua said. "Outside suits me for now."

Alphus understood and nodded. "I'll call you in a few

minutes, when it's all explained," he said, then vanished inside the shadowed interior.

Gabriel did not go home with them that night, and Alphus told Joshua it was because all of Gabriel's possessions, including his precious store of books, were at Thomas's small cabin near the store and were not ready to move. That was the reason Gabriel had given Alphus for not wanting to return, but Alphus didn't believe it any more than Joshua appeared to. Gabriel didn't want to come home because Joshua was there.

Alphus did not tell Joshua of the angry reaction Gabriel had displayed when he heard that he suddenly had a new "brother" and was expected to treat him as such. He was sure that Joshua knew of Gabriel's feelings in any case, for Gabriel had stormed so loudly that Joshua must have heard him through the tent's thin walls.

Alphus's relationship with Gabriel had never been as close as he would have liked, partly because Gabriel was such a different sort of person than he and partly because he had never been able to give Gabriel the same type of love a mother would have. He had done his best for the boy, but there was something lacking, and Alphus had always known it.

Alphus sat at his slab-top supper table, picking at the salt pork and beans Thomas had sent as a welcoming gift. He tried to act casual and cheerful, but the truth was he was wondering if offering Joshua a permanent home and his own last name had been wise.

Yet what else could he have done? It wouldn't have been right to abandon an orphan, and the fact that Joshua had come to him in such an unlikely manner and place seemed almost like a sign that such a thing was supposed to have happened.

"Is your food suiting you?" Alphus asked.

"It's fine," Joshua returned.

Usually silences between Joshua and Alphus were comfortable, but this one was different. Alphus could all but read the boy's mind, so he was anticipating the comment he made a minute later. "I think it will be best for me to go on to Virginia, like I first planned," Joshua said. "Though it was kind of you to offer to let me stay on."

Alphus took a swallow of water. "Gabriel being your reason, I suppose?"

"He's your natural son. He belongs here. I don't."

"You do belong here, now."

"Gabriel doesn't think so. I heard him today inside the tent."

"Joshua, you must understand that this is all new to him. It may take him time, but he will come 'round right. It's a strange thing to be handed a brother unexpected, especially when you are one such as Gabriel. He's a different sort than you and me, Joshua. He loves towns and streets and stores and books and such the way you and me love the wilderness. And he likes being at the center of things, not having to share himself much with others. I don't always countenance everything Gabriel says and does, but I do understand him. And having a brother of my own maybe helps me understand even more how he's feeling at the moment."

Joshua looked Alphus in the eye and said quietly, "I have a brother, too."

Alphus frowned. "But you told me all your family was . . ."

"I have a brother," he repeated. "He was still a new baby when I left him. His name is Samuel."

Alphus, honestly stunned, laid down his three-pronged fork and sat back to listen. For the next quarter hour Joshua spilled out his story, not just the partial version he had given Alphus before, but the entire tale, including the birth of Samuel, the ransoming of himself and the others by Henry Dorey, and the details of his departure from Dorey's party. Alphus listened, fascinated and somewhat awed to hear of all Joshua had endured and experienced at such an early age. No wonder, he thought, this boy seems so much older than his years.

Alphus fired a pipe when Joshua was finished with his story. "I've heard you call the name of Samuel in your sleep," he said. "I wanted to ask about it, but it didn't seem my place to do it. Do you think often on him?"

"I do. I wonder if I was right to leave him, and if he is alive. I'm thinking maybe it's best I go on and look for him."

"Where would you look?"

Joshua had no answer for that.

Alphus sent out a cloud of tobacco smoke. "This Henry Dorey could have taken them anywhere. Where was he from?"

"North Carolina, I think."

"Well then, perhaps he brought them back to Carolina. In any case, you'll have a devil of a time finding out. You can't track without sign, you well know."

"No. But how can I hope to find any sign of them by staying here?"

"You can ask questions, to start with. This country is reopening. There will be more travelers, and travelers have eyes and ears. If there is aught to be known of little Samuel and the others, in time we will know it. I'll speak frank with you, Joshua. I don't want you to go. 'Twould not be wise or useful. I want you here, and need you besides. Gabriel's time is spent at the store, and I'll not take him from it, for Thomas depends on him, and the truth is that Gabriel's poor help about a farm in any case and 't'will be all the worse for a game foot. I want you to stay, if you will. If you do, I'll ask questions myself about Dorey and Samuel, and perhaps we'll find their trail."

Joshua thought it over, then nodded. "Stay I will, then."

Alphus smiled. The pipe smoked furiously.

As soon as he heard the loud yelping howl that came ringing across the barnyard, Alphus knew that Gabriel and Joshua were at it again and that as usual, Joshua had gotten the best of his reluctant foster brother. Alphus lited his eyes skyward in a silent prayer of supplication, then tossed down the adze with which he had been smoothing a log that would become part of a new woodshed. Though the farmstead had escaped Indian damage, Alphus had been planning for a long time to rebuild his toolshed and this early May morning had the time for it.

As it was, though, no job about the farm was going particularly well, given the hostility Gabriel was showing toward Joshua. Almost a month had passed for Gabriel to get used to having Joshua about. Not only had he not done so; he hadn't even tried—not in any way that Alphus could detect, at least. Today, with Gabriel working at home for once instead of at Thomas's store, tension had hovered palpably between the two boys.

The frontiersman stomped across the barnyard, sending the new flock of hens scattering and the nervous just-purchased milk cow edging toward the paling fence. Another yowl came from behind the log barn as Alphus rounded the corner in time to see Joshua soundly pounding Gabriel on the chest and jaws. Gabriel was pinned on his back like an overturned turtle, his legs and arms waving in the air as Joshua straddled his chest. In one of Gabriel's hands, Alphus was shocked to see, was a scalp lock—a familiar one Alphus had kept well hidden and had not thought his son was aware of.

Alphus, strongly tempted to take up swearing at last, strode over, grabbed Joshua by collar and queue, and pulled him off Gabriel. The older boy, whimpering, scrambled to his feet and hugged his shoulder against the log wall.

"Now, what's all this about this time?" Alphus asked in exasperation.

Gabriel, his jaw quivering, at first looked trapped and scared. In a moment, though, he adopted a look of cunning very familiar to Alphus and held out the scalp lock. "Joshua had it. I tried to take it away because I knew it was yours. He attacked me right off, saying he was keeping it for his own."

"That's a damned lie!" Joshua shouted.

Alphus promptly knocked him down, not roughly enough to hurt him but enough to make him take notice. "You're no trader's son now," he said to Joshua, "and you'll mind your words. Now, give me your story."

Joshua stood and stepped away from Alphus a respectful distance. "He came back here with that scalp lock
and started shoving it in my face, telling me it was my
father's hair." Looking at Gabriel, he continued, new ice
in his voice: "Nobody makes sport of what happened to
my father, and nobody will ever shake a scalp lock in my
face again."

Alphus looked from boy to boy. "Aye . . . well, it's clear
that the both of you are scarcely able to share the same
colony, much less the same barnyard. Two tail-tied cats
strung over a clothes rope you two are! Now, I know little
and care less who began this, but I'll have no more
trouble from either of you, or you'll take a trouncing for
it."

"Nobody shakes a scalp lock in my face," Joshua repeated, still staring at Gabriel.

"Close your mouth, boy, or I'll close it for you. And
speaking of the scalp lock, how came you by it, Gabriel?"

The older boy's eyes bored intensely into Alphus's. "I
already told you!" He looked incredulous. "You believe
him above me, by God!" Now it was Gabriel who was
knocked to the ground. The scalp lock dropped from his
hand.

Alphus stooped and picked it up. Gabriel, chest heaving with fury, glared up at his father. Alphus realized he
had blundered. He had not wanted to reveal belief or
disbelief in either boy's story, though the truth was just
what Gabriel had surmised: Joshua's was the version
Alphus believed.

"I'll not have blasphemy from you, nor let you put
words into my mouth," Alphus said. "I'm not saying what
I do or don't believe."

Gabriel was angry almost beyond restraint. "Yes, you
are. You're saying you believe your chosen son over your
born one. You've made it clear enough from the moment
you came dragging him home that you prefer him to
me."

With that, Gabriel came to his feet and stomped away,
around the barn. Alphus ordered him to return, but he
didn't. The frontiersman stood fuming.

"I'm sorry I hit him," Joshua said.

"No doubt he did aplenty to earn it," Alphus muttered.

Joshua pointed at the scalp lock. "How did you come by that?" he asked.

Alphus quickly tucked the scalp lock under his arm to hide it. "That's no matter," he said. "It suffices to say I've had some fights of my own in my time. Now, you get back to the woodchopping I sent you here for. I've got another son in bad need of some talking-to."

He walked away in the direction Gabriel had taken, rounding the barn in his long stride.

The mountains had greened visibly over the past week, not with the rich, full color the summer would bring, but with the watered-down, pale pigmentation of springtime. White dogwood blossoms, wet from a recent sprinkle that had sheened the road with mud and covered its uneven surface with shallow puddles, spangled the forest on both sides. An army of foot-high mayapples stood like woodland sentinels in bright green uniforms as Joshua Byrum Colter drove the wagon slowly down the rutted road.

None of these things Joshua saw in more than a peripheral way, for he was in a state most uncommon for him: lost lazily in memory. Almost dozing, he had not spoken for half an hour to Alphus, who slumped on the seat beside him, and now Alphus was asleep, waking only enough to mumble slightly when the wagon bumped on a rut or jarred through a hole. Joshua's hands gripped the reins, but it was unnecessary to guide the horses; they well knew this road and plodded toward Salisbury with easy familiarity.

Memories had meandered without pattern through Joshua's mind for the last several miles, but in the last few moments had come into focus on one man: Attakul-lakulla, the Little Carpenter. Joshua was remembering his first sight of him that morning in Fort Loudoun when Jack Byrum was in the guardhouse for the knifing of Henry Dorey. He also recalled Little Carpenter's sincere sorrow upon frightening him into the river and his be-stowing the name Ayunini—though Joshua now saw, with the wisdom of a more mature retrospect, that Little Carpenter had simply been talking, not name-giving, and had not intended the title as a permanent designation.

Ayunini . . . this mid-April morning in 1770 was the first time in a year or more that Joshua, now a man, not a boy, had thought of himself by that Cherokee designation. Well over a decade had passed since the August afternoon when Little Carpenter had encountered him outside Fort Loudoun. Those years had rolled quickly past, filled with spring plantings, cultivation, fishing, subsistence hunting in the summers, harvesting in the autumns, and hunting in the winters. "Long hunting," people had come to call it; men such as Joshua and Alphus Colter, "long hunters."

Joshua wondered how Little Carpenter fared. He had not heard much about him in the past few years, beyond cursory mention by a couple of peaceable Overhill Cher-okee hunters he and Alphus had encountered two years ago along the Nolichucky.

That long hunt was the first Joshua and Alphus had undertaken without Levi Hampton, who had been gravely injured that year by a tree being felled for an expansion of his cabin. Joshua and Alphus had been with him when it happened; never would Joshua forget Levi's scream when the heavy poplar crushed him into the earth, shattering both legs and one arm. It had required a jackhook and roller logs to move the tree off Levi, and as soon as it was clear of him, he passed out and looked to be dead.

But Levi hadn't died. He clung to painful life with a grip more stubborn than that of a grasshopper on a finger. But healing had been a long, difficult process, and when tragedy again intruded into the Hamptons' life, Levi had suffered a setback, and Joshua had felt certain that Levi would die from despair alone.

The tragedy was the death of little Amos, who took ill after falling into a cold spring and never recovered. Sina had put on a front of bravery and acceptance, though it was evident the boy's death shook her to the core. Levi had not even pretended to react bravely; he had cried and moaned for days, and become ill himself. Joshua and Alphus, who had taken over all Levi's work since his accident, had stood by, expecting to bury their old friend any day. Happily, Levi's anticipated passing never occurred. Slowly he came out of his despair and began to heal again.

Now he claimed to be well, just a bit stiff and slow of movement, and was talking of hunting again when the winter came. And in the meantime, he had fathered another child, a boy he and Sina named Zachariah.

"If you're up to conceiving children, likely you are ready to hunt again," Alphus had joked to Levi.

All the extra labor on the Hamptons' behalf had held one particular reward for Joshua: the opportunity to be near Tilly Hampton frequently. The girl-child he had first known had since Levi's accident grown to be an attractive young lady—attractive at least to Joshua, who found her freckled face marvelously appealing, despite its plainness, and her thin but womanly frame breathtaking. Though Tilly had been slow to accept his friendship, apparently seeing him as some sort of heathen refugee because of his earlier life among the Indians, of late she had been softening toward him considerably, and he was beginning to harbor strong hopes that she might develop affections toward him as strong as those he felt toward her.

Sometimes he looked at his own reflection in Hankins Creek and wondered how he appeared to Tilly's eyes. Over the years his skinny form had filled out with hard muscle, and his shoulders were now as broad as Jack Byrum's had been. He was grateful that his resemblance to Byrum did not go much further than that; in his own face he saw far more of Hester Byrum's looks than his father's. Whether he was handsome he had no clear idea, but he hoped he was, because of Tilly. Sometimes lately he had noticed Tilly covertly watching him work about the Hampton farmstead and at such times had felt a pleasurable tingle. There was no longer any question but that he cared deeply about the girl, maybe loved her, and now that he was a full twenty years old and Tilly was nubile, his mind was turning toward marriage. It didn't seem to him a man should let himself age too much before taking a bride, for life was uncertain on the border and even more so across the mountains. Waiting too long to marry could mean finding yourself in a grave or dead and scalped along some unmapped stream, the opportunity for life and love with a good woman forever past.

Joshua's thoughts continued to drift as the wagon rolled along the rutted trace. Thoughts of marriage led to thoughts of Gabriel, now twenty-four and still single, with no apparent inclinations toward marriage. Gabriel's life seemed to Joshua to be built exclusively around commerce. A year ago Thomas Colter, a widower like his brother but with no children of his own, had sold Gabriel an interest in the store, and since then Gabriel had been more dedicated to his work than ever. He now took no time off to help out around his father's farmstead and always seemed preoccupied with his business, even during his regular Sunday-afternoon visits after Sunday services in the tiny Presbyterian church house recently built on the banks of Hankins Creek. Gabriel had built himself a house near the store directly after Thomas made him a partner—or rather, Joshua and Alphus had built it for him—and now his life was all but cut off from that of his family.

As for his relations with Joshua, they were now cordial in a cool manner, but beneath the veneer was a lingering strata of mutual resentment. The only quality Gabriel possessed that Joshua much admired was his love of learning and a budding interest in religion. But those were hardly saving graces in Joshua's mind. Every Sunday afternoon, when Gabriel came limping across the yard toward the cabin, Joshua had to fight back the urge to close and lock the door. He found nothing to enjoy in his foster brother's company.

The wagon rounded a slight bend and bumped through a rut, splashing water up to the hubs. Alphus mumbled again in his sleep, something about Joshua going to fetch him that farrier's chisel yonder, and Joshua smiled. Alphus was always working, even when he dozed.

Alphus's sudden stirring mixed with Joshua's thoughts about Gabriel and brought to mind an occurrence seven years ago. Joshua and Gabriel had blackened each other's eyes in another of their eternal boyish squabbles, and Alphus had leaned both of them across a tumbril sledge and whipped them with a hickory stick. Gabriel, then seventeen years old, considered himself too old for such treatment and limped off angrily to sulk in the woods, complaining that the fight had been started by Joshua—which in fact it had.

That night, Alphus had knelt at Joshua's bedside and told him a story he never forgot. "You're too eager a fighter, Joshua," Alphus had said, "too quick to make a fist. And that will cause you grief if you don't overcome it. You make me think of a young Cherokee I heard tell of once. This was back some years ago when the Cherokees were getting set to fight the Shawnees. A big band of warriors was about to leave Chota and head north, and along comes this little Cherokee boy, wanting to go along. His father tells him no, he's too young. But this young fellow won't listen and sneaks ahead to the portage and hides himself in a dugout canoe. Well, the warriors come along and find him there, and he begs again to go—he wants to bring him back some Shawnee scalps. By now, the warriors are all laughing among themselves and talking about what an eager little warrior he is, and his father decides to give him a test. He tells the boy: 'You pick up that canoe and carry it across the portage to the water, and you can come along with us.' They all knew, of course, that the young fellow was too little to carry the canoe, so the Cherokees all set out for the river, figuring that's the end of it. But then, a minute later, one of them raises a shout: '*Tsi-yu-Gansi-ni! Tsi-yu-Gansi-ni!* He's dragging the canoe!' And the father turns to look. Sure enough, even though he's too young to carry it, the boy is dragging that canoe just as hard as he can, following the others. And from then on, that's what they called him: Dragging Canoe."

Fascinated, Joshua had asked, "And did the father let him go to war?"

"That he did," Alphus answered. "I reckon he saw there was naught to be gained by not letting the boy be what he was set on being. Some ways of a person are put in them by their nature, and nothing will change it. It's a thing I'm reminded of a lot in dealing with you and Gabriel both, and I admit it scares me some. You're like Dragging Canoe—always ready for a fight, too ready to suit me. But I despair of changing it. You're going to be what you're going to be."

Joshua thought it over. "And what of Gabriel? What is he going to be?"

Alphus smiled rather sadly. "A schemer, a planner, a gainer of wealth more than happiness, I'm afraid. He'll never be like us, more at home under the sky than under a roof. And what he sees through his own eyes he thinks he's seen through the eyes of God himself, and he expects the world to fall into place all around him, with him right at the center. As you get to know him better through the years, you'll come to see what I mean."

Alphus had risen to go to his own bed when Joshua asked, "Alphus, is the story you told true?"

Alphus said, "It was given to me as such. And by the way, Dragging Canoe's father is a man you've met. The Little Carpenter himself."

Joshua had lain awake for an hour after that, thinking over the story, which roused in him a peculiar sense of excitement and destiny, and when he slept, his dreams were of the days before the fall of Fort Loudoun and of Little Carpenter.

The road widened and became more smooth. Alphus shook his head and blinked awake. They had left the forest behind and now were passing several well-culti-vated farms lined with paling fences. Livestock grazing in one of the greening fields lazily watched the wagon roll past.

"Almost there, I see," Alphus said.

"Yes, and it's a strange thing to me you'd sleep on the rough road and wake on the smooth," Joshua said.

Alphus gave a good-natured *harumph* and dug out his pipe. They came to the town and grumbled down a cobblestoned street. Joshua looked about him with appreciation; though hardly a townsman by inclination, he did enjoy visiting Salisbury from time to time. Usually the visits were in the spring—to sell hides and furs at one of the trading houses here; they had made such a journey only a month before. This second trip was to allow Alphus to arrange a lease of some fertile lands adjacent to the farmstead. Joshua didn't favor the move, for he disliked farm work and deplored the idea of having even more land to tend, but Alphus was set on it, and the transaction was already complete but for signing papers and passing money.

In that process Joshua would not be involved; his plan was to visit a favorite tavern and enjoy a good flagon or two of ale while Alphus did his business. They rode up the street, passing through the jumble of pedestrians, vendors, carts, and drays, then turned at the next intersection toward the clapboard house where lived the landlord Alphus was to see.

"See you find no trouble while you're roaming," Alphus growled when he climbed down from the wagon.

"I'll find no trouble," Joshua said. "Good luck to you in your business." He snapped the reins, and the wagon clattered down the cobblestones.

The interior of the tavern was cool and rather dark. The floor was made of smooth wide boards oiled to a shine but very worn and covered with a mixture of dried mud, spilt liquor, crumbs of stale bread, and tobacco ash knocked from hundreds of pipe bowls since the last sweeping. Heavy studs and braces framed the noggings composing the walls, and heavy beams extended across the ceiling. From them hung blackened lamps, casting a shadowy light over the handful of drinkers seated on three-legged stools and leaning over the rickety tables throughout the wide low room. One side of the room was taken up by a long varnished bar of oak. Smoke and dust hung in the atmosphere, giving the place a stink that was improved only by an infiltrating fresh-bread aroma from the bakery next door.

Joshua smiled and nodded his thanks to the overfat and underdressed barmaid who was refilling his cup with a second round of ale. The ale was far from the best Joshua had ever tasted, but he liked it much better than the rum most frontiersmen preferred.

"Aye, but you're taller even than you were even a month ago, Joshua Colter," the woman said playfully, pulling back the dripping pitcher and deliberately pressing it to her plump bosom. "And twice as handsome."

"And you're all the prettier, Hannah," Joshua said, raising his cup in salute before taking a hefty swallow. "When in Salisbury, I say, it's always worth a visit to rest my eyes with the sight of you."

It was a flagrant lie; Joshua never had found Hannah Benjamin the least bit physically attractive. But he did find her flirtatious banter diverting and a little flattering, though he knew she gave the same to every man she served; it was part of her job.

"Oh, when will you come and carry me off with you and free me of all this?" Hannah asked coyly, waving her free hand about to indicate her surroundings. "Take me back to your cabin, and I'll make you the happiest of men." With that, she gave a wink.

"That much happiness might be more than I could abide," Joshua said.

At that moment, the tavern door opened, and a long-bearded man with the look of a trapper walked in, accompanied by another man, who because of the wind gusting in the doorway, had his hand clapped on top of his slouchy beaver hat, the brim of which covered his down-turned face as he entered. He was broad and wide, wearing a huge hunting shirt that despite its size was straining at the sides to hold his girth. His massive legs looked like sections of poplar logs stuffed into black trousers. Noting the loud clumping sound the man's feet made on the floor, Joshua examined him and was amused to see that he wore well-blacked shoes with shining silver buckles—footwear that looked totally ludicrous in combination with the rest of his rough frontiersman's clothing. The shoes reminded Joshua of those Gabriel had recently taken to wearing in the store—the newest of his eccentricities.

"Ah, mercy, there comes trouble for me!" Hannah whispered to Joshua. "I curse the day he first walked through that door, for he never gives me peace."

"Come now, Hannah!" Joshua teased. "You've never been one to dislike the attention of any man!"

"That one I can well do without," she responded. "Treats me like a common harlot, he does."

"Well, in that case, Hannah, you should take a stout wagon spoke, fetch him a good blow against the crown of his skull, and—" He stopped suddenly.

Hannah looked at him with a frown. "What's wrong with you, Joshua Colter? Have you swallowed your tongue?"

Joshua was stunned beyond speech. The man in the buckle shoes had lifted his head and taken off the beaver hat. Standing before Joshua was a graying vision from his past: Henry Dorey himself, fatter and older, but unquestionably Henry Dorey.

"Joshua?" Hannah inquired again, frowing again.

"It's nothing, Hannah, nothing," Joshua said. He looked away from Dorey and down at his cup, chagrined to find his hand trembling on the handle. It wasn't fear he felt but an overwhelming nervousness. Seeing Henry Dorey again was such an unexpected event that he was stunned and didn't quite know how he should react.

Dorey swept the room with his eyes; his wide face was twisted in a grin. "Hannah!" he bellowed—and Joshua noticed he sounded drunk already. "Come fetch rum to two of the finest men you'll ever have fortune to meet!"

Joshua felt compelled to look at Dorey again and found the big man looking back at him. A flicker of confusion played across Dorey's face. He broke from Joshua's gaze quickly and looked at Hannah. For a moment, Joshua wondered if he had been recognized but then doubted it. The years had changed him far more than they had Dorey, and it was doubtful Dorey could know him.

Hannah put on a brave but forced smile and tromped over to the bar. Going behind it, she walked around to Dorey and the other man. The men turned their backs on Joshua, and Dorey began talking, demanding his rum again and making a lewd joke about Hannah's tight dress.

Joshua was fighting a mental battle. At the bar stood the man who could tell him what had become of Christiana, Samuel, and Beth—and suddenly he wasn't sure he wanted to know. What if the worst had happened to them? It was difficult to go through life ignorant of their fate, but it might be even worse to know, if that fate had been a sad one.

At the bar, Hannah was doing a good job of keeping Dorey entertained and watered while managing to stay out of reach of his big paws. Joshua watched Dorey from the corner of his eye. The big man was drinking and talking to the man beside him now, telling a big tale, of which Joshua picked up about half, about his prowess in killing Indians through the years. When Hannah moved on down the bar and began swiping it with the tail of her apron, Joshua rose on impulse and took his drink to the bar where he leaned across to talk to Hannah.

"Is the big one causing you any trouble?" he asked, the question an excuse to draw closer to hear better what Dorey said. Perhaps he would mention of Christiana or Samuel in his conversation, and Joshua could learn what he wanted without confronting him.

"Nay," she said. "Today he's got trinkets to sell to his friend there—I've seen him try to sell them before. He makes his living trading and selling foul things—the scalps of Indians, cutoff fingers, and the like." She shuddered. "He's a loathsome thing, he is."

Joshua surreptitiously watched Dorey, who had

reached into his pouch and produced a scalp lock dried on a hoop.

"This ain't one I took myself, but I got it from the man who did," Dorey said.

The other man examined the scalp lock and looked dissatisfied. "It's old," he said.

"Aye, that it is. It was took during Grant's campaign," Dorey replied. "And it's just a squaw's. But don't worry—I've got much better than that."

He reached into his pouch again and pulled out another scalp lock, which was examined like the previous one and also rejected. Joshua felt disgust at both the men. He was a frontiersman and had spent enough years among the Indians to feel no revulsion at the idea of taking tokens of slain enemies, but he had no use for those who traded in such for their own sake, seeking to own scalps and other relics of those they had not slain in honorable battle.

Dorey had turned slightly during his most recent conversation, and the sound of his words had been blocked from Joshua. Now he shifted again as he dug another item from his well-stuffed pouch. This was a powder horn. He sat it on the bar with a loud clump. "Take a look for yourself—see that bit of hide stretched on the side here? That's his devil mark. This one I can vouch for myself, for 'twas me who killed him and sliced it from him myself." Dorey had a tone of pride.

The other man picked up the powder horn. Joshua saw that what looked like a small piece of leather had been decoratively stretched onto one side of the horn, held by rawhide ties. He could not see it clearly, but something about it, and the term Dorey had used to describe it, stirred something in the back of his mind and made him want a closer look.

At that moment, however, Dorey turned and looked at Joshua again. Once more that strange uncertain flicker passed through his eyes; it was obvious now that Joshua roused some sense of familiarity in him but apparently not full recognition. Joshua looked the other way, taking another sip of ale.

Dorey resumed his conversation with the other man. "And this here I got from him at the same time," he said. Joshua heard something else clatter onto the bar. "I'll sell that to you as well."

The other man spoke, the first thing he had said that Joshua could hear. "This is naught but a piece of colored skin," he said. "If that's the devil mark of Bloody Eagle, I'm the king of England."

At the mention of Bloody Eagle, Joshua dropped his cup and wheeled, forgetting his impulse to secrecy. He stepped forward and saw the powder horn more closely, and the patch of skin attached to it. On the patch was indeed the birthmark of Awahili, just as Dorey claimed. He stared disbelievingly at it, then swung his gaze to Dorey, who was facing down his companion.

"I tell you, sod, that's Bloody Eagle's own hide on that horn. I should know, for I kilt him and peeled it from his corpse myself, and took this from about his neck!" He held up an object on a cord—apparently the item that had made the clattering sound on the bar.

Joshua knew it at once—the Roman coin he had given to John Hawk ten years before. "Give that to me!" Joshua demanded, stepping forward. He had made the move impulsively and regretted it at once.

Dorey looked at him again. His eyes suddenly widened. "You?" he said in a half whisper.

The other man, who had taken no note of Joshua, waved his hand in disgust at Dorey and turned away, muttering an oath and calling Dorey a liar again.

Dorey was becoming agitated. His sudden recognition of Joshua obviously roused quick fear, which, combined with his anger at the other man's insults, made him launch out in self-protection. He roared out a curse and lunged toward Joshua, obviously thinking Joshua was about to attack him. As he lunged, he stumbled and jolted his companion. The other man mistook the motion for an attack. His hand swept to his belt and came up with a butcher knife of the sort many trappers and hunters carried. It sliced air, then flesh.

Dorey screeched. Hannah screamed behind the bar

and staggered back, overturning a tableful of crockery mugs. Dorey did a graceful turn and fell atop one of the tables, knocking it over and dumping a half-risen patron from his stool. The patron stood and backed away. A fountain of red spurted from a slash in Dorey's neck, and he slid to the floor.

Joshua went quickly to Dorey's side. The wound was gushing blood. Dorey clamped his hand over the gash and went white as pus. The man who had cut him calmly wiped the butcher knife clean on his trousers, sheathed it, swore at Dorey, and walked out of the tavern to the street with no more concern than if he had merely swatted a troublesome insect.

"Give me a cloth, Hannah!" Joshua ordered. The barmaid did not move; she was frozen in place, staring at the widening pool of red beneath Dorey.

"A cloth, and be quick with it!" Joshua demanded again. Still she did not move, but one of the remaining two patrons in the tavern darted to the counter and brought Joshua the soiled damp cloth Hannah had been using to wipe the bar. Joshua folded it and pressed it to Dorey's neck after pulling away the man's hand.

"Hold still and try to be as calm as you can," Joshua directed Dorey. "With any luck, we'll be able to stop the flow."

"Byrum! Jack Byrum's lad!" Dorey said.

"Aye—that I am. I'm the very boy you beat near to death time and time again ten years ago."

Dorey's eyes rolled up in their sockets as if he were trying to examine the inside of his skull. Joshua gave him a sharp slap on his bearded cheek to revive him, then said to the men leaning over him, "If either of you know of a surgeon, you'd best go fetch him." But no one stirred.

"Byrum!" Dorey said again, this time in a mumble.

"Listen to me, Henry Dorey," Joshua said, leaning into his face. "Whether you'll live or die I don't know, but in either case you tell me now: What became of Christiana Cox and the babies with her?"

Dorey's eyes rolled up again.

Joshua slapped him back to awareness. "Tell me!"

Even while dying, Henry Dorey proved capable of managing a look of great hatred. His breath wheezing, he looked up bitterly into Joshua's face. "Forever gone they are. What do you think of that, Joshua Byrum?"

"What do you mean by 'gone'? What happened to them?"

"Dead and gone, the lot of them."

Struck by those words, Joshua unwittingly loosened his grip on the cloth. Fresh blood squirted; Joshua clamped down again. "How do you know they are dead?" he demanded.

"Kilt them . . . myself." Dorey's voice, like his life, was draining away, yet he chuckled softly. "Kilt them with . . . my own hands. That . . . I did. Never had patience . . . with a woman who wouldn't give herself proper to her man . . . and crying little buggers . . ."

Joshua's breath came in great heaves. Dorey's eyes rolled up again and began to glaze. Rage overcoming him, Joshua tossed aside the cloth, but this time nothing but a tiny seep of blood came out of the ugly cut. Joshua was on the verge of wrapping his hands around Dorey's throat to choke him in fury when he realized that life was already gone from the man.

Hannah came to Joshua's side, very pale. Her hand touched Joshua's shoulder. "Is he dead?"

Joshua roughly swept her hand away. He continued to look into Dorey's dead face for a few moments. One of the other men commented that Dorey was surely as dead as a stump. Slowly Joshua stood.

Dorey still held the thong upon which the Roman coin swung. Stooping, Joshua took it from his hand and walked slowly out of the tavern. The others closed in around Dorey's corpse, watching it with the great interest always aroused by the freshly murdered.

One of them grabbed the powder horn and held it aloft, admiring it. "The devil mark of Bloody Eagle he said it was!" the man said. "Mine to sell, and don't anybody try to take it from me, hear?" None of the others paid attention. He tucked the powder horn under his arm and darted out the door.

Lost in a daze, Joshua walked down the street, almost being run over by a cart. The driver shouted at him, but Joshua scarcely heard him. Reaching his wagon, he noticed the blood on his hands. Normally Joshua was not much affected by the sight of blood, but he was already beginning to feel ill because of what Dorey had told him, so now the blood clotting on his hands made him nauseous, and he quickly washed off the foulness in a nearby watering trough. Then he vomited on the ground beside it, receiving horrified stares from two passing women.

Stumbling back to the wagon, he climbed aboard and took the reins. The wagon clattered on down the street through the horsedrawn traffic.

In the cabin of Levi Hampton the next evening, little Zachariah played on Joshua's knee, but Joshua was largely oblivious to him. Only when the baby found the cord on Joshua's neck and pulled the Roman coin from beneath his hunting shirt did Joshua react to him, and then only to place the coin quietly back where it had been.

Alphus had questioned Joshua about his unusual despondency during the ride home and had also noted that he looked ill. Further, he had seen the Roman coin hanging around Joshua's neck and asked about it, for he remembered Joshua's story about having given such a coin to a sick Cherokee boy years ago. Joshua told Alphus only that he had obtained it in town from a trader, because the coin looked like the same one he had given to the boy. No, Joshua said, he didn't know how the trader came by it.

Joshua had shrugged off all other questions, and Alphus then left him alone. They had driven home in silence, stopping off at the Hampton cabin so Alphus could inform Levi of the success of his business transaction.

Staring into the fire in Levi's fireplace, Joshua tried to listen to the conversation of the two frontiersmen, but his thoughts continually returned to what Dorey had told him. His greatest fear had been realized. Samuel was dead, murdered—Christiana and Beth too. He shouldn't have deserted them in the wilderness. If he hadn't, maybe he could have saved them somehow.

Zachariah slipped off Joshua's lap and toddled to his mother. Sina picked him up, planted a kiss on his dirty little cheek, then made a face. "You need a fresh rag about your bottom, judging from the smell of you," she said, rising and carrying the baby into the next room.

Joshua became aware of Tilly's flitting gaze on him. She was sitting across from him, on the other side of the hearth, stitching up a tear in one of Levi's shirts. Her father and Alphus were droning on about a recent problem that had beset the region: robberies, carried out by an unknown band of bandits who holed up somewhere in the mountains. Stores and farms had suffered, but no help had come from the North Carolina colonial authorities. It was just one more example to the border dwellers of the indifference of their own colonial government and was further fuel for the rebellion movement called the Regulation. Both Alphus and Levi had become enamored of the movement of late, though neither had fully affiliated with it.

Suddenly Joshua had no stomach for company and talk, or even for Tilly's usually welcome glances. He rose, quietly excused himself, and walked out of the cabin into the night. Outside, he paced about Levi's yard, fingering the Roman coin beneath his shirt, wondering why Bloody Eagle rather than his nephew John Hawk had been wearing the coin when Dorey murdered him, whenever and wherever that had been.

It was a depressing night, dark and overcast, matching Joshua's mood. Across the mountain, thunder rolled through the North Carolina sky. Joshua lifted his eyes, watched the mounting wind whipping the newly leafing trees, feeling as guilty for the death of his brother and friends as if he had taken their lives himself.

8

Alphus Colter tossed down his flinter's pick with a snort of disgust and looked at the chunk of flint he had just shattered and ruined. He wondered if it was a sign of age that he could no longer strike out a decent gunflint.

In truth, the reason for his failure, now thrice repeated, was no mystery. He was simply too distracted this September day to do the job. Blast it all, he thought, why does life have to be so complicated and young men so hard to understand? Matters had been difficult enough when there was only Gabriel with his peculiar ways to deal with, but for the past five months, even the usually staunch and levelheaded Joshua had acted as moody as an old maid. He had seemed continually preoccupied, slow to do his work, even slower to smile.

Joshua had also developed an even greater intolerance of Gabriel than before, and now the two hardly spoke. Sunday-afternoon meals together had become such a misery that Alphus had started looking for reasons to call them off. Now he and Joshua spent most Sunday afternoons at the Hampton cabin, and Gabriel ate at home

124

alone or dined with Thomas. It didn't seem right to Alphus. A family shouldn't be so divided.

He worried over it a lot these days, particularly over Joshua. It had been almost ten years now since he had found the bedraggled little refugee in the old hunter's cabin; in a decade, he would have thought, he rightly should have come to know and understand the boy he had given his surname. For a long time he had thought he knew and understood Joshua; now he wasn't sure.

Something was troubling Joshua these days, it was evident. And for the effects to linger this long, the something must be substantial. Alphus had racked his mind for months to figure out what it was. Love, perhaps? Early in the year, Alphus had suspected that Joshua felt a strong attraction to Tilly Hampton. Now he questioned that notion, for Joshua often acted as distant toward Tilly as he did toward everyone else.

So Alphus was left mystified and worried about his adoptive son. And the mystery might never be solved; the three times Alphus had dared question Joshua outright about his unusual behavior, the young man had all but snapped off his head. That too was out of character.

As the cool September wind explored the hillside behind him and rustled the leaves of the maple under which he knelt, Alphus began working on a new flint, chipping more carefully and slowly this time. Come the winter hunt, he and the others would need a good supply of gunflints—Levi especially, who was to rejoin them this year and who never could make a decent gunflint on his own.

Alphus looked forward to this hunt far more than to any hunt in the past five years, partly because of Levi's return but mostly for other reasons. There was certainly little enough to make him want to stay around here at the moment. North Carolina had for many years seemed a fine place to live, but what with Regulator uprisings, an apathetic-to-hostile government, and the growing problem of sometimes violent local banditry, the Carolina border country was becoming a place a man could happily leave. It would be pleasant to put the Blue Ridge between himself and Carolina, and make Tanisi his winter home again.

Not that Tanisi was exactly what it had been anymore. From wandering hunters Alphus had heard that settlers were beginning to build cabins and plant corn crops in the river country. Alphus knew well what that was a foretaste of. More cabins, then more and more again, plus stockades, ugly girdled trees, crop fields, roads, fences, diminishing game, schools, church houses. About such developments Alphus's feelings were paradoxical. He loathed seeing the wild lands become less wild yet also welcomed the settlement, for it meant that at last the time had come when he might be able to fulfill his own lingering dream of moving permanently across the mountains into the land he had loved so well these many winters.

Alphus's gaze dropped to the ground at his feet, and there he saw the moccasin tracks of Levi Hampton, who had come by for a visit an hour earlier. Along the route of Levi's tracks was a series of small round holes, left by the end of his cane. Levi seldom used the cane anymore, for now the stiff old-man gait his injury had brought him had mostly given way to his old steady stride. On damp mornings, however, his bones pained him, just as Gabriel's foot still pained him at such times, and he would take to the cane again.

Alphus wondered sometimes if Levi really was up to the rigors of a full winter's hunt. If a man got achy and stiff living in a warm log cabin, he would have a far rougher time of it in the wilderness. But Levi remained determined to go. Alphus did not blame him. Levi loved long hunting as much as he and badly needed the guineas a few good bales of skins would fetch at the Salisbury trade houses. Levi had been in a perpetual state of excitement, talking of nothing but the approaching hunt, for the past week. And Sina had seemed just as eager, no doubt having missed the extra income while Levi was laid up.

This morning, however, Levi had carried surprising news. Sina was beginning to balk at the idea of his leaving. Levi was puzzled by that and said he didn't believe Sina's excuse that she didn't think he was physically ready for it. He had pressed her for further explanation, but she had given none.

Sina. Thinking of her made Alphus ruin yet another flint. He tried to suppress the feelings that had come to plague him lately but as usual, failed. Anymore, it seemed he hardly spent an hour that Sina did not come to his mind at least twice, and that made him feel terribly guilty. It had all started shortly after Levi's injury when his survival seemed in doubt. Standing by Levi's bedside, watching Sina tend to him, Alphus had found himself wondering what would become of Sina if Levi died. Maybe, if that happened, he could step in and . . . He had cut off that thought aborning, but it had returned unbidden many times since.

Alphus had long thought Sina the finest of women. She was no beauty, had none of the grace of motion and affectations of style he had seen in women back east in the cities. She was a frontier woman, through and through, devoted to her family, home, and stern view of life, and could puff a pipe with the best of her breed. Perhaps such things would put off many men, but not Alphus Colter. Sina was the sort of woman who made a fine partner for a man, a loving companion, supporter, and friend in his old age.

There—he had thought it again, and it made him feel just as guilty as ever. It wasn't right to covet a neighbor's wife, though Alphus wasn't sure he was really doing that. Alphus's ideas about marriage were firm, clear, and moralistic. He had no use for the lechers who sought to steal the wives of others and even less for those men who feigned morality and family devotion on the east side of the mountains, then debauched themselves with Indian wives or mistresses on journeys west. Any thoughts Alphus had of taking Sina for his own were built on two big ifs: if something should happen to Levi Hampton and in that event, if Sina would consent to take Alphus in his place. Dangerous thoughts, Alphus reminded himself. He feared he might unwittingly wish down harm on his best friend by thinking them and so tried not to. In the process, he found that trying to not think a thought was the surest way to keep it ever alive.

Alphus picked up another flint and decided to give it one more try. Carefully, he began striking it with the flinting pick. Movement down at the cabin caught his attention. Joshua had come around from the back, out of the forest, a string of squirrels hanging across his shoulder. Alphus waved. Joshua did the same, then entered the cabin, leaving the squirrels hanging temporarily from a peg on the front wall.

Alphus smiled. Despite his current inability to fathom Joshua's mind, he still loved the young man deeply, more deeply perhaps than he loved Gabriel, his own flesh and blood. Another thing to feel guilty about. Alphus hadn't fought such battles with his conscience in many a year. It was young bucks who were supposed to have trouble controlling their thoughts and feelings, not well-settled old long hunters.

Alphus took a deep breath and settled to his work. This time, he made a perfect gunflint that glistened like one of the legendary Uktena stones the Cherokee conjurers were always talking about and wishing for. Alphus admired then pocketed the flint, hefted the pick, and walked down toward the cabin.

Joshua Colter became instantly awake. His hand shot toward his Pennsylvania rifle, which lay nearby with his moccasins strung to it. A moment later, he relaxed and scowled. Alphus Colter, reacting a bit more slowly, was only just now sitting up. The two Colters exchanged looks of slight irritation in the dim red glow of the banked fire.

Levi had yelled in his sleep again. He did it at least once a night, usually more. Levi murmured and settled into a steady rough-edged snore. He hadn't been like this in prior years; in fact, he had been the soundest sleeper of the three and had never snored except when under the weather.

Joshua and Alphus lay back down on their makeshift

mattresses of bearskin and leaves. The leaves rustled crisply beneath Joshua, and he silently vowed to replace them with softer and quieter pine needles, like those Alphus had used, when he got the chance.

The interior of the little cabin, located in an isolated hollow one ridge over from the Nolichucky River, was warm, if slightly smoky because of the wind that occasionally gusted down the short stick-and-mud chimney. This was a cruder station camp than the one Levi and Alphus had built half a score of winters before, the one Joshua had found while fleeing from Dorey. This one was nothing but a rough shelter to keep off the snow and rain, and provide just enough room for the men to sleep and eat. It was not tall enough for even Levi to stand in.

Tonight, sleep was coming hard to Joshua. He felt restless, and Levi's snoring and vociferations were proving particularly irritating. At last Joshua sat up, crawled off his bed toward the hide-insulated slab door, and sat down to put on his moccasins. He had to untie them from the rifle first; he and the others always kept their moccasins, pouches, and such tied to their rifles when they slept—a practice that Alphus had picked up a decade before from Daniel Boone back on the Yadkin River. This way, Boone had advised, if a man had to run from Indians in the night, he wouldn't have to grab for more than his rifle.

Alphus sat up again, looking at Joshua inquisitively as he pulled on his moccasins.

"Going out to make sure all is well," Joshua explained in a whisper. Alphus nodded and lay down again.

Slipping on a heavy coat he had made out of a bearskin and putting on a felt hat he had purchased during the summer in Salisbury, Joshua pushed open the door and left. The dogs snarled at him, then wagged their tails in recognition and meandered about his feet.

The night was dark and cloudy, and a late-January snow was falling at a fair rate. Rains a day before had dampened the leafy forest floor and then frozen into ice that gripped and held the snow as soon as it touched. Two inches of it lay on the forest already, and the barren tree branches and evergreen boughs were drooping with it. This was a damp clinging snow of the sort that typically fell when the temperature was not much below the freezing point. Studying the sky, Joshua guessed another couple of inches, maybe more, might lie before morning.

He walked over to the tall elkhide-draped scaffolds that held the hides and furs high enough off the ground to frustrate predators that might be drawn by the scents. So far, the scaffolds held only two small stacks of hides. Hunting this year had not been as good as the year before, and Joshua had already prepared himself for a lower income come spring.

The hides were in good order, but still Joshua did not feel ready to return to his bed. Checking on the hides had been an excuse for rising anyway. Standing completely still, Joshua leaned on the hexagonal barrel of his rifle and looked at the dark land around him. His night vision was good, but tonight he could not see more than a few yards. The sky fired down a blast of cold wind at the long hunter, but the icy slice of it failed to cut through the heavy bearskin coat. Joshua closed his eyes and dozed lightly where he stood.

A clump of snow shaken down by the landing of an owl somewhere above him roused him a few minutes later. He shifted to the side and leaned on his rifle again. Looking about, he found himself pondering what it would be like to live in this country. Might as well think about it, he reasoned, for obviously Alphus was going to settle here before long. His actions and talk made that evident.

Two weeks ago, up in the Holston country, the three long hunters had discovered a newcomer to the region. The man, from Frederick County, Maryland, named Evan Shelby, said he had come to the Holston with an eye to permanent settlement. Shelby, Joshua had gathered, was pressed financially because of losses suffered during Pontiac's conspiracy to the north and had come south to rebuild his fortune. His eye had originally been on North Carolina, and in April of 1768 he had even gone to

Salisbury to acquire seven hundred acres on Carolina's Swearing Creek, but now his sights were on the Holston country about Sapling Grove.

Shelby said he planned to return to Maryland to settle his estate there, then come back as soon as possible and build a new home and stockaded fort. A fort for whom? Alphus had asked. For the men who will soon be settling this country, Shelby answered. Men of means, many likely coming from North Carolina. With that, Shelby had looked meaningfully at Alphus.

Alphus had seemed interested in Shelby's hints. Later, he told Joshua what Joshua already had surmised: North Carolina would not remain his permanent home. Perhaps as early as the coming year he would move to the Sapling Grove area or maybe even farther southwest. He would like Joshua to come with him, of course—unless, he had said with a sidewise glance, there were other affairs that would make him want to remain in North Carolina.

Joshua had fully understood what Alphus was hinting at. He was trying to prod him to reveal his intentions toward Tilly, even though it had been a long time since he had given much evidence of feelings for her, or anything or anyone else, and indeed, had even been unsure lately of what his attitude toward Tilly really was.

Since the encounter with Dorey, Joshua had felt drained and purposeless. A sense of guilt haunted him, taking away the pleasures of life, making him feel cut off from those he loved—even Tilly. No doubt he seemed moody and cold to those around him. Joshua regretted that but did not know how to change it. He no longer felt he belonged.

Out here, far from cabins and towns and people, is where I fit, he thought. Here is the only place I can feel a real sense of peace anymore.

But any peace at that moment was shattered by another shout from Levi, this one so loud, it startled Joshua outside the cabin. Levi yelled again, then again—yells of panic. Joshua trotted through the snow toward the log hut, alarmed. He heard Alphus trying to calm Levi, then a loud dead *thump* as someone—Levi, probably—obviously tried to stand inside the low cabin and soundly bumped his head. After that the yelling stopped.

Joshua pulled open the door and entered headfirst. "What the devil . . ."

"Hush, Joshua—Levi just had a dream that scared him good. He's all right now. Bumped his head standing up, and that roused him."

Levi had seated himself again on his blankets. His hands rested atop his head. He said nothing.

Joshua poked up the fire, brightening the light in the cabin. "Levi, you're shaking!" he said.

"I'm fine, I'm fine," Levi replied, forcing a smile. "Just a dream, that's all."

"I'll wager it was of that tree falling on you again," Alphus said.

"No—'twas Sina. I saw her before me as if—" He paused abruptly and seemed self-conscious. "No, no. I'm muddleheaded. You were right. 'Twas just a dream of that tree, like you said."

None of them slept very soundly for the rest of the night, and when they set off the next morning on a planned extended hunt down toward the Nolichucky, all felt unusually weary. No one said much, Levi least of all.

A day and a half later, when the three split up for lone hunts, Levi strode to the top of a ridge, looked back at his partners, and waved his hand for a long time.

"Is something wrong with Levi?" Joshua asked, but Alphus had already set off in the other direction and did not hear him.

The wind was howling now, descending down the mountain slopes like an angry god, battering against Alphus and Joshua and hampering their progress through the snowfields and rapidly growing drifts. The sun, westering somewhere on the other side of the thick layer of snow-spitting clouds, was a borderless blob of pale light beyond the gray. The temperature was dropping as fast as the snow; already the creek beside them was freezing where it lapped the bank.

Alphus retied the rawhide whang he had bound across

his hat to pull the sides of the brim over his ears and hold the hat on his head in the stiff wind. "We're going to have to stop," he said, nearly shouting above the roar. "The night's coming on fast."

"But what about Levi?" Joshua asked.

"Levi will have to fend for himself," Alphus replied. "He's done it before, and he can do it again. All will be well."

Joshua looked into the white gloom all around him. "Not this time," he said.

"You've turned prophet, Joshua?" Alphus rather harshly replied. "Seeing Levi's fate through revelation?"

The truth was that Alphus was also concerned. He and Joshua had waited for two days for Levi to rejoin them at the designated meeting point on the bank of the Noli-chucky, but he had not come. The first day, Alphus hadn't worried; Levi was typically late. By the second night, he began to suspect something was amiss, and on the third morning, he and Joshua had begun a search. The weather went bad on them, then worse. Snow fell sporadically, obliterating any sign Levi might have left, and about dawn on this day had worsened to a near blizzard. Here, where mountains loomed toward the sky above the rich creek bottoms, the wind howled eternally, but now the howl was more a scream.

"I'm no more prophet than you are," Joshua said in response to Alphus's sarcasm, "but I do have a fearful feeling about Levi."

Alphus brushed stinging snow from his eyes. "Aye. So do I, as you well know," he admitted. "But the fact remains we can search no more today. And tonight we'll need something over our heads."

They found a sheltered spot between rock buttresses, and there Joshua hobbled and fed the horses. Meanwhile, Alphus went to work with his belt ax, felling saplings and stripping them of their branches. He dragged the poles to the base of a dirt-and-rock bank near the two rock buttresses. By now, Joshua had finished with the horses, and he joined Alphus in beginning a lean-to shelter of which the bank would provide one wall.

The two longest poles they leaned at a forty-five-degree angle against the bank, twisting and digging the ends into it several inches. They buried the other ends of the poles into the ground, and lashed smaller poles across the two roofpoles, from top to bottom, leaving several inches of space between them.

The men returned to the forest and began cutting evergreen boughs in great quantities, hauling them back through the storm to the shelter. The boughs they placed across the horizontal poles, up and down the slope of the roof, using the crotches of the boughs to hook them in place. These were built in overlapping clapboard-shingle style until the entire roof was covered. Some of the boughs they tied in place individually, but most they secured by binding more poles atop them.

When the roof was done, they rooted upright poles into the earth on the windward side of the sloping shelter, binding them at the top to the roofpole against which the poles leaned, and against these bound and stacked more boughs until the shelter at last had only one opening, facing away from the wind and driving snow. They swept the snow from the interior of the shelter and from the area just outside the door, and as Joshua piled snow atop and against the covered portions of the shelter, blocking out the rest of the wind, Alphus skilfully used his flint and steel to spark a fire just out from the doorway in the cleared spot. By now it was nearly dark. As the last sunlight faded, the pair gathered a large supply of wood and stacked it near the door of the shelter.

When full night fell, the storm continued, though the snowfall lessened somewhat. Inside the shelter the two men huddled in their blankets, protected from the wind and much of the cold by the walls of wood, boughs, and snow above and around them, and the earthen bank against which the shelter itself stood. The snow that accumulated on it made it only more snug.

They ate silently of their trail foods, for this was no night to be cooking, and dried their damp footwear at the triangular door of the shelter.

"I hope Levi is making out all right," Joshua said, and Alphus nodded.

The night passed as comfortably as could be expected, though the fire had to be restoked continually. When dawn seeped over the eastern ridges and into the creek valley, the two long hunters arose to a world of stark but hostile beauty. Deep snow blanketed all the land except the rocky faces that would not host it and the leeward sides of deadfall logs.

"We'll find him today," Alphus predicted. "And if not today, then tomorrow, and if not tomorrow, then, I fear, never at all."

And with that, they set out.

When they took Levi Hampton's body down from the creekbank beech tree the next day, his frozen form remained in the same position in which it had hung, upside down, for the past four days, the face against the smooth trunk. The right leg, covered with frozen blood, was crooked at a painful-looking angle and pinched badly where it had been hopelessly caught in the crotch of the tree. The other leg was bent out and back in a sweeping curve, with the heel near the small of Levi's back. His arms, which had been dangling groundward when they found him, now reached gruesomely above his head in a terrible imitation of an ecstatic worshiper. His white face, deeply scratched by the claws of the wounded bear that had chased him into the tree, was horrible to see, and when they had him down from the crotch, they quickly covered him so they would not have to look at it.

The bear lay nearby, dead beneath the base of the hollow oak from which Levi had driven it. Levi had always loved hunting bears during winter, using the old Indian technique of rousing them with a vocalized imitation of a distressed cub's noise, then driving them from their hibernation tree with burning cane. Normally such hunting was done by at least two men, but Levi had tried it alone, with the worst of results. He had fatally wounded the bear, but it had lived long enough to attack him and send him scurrying up the beech tree. Perhaps he had slipped, or perhaps the bear somehow grabbed him, but for whatever reason, he had fallen, the crook of his knee caught tightly in the crotch, and he had swung there upside down, mauled by the bear until it died moments later, leaving Levi to suffer the rest of his time alone.

Alphus dug Levi's empty rifle from the snow beneath the tree and brushed it off. He choked as he spoke. "I just hope to God it wasn't as bad a death as it looks to be. Maybe there's mercies at such times we know nothing of."

"Maybe there are," Joshua replied softly. He didn't believe it any more than Alphus did, but it was a comforting thought.

"Levi never could climb a tree to save—" Alphus had started to say, "to save his life," but the irony struck him, and he didn't finish. "God above—poor Levi, poor Levi," he said.

Joshua, his face unusually white above the line of his sparse beard, wiped his hand down across his mouth and licked his lips. Alphus knew the younger man was trying to keep his emotions in check, just as he was. It had always seemed peculiar to Alphus that loved ones, of all people, were those to whom it was most difficult to display sorrow, but that was just the way it was.

Joshua noticed Levi's knife on the ground at the tree base. He picked it up, then noticed something else. "Alphus, look there." He pointed.

Alphus saw it too. He walked to the base of the broad beech tree and brushed away the light skim of snow clinging to the bark.

Levi had carved letters into the bark—upside-down letters, poorly formed and barely scratched in some spots but legible when Alphus twisted his head to the side. He read Levi Hampton's last message silently, haltingly, for he was not good with his letters, and then read them aloud: "*Alphus see to my family—bury me where I will not be forgot—Levi James Hampton, Gone to God February 2, 1771.*"

Joshua could no longer choke back his tears as Alphus read the message, which had surely been carved despite great pain and distress. He turned his back and wiped his eyes with the heel of his right hand. Alphus stood, staring at the message, and though he was not often prone to think obscure thoughts, what he thought right now was how sad it was that the final etching of a man who died not wanting to be forgotten would be distorted by the tree's growth through the years until at last it could be read no longer, and then the tree itself would die and rot away until nothing remained and no one remembered.

Joshua, having regained his composure now, turned and said, "I wish we could straighten him. It seems wrong to bury Levi all twisted up like that."

"He's froze, son," Alphus replied. "We'd have to break him to straighten him, and that seems worse than leaving him."

Joshua said, "It's going to be hard to put him in the ground, as cold as it is."

"We'll find a cave or a hole or someplace, and put him to rest there," Alphus replied. "In the spring, we'll come back and dig a proper place for his bones, like he wanted."

He looked at the rifle in his hand. Levi's favorite rifle it was, a fine Pennsylvania-made hunting tool. Because of the bitter cold, the snow had been too dry to do it much harm. "Here," Alphus said, extending the rifle to Joshua. "It's yours now."

"It ought to be yours, Alphus."

"He'd be proud for you to have it, and it's a better rifle than yours. You carry it proud."

"I will," Joshua said, taking the weapon.

They wrapped Levi in blankets and buried him in a wide rock crevice. Then they dug stones from the frozen hillside and creekbank until their fingers were raw and bleeding, and with the stones covered the body well enough to keep out wolves. When they were finished, they stood, shaking in the cold wind, and bowed their heads.

"Ashes to ashes, dust to dust. The Lord giveth and the Lord taketh away," Alphus said. "We thank you, Lord, for having given us Levi Hampton, a good friend and neighbor, for these many years. Now you've taken him back, and we will miss him, but this is your world and not ours, and your ways are above us. We pray you will give mercy to his family and promise we will do all we can to help them. Thank you again, Lord, for Levi Hampton, and bless his soul in your glory forever. Amen."

"Amen," Joshua repeated.

The hunt was over after that. Both Alphus and Joshua lost the will to remain in the wilderness and decided to give the profits from what skins they had harvested to Sina and her children. After the weather broke long enough to clear out some of the snow, they returned to their main camp and packed hides on the packhorses, and headed home again.

Not wanting to take the more direct but difficult Blue Ridge route back home, they went home by way of Fancy Gap and Fort Chiswell, descending to North Carolina from Virginia. Then, laden with a heavy feeling of dread, they reached Hankins Creek, paused long enough to store their hides at the farmstead, and headed for the Hampton cabin.

As they entered the yard, Sina came to the door, Tilly looking over her shoulder, Zachariah riding on her left arm and hip. Joshua and Alphus dismounted and stood beside their horses, solemn and silent.

"He's gone, then?" Sina said.

Alphus nodded.

Sina looked down, then up again. "Aye. I've known it for days. He came to me, you know."

"Who?"

"Levi. Levi came to me. In a dream, it must have been, but he was with me, beside our bed, as plain to my sight as ever I've seen him. The twenty-eighth of last month, middle of the night." Only now did her voice quiver. "He came and told me good-bye."

Tilly began to cry and ran back inside the cabin. Zachariah, too small to understand, nevertheless sensed the strong emotions around him and began to wail in

Sina's arms. The frontierswoman put a thin hand on the child's back and gently massaged it.

Alphus looked at Joshua and could tell they both had realized the same thing: Sina's dream had come on the same night Levi had awakened in the station camp in such a fright. Alphus felt a cold shiver. He had heard of such dream visits but had never seen the actual playing out of one and had hardly believed in them until now.

"Come inside," Sina said. "It's too cold to be standing about, and there's food enough for us all on the table."

They put the horses in the shed. A new snow had begun, light and gentle.

Alphus stepped out of the shed and watched the snow thoughtfully. "Poor Sina—first little Amos, and now Levi. What bad will come next for her? It's the good ones, like Sina, and the innocent ones, like Tilly and Zachariah, who suffer most in this world," he said. "Why it's that way I don't know, but so it is."

Joshua could not answer, for the comment had put him in mind of Samuel again, and it hurt too much to speak. He walked beside Alphus to the cabin. It was almost sunset.

9

The months that immediately followed the death of Levi Hampton were difficult yet healing ones for Joshua Colter. Hampton's passing jolted Joshua out of his self-absorption, and he quit brooding so much on Samuel, Christiana, and a past he could not change. The Hampton family's welfare began dominating his mind and time, and his stepfather's as well, and bit by bit, Joshua became more his former self.

Sina accepted Hampton's death with the same determined stoicism with which she took all of life's blows. It was Sina's opinion, Joshua deduced, that human beings were made to suffer but not to complain about it. She would have made a fine Indian, he felt. Indians put high value on the ability to endure suffering without complaint; indeed, to them, a condemned captive could bring great honor upon himself by taking his death tortures without complaint—and if he had the grit to throw a few taunts at his tormentors, all the better. Joshua found it blackly humorous to imagine secretly how Sina would respond to such bad treatment. "Ah, well, do what you must, you heathens," she would say. "Likely I've been through worse, and the Lord above never promised us comfort."

On the afternoon of Monday, July 8, 1771, Joshua was perched on a log-section stool at a table in the little log tavern the Hankins Creek locals called the Jones House. Tye Jones, the owner and operator, had indeed lived in this cabin at one time, until he had built a better one just behind it and turned this one into a nighttime business to supplement his wheelwright work. The Jones House had proven so successful that now he devoted more time to it than to his main profession.

Sitting across from Joshua were Alphus, a neighbor named Ben Slye, and Slye's visiting cousin, Jim Grindell, born in Wilmington and now living on the other side of Salisbury. Joshua was doing little talking tonight, mostly listening, and the subject was the big fight at Alamance back in May, in which the governor's forces had at last defeated the Regulators. The Alamance fight had for weeks been the second most-talked-about items in the Jones House. The most common subject was the worsening problem of bandits from the hills and the growing need for local action to be taken against them. That topic had been thoroughly chewed over tonight before talk had drifted over to events at Alamance.

Grindell had been at the Alamance battle and though he had not been a participant, had suffered a slight wound in the left hand from a stray ball. At the moment, he was showing the pink depression in his palm where the ball had grazed across it.

"Lucky it glanced. Much deeper, and it would have gone clean through," Slye commented, exaggerating as he always did. The wound didn't look to Joshua to have been deep at all.

"Luckier yet it struck your hand instead of your head, by Joseph," Alphus commented. He took a sip of rum. "You know, I thought of Levi when I first heard of the battle. Peaceable as he was, he was in great enough sympathy with the Regulators that he well might have joined that fight, had he been about."

"Aye. Speaking of Levi, how are Sina and the children faring?" Slye asked.

"Well enough, given their situation," Alphus replied. "Sina is a strong one—always has been. The children take it worse, I think. Matilda maybe worst of all. But Joshua could tell more of Tilly than I could."

Slye cast a twinkling eye on Joshua. "A case of impending wedlock on our hands, perhaps?"

Joshua, who did not take well to such teasings and was particularly sensitive where Tilly was concerned, started to fire back a snide comment when suddenly the tavern door burst open and a farmer named Ethan Wexell came pounding in, out of breath. Every eye in the place turned to him.

"My brother's shot!" he declared loudly. "Shot through the head, and little Elijah's skull knocked in with an ax!"

Colter stood so quickly his stool overturned. "Robbers?" he asked.

"Aye, the same bloody sods as the other times, I'll warrant. But be quick—I left them both still alive, but how long they will remain so I cannot say."

Every man in the tavern had already risen, even as Wexell spoke. Not a man was without his rifle; frontiersmen such as they would go nowhere without their weapons. In less than three minutes, they had formed an armed party of ten and were riding at full speed toward the cabin where lived Tom Wexell and his eight-year-old son, Elijah.

Tom Wexell's wife and only other son had died two years before in a building collapse in Williamsburg, Virginia. Since then, Tom and Elijah Wexell had gotten by alone, and rumor had it that Tom got by well indeed in that his late wife had come into a substantial inheritance a year before she died. Ethan Wexell said the stories of his brother's wealth were greatly exaggerated, but they continued to circulate. It was no surprise, given such tales, that the robbers had struck at the Wexell cabin.

The riders found the cabin scorched; obviously an attempt had been made to burn it. When they entered, they found both Tom and Elijah lying in clotting blood.

Wexell had died since Ethan had ridden off for help, but the boy was still alive. How that could be mystified Joshua, for the side of Elijah's skull was broken open so badly, the brain was exposed. Yet the boy's eyes moved, his lips spoke, his body responded to touch. Whether his clinging life was a blessing or curse Joshua could not say, for he doubted such a terrible wound would ever heal. The boy was probably doomed to a short life of suffering and isolation.

Ethan Wexell rose from his brother's side and staggered in grief to the cabin door. Fighting down nausea, he lifted his eyes to the wooded hills from which the robbers had come. "Damn their murderous souls," he said through gritted teeth. "Damn them to hell!"

"This is the worst they've done yet," Alphus said. "It's fast coming time that we take the problem in hand and quit waiting for help from men with soft hands and silver snuffboxes and long titles after their names."

"What are you saying, Alphus?" Slye asked.

"That when we lay hand on any one of these bandits, or any man who's given them aid, that we stretch a rope or two from the nearest branch."

In answer came a murmured chorus of agreement. In the silence that followed, Elijah Wexell moaned and tried to put his bloodied hand on his split head, but Joshua restrained him.

The heavy door of the Colter Store creaked open, and Gabriel Colter, holding a cocked flintlock pistol, paused a moment before entering. So homely and pleasant during the day, the store tonight seemed grim and foreboding. From its shadowed interior wafted familiar smells: oiled guns and traps, coffee, peltries, cloth, wood, tools, bar lead, and others. Gabriel limped inside and fumblingly lighted a tallow lamp that cast only the faintest of flickers inside these light-absorbing log walls.

Gabriel cleared his throat nervously. "Who's in here?" he demanded, trying to sound fierce. It didn't work. His voice was as feeble as the lamplight.

For a long time, Gabriel said nothing more but stood,

listening. Outside, the darkened world was ringing with the deep croaking of frogs in the nearby marsh, the shrilling of crickets in the trees and grass, the rustling of opossums and raccoons on the leafy ground, the calling of owls in the forest. It was a hot night, humid and sticky, heaven for mosquitoes. Sweat dampened Gabriel's temples and pooled at his hairline, despite the cold prickles of fear that tightened his scalp.

After a few moments, he began to relax, to suspect that the boy who had come knocking on his door fifteen minutes earlier, rousing him from sleep, had lied to him. "There's somebody in your store," the boy had said. "Saw them go in myself, and it's them robbers from the mountains as sure as sunrise. You'd best get down there with a gun or you'll find your store near empty come morning."

The boy had run off after delivering the message, and Gabriel had stood indecisively, wondering whether to believe him. He was far more familiar with these mountain bandits than were most around here, though no one in the community knew that, to his relief. Since the attack on the Wexell cabin four days earlier, the men of the region were more alarmed than ever and determined to punish the perpetrators severely. Gabriel had heard that even his own father now advocated hanging any captured bandit and anyone found helping them.

After the boy had delivered his message and left, Gabriel faltered but finally loaded his pistols, thrust one in his belt and hefted the other in his hand, and limped down to the store, his heart beating out of his chest.

Now, as he finally became convinced that the store was not being robbed after all, he took a deep breath and uncocked the pistol. He was quite confident no one else was here—though a final look might be in order. He lifted the lamp and took a walk through the store, letting the light fall around the crates and barrels stacked along the walls, and explored the dark places behind the counter and rows of shelves. His heavy buckle shoes clumped loudly on the floor. No sign of life. Gabriel smiled and shook his head, so relieved that he could muster only mild anger at the boy who had disrupted his night's sleep. He turned to leave.

The flat palms of two massive hands struck him hard on the chest, knocking him back to the puncheon floor. One of the pistols fell from his belt and slid out of reach. The man who had struck him reached down and deftly pulled the other from his belt.

Through Gabriel's mind flashed an image of his skull's being pierced by a ball from his own pistol. He opened his mouth to yell, but his attacker quickly raised and lowered his moccasined foot, and a moment later Gabriel was pinned to the floor, the foot pressing so hard on his neck that he could not even breathe. The tallow lamp had fallen beside him but not overturned, and the flame, which had almost gone out during the fall, now sputtered up again.

The man above Gabriel leaned down slightly; light played on a face that was unpleasantly familiar to Gabriel and glittered in eyes that fired down an ugly hateful look. "Come looking for us with a pistol in hand, eh, Shoebuckles? Why oughtn't I snap your neckbone?"

Gabriel, choking for air, felt his head begin to spin. He writhed, but the foot only pressed his throat the harder.

"Kill you we could—but we won't, for it's us who sent the boy for you. Now, I'll lift my foot if you pledge not to raise a noise."

Gabriel could manage only a faint grunt and nod. The foot lessened its pressure slightly, then completely. Gabriel sat up. "No call . . . for this. I . . . I helped you . . . paid you . . . to leave this store be," he gasped.

"So you did, so you did!" the man said. "But it's become our opinion that maybe you didn't do quite enough, Shoebuckles," the man said. He was one of the stockiest man Gabriel had ever met, no more than five feet tall but wide as a barrel. He wore a tricorn hat and crude dark trousers, apparently made by his own hand and following no standard pattern, so that his legs seemed to be wrapped in shapeless tubes of cloth. His shirt, though, was obviously a store-quality garment, made of cotton, as Gabriel's trained eye had quickly noticed. Cotton clothing was a rarity on the border and was usually imported at prices most were unwilling to pay. Likely this fellow had not paid for it either.

A second man walked to the edge of the lamplight circle now. Of him Gabriel could see little, but one thing he noticed: despite the heat, the man wore a woven cap that hugged his skull closely and rode down to the tops of his ears. He carried a heavy Jaeger rifle in his right hand and stared silently down at Gabriel. The tricorned man Gabriel had met once before; this second one was new to him.

Gabriel cleared his throat three times and loosened his voice. "May I stand?" he asked.

"You may not. No need for it. You stay right where you are and listen to me," the man in the tricorn said. "We got another thing or two needing doing for us."

Gabriel's brows lowered over his blue eyes. "I've already done more for you than I should have, and at quite a risk to myself. If it were known I stored stolen goods for you, I'd be jailed or hanged for it."

"Aye, but hanged you're not, nor are we, and so our commerce can yet go on, eh? Listen. We've got more goods needing a safe hiding place, and skins that need a quick and quiet selling. You're going to buy those hides from us, Shoebuckles. After that, they're yours to do with what you want. Take them to Salisbury and turn them into money, and you're out nothing for your trouble. Do that for us, and your place here will remain untouched by us."

"Look, you—that promise was made me before, with nothing said about having to deal with you yet again. If you want to sell your skins, take them to market yourself."

"Don't be so stupid a sod, Shoebuckles. All in our band have cause not to show ourselves in the towns. But such as you can come and go and trade freely."

Gabriel, though still frightened, felt anger rising. "Listen to me. You're asking too much. This store is my uncle's, and he keeps close watch on the peltries. And we pay no cash for them here, but trade out in goods for what is brought in. If I pay in cash, he'll know of it."

"Then pay from your own purse, not his. You look well-off enough for that. And believe you me, refusing will bring far more loss to your uncle than you'll know otherwise, and to you as well." With that, he twitched the pistol meaningfully.

Gabriel's eyes lit with fear. "Very well," he said. "Bring in your peltries, and I'll pay for them out of my own pocket. And after that I intend never to see you again."

"Wrong on two scores, Shoebuckles. We'll bring naught to you here. When the way is safe, we'll come fetch you in the night and haul you where we need you. And you've hardly seen the last of us. We like you, Shoebuckles. You're our partner now, and we'll be trading like this right regularly."

Gabriel's face blanched. "And if I say no?"

The tricorned man waved at his partner. "See my friend there? He's fond of that blade he carries. Likes to use it in interesting ways. I've seen him cut a circle about a wolf's neck and peel his neckskin up over the eyes, just to bring about a good prance and howl. What he might do to a man, or a man's kin, I'm afraid to say. You think on that a bit if ever you begin to feel unfriendly toward your new partners. Good night to you, Shoebuckles. And don't fret yourself. Once you've dealt with us a few times, you'll find it becoming a lot easier."

Gabriel watched them take his pistols and leave, and wondered how he could have been so foolish as to get drawn into commerce with such. He hadn't intended for this to happen. The first time he had cooperated with these men, it had been out of fear and a sense of practicality. In return for temporarily hiding a bale of skins and some assorted stolen items, he had been assured that Thomas Colter's store would never be robbed. Gabriel had believed the promise. Now he felt foolish for it.

He remained on the floor long after the intruders were gone. When he stood, he was shaking. He thought about going to his father and begging his help, but he was too afraid. He put out the lamp, returned to his house, and slept no more the rest of the night.

Tilly Hampton gently bathed the face of Elijah Wexell with a damp cloth and softly urged the boy to hush his rantings. He was lying on a cot near the open-shuttered window at the front of the Hampton cabin. He had alternately raged and mourned for the last hour, a pattern to which Tilly had become accustomed.

Sina, as tenderhearted as she was gruff, had taken in Elijah Wexell, who still lived despite the horrible skull injury inflicted upon him more than three weeks ago. Lived—but his life was merely a pitiful and mindless existence. Sometimes he would stare listlessly out a window or into a corner, responding to nothing said or done around him, a half inch of his pinkish brain visible through the cavity in his head. Other times, he would thrash and wail, as he was doing now, raving about the attack and bemoaning his inability to stop the men who had killed his father and injured him. Sina or Tilly would try to calm him, but there was nothing to be done but wait out the spells.

When first he had been brought to the cabin, Tilly had not been able to look at the disfigured boy without revulsion. Sina, never weak of stomach, had shaved the hair away from the wounded part of the skull, clearing a patch around it so the cavity could be kept clean enough to heal. The bare white skin outlined the cavity and made it look all the worse. Now that Tilly had grown used to it, she hardly noticed it.

"Hush, Elijah, hush," she whispered softly into his ear. "All is well now, all is well."

The boy sometimes responded to such soft cooings, but today he didn't seem to hear her at all. He thrashed with his right arm, almost striking her. Firmly she took hold of his wrist and forced his flailing arm against his chest. He breathed deeply three times in succession, then sank into a sudden quiet. Tilly felt relieved. Experience with Elijah had let her know that now he would remain peaceful for at least another hour or two. She felt great pity for the boy. Clearly the wound was not healing and likely never would. Tilly had ceased praying for his survival and now often petitioned for an easy, merciful passing.

The door opened, and Sina came in, bearing a bucket of springwater. Elijah stirred and murmured at the sound of the latch, waved his hands above him once, then became quiet again.

"Oh, I'm sorry to have disturbed him," she said. "Has he been thrashing about?"

"Yes. But I think he's weaker today."

Sina put down the water and walked to the side of the cot. She examined the wound. "Looks no better and no worse. But if he's weakening, that's not a good sign." She paused. "Or then, perhaps it is."

Tilly said, "Mother, I've felt badly for thinking it best that he should die. Am I wrong to feel that way?"

"That I don't know, daughter. But don't worry yourself for it, for you've thought nothing that hasn't gone through my own noggin a hundred times over." She put a lean arm around Tilly's waist. "You look too pale, my girl. Go outside and walk a bit."

Tilly was glad to obey. Leaving the cabin, she took to the path that led down to the spring. At the spring she knelt on the flat rock that jutted out slightly above the cool water. She drank from her hands, then splashed more water across her face and into her hair. When the water settled, she looked at her reflection until it was distorted up by the little stirrings generated by a skittering water strider. Tilly wondered if she was pretty. She didn't think so, not often, though sometimes Joshua's glances made her feel that way.

Rising, she jumped lithely across the spring and walked into the woods beyond it. Tilly loved the woods, especially in deep summer when it was so thick and lush and soft that it seemed she should be able to sweep it to her in her arms like heaps of cotton. The light beneath the overspreading leafy branches was muted and crystalline, a delightfully cool lure away from the searing rays that scorched the treeless meadows and fields. She

walked along the path she had beaten earlier in the
summer when she regularly made her way to the far
meadow to pick blackberries and watched a jay scolding
a squirrel somewhere up in a cedar tree.

A few hundred yards into the woods, she stopped and
sat down on a fallen maple that had come to rest against
the base of a spreading oak. She leaned back against the
oak's trunk and let her eyes drift out of focus so that the
mantle of leaves above her melted into an arch of mottled
green. This was her cathedral, her place of rest and
escape, just a short distance from the cabin yet seeming
a thousand miles away. Tilly relaxed, slumping back
comfortably against the rough bark. Her breathing stead-
ied, and she dozed off.

When she awakened, a man stood before her, not ten
feet away. Still in a sleepy stupor, Tilly for a few seconds
did not react to him but then bolted to her feet. She
tripped over a dead limb branching off the fallen maple
upon which she had been sitting. She sprawled on her
face and knocked the breath from her lungs. That was
all that kept her from screaming when the man stepped
forward and reached down.

He was a strongly built man with broad shoulders and
a unappealing flat face covered with a month's growth of
beard. On his head was a knitted cap that hugged his
skull tightly. Curls of dirty brown hair piled out from
beneath it around his ears and down the back of his
neck. He smelled like rum and sweat. Tilly recoiled as
his hand touched her shoulder.

"Let me help you up, there, pretty thing," the man
said. Feeling her pull away from him, he frowned. "Hey,
now—I'm doing naught but trying to help you up."

Tilly by now had regained her breath, and she scrambled to her feet. "Don't touch me!" she demanded, whirl-
ing to face the man. His eyes narrowed, and she knew
she had offended him. From the moment she had seen
him, Tilly had reacted to him defensively, instinctively
feeling he intended her harm. That he really might mean
no harm at all was a possibility that only just now came
to mind. She wondered if she had overreacted.

"I'm sorry," she said hesitantly. "Please pardon me—it's that you startled me so."

A clear drop of sweat emerged from beneath the knitted cap and ran down the side of the man's face. By the time it vanished into the forest of his ragged beard, it was brown with grime. "You think me a frightening sight, do you?" he asked. His smile was disconcerting.

"No, no—I was just startled. Good day to you, sir." She touched her dress in the sort of modest curtsy Sina had taught her and moved as if to step around the man. But he sidestepped and kept her from it.

"Hold your horses, little lady. There's no cause to run away. Stay and talk to me."

"Please, sir. I must get home."

"Home," he repeated, his smile unfaded. "Is that your home yonder in the clearing?" He thumbed back toward the Hampton cabin.

Tilly did not want to answer him, she did not want this man to know where she could be found. Her reluctance made her stammer, and that was as good as a confirmation.

"Come here, little lady," the man said, reaching out to her. "Let me show you something."

Tilly put aside any pretense of civility. "I'll not come to you," she said. "You leave me be!"

"Come now, girl, I won't hurt you! You can trust me—no! Don't go singing out!" Tilly had opened her mouth as if to scream. "Just calm down a moment and come here."

Tilly's eyes rapidly scanned the forest around her. Against a tree nearby the man's rifle leaned, a shot pouch and powder horn hanging from it. That let her know he had watched her for at least some moments before she awakened, for he obviously had set down his burden before advancing to her. She wished she could get to the rifle, but that was hopeless. Tilly backed away one step and almost tripped again. Glancing down, she noticed a large knarled stick at her heels and in half a moment swept it up and hefted it.

"Go away from me!" she ordered, crouching and holding the stick before her with both hands, like a club. "Leave me be, I say!"

The man chuckled. More sweat poured down his face. "That's right, pretty thing. I like it when a girl puts up a good fight." He took a forward step. Tilly swung the club, but he deftly ducked it.

"Quite a breeze you stir with that thing!" he said. "You think you can pound out my brains with a dead stick?"

Tilly backed away, furtively eyeing the path but afraid to wheel and run. She did not want this man behind her. The thought of screaming came again, but she decided against that as well. Her mother would come running, indeed, but would only endanger herself.

"Come on, my girl, put down your stick and fetch yourself over here. You won't regret it—"

The next swing of the club caught him on the side of the head. It was not a hard blow, for it glanced upward, but it did catch the woolen cap and pull it from the man's head. Tilly's eyes widened, and she gasped.

The man lost his smile with his cap and clapped his hands over his skull. Tilly wilted away from him, even more horrified of him now, stunned by the ugliness before her.

"Turn away from me!" he bellowed. "Don't look at me!" He went scrambling toward the cap.

Tilly saw her advantage and took it. With a great swing of the stick, she struck the man as he reached down for his cap. The blow took him between the shoulder blades and pounded him to the ground, forcing a loud grunt from his throat. Tilly hefted her club and ran, hard as she could go, to the path, then toward home. Near the edge of the woods she stopped and turned, stick ready. The man had not followed her. She closed her eyes and took a deep breath. Remembering all at once that he had a rifle and in his anger might even now be hidden out there drawing a bead on her, she spun and entered the clearing, heading for the cabin.

Sina was on the far side of it and did not see her come. Should she tell her mother what had just happened? She decided against it—the whole thing seemed foul and terrible, and she wanted simply to forget it.

Elijah Wexell was still asleep. His wound looked raw and festered—but less revolting than before, at least to Tilly. What she had seen when the man lost his cap had been far more repelling to her.

The dog's barking awakened her. Tilly sat up in her bed, mysteriously alarmed. It was common for the dog to bark in the night, for the dark forest held many things to stir it, but tonight something was different. With a chill, she realized what it was. The barking had begun, mounted furiously, and then stopped abruptly. For a few moments there was no noise at all, but then she heard Sina rising from her bed in the cabin below, and Zachariah began to cry.

Tilly rose. She wore a long pale homespun gown. On bare feet, she descended from the cabin loft to the main room below. In the corner, Elijah Wexell made a mindless noise and moved in his sleep. Sina was already up and had the rifle leveled at the door. The thin woman looked up sharply at Tilly.

"What is it, Mother?" Tilly asked.

Sina said, "I don't yet know. Something or someone is outside, and I think the dog is killed."

Tilly strained her ears to hear sounds of movement beyond the door, but Zachariah's crying was too loud.

Sina, her voice gruff with tension, said, "Take Zach and carry him into the loft with you. Get in your bed and remain there."

Tilly obeyed, now very frightened. Zachariah clung to her tightly as she picked him up. Clumsily balancing him, she climbed the loft, put him into the bed with her, and pulled her blanket up over them both. Zachariah quit crying.

What happened after that happened quickly. The door exploded open, the latch breaking under a great force from the outside. Sina's rifle barked at once; a man screamed, others shouted. There was a terrible thud. Sina moaned fearfully, and another thud followed. Elijah

Wexell sent up wordless calls from his cot and thrashed noisily. A man swore, another thud sounded, and Elijah's noise cut off as quickly as had the barking of the dog shortly before. Zachariah wailed again.

Male voices rose in a jumble. "William's shot—the rutting old strumpet shot him clean through." "Look there—why, that's the same boy William hatcheted on the topknot." "The girl, where's the girl?" "Above, she'll be—in the loft—"

Tilly's thoughts focused on the protection of her baby brother. She pushed him down into the bed, rose, and picked up the only makeshift weapon she could find—a small but heavy oak chest her father had whittled out and pieced together during his recovery after his accident with the falling tree. She went with it to the edge of the loft, peering down. Her mother lay to the side beside her fallen empty rifle. Whether she was alive or dead Tilly could not tell. Elijah Wexell was murdered, tomahawked, his head crushed.

One of the men—the same one she had encountered in the woods—was climbing the ladder to the loft. She raised the oak chest, threw it down at him, and was dismayed when he dodged it by hugging the ladder. The wooden box crashed against the puncheon floor and came apart at the joints. Zachariah cried all the louder.

Tilly backed away from the loft a short distance, then waited for the climber to stick his head up at the top of the ladder. When he did, she kicked, but again he deftly avoided harm by ducking to the side. A burly hand came up and grasped her ankle as she kicked again. With a twist, he pulled her toward him. Fighting, Tilly tried to pull the other way, but managed only to lose her balance. She pitched out from the loft and fell headfirst toward the floor—screaming, reaching out to try to cushion her fall.

When she hit, terrible pain spasmed down her nerves from her skull to the tops of her legs. She lay still, wracked by pain, unable to see clearly. She was conscious of men circling around her, looking down at her, then of the foul stench of the man in the knitted cap, and his face descending toward hers. She felt his kiss on her dry lips as she passed out, and then it all began growing dark. As she lost consciousness, she was aware of nothing but Zachariah's pitiful crying in the loft above.

10

Alphus Colter lifted his hand and halted the party of fifteen armed horsemen behind him. Closest to him was Joshua, who glared with open displeasure at the delay. Alphus glanced at him and noted the fury burning in Joshua. He understood how the young man felt. He felt the same.

But there was good cause to stop here, for he had spotted movement in a briar thicket down the slope from the trail. Alphus's hunter's eye knew the difference between human and animal movement at half a glance, and this was no animal. Joshua, who had let his anger distract him, was slower to see what Alphus had, but when he did, he dismounted rapidly, bringing his rifle with him in one smooth descent.

"You, down there!" Alphus called. "We see you, and there's no hiding now—you'd best come up peacefully!"

A few in the party glanced at each other, for they had not yet seen the man at whom Alphus shouted. Farmers, for the most part, were decent enough woodsmen but lacked the quick and sharp eye of hunters like Alphus. Even the slowest among them, however, saw the man clearly enough once he rose to his knees and thrust his hands to the sky. The hands shook, and there was blood on them.

"Who you be?" Alphus demanded.

"William Sloat!" a quavering voice answered. "Don't shoot—God above, I'm shot bad enough already. I won't resist you—don't have the strength."

"Are you one of the damned sons of whores who entered the cabin of Sina Hampton last night?" Joshua asked.

Sloat rose the rest of the way, tottered, and advanced to let them see his face, which was drained of color and frozen in fright. He wore a hunting shirt dyed scarlet with his own blood. "Please—I did no harm to anyone! The woman shot me first thing through the door, and now I'm bleeding again! Help me, please! My own companions, they left me here, left me in the night to bleed to death."

"Bloody hell!" Joshua bellowed. "You'll learn to bleed when my rifle ball cuts out your eye!" He lifted his rifle. Sloat sent up a wail and fell to his knees again, putting his blood-drenched hands across his face.

"No!" Alphus roared. He swung up his arm and knocked Joshua's rifle up just as it fired. Sloat screamed and fell to the side, but it was fear and loss of blood that made him do it, for the ball had sung off into the sky high above him.

"Why in hell's name did you do that?" Joshua stormed at his foster father through the cloud of powder smoke. "He's one of the very devils who—"

"I know well enough who he is," Alphus snapped back. "And if you'd let your head catch up with your anger, you'd see he can do more for us alive than dead. You calm yourself, boy, or turn around and go home, for you're dangerous to us all, the way you are."

Joshua's frown of anger softened into one of realization. Slowly, almost meekly, he began reloading his rifle as others of the party descended to drag Sloat up to the trail.

Alphus, though no constable or sheriff, was recognized by all as the unofficial leader of this party, partly because of his closeness to the Hampton women and his past advocacy of strong response to the robbery problem. One of the other men, a tall second-generation German named Jacob Brecht, had tried to have himself declared head by vote, but the others had declared there was no need for such formalities. Now Brecht, who had never liked Alphus, sulked at the rear of the band.

The men shuffled Sloat up before Alphus and had to hold him erect, for he had lost much blood.

Alphus coldly eyed him up and down. "Looks to me like you're going to die," he said. "I'm surprised you survived the night."

"Help me, please . . . I'm hurting bad."

Alphus nodded. "I'd say you've got good reason to hurt. And I'd say further that any of us here have just reason to make you hurt more."

Sloat's face was lined with deep creases and tear tracks. "Please, I beg you, don't harm me. I'll do whatever you ask, if you'll only get me patched. I don't want to die."

"I don't recall Tom or Elijah Wexell asking to die, either," Alphus replied. "Nor, I expect, did Sina and Tilly Hampton ask to be beaten and treated like strumpets by a band of fornicating swine." Alphus spat at Sloat's feet in a gesture of contempt. "The best that can be said for you is that at least you left the baby alive."

Sloat slumped against one of the men beside him, and the man shoved him upright again. When Sloat's head weakly lolled back, one of the others shoved it up straight and forced Sloat to look squarely into Alphus's face.

"Did you yourself dishonor the women?"

"I did nothing! 'Twas Jack alone who led us to that cabin, and him alone what went after the women! I swear it!"

"Who is this Jack?"

"I don't know—Jack's the only name I ever heard called."

"Aye, well, we'll find him and see that he gets his proper punishment, along with the rest of you bloody bastards. And you'll help us, Sloat. You'll tell us right now where we'll find your old partners."

Sloat fainted. Alphus slapped him awake and repeated his question. Sloat, his voice barely audible, slurringly described the route to the band's usual refuge—a well-hidden enclave accessible only by a difficult and narrow gap.

"I know the place he speaks of," Joshua said. "I've hunted there."

"And so have I, though not in years," Alphus said. "Come—let's go after them."

"What about this one?" one of the men holding Sloat asked.

"Tie up his wound and strap him to that tree. We'll come back to deal with him later."

"I'll die if you leave me!" Sloat pleaded feebly.

"Aye, and if you do, consider yourself lucky, for if you're yet alive when we return, that up there"—he pointed upward—"is the very limb you'll swing from. There's a good man, name of Tom Wexell, in his grave because of you and your band, and a boy, name of Elijah Wexell, hatcheted to death for like reason. And what you did to the women is alone cause to snap every one of your necks, and by Joseph, snap them we will."

They went on, leaving Sloat shouting after them, reasserting his innocence in the rape of Tilly and Sina. Ignoring him, they ascended through the forest. The sun rose higher, piercing through the branches above them with pale green-tinted light.

Joshua reloaded his rifle with a speed and grace developed during his years of long hunting when every discharge of a rifle was a potential invitation for attack from unseen Indians lurking about. Many a hunter had died during the interim between firing and reloading, and Joshua had been well trained by Alphus to rearm himself speedily. Today the skill was of particular value, for Joshua and his companions were embroiled in a battle with the band of thieves they had tracked down.

The young frontiersman slammed the hickory ramrod

back into its slides beneath the barrel. Beside him, Ethan Wexell groaned and gripped a bleeding leg.

"I think I wounded the bloody devil," Joshua said. "How is your wound, Ethan?"

"Hurts like blazes, but a clean hole," Wexell replied through gritted teeth. "But I'm done-in for running."

"Bind it up as best you can, then, and I'll go after him alone," Joshua replied. "Is there anything you need before I do?"

"No—just get on. I don't want that bugger to get away."

Joshua rose carefully and scanned the forest. Beyond the rocky ridge behind him, the sound of gunfire continued as the frontiersmen battled the robber band in and about the hollow where they had found them. Sloat had given accurate information, and Alphus's riders had found a full dozen men holed up. But a sentry had spotted the coming avengers and sounded a warning, and shooting had begun.

In the course of the fight, Joshua and Ethan had spotted one of the robbers, a stocky man in a tight-fitting woven cap, scrambling away from the battle. They had followed him and for several moments had lost sight of him until an unexpected gunshot had put a hole through Ethan's calf. Joshua had caught a glimpse of the rifleman and fired at him, and felt reasonably sure the shot was good, even though the man had scrambled away.

Rising, Joshua slipped along behind a line of trees toward the hill from which the robber had fired. His deerskin clothing blended with the color of the forest floor and the tree trunks among which he crept, yet he felt dangerously exposed. Whoever the gunman was, he was a good shot, or at least a lucky one.

Joshua reached the hill and found, as he expected, that the man was no longer there. Peering through a laurel thicket, Joshua studied the lay of the land around him. The hill sloped down and away from him toward the north, and at its base leveled along the foot of an east–west-running ridge. At the west end of the ridge, a creek ran through a deep gully lined with rocks and furred with soft ferns. There Joshua saw the man scrambling along, rifle in hand. Even from this distance he could see blood on the man's thigh. Obviously he was wounded, but not badly, for he seemed relatively unimpeded by his injured leg.

The woodland air was growing hotter and sticky, and bit by bit, the clear morning sky was becoming murky and gray. The afternoon would surely bring rain. Joshua, though strong and fit, was already beginning to sweat heavily, for the breeze had stilled and the air was thickening with humidity. Joshua moved down the slope, keeping his quarry in sight as long as he could, but at last the wounded man disappeared around the end of the ridge. As he drew closer to the ridge's end, Joshua stopped and again assessed his situation. He heard no sound of movement nearby. Finally he advanced, carefully rounding the end of the ridge.

A rifle blasted, and the ball thunked into the ground at his feet. The young Carolinian immediately ran forward into the open, hoping to spot the gunman before he could hide himself and reload. A cloud of powder smoke, hanging almost motionless in the still air, directed Joshua's gaze to an ancient fallen cedar on the other side of the creek, slightly up the bank. After a few moments, Joshua saw the crest of the man's cap over the tree and noted the furious movements of hurried reloading. Without hesitation, Joshua ran forward.

The man rose and saw Joshua. His face became stark with fear—and Joshua stopped abruptly. The face looking down at him was too far away to see clearly, but in it was something so familiar and disturbing that it halted him on his heels.

Joshua's delay was ill-advised, for the gunman dropped behind the cedar deadfall again, abandoned his reloading, and came up with a flintlock pistol. He fired before Joshua could seek cover.

The ball snapped Joshua's powder horn strap cleanly in two, making the horn fall, but Joshua was uninjured. Sensing an advantage in speed, he did not pause to retrieve his powder horn. Instead, he let out an Indian yell to unnerve his foe and splashed across the creek toward him.

The man, panicking as Joshua had hoped he would, flung a tomahawk, and in his haste, Joshua failed to dodge it. It struck him in the chest, knocking him down as he came up the bank. The tomahawk had hit on the flat, however, so did not pierce him. Joshua fell backward and slid three feet down the muddy bank, leaving him lying with his feet higher than his head, his rifle butt caught beneath his back. Before he could get up again and swing the weapon into firing position, the man climbed onto the cedar, drew a knife, and leapt toward Joshua.

Joshua rolled just as the man struck, but now he was completely on top of his rifle. The man began slashing at him with his blade, and Joshua yelled as the sharp edge sliced a quarter-inch-deep furrow into his shoulder. His position keeping him from gaining good momentum, nevertheless he struck his attacker as hard as he could, spasming the man's jaw. At the same time, he knocked off the woven cap, revealing a rough, bony, ugly expanse of scar tissue that extended from the brow halfway back across the crown and slightly down the left side of the head, like a promontory of scar thrusting into an ocean of matted hair. This fellow had been scalped alive sometime long ago and kept the ugly scar of it covered with the woven cap.

The fight was now a close-quarters wrestling bout as the two men strained and struggled, the scalped man trying to embed the knife in Joshua, Joshua trying to deflect it and reach his own knife at the same time. Mud smeared them as they tumbled and writhed, edging ever toward the creek and at last plunging into it. The fall into the water broke their grip, and Joshua spun away, sending up great splashes, and came to his feet.

Joshua did not know just when he had realized that the man he was fighting was Jack Byrum. Sometime in the struggle, the realization had come upon him, and he had accepted it with surprising dispassion. Bloody Eagle might have taken Byrum's scalp in the forest eleven years ago, but he had failed to take his life.

Joshua knew Byrum, but Byrum apparently did not know Joshua. The two faced off. The older man, chest heaving, stood in a slight stoop, like a fighting hound on its hind legs, knife twitching in his hand. Only now did seeing his natural father alive before him, like some living phantom, begin to awe Joshua.

He opened his mouth to say "Father," but the word would not cross his lips. Alphus Colter was now his father, not this scarred human beast before him, who by rights should be dead and gone. So Joshua did not say "Father" but "Jack Byrum!"

Byrum had just begun advancing through the creek toward Joshua. Hearing his name called made him stop and look closely at Joshua. His brows drew together, and he looked confused. In the silence they heard the clatter of continued rifle fire across the ridge. The fight at the roost of the mountain bandits obviously was still under way.

"How do you know my name?" Byrum asked.

"Look at me—don't you know me as well?" Joshua answered.

Byrum studied him even more closely. Suddenly his breath drew in, his brows lifted, and his eyes lighted in recognition. "Joshua!" he said. "God, boy, I thought you were dead long ago, killed at Cane Creek!"

"And I thought you were dead—I saw your scalp hanging on Bloody Eagle's pole."

"Many a man has lived through a scalping."

Joshua took a long stare at Byrum, head to toe. "There was a time, right after Bloody Eagle waved your scalp under my nose, that I wished you were still alive, even after all you did . . . and didn't do, for Mother and me and Samuel. Now I know how foolish a wish that was, for it's not right, just not right, for you to have been spared while little Samuel had to die."

"Samuel?"

"Aye, Samuel! Your own son—the newborn boy you abandoned, the baby your own wife died bringing into the world, the boy Christiana Cox took for her own. They're dead now, Samuel and Christiana, and her own little baby, Beth. Killed in the wilderness by Henry Dorey."

"Dorey!" Byrum squinted. "How know you all this?"

"Dorey told me himself, the day he died, knifed to death in a tavern in Salisbury."

Byrum's expression showed surprise and pleasure. "Dorey was killed? Well, I'll be damned!"

"That I don't doubt."

Byrum paid no heed to the comment. "Boy, don't you know a man born lying, like Dorey will die the same way? Christiana Cox is as alive as me and you, and married again, from the look of it. I seen both her and her fat-bottomed husband in Wilmington, and two children with them, both girl and boy."

"Girl and boy . . . how old?"

"Eleven, twelve—I don't know. The boy's face looked mighty like Hester's—that's what drew my eye to him. I watched them cross a street together, I did. Yonder goes my living son, born in Fort Loudoun, I told myself. That's him alive and in the flesh, with Nathan Cox's old wife beside him. There was a big-arsed man with them. Looked rich. I never let them see me."

Joshua was overwhelmed. "Samuel . . . alive!" he said, scarcely able to believe it. He stood like a statue, letting himself absorb the astounding information.

"So how did you make it through after Fort Loudoun, boy?" Byrum asked.

The question stirred old memories and old angers. "With no help from you, that's how," he answered. "You ran out and left me to be slaughtered with the rest at Cane Creek."

Byrum shrugged. "I offered you a chance to run with me. You turned it down."

"Turned it down because I wouldn't leave a newborn baby alone in a time of danger, like you did."

"Well, you must have left him sometime or another, for you surely ain't with him now."

The words struck Joshua's hidden sense of guilt. "You shut your mouth," he said threateningly.

Byrum laughed. "Well, I think I've touched a hot iron to a tender sore! Got something you feel bad about, boy? Maybe you're no better than your old pap after all, eh? It's like I told you long ago—that's my blood running in your veins, and like me you'll finally be."

"I'll kill you!" Joshua roared.

"Come and do it, then! Hell, you were trying hard enough to kill me a minute ago, you and your righteous bunch of Carolina angels! Was it what we done to them women that made you finally decide to run the demons out of the mountains?"

In the astounding events of the past minutes, Joshua had almost forgotten what had prompted this battle in the first place. Now Byrum's words brought back the fresh image of the battered, bruised form of Tilly Hampton as she had appeared in his cabin doorway this very dawn, holding her torn gown about her body, quakingly telling of what had happened in the night back at the Hampton cabin.

He remembered finding Sina's pitiful thin body lying on the puncheon floor, covered only with the blanket Tilly had thrown across her before she fled to find help. He remembered also the gasping cries of Zachariah up in the loft; the child was too small to comprehend what had happened but not too small to sense the horror of it. And clearest of all, he remembered young Elijah Wexell, lying dead on his cot with his skull caved in for the second and final time by men who cared nothing for any lives but their own.

Then another memory, even fresher: Sloat had said the actual violence against the women had been done by a robber named Jack . . . and Tilly, this morning, had muttered something about a strange cap and a scarred head.

Joshua's face went livid as comprehension dawned. "It was you, you yourself, who hurt them!" he exclaimed. "God help me—my own father!"

Byrum grinned. "Hell, I was just doing what a man is

driven to do! You ain't a child—you know what I'm talking about, the way a man feels when the fire's up within him. Look at me! Look at this skullbone of mine sticking up here like a rock on a ridge! When Bloody Eagle took my hair, he left me looking mighty frightful. Women don't take much to a frightful-looking man. When I want a woman anymore, I got to reach out and take her, or do without. And I've never been much for doing without for long—and last night, I didn't."

Rage overcame Joshua. He roared like a wounded bear and charged at Byrum, who met him with a swing of the knife. Joshua managed to dodge it and put one hand to Byrum's throat, another around the wrist of his knifing arm. Byrum fell backward, but as he did so, drew up his right foot and wedged it against Joshua's abdomen. With a yell of exertion, he straightened the leg and sent Joshua flipping backward, over his head.

When Joshua came up again, Byrum had splashed to the bank and recovered the tomahawk he had thrown earlier. Joshua lowered his shoulder and bulled into his father, but Byrum managed to sidestep most of the blow. Joshua fell headfirst into the bank, and before he could push himself aright, felt a tremendous exploding force on the back of his head. He saw a fierce burst of light that seemed to come from behind his eyeballs. Then the light twinkled away to inky black. The last thing he was aware of was the pop of repeated rifle fire echoing across the ridges as the battle went on.

Water splashed Joshua's face, and he opened his eyes. Looking down at him, a worried expression on his face, was Ben Slye. Beyond Slye was a sky of tossing black clouds, filled with wind and the promise of storm.

"Good, now, that's right—come awake. You're all in one piece, my friend, and unless you want a good hail pelting, you'd best come around."

Joshua groaned and sat up. He had been lying half in, half out of the creek. He was drenched and so covered with mud that he seemed dressed in it. As he rose, his ears rang in a dissonant throbbing chord, and his head pounded in time to the ringing.

"That's quite a knot on the side of your head, Joshua," Slye said. "Big and red as a ripe apple."

Joshua carefully felt the knot and found that this time, Slye was not exaggerating. Byrum's tomahawk had raised quite a lump, and it hurt like the devil.

Byrum—

"Where is he?" Joshua asked, looking around. He saw nothing but wind-mangled forest, every leaf showing its underside and tugging as if to free itself from its host. A hot bolt of lightning cracked the sky, and now the air was cool, not hot and heavy as it had been earlier.

"Where is who? I found no one but you, though there are prints heading off down the creek yonder. You were after one of the thieves, I suppose? You'd best forget him, for he's gotten away, and took your rifle with him too. Far luckier than his friends he is."

"What do you mean?"

"Come and see for yourself."

Every step jarring his throbbing skull, Joshua followed Slye toward the lair of the bandits. There was no gunfire now. From where the sun backlighted the clouds Joshua could tell it was about noon, though had he been judging by the daylight, he would have guessed closer to five or six. The storm that was on its way would be a typical summer storm of the hills—fast, driving, windy, and over in minutes.

"Take a look at a good day's work," Slye said when they came in view of the hollow.

Below stood the band of bordermen, who obviously had defeated the bandits. In a heap to one side were piled seven bodies—bloodied, apparently shot to death. From the limbs of two stout trees at the center of the hollow swung four more, hanged by the neck.

"We lost not a man, though some have a new hole or two in them. Only one of the scum we came after got away, that being the one that pounded you. Most were killed in the shooting, and you can see what happened to the rest. . . ." Slye trailed off and squinted at the men below. "Well, I don't understand this! It appears there's yet another prisoner. Perhaps they found one hiding."

As Joshua and Slye drew near, the men below turned to watch them. Ethan Wexell limped over to meet them, his expression serious.

"Joshua, thank God you're alive," he said. "I feared for you. But listen to me. Something bad has come up."

"Bad?"

"Aye. We found another one hidden among some stolen skin bales just now. It's—"he stopped and swallowed, "I'm afraid it's Gabriel."

Joshua stared disbelievingly at Slye, then examined the crowd. Alphus turned to look back at him, his face ashen and anxious. Near him stood Gabriel, white as milk and looking more frightened than Joshua had ever thought a man could.

"There's a mistake of some sort," Joshua said. "There has to be a mistake."

He strode over to Alphus. "What is happening here?"

Alphus looked old and tired—the first time Joshua had ever seen his foster father like that. "It's Gabe," he said in a voice that wasn't his. "They're talking of hanging Gabe."

"He was hidden among them, and there's no question he was of their number. It's only right he should pay the same price—you yourself said that any caught dealing with these sods needs to stretch a rope." The speaker was the broad-jowled white-haired Jacob Brecht, Alphus's longtime antagonist.

"This is not some stranger come in from the outside. This is my son!" Alphus said. The defense sounded feeble, even though he spoke forcefully.

"He's a thief, like the others," Brecht said, lifting his head and looking down the length of his nose at Alphus.

"I'm not a thief, I tell you!" Gabriel said. "I was never part of them. They forced me into anything I did—they threatened me and my kin if I wouldn't agree to hide some goods for them and buy a few skins. That's all I did . . . I had no choice."

"That's as good as a confession, in my view," Brecht said.

Alphus stared bitterly at Brecht, working his lips but finding nothing to say.

Joshua stepped forward and faced Brecht squarely. "If you lay a hand on him, you'll answer to me," he said.

Brecht's eyes flashed. He was a good four inches taller than Joshua and twice as broad, and he stretched and spread himself to full advantage, like a cock spreading its feathers for a mate. "Is that supposed to be a threat?"

"No. Just a fact."

Gabriel was looking at Joshua strangely, and Joshua understood why. The two of them had never been anything but near-enemies, enjoying none of the pleasures of brotherhood. It felt as strange to him, defending Gabriel, as it did to Gabriel being recipient of that defense, but Joshua would not stand by and let Alphus be humiliated in the way Brecht was trying to do.

Brecht looked around the group. "See there? The Colters are quick enough to put the neck of strangers into the noose, but when the noose threatens too familiar a neck, they change their song bloody fast."

Slye said, "Shut your flaps a few moments, all of you." He looked around a little nervously and swallowed. "I don't know the right or wrong of it, but I'll not be party to hanging the son of Alphus Colter, especially not on the urging of a man who has looked for an opportunity to see harm done him."

One of the others said, "There's still the fact we hanged the others. 'Tain't right to hang some and not all."

"This man is my brother, or as good as," Joshua said. "That's all that counts to me. You hang him, you have to come through me to do it."

"You don't even have a rifle," Brecht muttered contemptuously.

"I can deal with you, rifle or no rifle," Joshua snapped.

"Blast and blow it, we know the right thing to do is hang the bugger!" Brecht bellowed. "Now let's be men about it and get the job done!"

Joshua struck Brecht in the mouth, knocking him

down. Brecht came up, blood on his lip, and lumbered toward Joshua. Four others circled in and grabbed him; two more grabbed Joshua.

Slye waved his hands in the air. "That's enough! We'll hang no one else today—this is something that needs thinking about. I say let's go back to our homes and mull it over."

"What? And let that one run off?" Brecht said, nodding toward Gabriel.

Slye slowly nodded. "Aye. Perhaps that's the best answer yet. Gabriel is guilty, that's no question, but he says he acted under threat. That may be true, and none of us can prove otherwise, for there is none left living to dispute it. I can't support what Gabriel has done, but if in fact he was threatened, that softens it somewhat, does it not?"

The others, none of whom seemed nearly as eager as Brecht to see Gabriel hang, voiced their assent.

"Well then, perhaps the thing to do is let him go, but send him off. Make him leave the country and not come back."

"No!" Gabriel burst out. "I don't want to leave here! I have work, a home—"

Alphus stepped up. "Gabriel, shut your mouth, and maybe you'll avoid dying today."

"But the store—"

"All that is done for you now. Shut up, and maybe we can keep you alive."

"There is one yet living who might give information to settle this question," Brecht said, shaking loose from the men who had grabbed him and dusting off his sleeves. "That Sloat man, tied to the tree." He glanced meaningfully at Alphus Colter. "The man, you may recall, that Mr. Colter here promised a swift hanging upon our return."

"Aye, that's true," someone said.

Alphus looked like he might pass out. His own words had trapped him. Joshua stepped close and put his arm across his foster father's shoulder.

Slye, still trying to talk Gabriel out of the shadow of a

noose, licked his lips. "Aye . . . aye. Well, then let us get back to Sloat and see what he has to say. If he is dead, I say let Gabriel be banished."

"And if he is alive, and his words condemn young Mr. Colter there, then let both Colter and Sloat be hanged," Brecht said. "Agreed?"

Slye looked nervously around at the others. "Agreed." He turned to Alphus. "I'm sorry. There's no other fair and just way."

As they rode back toward the place where they had left the wounded bandit, Slye drew close to Alphus and Joshua. "Pray hard that this Sloat's black soul has traveled on," he said. "If he's alive and speaks against Gabriel, there's naught we can do now to save your boy."

They found Sloat tied to his tree, lying on his side. The men gathered around. Slye knelt and felt Sloat's neck, then looked up.

"Dead?" Brecht asked.

"Dead," Slye said.

Brecht swore.

Alphus Colter closed his eyes and took a deep breath, and Gabriel burst into tears of relief.

11

Long before they reached Gabriel's log house, the storm began, pouring down rain and hail the size of rifle balls. Alphus, Joshua, and Gabriel sheltered beneath the spreading boughs of a leafy oak and avoided the worst of the hail, but the rain drenched them. Alphus stared listlessly into the gloom, hardly seeming to notice it. Gabriel had ceased weeping and seemed dazed.

In minutes, the fiercest part of the storm had passed, and they went on. Joshua glanced behind him and saw other figures farther up the road, watching them.

"They're there," he said.

"I know," Alphus replied. "There can be no time wasted, Gabriel. We must get you off before their patience is gone. We'll ride with you far enough to be sure no one is waiting to have their hanging after all, once you are out of sight."

Gabriel closed his eyes and began to cry quietly again. Joshua watched him, trying to decide how he felt about his foster brother. He had defended him staunchly, yet he still felt no real love for him, no kinship beyond that forced upon them by relationships neither controlled. It had been primarily for Alphus's sake that Joshua had defended Gabriel.

Saddening though the affair with Gabriel was, Joshua also felt an inward thrill of happiness each time he thought back on what Jack Byrum had told him. That Christiana, Beth, and Samuel were still alive was marvelous news—if it was true. He was almost afraid to believe it was, but if Jack Byrum could still be among the living, maybe others thought dead could be as well.

Joshua counted himself fortunate to be alive. Byrum might have killed him back at that creek. It was surprising, when he considered it, that Byrum had not. Maybe there was some vestige of love for his offspring buried in the scarred, callused soul of the man.

Joshua had not revealed, even to Alphus, the identity of the robber he had battled by the creek, and he felt no desire to do so. Better that others should believe his blood father was dead. And dead he might as well be, now. Likely Joshua would never encounter him again, and that suited him fine.

They reached Gabriel's house and entered. Alphus began gathering clothing and goods for Gabriel, who moved mechanically about the house as if lost in a fog. Joshua had been in Gabriel's home only a few times, and each time he had noted, as he did now, the impeccable neatness of it. Gabriel kept house better than most women. Joshua wondered if Gabriel had ever thought of taking a woman for his own. The man seemed to feel no need of feminine company. His sole loves were his business and his books of philosophical and religious speculations, which filled three long shelves on the west side of the main room.

"Go into Virginia is my advice," Alphus said to Gabriel. "You could find work in Salisbury, but that is too close. If you won't have Virginia, then go to Charles Town, or at least Wilmington. You must put many miles between yourself and your trouble here."

"What of Thomas?" Gabriel asked.

"It's too late for you to worry about him. That you should have done before putting his business into so bad a situation," Alphus answered. "I'll wager that Brecht and some of the others will try to make my brother look as guilty as my son, and no doubt his business will suffer. Few will want to trade at a place they see as having done commerce with murdering rabble such as those you dealt with."

"But Thomas had nothing to do with it. He knew nothing of it, and I used my own money, not his, nor the store's."

"It's not the truth that hurts sometimes, Gabriel. It's what other people think is the truth."

Joshua went to the window and peered out through the shutter. "They are still out there, watching," he said. "And not trying to hide themselves."

"Aye. We must move quickly and satisfy them that Gabriel is truly leaving. Quickly, son—gather what food you have that will travel. You must be off."

"It looks as if it may storm again," Gabriel said. "Can't I wait until—"

"A storm will not hurt you nearly so much as a rope around your neck, Gabriel. Please—you must hurry."

Gabriel sniffed back his tears and complied. Joshua watched him with a combination of pity and distaste. "I'll get you a spare horse," he said to Gabriel. "You'll want to move far and fast." He paused. "I'll go along with you the first day or two, if you wish."

Gabriel nodded and smiled. "That's good of you, Joshua. Good of you."

They felt eyes upon them when they rode out of the yard and through the wicket gate, felt them when they headed up the muddy road, felt them until they had put five miles between them and Gabriel's house. Gabriel rode in a straight, uncomfortable posture, eyes fixed straight ahead, staring out before him with the same expression of unbelief that marks the faces of condemned men.

Joshua could guess how he was feeling: stunned, unable really to believe that he was leaving Hankins Creek for the last time, and barely escaping the hangman's noose, at that. Joshua pitied him in a distant way, but pitied Alphus more. Gabriel, after all, was getting only what he deserved—maybe less than he deserved. Alphus was suffering through no fault of his own.

Darkness fell as the wind blew out the clouds and blew in clear skies. The new storm Gabriel had anticipated had never come. In near silence, the three men made camp, cooked corn cakes by the fire, and boiled dried beef in tallow. The meal was devoured with a minimum of conversation.

Joshua sat off to himself, thinking about Byrum, Samuel, Beth, Christiana—a dead past suddenly seeming fresh and alive again, stirring both hope and old hurts. As he mused over it all, he fingered the Roman coin that still hung around his neck and thought of the day in Tikwalitsi that he had given it to John Hawk and the peculiar way fate had given it back to him. The more he considered it, the more Joshua was struck by the strange turns life took. Years in the forests had taught him the skill of anticipating changes in trails and terrain, sudden drops, hills, valleys. But so far, he remained unable to anticipate the turns the path of his life made. When they came, they came without warning, and where they led could not be known.

They parted from Gabriel the next day. Joshua felt no real sorrow and refused to feign any, but Alphus barely restrained his tears. Joshua turned away to allow the father and son some private time.

Gabriel seemed as disbelieving and stunned today as he had yesterday. Before he left, he walked up to Joshua and uncomfortably thrust out his hand. Joshua shook it, noting the softness of it compared to his own. Gabriel's life had been a merchant's life of quills and ledgers, casks of flour and gunpowder, bolts of cloth, bales of hides, barrels of paint. He knew little of the hard labor of farming and the strenuous endeavor of long hunting. As he shook Gabriel's hand, Joshua pondered how little he really understood his foster brother after more than a decade of knowing him.

"You defended me as your brother before those who would have hurt me," Gabriel said, self-consciously clearing his throat. "I know we've had our differences, and may never see things in the same way—but I do appreciate what you did for me yesterday."

Joshua looked Gabriel in the eye. "I would be lying if I said I did it for you. It was for Alphus."

"I know that," Gabriel replied.

"Good-bye, Gabriel," Joshua said. "I'll see you again someday, I'm sure."

"Maybe so—and I hope so, I truly do. Good-bye, Joshua."

Joshua watched Gabriel ride away for as long as he could see him. Alphus did not. He looked west, toward the blue line of mountains, beyond which lay the land where he hunted and hoped to settle someday.

"Let's go, Alphus," Joshua said.

Still gazing at the horizon, Alphus misinterpreted him. Slowly nodding his head, he said, "We will go, Joshua. That we will, and soon."

Alphus Colter got drunk as soon as he returned home, and to Joshua it was a novel and saddening spectacle, for he had never seen Alphus drunk in all the time he had lived with him. When Alphus passed out at the table, Joshua picked up the big man as if he were made of feathers and dumped him in his bed. Then Joshua fetched what had been his spare rifle, slipped on the straw hat Sina had compelled him to wear in warm weather, and walked to the Hampton cabin to see how the women were faring.

Ben Slye's wife, Junie, along with the wife of Slye's visiting cousin, Jim Grindell, had moved in with Sina and Tilly to help take care of Zachariah while the women rested. Visitors were being discouraged, but Joshua felt he was no usual visitor, given his and Alphus's history of supporting the Hamptons since Levi's death. He was therefore surprised when Sal Grindell, a broad-shouldered muscled creature whom Joshua perceived as nothing but a slightly feminized version of a man, blocked him at the doorway and told him to head back home.

He tried vainly to argue his way in. Sal Grindell stood

her ground. "She wants to see no one, and she's made that clear," she said. "The poor girl has been through a shaming experience, and the sight of a man is hardly what she needs."

Joshua tried to understand but felt wrongly rebuffed nonetheless. Did not Tilly appreciate the risk he and the others had taken for her, riding after and punishing the perpetrators of her humiliation? He had fought the very man who had raped her. But Joshua let that thought go no further, for he did not like being reminded that his natural father was the guilty man. That was one thing Tilly would never find out; he would make certain of that.

Leaving the Hampton cabin, Joshua walked back home. Alphus had fallen out of his bed and crawled over to a chair where he sprawled, legs outspread. He had his rum with him again but didn't appear to have touched the crockery cupful that sat on the table beside him.

He looked up coldly as Joshua entered. "Where you been?" he slurred.

Joshua, repelled by the sight of his foster father in such a state, deliberately gave a minimal answer. "Hamptons'."

"You see Sina or Tilly?"

"No."

Alphus scratched beneath his neck and rubbed his jaw, eyes closed. "No? Why the devil did you go if not to see them?"

"I did go to see them. They wouldn't let me in."

"Why not?"

"I don't know. They just don't want to see anybody at the moment, I suppose."

Alphus laid his head on the table, mouth lolling open. For the first time, Joshua found himself disliking the man. "Look at you—this isn't right for you," Joshua said. "Let me get you back to bed."

Abruptly Alphus sat up and pointed a forefinger at Joshua's face. "You leave me be!" he said angrily. Joshua was surprised at the level of venom in his tone.

"Aye, certainly," he said meekly, not understanding why Alphus seemed so angry.

"Aye, good," Alphus said. "You leave me alone. God knows that if I'd left you alone, maybe this would not have happened."

"What are you talking about?"

Alphus's anger became even greater. "What do you think I'm talking about? Gabriel, my son—my real son—that's what I'm talking about! It's my fault he's been so shamed. I treated you as my son and neglected the one the good Lord sent me, and this is what's come of it!"

"You're holding me to blame for what happened to Gabriel?"

"Had you not come between Gabriel and me, forcing us apart, I could have raised him better, taught him better not to do the sort of thing he did." Alphus wiped drunkard's drool from the corner of his mouth. "I let myself believe the fool's notion that a lad had been sent to me to replace the infant son I lost years ago . . . and now I've lost yet another true son and let my own brother be shamed besides."

Stung deeply by his second rejection of the night, Joshua could only stand and watch Alphus, who now lifted his cup and drained off a swallow of rum. A quarter of the cup's contents spilled down his chin and soaked his already wet linsey-woolsey hunting shirt. He swiped his sleeve across his damp face and pointed a trembling finger at Joshua. "You're not my son . . . never will be, never could be," Alphus said as he clunked the cup back onto the table, splashing rum across its brim. His eyes became swollen, red, wet; his lip quivered. "God forgive me, but I've let myself come to love you more than I loved my own flesh kin. It's God's punishment against me for it that Gabriel has come to the end he has."

"Gabriel's come to no end. He's yet alive, and even this will be forgotten in time."

"I'll never forget. My brother will never forget, nor my neighbors."

Joshua looked at Alphus a long time, then said, "It's clear the time's come for me to go. I'll take to the woods and leave you be from now on."

Alphus waved him off contemptuously, turned sidewise in his chair, and refused to look at him anymore. With a trembling arm, he lifted his cup and drank some more, then laid his head on the table again.

Joshua turned on his heel and walked to the little room where his bed and few possessions were. He gathered what he needed, growing more angry all the while. When he was finished, he walked back to where Alphus sat, head still on the table.

"I've remained here too many years in any case," Joshua said. "I'm no longer some little boy running loose in the wilderness and needing an old man to look after him. It's past time I lived on my own. Maybe soon I'll take me a wife and make my own family. True kin, the kind that won't turn on you, won't treat you like a piece of dung."

He wheeled and walked away. Alphus, almost unconscious, did not seem to have heard his diatribe. Slamming the cabin door shut behind him, Joshua strode up the hill to the stable to get his horse and saddle. One of the dogs came wagging around his feet, and he kicked it away.

Joshua roamed and hunted for a week in the forest but for the first time in his life found no pleasure in it. So he turned to the town, traveling to Salisbury and spending another several days in the company of drunkards, gamblers, thieves, and bad women. At first he found it diverting and exciting, but one evening, as he sat half drunk in a tavern with a painted woman on his lap, it all suddenly seemed foul and ugly, and he pushed the woman aside and staggered out into the street, feeling ill and worthless.

Later that night, he at last faced the truth and knew what it was he really wanted. The next morning, he set out for home.

The wound left by Alphus's rejection no longer carried a sting but a dull ache. Joshua tried to believe that what Alphus had said reflected his drunkenness more than his feelings, but it made little difference. Perhaps what Alphus had said under the tongue-loosening influence of rum had been his true inward feelings, long held back. The truth was, Joshua could understand how Alphus could feel as he did. Looking back on the past decade or so, it did seem that Alphus had favored Joshua above his natural son. Gabriel had gone off to live in his own house; Joshua had remained with Alphus. Gabriel and Alphus spent little time together and had less to talk about when they did; Joshua and Alphus shared entire months, hunting and enjoying interests Gabriel cared little about.

No wonder Alphus had felt so responsible, or irresponsible, and blamed Joshua when Gabriel got himself into trouble.

Understand Alphus's feelings Joshua might, but accept them he could not. He had devoted himself to Alphus almost from the first day he met him, sharing his life and work, filling a void that Gabriel never could or would fill. To be tossed out after all those years in a fit of rare intoxication was not right or fair, and the more Joshua brooded on it, the more he resented Alphus's words.

When he rode back toward Hankins Creek, it was not to seek peace with his foster father, though he hoped they would reconcile. That was for later, though; Joshua's immediate intent was different.

His horse plodded back up the familiar road and reached the place where a smaller road branched off toward the Hampton cabin. As the horse walked down the slight decline toward the cabin, Joshua felt his throat growing dry. He had not seen Sina or Tilly since their rape three weeks before. Three weeks . . . it seemed much longer ago than that, lost in a distant haze. Would Tilly still be isolated? She might decline to see him again, in which case he would not have the opportunity to do what he had come for. As the Hampton cabin came into view, he vowed that he would not be as easily put off this time.

He stopped just in view of the log house, puzzled. The Hampton cabin was empty. The garden was growing, and the nearby field was full of corn, but the cabin, the barns, the stable, the chicken coop—all were vacant. An eerie sense—that more time had passed than really had—grew stronger, making Joshua uncomfortable.

He dismounted and walked around the cabin, then opened it and went inside. Nothing. It was empty. One unlatched shutter tapped lightly in the hot August breeze. Joshua latched it shut and walked back into the yard, scratching his neck beneath his long queue of hair.

Where might they have gone so abruptly, and why? Discomfitured, he walked to his horse, grazing in the lush wild grass at the edge of the road, mounted, and rode toward the place that would likely hold the answer.

The doors and windows of the Jones House were flung open wide, exuding a smell of cooking pork, liquor, and sweating patrons. Flies buzzed in and out with impunity, mostly ignored, sometimes slapped at when they became too annoying. Joshua tied his horse to a dogwood sapling and walked down to the tavern.

A score of eyes turned to him as he entered, examining him with great interest. He felt self-conscious and slightly irritated; obviously his rift with Alphus and subsequent absence had generated lots of gossip. He returned the stares, one by one, and quickly the gawkers turned back to their cups, except for one—Ben Slye, alone at a corner table.

He waved Joshua over. "You've missed quite a stir these past three weeks," Slye said in low tones. "Somehow word got to Salisbury of our little battle in the hills. For days we had sour-looking men sent by the sheriff asking lots of questions." Slye smiled foxily. "They found very few answers. Many memories have gone remarkably bad."

"A good thing," Joshua said. The possibility of legal consequences for the raid on the robbers' camp had never occurred to him; like the others, he had seen himself as involved only in the disposition of a justice no one could argue with. "What of the bodies?"

"Long gone before they could be found. Several of us buried them well the day after the fight, and the recovered goods we distributed as best we could to those who had lost them. A good portion had already been sold by

the scoundrels, though." Slye's expression became more
serious. "I must tell you that it's been a hard go for
Thomas Colter, now that Gabriel is gone. His business
has declined, and Brecht and a few others are spreading
bad word about him. A real shame. It wouldn't surprise
me if he sold out and moved."

"Aye. I feared as much might happen." Joshua asked,
as nonchalantly as possible, "And how is Alphus?"

"A saddened man, hurt both by Gabriel's wrongdoing
and your departure. I'm a man who believes in minding
his own affairs, not his friends', but you must know that
your leaving is widely known."

"I felt that as soon as I walked through that door."

"Joshua, there is news you may not yet have heard.
Alphus has gone and gotten married. Two weeks ago."

Joshua was so stunned, he could not speak for a
moment. "Sina?" he asked.

"Aye. She and Tilly and Zachariah have moved into
your cabin—Tilly in your room, in fact. Alphus worried
over it, knowing that if . . . when you came back, you'd
be faced with quite a surprise. Maybe it wasn't my place
to bear the news, but I would want to know in your
shoes."

"Yes . . . thank you." Joshua replied. "You've answered
a question for me before I could ask it. I came to Sina's
cabin and found it empty. Alphus and Sina, married! It
will take me time to grow accustomed to that."

"It's the one joy he's had the past month, I think. In
truth, I'm surprised he took this long to hitch himself to
the old girl; they've long been thought of as shoes from
the same pair, you know. Just as you and Tilly have."

Joshua took on a self-conscious expression at that last
comment and cleared his throat. "Ben . . . when a man's
foster father marries the mother of a girl . . . does that
girl become the man's sister?"

"What a question! But I see your point. It's clear you
are speaking of your own situation. I'm no educated man
in such matters, but my answer would be no. You're not
Alphus's natural son, and you're full-grown and independent. Tilly has no blood link to you at all, whether her

mother and your father are married or not." Slye grinned.
"I take it you might have marital intentions of your own?"

Joshua smiled. "I thought you were a man who believed in minding his own affairs." He stood. "I'd best be
going now."

He was about to leave when he stopped and returned
to Slye's table. "Ben, one more thing—Tilly . . . is she
well?"

Slye flickered his brows up and down. "I don't truly
know, Joshua, for I've seen her but once since the—since
the trouble. The truth is, she looked badly to me. Pale
and sickly. What happened to her has brought much
shame on her, at least in her own mind."

"Why? 'Twasn't her fault, and she should feel no guilt
for it. Though I understand, when I consider it, how she
must feel," Joshua said. "Well, good-bye for now, Ben."

The horse had pulled free from the sapling but hadn't
wandered far. Joshua mounted, took a deep breath, and
began riding toward Alphus Colter's cabin, feeling edgy
with anticipation and dread.

Slye had been right. Tilly did not look well. Pale, gaunt,
sad-eyed . . . and she had about her something different,
something Joshua could not put his finger on. It disturbed him, deadening the happiness that had unexpectedly come to him when Alphus met him at the doorway
of his cabin, threw his arms around him, and begged his
forgiveness for what he had said the night Joshua left.
Joshua asked his pardon, and any bitterness he had felt
toward his foster father melted away at once. The two
were again at peace. Joshua was welcomed in and fed.

Afterward, Joshua and Tilly, Sina's good supper freshly
inside them, walked together along the path leading to
an old, now unused smokehouse that stood in the forest
surrounded by weeds and undergrowth. Joshua risked
putting his arm around Tilly's waist, but she recoiled
from him.

When that happened, he almost gave up the idea of
asking what he had come to ask. But then the opportu-

nity arose, and he took it, then waited breathlessly for her answer.

Her eyes were soft as a doe's and dampening as she spoke. "Oh, Joshua, I cannot marry you. Can't you see that now you are my brother?"

"No, I cannot. We have no kinship by my reckoning. I am not Alphus Colter's natural son."

She shook her head—too firmly, it seemed to Joshua, as if she were fighting the very idea he had presented.

"But to me you are a brother. You've always been a brother. Helping us, befriending us, always being close at hand . . ."

"A husband is also a helper and friend, and closer at hand than anyone. Tilly, often I've hidden from you the way I felt, and sometimes I've hardly even known what my feelings were. There are things that have troubled me, things from my past . . . but now it is different. I love you, Tilly. I have loved you a long time, and I want you to be my wife."

"Joshua, I cannot."

"Yes, you can." He looked closely at her. "It isn't because you see me as a brother that you are turning me down, Tilly. I can tell that from your manner alone. There's something more. Tell me what it is."

Tears fell, and she ran from him toward the back of the cabin where she knelt, put her forearms against the wall, and cried. Joshua started to go after her but stopped and withdrew, standing awkwardly and watching her from a distance until finally he saw the futility of further talk and walked away to trouble her no more.

That night he slept in the barn, and the next day went into the forest and built a lean-to shelter for himself. There was no room for him in the cabin, and for that he was really grateful, for it was difficult to be beneath the same roof with Tilly now that he had bared his heart to her. She remained in bed a full day after rejecting his proposal and half of the next. "Just a little sickness that will pass," Sina explained to the men, looking more worried than she was trying to sound.

Just before dawn the next day, Joshua was awakened

in his lean-to by the approach of someone. It was Alphus, who stooped and looked inside with a terrible expression on his face.

Joshua knew at once. "Tilly . . ."

"Listen to me, Joshua. Listen—and it will be hard to hear. I know no soft way to tell you. Tilly is dead."

"No . . ."

"Yes, yes. She cut her wrists with a knife last night as we all slept. We did not know until this morning when Sina found her." Alphus's eyes softened and grew wet. "She left a note to Sina. She said she was sure there was a child in her, Joshua. A child planted by the man who attacked her and Sina. The thought of it bothered her so that she could not bear to go on living." He stopped, choking with emotion. "God. God in heaven help us all."

This is Jack Byrum's doing, Joshua thought. His fault and no other. His doings have taken another I loved from me now, just as they took my mother.

They buried Tilly that very afternoon, for it was hot and interment could not be delayed. A traveling tinker who preached on the side stood by her graveside, praying and talking to the sky, as Joshua stared at the gaping hole, hearing none of it.

When Alphus went out to Joshua's lean-to the next morning, he found a note written on the inside of a piece of hickory bark. He read it and was not surprised.

He carried it back to the cabin and showed it to Sina, who read it silently and nodded. "Gone, across the mountains," she said, laying the bark note in her lap. "And who can blame him? May God go with you, Joshua Colter."

"God go with you," Alphus repeated. "And may he bring us back together soon."

HAVERLY FORT

12

For months after Tilly's suicide, Joshua remained alone: hunting, exploring, losing himself in the deep forests and avoiding human contact. The lingering pain of Tilly's death was his only companion besides his packhorse and dog. He grieved for Tilly deeply but also fought an impulse to hate her for what she had done. She had forever taken herself from those who loved her, and Joshua had trouble forgiving that.

He prayed for Tilly sometimes, having no idea if such could do her any good. If nothing else, it made him feel better, so he did it quite often—in the back of his mind and sometimes aloud.

He left North Carolina and traveled into Virginia, crossing the New River along the road leading to Fort Chiswell. Turning southwest, he passed rapidly through Wolf Hills and into the Holston region, moving down the great valley that extended into Tanisi, or Tennessee, as many now called it. Near Sapling Grove, where he, Alphus, and Levi had met Evan Shelby many months ago, he took a more westerly course and traversed the rolling hill country over to the famous Long Island of the Holston River,

an important military site for both white and red men
and a historic treaty ground.

Here, at the head of a long mountain ridge that extended southwest for more than twenty miles, he turned
northward along an ancient Indian route and passed
through a gap sliced by nature through Clinch Mountain.
He went west along the line marked by the northern
slope of Clinch Mountain for about six miles, then turned
north up a creek that followed the contours of the hill
bases like a long curving snake until at last he reached
the rocky slopes of Powell Mountain.

Just beyond Powell Mountain was the northwestern-
most section of Wallen's Ridge, a familiar landmark to
hunters and explorers. The ridge, named for a 1760s
long hunter whom Alphus Colter said he had met many
years before, extended parallel to Powell Mountain for
many miles, with Wallen Creek running between the
mountain and ridge.

Joshua turned west along the creek to hunt, planning
to travel the full length of the ridge. He went only a short
way, however, before changing his mind and cutting
north across a high gap in the ridge and entering the
valley of the Powell River, which meandered through
some of the most beautiful land Joshua had ever seen.
Joshua decided to follow the river, along whose banks
one Ambrose Powell had more than twenty years before
carved his name into the bark of streamside trees, leading Wallen and other long hunters to call the river by his
name.

As weeks passed, the sharpness of his pain wore away,
and his thoughts turned more often to the daily activities
of his solitary life. Autumn came, cooling the air and
turning the mountains scarlet and golden. The fresh
smell of crisp fall leaves gave the air a clean sharp edge
that made every breath seem purging and full of health.
The cooler temperatures allowed for longer and more
strenuous treks, and Joshua covered vast distances, especially when traveling along the abundant Indian paths
and buffalo trails that were the highways of the forest.

Joshua traveled slowly through the valley, with the

high ridge of the Cumberland Mountains to the north, Wallen's Ridge and Powell Mountain to the south. At length he turned north again, moving toward the base of the Cumberlands and onto the Indian war trace there. He found the remains of a settlement that one Captain Joseph Martin had begun in 1769 but had abandoned under the harassment of hostile Cherokees. He continued westward until the white rocks along the top of the Cumberland ridge told him he was nearing Cumberland Gap.

The gap, which first revealed itself awesomely to Joshua in the glare of a nighttime lightning flash, was a deep wide slice through the otherwise impenetrable Cumberland Mountains, beyond which lay the fabled country the hunters called "Caintuck," or Kentucky. Joshua traveled across the long sloping hump of the gap's low point and down into the level of the creek beyond. Crossing the creek, he noted occasional seams of coal in the nearby rocks, found abundant reeds and cane, and struck a wide buffalo trail that marked a clear northward route. Following it, he forded the Cumberland River and passed through another mountain gap some miles beyond it.

Until the winter came, he hunted and explored through the endless mazelike forested Kentucky hollows, valleys, and passes. This was rugged rocky country, full of vast trees overtowering scrubby dogwoods, rhododendron, laurel, sumac, and other underbrush. It was level nowhere, easily confusing, even to an experienced woodsman, and Joshua occasionally was uncertain for several hours of his exact location. He began using the Cumberland River as his point of reference and after that explored throughout the region without much difficulty until winter came on and he turned south again.

At Cumberland Ford, the dog tangled with a bear Joshua had stirred from its winter den and came out the worse for it. Joshua killed the bear, then with a heavy heart shot the hopelessly injured dog. He lingered long enough to bury the dog and to make a new winter cloak for himself from the bearhide, then continued south.

Passing back through Cumberland Gap, he crossed the
Powell and Clinch rivers, climbed the northwest slope of
Clinch Mountain, and descended into the flat bottomland
on the far side. Here he hunted, living in a little hide-
covered lean-to built near a clear spring that bubbled
from a hole in a rock. Tiring finally of this area, he
headed farther south and then east as snow dusted the
landscape. He was now closer to the hunting grounds
that he, Alphus, and Levi had most often used.

These months of long and seemingly pointless wander-
ings were serving a purpose for Joshua. Every day, his
mind was less weighted by the death of Tilly. He thought
increasingly about Alphus, Sina, and the others, wondering how they fared and if Alphus had made good on his
talk of moving west. If he had, then he might not be far
from here. Perhaps at Sapling Grove in which he had
seemed so interested during their talk with Evan Shelby.

Traveling up Lick Creek, Joshua came to within a few
miles of Long Island in the Holston and considered
heading across to Sapling Grove. But after considerable
debate, he decided instead to explore the Watauga River,
along which he, Alphus, and Levi had hunted and
trapped so often. There, surprisingly, he found many
signs of settlement. The cabins and farmsteads he kept
away from, not yet desirous of company, particularly that
of strangers.

Traveling slowly, building one crude lean-to station
camp after another, Joshua by chance found a beech tree
marking the spot where Daniel Boone had killed a bear
in 1760 and recorded the event with his knife on the
tree's smooth surface. There were several cabins nearby
now, and more in the nearby Watauga Old Fields—
ancient fields cleared of their virgin forests long ago by
the Indians.

Joshua all but felt the presence of Levi Hampton,
partially because he had hunted in this area with him,
partially because Boone's carving on the tree reminded
him of Levi's final carved message. He eventually
reached Great Limestone Creek and followed it to the

Nolichucky River, along which he searched for the little creek marking the place Levi had died. He found it.

The tree still bore Levi's message and would for scores of years to come, but already growth and healing had begun warping the inverted words. Joshua read the message and felt tears burn his eyes. A sense of failure overcame him as he read Levi's plea to be buried in a place where he would not be forgotten. Despite all their intentions to come back and recover Levi's remains for a better burial, Alphus and Joshua had never gotten around to it. Joshua determined then that he would not leave that duty undone much longer. As soon as he could, he would come back here, recover Levi's corpse, and reinter it in a proper burying ground, with a stone and a fence and people around to see it. With that thought in mind, he went looking for the place he and Alphus had laid Levi's body.

Joshua found it and stopped, shocked. The grave was empty. It had recently been dug up, and not by wolves, as he might have expected, but a spade. Someone had deliberately removed Levi's body.

The frontiersman knelt beside the empty grave, wondering who would have emptied the grave and why. He finally concluded that some other wandering hunter or trapper must have found Levi's carved message and his grave, and reburied the body at some place he thought more permanent.

"Well, whoever it was likely did better by you than Alphus and I have, Levi," Joshua said to the sky. "I'm bloody sorry we didn't get it done ourselves." He stood, tossing a pebble into the snowy hole. Turning away, he stopped abruptly. "And, Levi, if you can really hear me, I hope you'll tell Tilly, next time you see her, that I miss her. But tell her I can't go on thinking on her all the time anymore. Life has to go on for me, even though she decided it shouldn't go on for her. I wish she had stayed around to share my life, but that was her choice, and I can't change it. I reckon that's all I got to say at the moment, Levi, except good-bye. And now, if you'll excuse me, I think I'll go to Sapling Grove and see if maybe

Alphus has come through, for I'm ready to see him again."

The settlement north of the Holston had grown extensively even since Joshua's previous pass through the area months before. As he traveled beneath a gray late-winter sky, he found abundant new cabins, cleared fields, fields of corn growing beneath girdled trees or around fresh stumps, and occasional small stockades either completed or under construction. He traveled along a new rutted road beaten through a belt of woods, and when he came out on the other side, he stopped to investigate what appeared to be a substantial monument consisting of a tall chunk of limestone surrounded by palings, standing at the head of a mound of earth. As he drew closer to it, he realized it was a grave.

On the stone was a carved inscription in large letters, and as he read it Joshua shook his head in surprise.

HERE LIES LEVI JAMES HAMPTON, HUNTER AND FARMER OF NORTH CAROLINA, BORN MAY 18, 1712, DIED FEBRUARY 2, 1771. BLESSED IN THE EYES OF THE LORD IS THE DEATH OF HIS SAINTS.

"Quite impressive, is it not?" Surprised by the voice, Joshua turned. Approaching him from a cluster of log buildings ahead was a man, older than he and resembling Evan Shelby, though younger. The man extended his callused hand, and Joshua shook it. "Hello to you, sir. My name is Isaac Shelby."

"Hello. You're kin, I would guess, of Evan Shelby?"

"Yes. My father."

"Aye, I saw the look of him in your face. My name is Joshua Colter."

"Colter! I've heard of you, and not long ago."

"Your father must have spoken of me, then. I've met him."

"Oh, many times I've heard your name, Mr. Colter. They say you once traveled the wilderness alone when you were just a lad, fresh out of captivity among the Cherokees. Quite a tale, that one. But that's not the mention of your name I was talking of. There was a man through here who spoke much about you, the very man who made this grave and stone here. His name was—" Isaac Shelby screwed up his brow, searching his memory, "Alphus Colter. He's your father or foster father, I gathered."

"Aye, yes! When did you speak to him?"

"Not a month ago. As I said, he came bearing the bones of this Levi Hampton, wrapped up in bearskin, and put this grave here by the roadside—with my father's permission, for this is one of his parcels. He said it was important that the grave be where it could easily be seen."

Joshua felt a warm surge of emotion. "It was what Levi wanted. He wanted to be buried where he would not be forgotten. Tell me, did Alphus appear to be hunting, or coming to settle?"

"To settle. He talked much about it. He had with him a woman and little boy."

"That would be Sina and Zachariah. Formerly Hampton, now Colter. Sina was Levi Hampton's widow, now my father's second wife."

"I see. You well knew this Levi Hampton and his brood, then."

"Aye. Levi was a good friend, and a neighbor when I lived in North Carolina. I hunted with him often. It was my father and I who first buried him."

"Down by Gone to God Creek?"

"By a creek, yes, but I've never heard it called by that name."

"It's a new name, I think, so called by hunters who come to trade at the store yonder. They took the name from some carving by this Levi Hampton on a tree— letters turned top down, for some reason. . . ."

"Levi carved it while he was dying. It was a bear mauling that killed him. He died hanging head down from a tree crotch. That's why the letters were like that."

"Merciful heaven! What a sorry way to die!"

"Yes. But I have no doubt Levi bore it well. He was the sort who would. Tell me, where is Alphus now?"

"I cannot say. He spoke more to my father than to me. Come up to the store, and we'll see what we can learn from him." Isaac Shelby eyed Joshua's laden packhorse. "You've got skins to sell?"

"About a hundredweight, maybe more. Mostly deer-skin, some otter and beaver."

"Perhaps we can serve you, then, if you're of a mind to sell to us."

"That I am, and thank you."

They went together to Shelby's store. Along the way, Isaac Shelby talked of the extensive settlement taking place throughout the Tennessee country.

"The land will not be the same if civilized men can keep their claims on it," he said. "There are five real settlements now. Down along the Watauga, on the Old Fields, is the oldest, with sixty, seventy families already there. William Bean used to hunt with Daniel Boone some, and that's how he came to know the land. The Cherokees might well have run him off, but they were too busy fighting the Chickasaws to deal with him. And by the by, there is a man down there to keep an eye on, a North Carolinian like yourself, name of Robertson, James Robertson. He put in corn on some of the Chero-kee Old Fields there, back shortly after Bean came in, and then moved in his family."

Isaac Shelby pointed more directly west. "Let's see now . . . over on the Holston, south of Clinch Mountain, a trader named John Carter set up a store in partnership with a man named Parker, but they're having trouble with the Cherokees, who want the stores closer to their own towns. As for others, there's Jacob Brown, way down on the Nolichucky. He does some small commerce with the Indians and hunters there. Then there is our own Sapling Grove settlement here—North of Holston, some are calling it, or Shelby's Station.

"Then there is the latest, a settlement being started by a man named Peter Haverly, from Wilmington. He's putting in a stockade on Sinking Creek, which runs into the Nolichucky southwest of here many miles, beyond Great Limestone. Haverly is quite an interesting man, a bit different than most. Very religious, very outspoken. He was here about the same time as your father."

"You spoke of Indian trouble?"

"Yes. There has been much argument and treaty making these past few years. You know of the old proclamation of sixty-three, the ban on settlement this side of the mountains? Aye, I thought so. And are you familiar as well with the Indian superintendent, John Stuart?"

"If he's the John Stuart who was an officer at Fort Loudoun, I am indeed."

"The same man. Some four or five years ago, he drafted out a treaty that softened the sixty-three proclamation a bit and gave those west of the mountains a little better foothold on their lands. Then, two years ago, he got the Cherokees to move the line some more, which cheered most everyone—until they got around to surveying the actual line. The final working-out of it is that those of us in North of Holston are on safe ground, but the Cherokees still have claims on the other settlement areas. Now Stuart is demanding that all the settlements on Indian lands be abandoned. But there are plans afoot to work this problem out."

"Sounds as if I've missed quite a lot, roaming alone these many months."

"Oh, it's been a busy time, no question. Here we are— step inside. My father will be wanting to see you."

They found Evan Shelby inside the store, which reminded Joshua of Thomas and Gabriel's store back on Hankins Creek. Its interior, dimly lighted by lamps today because the doors and shutters remained closed against the cold, was filled with casks, barrels, crockery jars, hide sacks, tools, gun parts, traps, stacks of cured deerskins, and jugs of liquor.

Shelby remembered Joshua at once and immediately mentioned the recent visit of Alphus and the reburial of Levi Hampton's bones. "That grave is noticed by all who pass," he said. "If it was a visible grave the departed Hampton wished, he's resting happy now."

"I'm glad of it. Isaac tells me you might know where my father went when he left here."

"Indeed I do," the senior Shelby said. "He was on his way to Haverly Fort, on Sinking Creek, looking to settle. I gathered he had come under Peter Haverly's hire, in some way or another, to oversee building the stockade and such."

"In that case, it's to Haverly Fort I'll be going, as soon as I put a good meal beneath my belt and sell those hides outside."

The transactions took only a short while and left Joshua satisfied. Having almost exhausted his ammunition supply over the past several months, he took part of his payment in powder and lead. Not that Joshua planned any major new hunting or trapping excursions at the moment. He had it in mind to reunite with Alphus if he could find him and perhaps establish a home of his own, at least for a year or two, somewhere in this new country. He had had enough of solitude to last him a long while.

The two Shelbys had Joshua's horse fed and provided Joshua a meal of fresh bread, which they sopped in bear grease and washed down with cold water. As they ate, Joshua asked Evan Shelby about his views on the future of the Tennessee country. Could it be retained in spite of the British-backed Indian claims to it?

"Oh, we'll keep this land, never fear," he answered, wiping a trace of grease from his lip with a forefinger. "For one thing, the Indians speak out of two mouths where white settlement is concerned. Why, Little Carpenter himself helped Jacob Brown mark off his lands down on the Nolichucky and also agreed to a shifting of the survey line last year, to the advantage of the northernmost settlers. The older chiefs can be dealt with—they are accustomed to years of negotiation and trade with the British. Some of the younger ones, they'll prove more a problem. Still, we'll overcome it somehow. We'll keep our lands."

"But if the lands are forbidden for purchase," Joshua asked, "how can they be kept?"

Shelby's eyes twinkled cunningly. "A sale may be

forbidden, but as Jacob Brown has said, we've heard nothing forbidding a lease."

Joshua understood. "And a lease, once in place, would almost certainly become equivalent to a sale."

Shelby shrugged one shoulder and smiled. "Suffice it to say that land once settled and occupied would be unlikely to go back to its previous state."

Joshua dabbed a final speck of bear grease from his wooden trencher. "It would, at that." He paused, thinking. "No wonder the younger Cherokees arc astir. Their ancestral hunting lands and warpaths are precious to them, and some of their fathers and grandfathers let them go with the stroke of a quill."

"One might feel you sound more Cherokee than white at the moment," Isaac Shelby said, chuckling but also looking at Joshua with vague concern.

"Just thinking aloud when I should think in silence," he answered. "I lived among the Cherokees for some years, as a boy. Perhaps I picked up some of their thinking and ways of feeling. The times are changing for the Cherokees, and once changed, they'll never change back. And now, gentlemen, I'll be off, and thank you for the feeding."

Outside, fresh snow was falling lightly from the gray sky. Joshua removed the hobbles from his packhorse and set off, the wind tugging at the brim of his felt hat, snow settling into his beard and eyelashes.

Joshua Colter stood like a statue, his still form almost invisible against the backdrop of poplar trunks and leafless groping dogwoods. He was one hurried day's trek from Shelby's Fort, deep in a forest of poplar, maple, oak, and beech. His rifle was almost level, the weight of its long barrel resting in his left hand. Before him, blending with the dead brown leaves of a beech tree, a doe nuzzled at the forest floor. Joshua slowly leveled the rifle a little more, almost getting the butt to his shoulder when the doe's white tail flickered and the head shot up.

Joshua became still again, and the doe did not see him. The tail flicked once more; the doe lowered her head.

Deliberately, Joshua lowered the rifle and put the butt against his shoulder. He aimed, then carefully squeezed the trigger. The gunflint struck the frizzen, a spark jumped to the pan, pan powder flared into the touchhole, the powder charge in the barrel exploded, and the lead ball twisted through the riflings and toward the target. But in the half second before the rifle had fired, the sound of another shot, from at least a quarter mile away, cracked through the forest. The doe lifted its head, shifting out of Joshua's sights at the moment of his firing, and bolted away.

The frontiersman lowered the rifle and shook his head. "Blast," he muttered. The rifle ball had thunked soundly into the beech trunk as the deer sped away through the forest.

Nothing fretted Joshua worse than wasted ammunition. With a frown, he reloaded the rifle, wondering as he ramrodded a fresh ball and patch down the forty-inch barrel if the distant hunter whose shot had run off his quarry had done better than he. Suddenly he cocked his head, listening to a new sound in the wind coming from the same direction the rifle blast had.

A moaning, a howling . . . no, a human voice, both moaning and speaking. Though it came from too far away to be understandable, Joshua felt sure that whoever was speaking was in pain or despair. He slipped the ramrod back into place beneath the long barrel, hefted the rifle, and began tracking the voice, his moccasins moving silently on the snow-dampened forest floor. His horse was hobbled in a thicket, and there he would leave it until he knew what the wailing was all about.

Eventually he caught the scent of horses. Here the voice was much louder, and he began to understand the words. A man, obviously in despair, was alternately praying and crying. The noise of it, wafting through the forest in the shifting wind, sounded as mysterious as some of the Cherokee conjuring chants he remembered from childhood. The horse scent was much stronger now.

He topped a bluff about fifteen feet high that looked

down into a narrow defile and in the defile saw the praying man, kneeling beside an apparently dead body that stared skyward with unseeing eyes.

At first, Joshua could see no sign of injury on the dead man, but then the praying man brushed back the corpse's hair, exposing the brow, and squarely in the center of the forehead Joshua saw a round hole, obviously from a rifle ball. The despairing man sent up a great sob and put his hand across the round hole, gently stroking the hair back again and again. He moved a little, and his shadow shifted. Now Joshua saw a pool of blood still broadening around the back of the corpse's head where the ball had come out the top of the skull.

Behind the kneeling man, who had thick sandy hair tied with a thong behind his head and appeared to be some years older than Joshua, lay a fine Pennsylvania rifle, tossed aside. Joshua figured it for the death weapon. Given that there was no one else about to have done it, he supposed the crying man was the one who had fired the fatal shot.

Movement in the forest caught Joshua's eye. Two fine Chickasaw horses laden with saddlebags and packs wandered into the defile. Likely the shot had spooked them, but curiosity was drawing them back. One of them walked up to the dead man and sniffed at his head. The kneeling man flew into a rage and hit the animal between the eyes with his fist. It stumbled back, turned, and bolted out of the defile again. The man stood, wiping tears on the back of his hand. At that moment, he seemed to become aware of another human presence and looked around furtively.

"I'm up here," Joshua said quietly. The man started at the sound of his voice, stepped back, and tripped over the rifle. Landing on his rump, he stared upward at the lean frontiersman.

"My name's Joshua Colter," Joshua said. "Looks like you've had some trouble here."

The man stood, weeping lightly, and dusted leaves and snow off his backside. He was wearing a store-bought wool coat that hung nearly to his knees and tall shining boots that looked to Joshua as if they would be very uncomfortable.

"My name is Israel Coffman," the man said, his voice scratchy. "And this is . . . was my brother Jordan." He buried his face in his hands. "I just killed him."

"So I see," Joshua said, turning and beginning to climb down the edge of the defile. When he reached bottom, he walked over to the body and looked at the nicely centered brow wound. "As clean a shot as I've ever seen," he said. "I doubt he felt a thing. Did you kill him on purpose?"

"Oh, in heaven's name no! I didn't mean to do it at all. We heard a sound in the forest and thought it was Indians. I got my rifle, cocked it—somehow I bumped it on a tree and pulled the trigger. When I turned, Jordan was . . . like this. Oh, God forgive me for murdering my own brother!"

"If you didn't mean to do it, I doubt there's aught to forgive, and it was certainly not murder in any case. Come on, now, calm yourself, Mr. Coffman. You can't cry or pray him back alive again, and we've got some burying to do. We can make him a wood cross and say some words over him if you like. It's only too bad we don't have a preacher about to do it proper."

Coffman laughed mirthlessly. "Ah, but we do," he said. "A preacher's the one thing we do have."

Joshua blinked, uncomprehending, then suddenly understood. "You're a preacher?"

"That I am. A preacher who has just killed a man who was not only his own brother but also his joint laborer in the Lord."

"Jordan was a preacher too?"

"Indeed. A finer one than I. Together, at Haverly Fort, we were to begin a church and school. Lord Jehovah help me, but what will I do now? What will I do now?"

Joshua was at a loss about what to say to comfort a preacher, it usually being the situation that a preacher was the one expected to give comfort to someone else.

Fumbling for words, he finally stammered, "At least it was a good . . . and painless shot." As soon as he said it, he knew it was the worst choice of words, but Coffman either didn't hear it or chose to appreciate the intent rather than the meaning.

Joshua made no further progress toward Haverly Fort that day. The burying proved difficult, for the ground was rocky and the Coffman brothers had brought no tools but a single hoe, to be used in corn cultivation. With it, Joshua hacked and scraped at the ground until finally he had dug out a shallow grave. Israel Coffman helped out some but tired quickly and did a generally clumsy job that Joshua was too impatient to stand and watch.

It was almost sunset when at last they laid Jordan Coffman to rest. Expecting a long sermon from the surviving Coffman, Joshua was surprised when the preacher merely quoted some scriptures, said a short prayer, and turned away, gesturing for Joshua to fill the grave. Coffman refused to watch the muddy earth go atop his brother and seemed relieved when it all was done.

"I'll go swill this dirt off my hands at the creek yonder," Joshua said. "Then I'll see what I can find to make us a meal."

"The meal I can provide," Coffman responded. "Jordan was a better hunter than I, and just this morning brought down a fine doe. He carved out the tenderloins for us to roast and eat tonight . . . though now it appears it will be you instead of Jordan I share that meal with."

"Sorry it has to be like that, though I do appreciate you feeding me," Joshua said. He walked to a small creek about a hundred yards away and washed his hands and arms in the bitter-cold water, sending swirls of mud down the stream. The water chilled his hands to stiffness; having long ago given up his old habit of a Cherokee-style cold-water plunge each morning, he had lost some of his insensitivity to cold washing.

When he returned to Coffman, he found him vainly trying to light a fire with flint and steel. Not wanting to embarrass the obviously inexperienced preacher, Joshua took the opportunity to go off and retrieve his packhorse. When he returned, there still was no fire, and it was almost dark.

"Perhaps I can give you some help there," he quietly suggested.

Coffman gladly handed over the flint and steel, and watched with interest and undisguised jealousy as Joshua deftly got a blaze going.

"I've never been able to do that well," Coffman said meekly.

"You'll learn with time," Joshua said. In truth, he was beginning to worry some about Coffman, who was obviously completely out of his element in the forest. He had already decided to accompany Coffman to Haverly Fort, partly because it was the destination of both of them and partly because he seriously doubted Coffman's ability to proceed alone safely. If Coffman's directional skills were as poor as his riflery and fire-building abilities, he probably would try for Sinking Creek and wind up on the Ohio River.

Coffman proved to have at least one capability. He roasted the tenderloins to perfection, spitted on sticks near the fire. Joshua enjoyed one of his best meals in memory, eating pones of corn bread that the brothers had packed and drinking English tea that Coffman confessed was his one seemingly unbreakable habit. Joshua informed him as gently as possible that he might have trouble sustaining his tea supply on the frontier; he might have to make do with walink, or dandelion-root coffee.

After they ate, Joshua leaned back against a maple and listened as Coffman told his story. He was thirty years old, Presbyterian, single but engaged. He had been born in Massachusetts but had most recently lived in Maryland and New Jersey, studying at the West Nottingham Academy in the former and the College of New Jersey in the latter. His theological tutelage had been under the Reverend Uriah Blanton of New Jersey, a staunch Presbyterian leader whose daughter Virginia had caught first

Coffman's eye, then his heart. He was now engaged to marry Virginia, though no date had been finalized.

Joshua asked what had brought Coffman to the wilderness, and Coffman said he had no good answer except that he had for about three years felt sure he would end up as a frontier preacher and educator, together with his older brother whose life and education had followed a path similar to his own. Blanton, knowing of his future son-in-law's interest and favoring it, even though it ultimately would mean seeing his daughter carried away for life to some distant wilderness, introduced Coffman to Peter Haverly, of Wilmington, North Carolina, a dedicated if somewhat independent-minded Presbyterian and operator of a large trading firm who had begun planning a settlement somewhere west of the Blue Ridge and had sent agents to begin treating with the Cherokees for land. Haverly, apparently taking a liking to Coffman, invited first him and then his brother to lead the religious and academic education of his new settlement, and the brothers accepted.

"And now," Coffman said, "here I am—and there beneath the earth lies Jordan, all because of my own foolishness."

" 'Twas an accident, and such happen," Joshua said. "You can do nothing by grieving over it. Tell me, what kind of man is this Haverly?"

"A good one, I think, though hard to know. He's big and broad, very much a man of the city but strong as an ox and far more experienced than I in the wilderness. He's dedicated to his God and his church, not to mention his business, but he's also—" He faltered and looked uncertain about continuing.

"Yes?"

"He's . . . harsh. Loud. A man who expects to be followed, who listens to no thoughts contrary to his own."

"You reckon you can work for such a man?"

Coffman smiled. "I work for a greater One than Peter Haverly, and it's in him I put my trust. As Jordan always says—" Coffman's smile drained and he suddenly looked very sad and said no more. Joshua knew bereavement well enough to understand what was happening to Coffman: from one moment to the next, he was forgetting his loss, then remembering it, again and again, with sharp new stabs of grief upon each remembrance.

"The hurt won't be so bad after a while," Joshua said. "Just remember that there's nothing that's happened to your brother that hasn't happened to untold many more before him and everyone who will come after. The path he stepped onto is well-trod. Maybe that's not the wisest thought ever to pass through a mind, but I've found it helps me sometimes when I'm grieving over my own kin and loved ones who have gone on. Maybe it will help you too."

Coffman thought it over. "Aye, it does at that."

13

There was no real road to Haverly Fort, just a trace cutting through the forest, following a game trail. Joshua Colter and Israel Coffman plodded along slowly, leading their horses, which stepped carefully around the many stumps and over the occasional fallen trees that hampered their route. All the snow had melted, for the weather had grown unseasonably warm, and the trace was very muddy at spots, soaking Joshua's deerskin moccasins and chilling his feet. Coffman, in his high boots, was drier and warmer but suffered from abrasions created by the too-stiff leather. He walked gingerly, taking two strides to Joshua's one.

The preacher was becoming visibly excited as his destination drew near and a mile earlier had begun talking rapidly and endlessly, thanking Joshua over and over for his aid and telling him he had been sent by heaven to help him in a time of tragedy.

Joshua accepted Coffman's praise uncomfortably, trying to downplay his help to the distressed preacher as nothing but the common courtesy any neighborly soul would have provided. He saw their meeting in less cosmic terms than Coffman; they had simply been traveling to the same place, and their encounter required no sophisticated explanations.

"Ah," Coffman responded, "but it is in the commonplace and seemingly chance events of life that the hand of providence is most active."

Joshua shrugged and said, "Maybe so."

They encountered a farmstead in a clearing off the trace and there met a lean sun-browned man who told them Haverly Fort lay about three miles ahead. It was not yet properly a fort, he said. The winter's weather, though relatively mild overall, had yet been too unstable to allow a stockade to be completed. His own cabin had been built the previous autumn, just before the first snow. The man was pleased to hear that Coffman was a preacher, saying that his wife, remaining back in Virginia with his family until he could finish clearing some fields and get his first corn crop in the ground, had worried that their children would grow up without the influence of a church.

Coffman was cheered by the reception and when he and Joshua proceeded on the final stretch to Haverly Fort, was even more enthusiastic than before, his spirits darkening only once when he commented that he wished his brother could be with him to enjoy the moment of arrival.

That moment was delayed in any case, for a mile from the station, Joshua and Coffman came upon a tense scene. Earlier, Joshua had seen fresh tracks, indicating a party advancing ahead of them; his assessment was that there was but one man walking with the group, and he was obviously lame, for his tracks fell at uneven depths into the muddy ground. The only other human tracks were those of a moccasin-clad boy or a woman. Joshua suspected the latter from the narrowness of the marks. As Joshua and Coffman rounded a bend in the trace, which here had widened to nearly a road, they encountered the party that had left the sign and a second man.

That second man was a big brutish unshaven frontiersman clad in a poorly made bearskin cloak, wearing a raccoonskin cap with no tail pulled low across his ears.

Dirty brown hair strung out, unbound, across his shoulders. He held a long battered flintlock rifle in front of him, using the flat of it to shove a much leaner shorter man before him.

The smaller man, wearing a hacked-out deerskin vest over two linsey-woolsey wamus jackets with a dried dead wolf spider on a string around his neck to ward off the ague, had no weapon but a butcher knife. Though his hand was on the knife's handle, the blade was still sheathed at his right hip. The man was crippled, his left leg bent oddly. His felt hat was gone from his head and lay in the mud between the hooves of the first of his four well-laden horses.

Two of the horses wore packsaddles piled with sacks and boxes; the other two bore a pair of elderly people, a man and a woman. The old man was staring off into the forest, seemingly unaware of what was going on around him. Joshua noted an old broad scar on the left side of the old man's face, running up into his hair, and the left ear also looked mangled. The old woman, a thin sliver of a human being, had her hands to her mouth and was looking on in horror as the bigger man harassed the smaller.

All these things Joshua saw and assessed at a glance, but a final vision he gave more than a glance. Standing beside the first packhorse, holding a rifle, was a young woman, dressed in a plain wool overdress that reached just below her knees, brushing the tops of her tall moccasins. Most of the dress was hidden by a long slightly oversized rifleman's coat that Joshua figured must have been made for one of the men. Her hair was pulled back beneath a German-style cap with two laced flaps that hung down either side of her freckled face. Her right hand seemed too small for her arm and was slightly misshapen and stiff. Her forefinger was hooked around the trigger of her cocked rifle, and Joshua had the clear impression she was pondering shooting the bigger of the two men.

As Joshua and Coffman came around the bend, she

turned and looked imploringly at them, then called, "Please, sirs, can you help my brother?"

Joshua shifted his rifle from the crook of his right arm to that of his left and stepped forward. Coffman hung back a moment, then came forward as well, looking around from face to face. Joshua looked only at the young lady, whom he guessed to be nineteen or twenty, and at the two disputing men, both of whom now turned to face him.

The big man drew his thick brows together until they were one shaggy line above his black eyes and snarlingly lifted one side of his bearded upper lip. The look of the smaller man, who had wide intense eyes, was that of a cornered hare.

"What's the trouble here?" Joshua asked quietly, taking one more step forward and then stopping, his rifle cradled casually but in a position for quick use.

"No trouble, just private business that's none of yours," the big man said. "If you be heading to Haverly Fort, it lies yonder, and you can be on your way."

Joshua flicked his glance to the pleading face of the young woman, feeling a subtle pang of hurt as he saw that she looked a little like Tilly. He looked back at the speaker. "I'll go on when I'm satisfied all is right here."

"He's trying to steal our packhorses," the young woman said.

"Steal, hell. I'm buying these animals," the man said. "Now get on and leave us to our business."

Joshua looked at the lame man. "You don't look to be an eager seller, sir."

"I'm no seller. Like Darcy said, this bugger is trying to steal these horses. He walked up on us, told us he was taking them and would pay us later."

"That takes some brass, I must say," Joshua commented. "Are you wanting to give sale credit to this man?"

"Nay, not at all. I intend to keep my horses."

The big man shoved the other with his rifle again; the lame man fell back on his rear in the mud. "You're a damned liar, cripple. This is a fair transaction, and my credit is as good as my word."

Joshua said, "I think maybe you'd best make your fair transaction with some other seller. You just heard this man say he wants to keep his horses."

"And I say he's a liar. He offered the horses with his own lips."

The young woman said, "You're the liar. I'll shoot you through the entrails, you devil!"

"No need for that," Joshua said, striding forward so quickly it surprised all of them. The big man started to swing his rifle around, but Joshua lifted his own and rammed the butt of it into the man's forehead. With a grunt, the brutish man jolted backward and fell.

The old woman leaned forward in her saddle and moaned loudly.

Coffman exclaimed, "I say now, Joshua, don't you think . . ." and then faded out.

The crippled man scrambled as best he could to his feet, a look of pleased amazement on his face.

Joshua reached down and took the rifle from the hands of the stunned man. He looked it over and said, "This looks to be a fair weapon, if a little the worse for wear. I think I'll buy it from you. And have no fear—my credit is as good as my word."

The big man, stunned but not unconscious, swung up his hands, groping for the rifle. Joshua stepped back. "Then again, perhaps I'll change my mind. A sod like you would not take good care of his weapon. If I change my mind about the purchase, you'll find this rifle leaning on a tree somewhere ahead, near the station. I suggest you not come for it for at least two hours, for if I see sight of you following us, I might be tempted to test its accuracy on a moving target. I might even let my friend back there in the high boots give it a try, and the last man he shot took the ball square through the forehead. Do we understand each other, my friend?"

"Go to the devil," the man growled, looking at Joshua with hatred but also fear.

"We have reached an agreement, then," Joshua said.

He turned to the crippled man. "Sir, Mr. Coffman and I would be pleased to accompany you to Haverly Fort, if you'll not mind the company."

The man walked crookedly over to the first packhorse, and retrieved his hat. As he brushed it off, he said, "We'll be pleased to have you along." He put on the hat and stuck out his hand. "My name is Will Fiske."

"Joshua Colter. And this is Israel Coffman, the Reverend Israel Coffman, I should say."

"Reverend! Well, preacher, do you often travel in the company of so fine a guardian angel?"

Coffman smiled. "Only since yesterday. But I must explain his comment about my having shot a man through the forehead, for I certainly wouldn't have you think—"

"You can explain it later, Reverend," Joshua said. "And you have my apology for having said that in any case, for I doubt you cared much for it."

"No apology necessary." Coffman paused, then smiled broadly. "Under the circumstances, I rather liked the sound of it. You have a keen wit, Joshua, if rather coarse."

"This is a coarse country." Joshua shifted attention to Will Fiske. "Where's your rifle?"

"Out of fix, strapped to the horse there."

"Quite a danger to travel in such country with a rifle out of fix. We'll hope for a smith at Haverly Fort, and if not, we'll have a go at fixing it ourselves. Now, let's get on."

The big man, hate in his eyes, watched the party leave. As the last horse passed, he began to rise, but Joshua turned and looked sternly at him, and he lay down again, and there he remained until the party lost sight of him.

Will Fiske, crippled long enough to be used to it, walked roughly but with surprising speed. He stumped along beside Joshua, talking so rapidly that even Coffman could not get in a word. Joshua quietly marveled at how what he had intended as a quiet and solitary trek to find his father had turned into such a parade.

Fiske described his family. The old man, his father,

was named James and had for ten years been "empty-headed," a result of head injuries suffered in the same New York wagon accident that had crippled Will's leg and damaged the hand of his sister, Darcy. The old woman was his mother, Mary, and she was well enough in body but slowing mentally with age. The move to Haverly Fort had been Will Fiske's idea. He had been struggling to keep them all fed on a little farm in Virginia, but the land was poor and debts were high, so when he heard through a friend that a man named Peter Haverly was beginning a settlement in the Tennessee country, he had decided to become part of it.

Along the way, however, he had found seemingly endless trouble from men like the one who had just attacked him, and now he was unsure he wanted to live in such a difficult country after all. Now that he had met Joshua, however, he was encouraged. Perhaps Joshua's fortuitous aid was a sign that his luck was improving.

Nearing the station, the party passed two more new farmsteads and finally came in sight of the partially completed stockade, which stood within rifle distance of a gently flowing stream that wound through a beautiful long grove. The winter day had grown so atypically warm that a sheen of sweat dampened Joshua's brow. He loosened his rifleman's coat and pushed his hat to the back of his head as he led the group through the muddied clearing toward the fort.

Now it was Joshua's turn to feel excited, for somewhere hereabouts he would surely find his foster father. Work was going on vigorously in the stockade as its builders took advantage of the warmer weather. Two walls of palisades were already complete, and through the broad double gate in one of them Joshua led the group. Coffman began singing a hymn of thanksgiving, looking around the station as dogs scampered about his feet and barked to herald the arrival of strangers.

Joshua looked for Alphus Colter but did not see him among the workmen. He noted the fine job being done on the stockade wall. This was not a crude round-log fort of the sort sometimes thrown up in new settlements but a carefully crafted enclosure made of logs split from end to end and rooted in a ditch, flat sides inward, with other flattened logs put in place over the spaces between the first ones so that there was no gap through which a stray rifle ball could pass in time of siege. A tall blockhouse stood at the one completed stockade corner, its oversized upper portion jutting out three feet beyond the walls to allow riflemen a good sweep of the twelve-foot-high palisades.

Inside the walls were a line of half-faced cabins, the slopes of the roofs descending toward the interior of the enclosure, providing both coverage for the cabins beneath them and places where armed defenders could shoot from a lying position and still be protected from rifle fire from outside. At the few places where half-faced cabins were not built were rifle platforms, reached by ladders built against them and strapped into place.

Judging from the size of the ditch already dug to hold more walls, Joshua estimated that the entire fort would enclose nearly half an acre of land. In the center of the enclosure a well was being dug; near it sat a half-finished watering trough, being hollowed out of a great log, much as a dugout canoe would be, by alternate use of fire and chipping. Outside the fort walls were stock pens, already filled with cattle, hogs, and horses, from which livestock could be quickly driven into the stockade in times of attack.

A man splitting logs for palisades watched the newcomers enter, put down his mallet, and walked up to Joshua, blistered hand thrust out before him. Joshua did not know why the man had come to him in particular, for he was largely unaware of the aspect of his presence that made him stand out authoritatively among almost any group.

"Callum McSwain," the man said with distinct Scottish inflections. "Welcome to you, sir. You are a newcomer to this land?"

"I've hunted here in years past, but beyond that, new I am." Joshua introduced the others with him. McSwain's eyes lit up when he met Coffman.

"Ah, we've been awaiting your arrival, Reverend. But was there not to be a second Coffman? So Mr. Haverly led me to believe."

Israel Coffman lowered his head. "A tragic loss, I'm afraid. And my fault."

"Jordan Coffman was killed accidentally on his way here," Joshua said. "A gunshot accident."

"No! How came it to happen?"

Coffman started to relate the story, but Joshua knew he would lapse into more self-derision and interrupted him before he could really begin. "A rifle was jolted in some manner, and the ball struck the gentleman in the head. He died a quick death, never suffering."

"Mercies in tragedy, then. But I truly am sorry to hear of it, as Mr. Haverly will be when he returns. Still, Reverend Coffman, we are glad you at least have made it safely to us."

"To that I owe a great debt to Mr. Colter here," Coffman said.

"And us the same," Fiske chimed in.

"Colter?" McSwain said inquiringly. "You are Joshua Colter, of whom Alphus Colter has spoken so much?"

"I am. Is he here?"

"Gone to the woods, fetching logs. Here, climb up on the shooting platform, and we'll probably catch sight of him."

Joshua followed McSwain up the ladder. On the platform, McSwain pointed. "Look there—he's coming now."

Joshua had already seen him. A warm, happy feeling spread over him as he watched Alphus Colter leading in two horses, each dragging a fifteen-foot log about fifteen or sixteen inches thick. Despite his nearly sixty-two years of age, Alphus had the form and stamina of a man twenty-five years younger. Joshua did not realize until now how much he had missed his foster father.

"Alphus Colter!" McSwain called. "Why you be so slow? See here who's waiting for you!"

Alphus stopped, shaded his eyes with his hand, and looked up at the two figures on the rifle platform. Joshua smiled and waved his hand above his head. Alphus froze for a moment, then waved back. Dropping the leads, he ran across the muddy expanse between the forest and the fort, leaping stumps and mudholes like a boy, making Joshua laugh to watch him.

At Alphus's table, Joshua told his foster father and Sina about his recent travels and described his finding Levi's empty grave and the new grave at Sapling Grove.

"It was something that needed doing," Alphus said. "I could not rest easily until I had fulfilled Levi's last wish. I hope he would have been pleased by it."

"I think he would be pleased—or is pleased if he can know of it," Joshua replied.

Alphus forked another slab of cold salt pork onto Joshua's wooden plate, then two more pones of corn bread, despite Joshua's protest that he had already eaten his fill.

"You're thin as a ramrod, Joshua, and I'll not see you turn down good food." Alphus took another chunk of meat for himself. "Besides, you'll hurt Sina's feelings."

Sina's responsive smile was a mere flicker across her lean brown face; then she hid within the same shell of withdrawal she had been in since Joshua returned. Sina had hardly spoken to him since he had arrived at Alphus's cabin, which stood within sight of the stockade in a clearing barely big enough to accommodate it.

"The food is good, Sina," Joshua said. "I often missed your good cooking while I was roaming."

Again the flicker of a smile, then withdrawal. Joshua and Alphus shared a quick glance, then returned to eating.

"So what did you think of Kentucky?" Alphus asked, shifting the conversation back to Joshua's travels. "Did you reach the big meadow country?"

"I never traveled that far. I kept to the mountains. Good hunting grounds, though rugged. But it wasn't really for hunting that I was there. It was just for the being alone."

"Aye. So I reckoned."

Even such a veiled and indirect reference to the pain of the death of Tilly seemed to affect Sina. She stood quickly, picking up her plate. "I'd best get to washing.

You men mind that you don't wake Zach, or it will be you left to deal with him."

"I wouldn't mind that," Joshua said. "I've missed the lad."

"Ah, but he's now such a handful that you'd quick get your fill of the job," Alphus commented. "When we're finished here, Joshua, we'll walk outside, and I'll show you more of the station."

Ten minutes later, the two frontiersmen left the cabin and strode slowly toward the stockade. Alphus smoked his long clay pipe. A bright winter moon sailed above them, making Alphus's clouds of tobacco smoke faintly visible as he spoke.

"Sina's been the way she is since Tilly's passing. Stern, severe, much colder than before. Yet I think she's coming out of it, slowly. Quite a blow it was to her. You were gone too soon to see how badly Tilly's death affected her. For days she would sit on her stool, staring out the window, arms all wrapped around her middle, and rock back and forth, back and forth. For days it went on like that, her crying sometimes. Finally I talked to her of it, and she broke out crying and said that all she could think of was Tilly as a baby, and her rocking her. When she said that, I couldn't hold back from crying myself. God, I hope I never have to live through aught like that again—someone close killing themselves like that. But listen to me, talking as if it was my grief that mattered. I'm not the one who really suffered. That was Sina. And you too."

Joshua nodded. "I doubt I'll ever fully put Tilly out of mind. Just learn to live with her memory, like Gabriel with his limp or this Will Fiske fellow with his crooked leg."

They reached the stockade, and Joshua waved toward it. "You designed it?"

"So I did. What do you think of it?"

"Oconostota with five hundred Cherokees couldn't best a force in that fort, once it's finished."

"I hope that's true—but never tested out. The thing is to be fortified so well, nobody will even try to best you."

"How stand matters with the Indians?"

Alphus puffed his pipe, the smoke trailing back across both sides of his face to rejoin in a cloud behind him. "Peaceful enough, at the moment, though some of the touchier ones are not much happy to see their hunting lands settled. What I fully expect to see is some sort of lease agreed upon."

"I heard mention of that at Shelby's Fort."

"Did you? The notion is spreading, then. Have you heard talk of formation of some sort of government as well?"

"No."

"Well, that's coming too, if the lease can ever be worked out, which I am sure will be done, in that Haverly came here with advance assurance from some of the Cherokee headmen that he could obtain some sort of rights to these lands. There's a story behind that, but Haverly hasn't told me what it is. In any case, Haverly has already been talked to about working out some sort of government compact with the Wataugans. The problem is the survey line that was run last year. Most everyone from the Holston down to the Nolichucky thought they'd find themselves in Virginia, but it winds up that only North of Holston is properly in Virginia."

"So what of the other settlements?"

"Not in Virginia, that's clear, and they're of little interest to North Carolina, leaving it all murky as mud. Any government here will have to be of our own making, it appears."

"Will you be involved?"

"I hope to be." Alphus stopped and looked at his foster son. "I like it here, Joshua. Like it every bit as much as I thought I would. Peter Haverly has put a lot of trust in me, and made me what amounts to his agent."

"Where is Haverly now? Everyone talks of him, but I haven't seen him."

"He's gone back to North Carolina—something to do with his business there. I expect to see him back any day now. He's a wealthy man, very powerful within his circles. Later, once the stockade is done and some crops put in, he'll return to Carolina again and bring his family back here with him."

"It all sounds very fine, Father. He must be a man of judgment, for he was wise to put his faith in you. Though I admit, I'm fuddled a little over why he would do that, never having known you."

Alphus took his pipe from between his teeth and looked at Joshua with a peculiar soft expression like that a man would use in discussing a beloved child or a new bride. "Do you want to know why he did that, Joshua? Listen to it, for it's worth hearing. It was Gabriel's doing. That's right—our own Gabriel. When he left Hankins Creek, he didn't go into Virginia, like I thought he might, but to Wilmington. He chanced to meet up with Haverly, helped him out somehow, and got himself a job in Haverly's trading firm. It was Gabriel who talked about me to Haverly, telling him I was a good and capable man, and interested in settlement hereabouts. Haverly himself came to Hankins Creek and found me, hired me to help him get his settlement going, and this just barely a month after Gabriel was gone. Think of that, by Joseph— my boy there in Wilmington, running from trouble and shame back home and talking good about his old father all the while. Almost makes me well up to think of it. Anyway, when Haverly came, I had already decided there was no staying in Hankins Creek, not with Gabriel's trouble and then Tilly taking her own life like that. So I took him up on his offer, and before the autumn was out, we were here, putting in cabins and starting on the stockade."

"Peculiar time of year to be starting a settlement."

"Aye, but Haverly's not a man who waits well. He packed in food, tools, guns, and such, and we've fared very well. And with this warm weather, we're ahead of the plan."

Joshua shook his head thoughtfully. "And all because of Gabriel."

"Aye—and here's the best of it, Joshua, the part I've

been saving up all day to tell you. I fully expect that
when Haverly returns, he'll have Gabriel with him."

"Gabriel . . . he's going to be here too?"

"That he is, or so stands the plan. I'm grateful for how
we're all coming together. Me and Sina, Zachariah and
you, all here together, and now Gabriel coming too. It's
as it should be, and I'm a happy man."

14

In the days following, Joshua was a happy man as well. Because Alphus's cabin was too small to accommodate another adult comfortably, Joshua moved, according to the frontier custom for newcomers, into one of the stockade cabins where he would remain until he had time to build a cabin of his own. Sharing the little cabin with him was Israel Coffman, whom Joshua found he liked more each day, despite their tremendous differences in personality, skills, and background.

Joshua's theological education was almost nil, deriving mostly from what Christiana Cox had told him during the Fort Loudoun days and what he had picked up from religious services on Hankins Creek—all this intermixed with various Cherokee legendry and formulas, long hunter superstitions, and ideas he had developed on his own. He wondered sometimes if Coffman regarded him as a complete pagan, for the preacher sometimes asked delicately worded questions but at the same time was never intrusive. For his part, Joshua supported Coffman's plans for the religious and academic education of the community and gave a pledge to help him build a combination meetinghouse and school building as soon as feasible.

Into the next cabin down the line the Fiskes moved, pending construction of their own cabin, and often Joshua and Coffman had to lie awake, listening to Will Fiske chatter on late into the night. Argumentative, hotheaded, and loud of voice, the little crippled man nevertheless was likable and obviously held Joshua in the highest esteem for the help he had given him, though his experience with the bully on the trace obviously had soured him on the Haverly Fort area.

Fiske spread widely the story of how Joshua had bested the troublemaker, embellishing the story enough to make its hero seem almost superhuman. Joshua soon began to notice that the people around him were treating him with unusual respect, largely, he suspected, because of Fiske's story and Colter's bragging. The attention was both vaguely uncomfortable and slightly amusing.

Weather being cooperative, work on the stockade advanced rapidly. Joshua became involved, mostly in splitting the logs that Colter and two others brought in from the forest. The splitting was achieved by mallets and locust wedges that gradually worked a crack up the length of each log until it divided end-to-end. There were also more half-faced cabins to be built, requiring bark skinning and notching, in which Joshua also participated. Fiske proved to be a capable splitter of oak shingles and with froe and hammer turned out stack after stack of them to be affixed to the cabin roofs with long weightpoles.

Two weeks and one day after Joshua's arrival at Haverly Fort, a workman up on one of the rifle platforms stood, shaded his eyes as he looked into the distance, then sang out, "Haverly! Haverly's returned!"

Joshua and Colter, who were using a "log dog" to pin down a poplar log for hewing, shared a quick glance. Then Colter called up, "How many with him?"

"Three," the herald called back.

"Gabriel's here, then," Colter said excitedly, throwing

down his mallet. "Haverly had only two with him when he left."

At a run, Joshua and Colter left the stockade and circled around to where the newly arriving party was emerging into the cleared flat at the edge of the woods. Joshua stopped on his heels and held back as soon as he saw them, deciding that Colter should be the first to greet Gabriel, who would surely be surprised to find his foster brother here, for when Haverly had left for Wilmington, Alphus had been the only Colter at the fort. There was no knowing how Gabriel would respond to Joshua's presence; though the two of them had parted on better terms than they had known previously, their relationship had hardly been warm, even then.

From a distance, Joshua watched Gabriel leap from his horse and limp at a half run toward Alphus Colter. The two men embraced, big smiles on their faces, making Joshua smile to see it.

The other arrivals also watched, then continued riding past, leaving father and son to reunite more privately. As the three riders passed, the one in the center, whom Joshua took to be Haverly, looked around pompously, examining the growth of the station. He was a huge man with short heavy legs, a broad rump, a thick fatty belly, hammy shoulders, and a flat wide face framed in overlong hair that once had been yellow and now had gone white, with just enough blond lingering to make the tied-back mass look dirty beneath the tricorn he wore. He slumped so heavily in his saddle that Joshua almost pitied his horse.

As he passed, Haverly looked down at Joshua, smiled lazily, and touched the brim of the tricorn. Joshua nodded back, then returned his attention to Colter and Gabriel. They were coming toward him. Joshua nodded at his foster brother and put out his hand. Gabriel took it, nodding back.

"Good to see you, Gabe. A surprise, eh?"

"That it is. Hello, Joshua."

And that was all either had to say at the moment. Colter, beaming like the noon sun, clasped his arm over

Gabriel's shoulder. "A rest from travel and work, and a cup of rum is what this calls for. And I've been saving a good jug of it for just such a time."

He took them to his cabin where Sina greeted Gabriel with as much warmth as she was capable of showing these days. Zachariah held back and stared at the newcomer until Gabriel made a humorous face and knelt beside him. The child grinned coyly and came forward, slapping playfully at the palm of Gabriel's upturned hand.

"I can cook up something if you like," Sina said to Colter.

"No need for that yet—bread and rum will do us for now, unless you want more, Gabriel."

"No, no. Bread and rum will be aplenty."

Carrying the jug, loaf, and crockery cups in a split-oak basket, Colter led his son and foster son to a sunny place in a meadow near the creek. He there led them in drinking to Gabriel's return and to their reuniting as a family. Joshua drank but thought to himself that Colter was exaggerating matters. He and Gabriel had never really been part of one family. They had simply shared the same man as father.

At Colter's urging, Gabriel filled in the details of his life since leaving Hankins Creek the previous summer. So neatly had the broken pieces come together that Gabriel now had become a strong believer in destiny.

"I met Mr. Haverly almost as soon as I reached Wilmington, and he hired me a day later," Gabriel reported. "My experience at Thomas's store, my trading and selling, all matched what he was seeking. From something bad, a good thing has come."

"And did you tell him about the 'something bad'?" Joshua asked, swishing his rum in his cup. Colter looked at him so as to imply the question was not well taken.

"Aye, I did tell him. Though I was sore tempted not to. But no, I told myself, no, I won't withhold the truth. From now on, I'm an honest man, for I've learned what the cost of lies and dishonesty is. So I told him, and expected to be put out on my backside. But instead of putting me out, Mr. Haverly hired me and told me it was my honesty with him that was half the reason."

"Must be quite a man, this Haverly," Joshua commented.

"Oh, yes," Gabriel went on, almost gushing. "Powerful, confident, wealthy, influential, devout—he's what a man should be. I admire him, and owe him much. He has my loyalty as long as he'll keep me in his hire."

Alphus said, "Loyalty is a fine thing, Gabriel. Just be careful not to give it too freely to any one man, especially in exchange for money. Once you do, you've become a slave."

Gabriel seemed offended. "Father! I never expected such talk from you, especially not after what Mr. Haverly has done for you!"

"Oh, I appreciate all that, don't take me wrong. But I'll not have Haverly or any other man doing my thinking and planning for me."

Gabriel, obviously not wanting to argue, fidgeted, then said, "Well, I see it to my best advantage to be the best worker for Mr. Haverly that I can be. That's my choice, and hardly slavery."

"I'm sorry I spoke as I did," Alphus said. "This is no time for argument. Put away your frown, Gabe—we're together again, here in a good land, and we have no cause to be unhappy." He poured more rum all around. "To a new life," he said, lifting his cup.

"To a new life," the younger men repeated, then drank.

Good weather held until the stockade had been completed, then was chased out by the last advance of winter. Temperatures plummeted; snow, sleet, and cold rain fell frequently; and work on the new settlement slowed and then stopped, except for what could be done indoors. Joshua and Coffman continued to share their stockade cabin, and through him and some direct contact of his own, Joshua began to know more of Peter Haverly.

Coffman, genial by nature and having cause to think the best of Haverly, who had called him here and pledged strong financial backing for his work, was initially positive about Haverly and the future. But as weeks passed, Joshua detected a subtle intensification of the worries Coffman had expressed early on. Finally Coffman spilled his concerns about Haverly in a flood of complaint to Joshua.

Haverly, he said, was loyal only to himself, his king, and his own concept of God, who seemed to be, according to Coffman, simply an expanded version of Peter Haverly himself. Haverly was arrogant, self-righteous, and so predestinarian in his thinking that he viewed all Indians as outside the scope not only of salvation but of God's love. They were therefore of no concern to the elect—of whom he obviously saw himself as chief— except as tools to be used and manipulated, even at the expense of honesty and decency. If lying to an Indian will lead him to do what you wish, then lying to him should be done—that was Haverly's view.

Coffman was stunned by the attitude, for it was his desire ultimately to include the Cherokees in his ministry and educational efforts. That perceived opportunity was part of what had motivated him and his late brother to come here in the first place. And his brother—that was another point. According to Coffman, Haverly seemed to hold it against him that instead of two minister-educators, he now had but one, and apparently the less desirable of the pair, at that. Such, at least, was the way Haverly made Coffman feel.

"I'm straining my Christian charity to the utmost to maintain any love at all for the man, Joshua," Coffman said. "He's hardly what I thought he was."

Joshua said, "Maybe you're judging him too soon. Give him time—maybe he'll prove different than you think."

"Oh, no. If there's one thing Peter Haverly can do, it's make his views clear. There's no mistaking where he stands."

"Well then, I'd say you two will not long keep company together."

"But he's my employer, really, and is to be the chief supporter of both church and school."

"Not for long he won't be. If Haverly is what I think he

is, he'll not long support anyone who doesn't simply repeat his own thoughts after him."

"Aye. Like his devoted follower Gabriel Colter." As quickly as he said it, Coffman looked embarrassed. "I'm sorry. I shouldn't have said such a thing. I forgot your relationship with Gabriel."

"Believe me, Israel, there's little relationship between us and nothing you could say about Gabriel that would likely offend me. We've never been friends, even at the best of times. And I know now what you speak of. Gabe too greatly admires Haverly."

"Gabriel is in my prayers," Coffman said. "There is much potential for greatness in him, whether you see it or not. But there is also weakness, and men such as Haverly can exploit it."

Coffman, who had been pacing about the half-faced cabin while venting his frustration, now sat down and began filling his pipe. "Ah well, at least we all will have some temporary freedom from friend Haverly soon. He's talking of returning to Wilmington when the threat of snow is gone and fetching his family." Coffman smiled mischievously. "They say his wife is fatter even than he is."

As the days passed, Joshua learned more not only of individuals and personalities about Haverly Fort but also of developments throughout the region. By now, talk of leasing land from the Cherokees had gone beyond speculation to definite plans. Negotiations went on quietly between the Indians and various leaders in the white settlements, Haverly and the Nolichucky's Jacob Brown among them. Colter, getting his information from Haverly, said the plan was that a delegation from the settlements would visit the Cherokee capital, Chota, and there work out details not only of a lease but also of friendship terms designed to preserve peace and understanding between the Cherokees and their new white neighbors.

Joshua, who knew that treaties with the Indians had a way of being broken promptly, expressed his doubt to Alphus about the usefulness of one more agreement.

"I agree with you, Joshua, but what else can be done?

There must be some terms for us to follow, else we will be like an unstable ship. A lease and friendship agreement would be a foundation for a government, with courts and judges and militias and such. God knows, we'll need it sooner than later."

Thinking back on Coffman's earlier complaints, Joshua asked Alphus, "What do you think of Haverly?"

Alphus glanced at his foster son from the corner of his eye. "Haverly, you say? Ah yes, Haverly. I think, son, that Haverly is Haverly, and beyond that I ought to say little."

"Is he honest?"

"That I don't know, not any longer. The more I'm about him, the more I—" Alphus shook his head. "I'll not speak ill of him, though, for I don't know him that well. It's Gabriel who is closest to him now. Since Gabriel returned, I've hardly spoken to Haverly himself but to tell him this or that about the stockade. And he acts as if he hardly has time even to hear that."

The winter at last began to fade, and even before the earliest blush of spring, Peter Haverly took Gabriel with him and headed back toward Wilmington to get his family and arrange for delivery of supplies to the settlement. He left Alphus in charge of the station, empowering him to make decisions on his behalf. This was all greatly to the old frontiersman's surprise, for he had come to believe Haverly thought little of him.

"Gabriel's doing, probably," he told Joshua. "He's been talking good of me to Haverly some more, I'll wager."

With Haverly gone and the pleasant days of spring arriving, the atmosphere of Haverly Fort became relaxed but busy. Work on Coffman's school and church building began, Joshua and Alphus taking the lead. Finding a good plot of land, Joshua built a lean-to shelter for himself about a quarter mile from Alphus's cabin, and a shed and corncrib, and began building a little springhouse in the creek.

He had just gotten a good start on the springhouse the day that Alphus rode in on a fine new Chickasaw horse and told Joshua to get his rifle and gear.

Joshua splashed up out of the creek. "Why?" he asked.

"We're going to Watauga, to meet a man named James Robertson," Alphus replied. "And then we're off to Chota. The Cherokees have agreed to the lease and friendship agreement, and we're to fetch back Little Carpenter to work it out."

"Little Carpenter!" Joshua repeated. The name stirred scores of old memories. "I haven't seen him since Fort Loudoun. But why take me along? I'm no leader here."

"You've got the respect of the people. You've been among the Overhills, know their language, and are a good trailsman besides."

"Who'll look after things at Haverly Fort?"

"McSwain. And Preacher Coffman's coming into his own, people liking him and all. He can lend a hand."

"If Israel tries to lend a hand, he'll likely get it chopped off. Maybe I ought to stay here."

"I want you with us, Joshua," Alphus said. "It's important to me."

Joshua patted the Chickasaw between the eyes. "You'll have me, then. Back to the Overhill towns . . . nothing's been farther from my mind. Well, if we're going, I'd best fetch my goods," he said, and walked toward his hut.

They set out for Watauga that day, camped near a canebrake for the night, and completed the final twelve-mile stretch the next day.

Joshua had heard much of James Robertson but, unlike Alphus, had never met him until now. His immediate impression as he shook the blue-eyed hunter's hand outside Robertson's cabin on Watauga Old Fields was of a serious, experienced man, wirier and taller than usual but a typical frontiersman in most other ways. About eight years older than Joshua, he had thick, dark hair hanging in locks across his forehead, and spoke in a quiet, even voice. He possessed an air of quiet authority, much like Alphus's, that inspired confidence. Initially, Robertson was taciturn, but as he became accustomed to his visitors, sharing with them meals, plans, and conversation, he told them about himself and his background.

Walking with Joshua and Alphus beneath a grove of

oak trees near the juncture of the Watauga and Doe rivers, Robertson told his visitors that he had first come to the Overmountain country in 1770, traveling through a mountain gap often used by the long hunters.

In Watauga he had visited John Honeycut, an early settler whose cabin was in the vicinity of William Bean's. During that visit he admired the Watauga Old Fields, cleared long ago by the Indians, and decided to make himself and his family, then back in Orange County, North Carolina, permanent residents. He cleared an Old Fields plot of saplings and undergrowth, planted and tended a crop of corn, and in August returned toward North Carolina.

He did not fare well on the journey, for as he headed into the mountains, heavy rains set in for several days. He became lost in an area overgrown with laurel and rhododendron and so rocky and wild that he had to free his horse and proceed on foot. He climbed trees and bluffs in attempts to find landmarks by which to guide himself, but to no avail. He began marking his route as he traveled, and found that he was crossing his own tracks repeatedly. His powder became wet, and since he could not kill game, he feared starvation. Finally he stumbled across two hunters who provided him a horse. Mounted now, his spirits lifted, and he successfully made it out of the mountains. He had been lost for two weeks.

In early autumn, Robertson gathered his family and sixteen fellow journeyers, and returned to Watauga, bringing goods, livestock, seed, and food. Since his arrival, his natural leadership ability had asserted itself, much as Alphus's had, leading to his choice as head of the delegation to Chota.

"What will our main purpose be?" Joshua asked. "Bargaining?"

"Not really—much of that has already been done, and what remains will mostly be dealt with when we return. Our primary purpose is for ceremony and escort for the Little Carpenter and whoever else he may bring."

The group set off. As they rode, Alphus related his own background to Robertson and told some of Joshua's.

Robertson was intrigued by Joshua's Fort Loudoun experience, but Joshua was reluctant to talk much of it, for it made the death of his mother seem fresh and painful again. He began wondering how he would feel once back among the Overhill Cherokees from whom he had been separated for more than a decade.

Once near the Overhill towns, Joshua felt as if he were being drawn into his past. Yet not the past as he had known it, for the towns had changed, some growing, some dwindling, some moving, some disappearing. Having arrived at Chota, Joshua had parted company with Alphus and Robertson and begun a private exploration among the towns, leaving the actual diplomatic business to his seniors. Alphus did not favor Joshua's roaming off alone, for there were some Cherokees greatly embittered and hostile toward the white settlers, but Joshua could not resist the lure of exploring an area he had not seen since boyhood, and as it turned out, he traveled unmolested.

He found that the late Bloody Eagle's old village of Tikwalitsi, where Henry Dorey had traded and where he, Christiana, Samuel, and Beth had been prisoners in the house of Kwali, was gone entirely. Lacking a townhouse, Tikwalitsi had been merely an impermanent Cherokee village in the first place and had vanished when its surrounding resources were played out. Joshua rode about the old site, finding the spot where Kwali's house had stood and then the site of Bloody Eagle's residence where Jack Byrum's scalp had been tauntingly displayed and he had found the ailing John Hawk.

From Tikwalitsi he rode to the ruins of Fort Loudoun, now simply an overgrown area surrounded by the eroding moat filled with underbrush, the thorny locusts having mostly died away.

His throat tight, Joshua crossed into the area where the fort had stood, finding only blackened traces of the palisades and buildings. A deep fond sadness filled him as he looked about, mentally restoring the weed-infested ruins to what they had been, seeing again the faces of

his mother, Christiana, the two Demeres, Nathan Cox
. . . and Jack Byrum. He explored the old parade grounds,
the corners where the bastions had been, and the site of
the soldiers' barracks—then, with an eager and heavy
heart, sought the place where Hester Byrum lay.

There remained nothing to mark the grave, but Joshua
searched until he found the place he thought it was and
stood alone beside it, missing his mother more than he
had since the days when her loss was fresh and feeling
anew bitterness toward the man who had forced his own
wife to come against her will into a country she knew
she would never leave.

Before he left the fort site, he cleared brush and weeds
from his mother's burial place and put stones atop it.
Someday, he thought, he might be able to return and
bring a permanent marker.

At last he turned away and walked back down to the
river where he boyishly tossed stones into the water in
the way he had the day Little Carpenter had startled him.
As before, he became wrapped up in what he was doing,
this time lost in memory instead of imagination, and as
before, heard a noise behind him and turned.

A Cherokee stood on the bank, looking down at him.
Joshua faced him squarely, looking the lean young warrior in the eye. He appeared to be about Joshua's age,
and in his face Joshua saw something familiar. A childhood playmate, perhaps? He had seen among the Cherokees here several dark faces that looked familiar.

"Hello," the Cherokee said in English.

"Hello," Joshua replied.

"You are one of the men come to talk friendship and to
buy land?" the Cherokee asked. His English was remarkably good.

"To seek friendship, yes. To buy, no. We wish to lease
the land for ten years, to pay for use of it."

The young Indian smiled very faintly. "You talk the
talk of the white men. This lease . . . it would not always
remain so, as you know. To occupy the land is to possess
it, and the white men will ever occupy any land they
settle upon."

Joshua looked back into the dark unblinking eyes and felt as if he and his race had been summarily probed and evaluated with accuracy. He smiled back, just as faintly. "You are a man of understanding."

"I am a man who knows the white man. For many years I have watched them, and learned from them what I could, when I could. The white men are the most interesting of the creatures of our world. Little Carpenter has taught me much about them. He has told me of their great cities to the east, and of even greater ones far across the water."

Joshua stepped closer. "You are familiar to me."

"Yes. And you to me."

"Where have I seen you before?"

"I cannot answer that. But it was here, or close. Many years ago. My village was Tikwalitsi; it now is gone. My mother's brother was called Bloody Eagle by the white men; he too is gone. My name is Tsantawu, and I have earned war titles besides, but for many years I have used the name of John Hawk."

Joshua drew in a deep breath, his eyes sparkling suddenly. He grasped the cord around his neck and from beneath his hunting shirt pulled out the Roman coin.

The Cherokee looked at it, then again at Joshua's face. Stepping down the bank, he came directly up to Joshua, reached out, and felt the coin.

"You are the one called Ayunini. You gave this to me when I was sick?"

"I am." Joshua was so overwhelmed to see John Hawk again that he could hardly speak.

"It has been many years since we have spoken, Ayunini. Do you remember our talk at the river beside Tikwalitsi, the day you and those with you were ransomed?"

"I do remember, very well."

"So do I. And it brings me great unhappiness that now I must kill you."

Joshua had hardly expected to hear that. He frowned and stepped back, pulling the coin from John Hawk's hands in the process. "Why do you say you must kill me?"

"This coin . . . how come you to have it now?"

Suddenly Joshua understood what John Hawk was thinking. The coin had last been possessed by Bloody Eagle. The presumption among the Cherokees by now surely was that Bloody Eagle was dead, as in fact he was. Because Joshua now had the coin, John Hawk could only believe it had been taken from Bloody Eagle himself, making Joshua the author of Bloody Eagle's death.

Joshua was on the brink of spilling out the story of his encounter with Henry Dorey in the tavern at Salisbury when another consideration made him hold his tongue. At the moment, he, Alphus, and Robertson were in the Overhill towns on a mission of friendship. Bloody Eagle had been a prominent, influential warrior, admired by his fellows. To reveal that he had been murdered by a white man could jeopardize the friendship mission, the lease, and perhaps even the lives of the emissaries.

Feeling trapped, Joshua did the only thing he could think of. He lied. "I found the coin beside the Watauga River," he told John Hawk, hoping he sounded convincing. "When I saw it, I knew it to be the very coin I had given to you many years ago, and that the great cycle of life had brought it back to my hands. I knew then that we would see each other again, and be brothers, as you said in Tikwalitsi years ago, and live at peace with each other. This coin is the symbol of that—and so I give it back to you now, to make the cycle complete."

John Hawk looked into Joshua's eyes. "Do you tell me the truth?"

Joshua felt a pang of guilt but hid it. "Yes."

He could feel John Hawk evaluating his expression, his gaze, his manner. For several fearful moments, he was sure the Cherokee had detected his lie. Then John Hawk lowered his head.

Joshua lifted the thong from around his neck and placed it around John Hawk's. "It is good for you to again have it," Joshua said. "The cycle is complete."

"Yes," John Hawk said. "It is good."

15

          Little Carpenter had looked far older than his years, even in the days of Fort Loudon. Now, twelve years later, the light of day made him appear ancient. Only by firelight did he lose some of his age, and so it was tonight, in the warm glow of the light of a fire built to drive away the chill from this spring evening in Chota. The Indian's face was ageless, neither young nor old, as he talked to John Hawk and Joshua about the days of his young manhood when he had journeyed from the Overhill country to the court of George II.

The Cherokee gazed out over the top of the leaping flames into the deep black sky. From his vantage point, Joshua could see behind Little Carpenter the townhouse of Chota where the sacred fire was never extinguished, the councils of the Cherokee people were held, and Little Carpenter's voice was often heard. That voice was steady and strong tonight, a voice that should have belonged to a physically large man, not one as diminutive as he. He spoke in a mix of English and the Overhill Cherokee dialect.

"I came from the Big Island in the river you now call

235

the French Broad," he said. "By the reckoning of the white men, my birth was about 1710. Among these people"—he gave a broad sweeping gesture indicating Chota and the Overhill Cherokee lands all about him—"I have spent my life. For the good of the Ani-Yunwiya I have given my time and my best labors, even when my brothers have called me a fool or an old woman. I have stood against Old Hop, my own mother's brother, when he led our people in ways I thought were wrong. My own son, Dragging Canoe, believes I am blind to the danger of the white men and talks of war like a hungry man talks of buffalo hump and marrowbone. I have known war, and do not fear it, but neither do I love it as the young warriors do. The slaying of enemies is good, and the taking of their scalps, but so also is a life of peace, when it can be had, and when war cannot prevail.

"I am not blind to the ways the white men sometimes deceive us. I know the white men well, particularly the English, both the good and the bad of them. I know the Englishman is powerful, and that he builds homes and fortresses of stone that are as mountains beside the biggest of our townhouses. Across the great ocean the white man is numbered like the stars in the sky. When he decides to occupy a land, he does so, with nothing stopping him, and to try to stop him is like trying to stop a flooding river from overflowing its banks. I have not sought to stop that river, as some of my brothers believe we can do, but to control its flow so that we may live alongside it in peace. The old days are gone, when the land could be that of the Ani-Yunwiya alone, though I am sorry this is so.

"I more than most of my people know of the life of the white man, for I have seen the place from which the English come. Long ago, in the summer of 1730, as the English number their years, I went on a long journey across the great water to the court of the king of the British. If you wish to hear of it, I will tell you."

"I wish very much to hear it, sir." Joshua had known since childhood that Little Carpenter had made such a trip and had hoped to obtain a firsthand description of it while in Chota. Little Carpenter's journey of forty-two years before was a far longer one than any made by Joshua, who had seen no city more substantial than the Charles Town of his early boyhood, and so his expression of interest was no mere politeness.

Little Carpenter smiled without parting his lips and lifted his head. He closed his eyes as if to see better into his memories. "In the days when I was younger—younger even than you, and not yet called Little Carpenter or Attakullakulla, but instead Okoonaka—there came among the Ani-Yunwiya a warrior of Britain who called himself Sir Alexander Cuming. This warrior, who had come to us on his own upon what he called an adventure, talked much of the great English father across the water, named King George. The warrior spoke of this great father of his people even in the tribal council at Nequassie, where he was allowed to visit, and told us of his greatness, his strength, his power, and his desire for the friendship and homage of the Ani-Yunwiya. In return for that homage, the warrior said, the great father across the water could do good for us. It was barely past this time of year when the English warrior talked of such things, so our minds were open and eager, as they always are when the earth is renewed. Soon my people, having heard so much of the warrior's pretty talk, chose to honor this great King George, and in turn the king's warrior gave the title of Emperor to Moytoy of Great Tellico.

"The warrior had with him an interpreter named Wiggan, and one night Wiggan came to my house and told me that the warrior wished that I, and maybe also others of my people, should journey with him across the water to his land of England, and there meet this great King George to whom we had given homage. I was young then, and answered him with great care, for I did not wish to do that which was not proper. I asked him about the distance to England, for I had heard it was far away, but Wiggan told me it was not nearly as far as I believed and that I could make the journey and be home again even by the late summer or fall. I considered what he said, and agreed to make the journey.

"On the morning of the next day, one of our people approached me. The warrior, he told me, had asked others to make the journey as well, but none had agreed until they heard that I had made my pledge. I was young then, and none thought I should make such a journey alone. So it was that six others, all older than I was, joined me in the long voyage. Together we traveled, I being the youngest of the seven.

"We went first to Charles Town, and there boarded a ship of the type called by the English a man-of-war, and named *Fox*, for the British give names to their vessels, as you know. For many days we were upon the water, more water than ever I had seen, stretching all around us so there was no land in sight, and the boat was like a small stick floating in a vast river. The motions of the ship were distressing to us, for it was as if the land beneath us swam, and many times the food I was given to eat would not remain in my stomach.

"When I had come to believe that the water had no land beyond it and that we would sail until we reached the ends of the world, at last we reached a place called Dover, and there set foot on earth again. The sun had risen and set more than thirty times since last my feet had stood on solid earth. But we did not remain long in Dover, but instead sailed again, until we came to a great city, amazing to see, and called London.

"Our lives from then until our return were no more like the lives we knew as Ani-Yunwiya, but like those of the white men. We were given lodging, first in rooms above a tavern and later in other rooms dug beneath the level of the earth, with a building above us.

"We were taken to a great stone castle called Windsor, built something like one of your forts but immensely larger and of stone, with high walls, many windows, and a round tower in the midst. There we met this King George of whom we had heard so much, and were given his hand to kiss, and the hands of others with him, whom we were told were also great and mighty people. We wore clothing and decoration as seemed right to us, breech-cloths and feathers and paint, but later we were given clothing that looked like that worn by the British men—very uncomfortable, but laced with gold and costing much money. A man was sent in with a thing like a skin stretched around a frame and brushes and paints, and he made us stand together, very still, me with my gourd rattle and knife, and some of the others with rifles and axes, and on the skin he painted our images, which we declared very fine, but were glad when it was done, for we were tired of standing so long.

"Many places we were taken, and many sights we saw, some of them beautiful and awesome to our eyes, others stupid and hard to understand. We saw a great building called Canterbury, where we were told the English prayed to the Great Man Above, and were taken also to a tower where jewels of great price, and belonging to the king and his family, were kept. Here also many prisoners had been kept awaiting their deaths, which were most often done by the chopping of their heads from their shoulders, they told us.

"We were also shown places where men and women in garments and hats of bright colors tossed themselves in the air to land on their feet, making those who watched them laugh and clap their hands. They did many other things that amazed us, such as tossing many balls again and again from their hands, all together, and catching them and throwing them up again, with none dropping. Here we smiled much and were happy. But when we were taken to a place with a great platform where people walked about and talked on a great platform, pretending to be people who they really were not, I grew tired and left, going back to the rooms where we stayed, for I wanted to be alone.

"I was young, and did not like being stared at forever by so many eyes. Yet I did not complain much of it, for I had the best part of the bargain. The English looked on me because they saw me as a strange creature—but as they looked, seeing but one such creature, I in turn could look back, and see thousands."

Here, Little Carpenter paused as Joshua chuckled at the last remark. John Hawk, having heard the story, which invariably included that same quip, smiled but did not laugh. Little Carpenter went on.

"You have come here seeking to bring me to your settlements to sign a treaty of friendship, Joshua. I know much of such treaties. Let me tell you now of the one my companions and I signed while on this journey to see King George.

"We knew little of the English tongue then, though I was learning it, and to us came the British, asking us to put our names upon a paper that they said declared friendship between our peoples, and a desire for trade and commerce. We put our names upon the paper, though we did not understand all its words. In this signing, Oukaynda was our spokesman, for I was the youngest and not suited for so important a task.

"When we returned to our place for sleeping, we asked that the paper we had signed be put out for us in our own language, and when we read it, we discovered the English had made us declare they had right over what they called the country of Carolina. Friends we wished to be, but not givers of land. We counciled together and at first determined that we must kill Wiggan the interpreter, and Oukaynda as well, as parties to this trick, but later we changed our minds, for we had no power to give lands in any case, and thus the paper meant nothing without the consent of the headmen. So we did nothing, and in the fall began our journey home with many gifts in hand. I had learned to love much about the great land of King George, and when I departed it, there were tears in my eyes. There was an old woman near the ship, selling fish, and I took her hand in mine. 'Thank you,' I said to her, for there were none other of her nation there to thank. 'Thank you, all,' I said to her."

Little Carpenter stopped and looked to his right, studying the faint line where the dark treetops melted into the black sky. "Someday I hope to go back again, once more before I am dead, and see the great house they call Windsor."

"I hope such a journey will be given to you," Joshua said. "Thank you for telling me this tale."

"And I thank you for letting me tell it, for telling it is much like living it again."

John Hawk stood. "And now," he said in his excellent English, "once again the white man seeks the name of Attakullakulla on a treaty of friendship, and once again he seeks the right to claim Cherokee lands."

Little Carpenter lifted his brows. "And what think you of this, John Hawk? I am age, seeking the counsel of youth. Should the Cherokees talk friendship with the people of Joshua Byrum, and let them occupy their lands, as they ask, even though I am loath to do it?"

John Hawk looked at his feet, thinking. Finally he lifted his head again. "In this case, youth has no answer. What will happen will happen. I go now." With that, he turned and walked away into the night.

"He is unlike his uncle was," Little Carpenter said. "Bloody Eagle was a man quick to act and then forget. John Hawk is a man who acts more slowly, and never forgets. He is a man of thought, and upon such men there are burdens that lie heavy as stones."

At the head of the procession of riders was Little Carpenter and his contingent, followed immediately by James Robertson, then Alphus Colter, and finally John Hawk and Joshua. John Hawk had both surprised and delighted Joshua when he accepted his invitation to return with him to the settlements for a visit as extended as he wished.

As he rode, Joshua learned that his newfound partner had more than the average Indian curiosity about the white men—and for that, surprisingly enough, Joshua himself got much of the credit. Joshua's gift of the Roman coin many years ago had greatly affected the ailing young Cherokee, so much that he had thereafter insisted on using the name Joshua had given him. Further, John Hawk's curiosity had been roused by the coin, and he had queried his seniors extensively about its origins. He had found few answers beyond some vague talk from Oconostota of ancient white men with long beards who supposedly were in the land before the Cherokees came.

Oconostota said the story had been passed to him from much older Cherokees, and they in turn had received the tale from their own ancient ones.

"Perhaps, among your people, I can learn more of this," John Hawk said. "There may be those who know what the markings on the coin mean, and what people made them."

Joshua had his doubts, for there were few educated men on the frontier and none he knew of with much knowledge of ancient times. Not wanting to discourage John Hawk, however, he said nothing of this. "How did you learn to speak English so well from the traders alone?" he asked.

"It was from the brother of a trader, who was in our towns for a year, that I learned most of it. The brother was a lazy man, never doing much work, but he had books and taught me to read them and to speak English words well. But when he was gone, he took his books with him. I was left with only this one that I had found myself."

John Hawk reached into a saddlepouch and pulled out a fragment of a book, which he handed over to Joshua. It was a portion of a Bible, consisting of the Apocrypha and about two-thirds of the New Testament, the rest torn out. It was very torn and yellowed, with no cover except a homemade one of deerhide that John Hawk had made for it.

Joshua studied the book, then asked, "Where did you find this?"

"On the field where those from Fort Loudoun died, and where you were taken prisoner." John Hawk looked more closely at Joshua. "Why do you look as you do? Is it my talk of Fort Loudoun?"

Joshua handed back the book. "No, no. It's nothing. Your book just reminded me of something. Nothing important."

In fact, it had reminded him very much of Christiana Cox's old Bible, the one she had used while teaching him to read. Whether this was the same Bible he could not tell, for his memory was dusty with age, and certainly there had been several Bibles in the possession of the Fort Loudoun refugees. Still, it might be the same book, and if so, this clutch of ragged pages was one more piece of his past intruding unexpectedly into his present, just like Henry Dorey's bearing the Roman coin in a tavern in Salisbury and Jack Byrum's turning up alive among a band of North Carolina mountain bandits.

Ahead, Little Carpenter was talking, with abundant hand gestures, to James Robertson.

Alphus slowed his horse until Joshua reached him, then pulled up to plod along beside him. He wore an amused grin. "Attakullakulla up yonder is telling about a time he got drunk on rum and chased the commander of Fort Loudoun, trying to break a bottle over his noggin," Alphus said. "Quite an interesting man that one is, by Joseph."

"Aye, that he is," Joshua said.

The rest of 1772 was crowded with events of importance to the Colter family and the settlements at large.

When Alphus, Joshua, and Robertson returned with the delegation from Chota, they found the Watauga settlers eagerly awaiting them, along with Jacob Brown from the Nolichucky and Peter Haverly, who had returned since the delegates had left for the Overhill towns. He had brought Gabriel with him, along with two slaves.

Joshua, not seeing Haverly's family, asked Gabriel if the family had not returned with Haverly as planned. Gabriel answered that Haverly's son, a fine-looking young fellow of about eleven called Cooper, had returned with them and was now back at the stockade, but Haverly's wife and daughter were ill and had been left behind in North Carolina yet again.

The slaves, two of three owned by Haverly, had been brought back to help Haverly and—here Gabriel swelled with ill-hidden conceit—to serve as laborers on a large new house Haverly was building for Gabriel. " 'Twill be the finest in the settlement, next to Mr. Haverly's. When it's done, I plan to purchase one of the slaves for myself."

"Proud of that notion, eh?" Joshua asked before walking away.

The work Little Carpenter had come to Watauga to do went along nicely. The treaty of friendship was drafted; in the meantime, other Cherokee leaders arrived, and the leases were finalized and signed. The Wataugans, Brown, and Haverly all signed separate leases, and when it was done, attention promptly was focused on forming what was to be called, at Robertson's suggestion, the Watauga Association.

The association, unprecedented west of the mountains, was a loosely defined government based on common principles of law and binding upon all who signed its formative document, protective of none who refused to do so. The North of Holston settlements did not fall under its scope, for they were seen as part of Virginia, but the remaining settlements all fell under the Watauga Association.

A court of five "commissioners" was established to serve both legislative and judicial functions. The members were chairman John Carter, for whom Carter's Valley had been named; James Robertson and his Virginia cousin, Charles Robertson; and Zachariah Isbell, who had once been a justice in Bedford County, Virginia. The fifth commissioner, to Joshua's pride, was Alphus Colter.

Joshua unexpectedly found himself holding a post as well. Due largely to Will Fiske's continual telling of how he bested the bully on the road to Haverly Fort, Joshua was asked to serve as under sheriff to the high sheriff, a newcomer named Valentine Sevier, Jr. Though reluctant to take on the job, Joshua agreed after Sevier assured him that his primary duties would be to keep watch on the area around Haverly Fort, which was under the Watauga Association government but away from the main Watauga settlement. In the event of major troubles, Joshua could recruit help from the populace at large or call on Sevier if logistics allowed.

Formalization of the Watauga Association brought a spirit of great cheer to all the settlements, and several celebrations were held. Peter Haverly hosted a great horse race near his fort, and it was here that Joshua noticed for the first time that Darcy Fiske, Will's sister, seemed to enjoy his company. Where Joshua was, there she would be, shyly watching him, sometimes venturing a smile or light comment upon the goings-on around them. She kept her withered hand hidden beneath her apron; it seemed to embarrass her for Joshua to see it, though he was in no way put off by it.

Nor, apparently, was Gabriel put off, for he shadowed Darcy in the same way Darcy shadowed Joshua. A slight ache of jealousy struck Joshua, surprising him, for he had thought after Tilly's passing that he would have an interest in no one else. Evidently he had been wrong.

Even so, he did not vie against Gabriel, for the idea of that hurt his pride. Eventually, when Gabriel finally got Darcy's attention, Joshua moved away from them and later saw them walking together along the creek, Gabriel talking vigorously, Darcy listening but looking none too interested. Probably Gabriel was talking about his new house or maybe the meat-packing business that Haverly was reportedly about to set up, with Gabriel in charge. These days, Gabriel talked only of business, his admiration for Peter Haverly, and his Haverly-influenced view of destiny, settlement, and religion—the latter, in Haverly's and Gabriel's version, including much bigotry toward the Indians, who Haverly believed were descendants of apostate Israelites.

Despite patronizing treatment by Haverly at Watauga, Little Carpenter came to Haverly Fort with Joshua, accompanied by John Hawk, and remained there several days, living in the largest of the stockade cabins. From him Joshua heard much Cherokee lore, most of it familiar from his Fort Loudoun childhood but some of it new to him. Born into a family of importance, Little Carpenter had been trained in the history and mysticism of the Cherokees and could recite the old legends and formulas with ease.

Because of his fame and influence, Little Carpenter received much attention from the Haverly Fort settlers

and to the delight of most, used events around him as
promptings for stories and expositions.

Seeing McSwain bringing in a possum, for example,
led him to relate, in a loud oratorical voice, the Cherokee
legend that told of the possum's original wide bushy tail,
which was sheared off, through the conniving of a jeal-
ous rabbit, by a hair-cutting cricket. After this, the possum became so ashamed of his ruined shorn tail that he
fell over and trembled each time anyone came near, as
possums forever after him did when confronted.

Likewise, a ghost tale related by Alphus one night
prompted Little Carpenter to talk of a Cherokee of some
years back named Yahula, who became lost in the mountains and was rescued by the immortal forest fairies
called the Nunnehi. Thereafter, Yahula lived among
them, singing songs that could be heard echoing through
the forest with no singer visible, until finally they faded
away and he was heard no more.

At last Little Carpenter returned to the Overhill towns,
but John Hawk remained. He built a small hide-covered
shelter near Joshua's log hut, which was too small to
house two men comfortably, and together he and Joshua
hunted and explored. Never had Joshua encountered an
Indian who could so naturally absorb and understand
the ways of the white men yet fully and pridefully maintain his Indian identity. John Hawk, an unusually
thoughtful and reflective man, seemed unsure of how to
view properly the swirl of changes coming to his world.
From him Joshua learned much and to him taught much,
so that their relationship was beneficial and pleasurable
to both.

John Hawk was curious why Joshua was twenty-two
years old but still unmarried. Joshua, though a little
reluctant to talk about a painful subject, told him of Tilly.
Asking for and receiving John Hawk's pledge of silence,
he even revealed that Tilly's rapist was none other than
his natural father. John Hawk was the first human being
to whom Joshua had unveiled that deepest of secrets.

John Hawk revealed that he had been married until a
year before, but his young wife had fallen ill with a

mysterious illness and died. "If I had possessed this coin," he said, lifting the Roman coin, "she might have been saved by it, as it saved me. But I did not have it. I had given it to Bloody Eagle, who had gone off to fight. I am sure he is now dead, or he would have returned long ago. Bloody Eagle must have lost the coin—otherwise he would have been kept safe from harm."

"Do you really believe there is power in a circle of metal?" Joshua asked, feeling a twinge of guilt at the mention of Bloody Eagle, whose murder by Henry Dorey was still a secret he hid from John Hawk.

John Hawk looked puzzled. "Do not many of your own people believe that a man can be cleansed of all the bad he has done by being dipped beneath water or having it sprinkled upon his brow by a priest?"

Joshua felt unqualified to debate such matters and referred the question over to Israel Coffman, who had been eager to get to know John Hawk in any case.

After the two were introduced by Joshua, they spent many hours locked in deep discussions about their views of God, the universe, and man.

Sometime afterward, John Hawk confided to Joshua that he initially found Coffman to be a "funny little man" but later came to like him. "He is much like the Jesus I have read about in the old book," he said, and when Joshua privately repeated that to Coffman, the preacher's eyes filled with tears at that finest of compliments.

Coffman had begun holding regular services and throughout the week was schooling the handful of settlement children. Though some of the settlers were typically rough frontier sorts, having little use for preachers and churches and books, many others supported Coffman's little church and school. As weeks rolled past, the preacher began baptizing several new converts, among them Alphus and Joshua Colter.

Joshua declined to affiliate fully with the congregation. "I'll not be part of a group that lives under the thumb of a man like Peter Haverly," he declared. When Gabriel heard of that, he was offended and expressed doubt about the validity of Joshua's religious profession, which had come as a surprise to him in any case.

For his part, Joshua saw more reason to doubt the sincerity and professed righteousness of Haverly, who was the most arrogant, condescending man he had ever encountered. Haverly seemed intent on dominating every part of the settlement's life. He even had difficulty fully accepting the idea that Haverly Fort was under the authority of the Watauga Association, especially since Alphus, and not he himself, had been appointed a commissioner in the new government.

Haverly had grown rather cold toward Alphus since that had occurred. He also had come to dislike Joshua, who had never given Haverly the deference he craved and as under sheriff had authority to enforce the Watauga Association's authority, which galled Haverly. The fact that Joshua respected and kept company with "red demons," as Haverly privately called Little Carpenter and John Hawk, deepened Haverly's dislike.

When Haverly saw that Israel Coffman also took a respectful attitude toward the Indians—and, even worse, did not believe slaveholding was morally acceptable— Haverly soured on the preacher as well.

Joshua saw Haverly's changing attitude toward Coffman and warned his friend to be careful what he said and did around the settlement's leader.

"I'll say and do what I think is right," Coffman replied, "and neither Peter Haverly nor any other man will stop me from it."

Joshua admired Coffman's stubborn stand but knew that ultimately he would find trouble for it. Haverly was not the kind to put up long with any resistance to his will, especially from a man more or less under his hire.

"The day will come," Joshua warned, "when Peter Haverly will have his fill of you, Israel. You'll find yourself with no congregation to preach to."

The preacher smiled. "If that happens, I'll become a hunter, like you."

Joshua smiled. "In that case, God preserve us all."

16

Darcy Fiske shifted her brother's heavy rifle on her forearm as she strode across the beaten dirt expanse between the stockade and Callum McSwain's smithy. The late-September breeze gusted across the smithy's cedar-shake roof and stone chimneytop, carrying down sooty forge smoke to enwrap her. Except for the smoke, the wind would have been pleasant; today it was neither chilling, as it would be within a week or two, nor hot, as it had been in August.

From the corner of her eye, she saw the front door of Gabriel Colter's ostentatious log house swing open. Before she thought better of it, she turned to look and was thankful to see it was not Gabriel at the door but the slave named Patton, whom Gabriel had purchased from Peter Haverly. Darcy nodded a greeting at Patton, who smiled and responded with two quick bows of his head and a slight wave of his fingers from waist level. Darcy pitied Patton, who seemed very unhappy here, and for that she could not blame him. Life as a slave was bad enough in any case; to be the slave first of the oppressive Peter Haverly and then of Gabriel Colter surely must have worsened his lot considerably.

Darcy was not pleased that Gabriel owned a slave. The concept of owning another human being did not sit comfortably with her. She had dared express those feelings to Gabriel at one time, and he had looked at her with one lifted brow, in that irritating way he had, and informed her coolly that he did not own Patton, just the right to Patton's labors. There was hardly a difference, she had replied, in that Patton could certainly not live a life separate from his labors. Gabriel had assured her that there certainly was a difference, even if she as an unread woman could not see it, and that in any case she should realize that slavery was a morally valid institution; the very scriptures instructed slaves to be loyal to their masters.

That was the sort of answer Gabriel was always giving. Consistently firm, never any doubt or wavering, delivered in a tone of condescension. It was just the way Peter Haverly talked, and Gabriel imitated it, just as he imitated almost everything about Haverly, from house to dress to gait. The most amazing thing about it to Darcy was that Gabriel obviously did not realize he was doing it or know that his idolizing mimicry of Haverly had earned him the nickname "Little Pete," played off Haverly's whispered nickname "Big Pete."

It was a shame, really. Darcy saw in Gabriel the potential to be a truly fine man, even a leader of the community. Sad she found it that he was so willingly overshadowed by the pompous Haverly, hampered from growing into the independent man he should be. Sadder still it was that Gabriel did not realize his situation.

Darcy approached the door of the smithy and heard voices inside. McSwain, in his full Scottish brogue, was asking a question. The voice that answered made Darcy's heart race. It was Joshua Colter's. She had not realized he was back in the settlement; the last word she had received was from her brother, who said Joshua had gone to Watauga to help Sheriff Valentine Sevier with some problem or other involving theft of livestock.

Darcy paused beside the smithy door, taking a deep breath and closing her eyes for a moment. Why did she feel so unsettled? Several months ago she had given up hope that Joshua Colter would return the affection she had for him—affection she had felt from that moment on the trace back in the winter when he had bested the man trying to take Will's horse. She had been hopeful that Joshua's initial interest in her would bloom, but bit by bit, that hope had faded. Gabriel had become more aggressive in his own clumsy attempts to impress and attract her, and as he had advanced, Joshua had retreated. It was dismaying . . . but perhaps understandable. Joshua was a fine-looking man, too fine-looking to settle for a woman with a damaged hand. The thought made Darcy draw up her stiff right hand and hug it against her body. She wondered so often why providence had chosen to deform her. Had she done something as a child to merit such disfavor? Had it not been for her bad hand, surely some man would have taken her for a wife by now, maybe even so fine a man as Joshua Colter.

She scolded herself. No point in such thoughts. The withered hand is there, and it's like Will says about both himself and me: "Too marred to be married." I should be grateful that Gabriel, a good, well-off man with a future before him, is interested in me. Joshua Colter is more than I can hope for, and I needn't let my heart flutter for one I can never have.

With that resolute thought, she stepped into the doorway of the smithy and walked inside the single smoky room. Joshua was indeed there, along with Alphus Colter and the Cherokee named John Hawk, who had been hunting with Joshua now since the spring and seemed alien and slightly frightening to Darcy.

The young woman fancied that Joshua's eyes widened as she entered, and despite her self-scolding of a moment before, her heart did flutter again. Without being aware of it, she drew up her right hand even closer in an unconscious attempt to hide it. Her left hand was wrapped around the stock of Will's rifle, the butt of which she rested on the hard-packed dirt floor.

"Good day, Miss Darcy." Alphus removed his straw

summer hat. Though the weather was cooling rapidly, he had not yet shifted to the felt hat he wore in winter.

At the moment, he was serving as blower and striker for McSwain, pumping the iron ring that hung from a rope tied to a crossbeam hung on swivel between two upright square-hewed posts. Another rope at the far end of the beam from Alphus attached to the bottom leaf of a six-foot-long bellows McSwain had built for himself from wood and oxhide. When Alphus pulled down on the ring, the other end of the crossbeam went up, drawing up the bottom bellows leaf and driving air down through its taper, through the tue iron on the end and into an opening in the stone forge. When Alphus let the ring go, the bottom leaf of the bellows would descend again, pulling in air through a hole in the top, covered on the underside with a leather valve flap that closed whenever the bellows did.

"Good day, Mr. Colter," she said. Then to Joshua: "And you too, Mr. Colter." To John Hawk, who looked back implacably at her, she gave only a brief tight-lipped smile.

"And how are all the Fiskes doing?" McSwain asked, smiling at her. She had no time to answer him, for suddenly he said, "Now, Alphus," and pivoted around, his long forge tongs in hand, and onto his anvil laid two white-hot flats of iron, side by side.

Alphus picked up a hammer he had set nearby and began pounding the flats until they welded together.

The ringing of his hammer made conversation impossible, so Darcy and the others quietly watched as the work went on. The fused pieces of metal went back into the fire for a reheating, then came out again for welding on the other side. After several minutes of intense sweat-inducing labor, some of which was hidden from Darcy by Alphus's intervening form, McSwain plunged the well-beaten metal into a bucket of cold water, generating a hissing rise of steam, and removed a fine axhead, which he examined with satisfaction.

"Aye, but you're soon to smith better than the smith himself, Alphus," McSwain said.

"By Joseph, I doubt that," Alphus replied.

McSwain spun toward Darcy. He was a man given to big movements and extreme expressions. "And you'll be forgiving me, I pray, for leaving you standing so long?"

" 'Twas a welcome chance to stand still, which I seldom get to do, Mr. McSwain," Darcy said. "I've come to bring you Will's rifle."

McSwain frowned. "No! Not out of fix again!"

"Aye, but it is. Will asked me to bring it by for you to work on again."

"Will's the worst I've ever seen to let a rifle get out of fix," Joshua said. "No offense to him or you, though, Darcy."

She smiled at him, noting again how handsome he was, and said, "Truth is truth, and there's no offense in it. Will's always hard on his guns."

McSwain came to her and took the rifle, examining it. He was a capable and important man at Haverly Fort, serving as blacksmith, gunsmith, farrier, occasional whitesmith, and puller of teeth. Few around the region had not used at least one of his services at one time or another.

"Aye . . . the lock again," he said. "I thought I had it fixed." He shook his head in disappointment, both in himself and the firearm. "I may have to make him a new one complete, or talk to Gabriel about having one shipped in. Hang it, I wish Will would let me make him a new rifle. I'd surely enjoy that."

"And Will would never find himself a finer rifle," Joshua said. He had hired McSwain to make him a rifle in the spring and had been vocal ever since about his pleasure with the results.

"I'll speak to him of it," Darcy said.

"Do, and in the meantime I'll see if there is aught to be done with this lock," McSwain said.

"Thank you," Darcy said. "Good day to you all." She turned and stepped out of the smithy into the brisk morning and began walking across the dirt yard.

"Darcy."

Recognizing Joshua's voice, she turned, a little too eagerly. He was coming after her.

"May I walk with you?"

"Aye, yes—you may, if you wish." Her face suddenly felt warm.

"Are you going home?"

"First to Gabriel's store, to fetch Will a bit of lead. He's let himself run out of rifle balls again, not that he could have used them with his rifle not working."

Joshua said, "Does Will have you do all his fetching and carrying for him?"

"It's his leg, hurting him bad this past week," she said, a little defensively. Will was sensitive about his lameness, and through sibling propinquity, she had begun reacting in the same way to any mention of it.

They turned toward Gabriel's store, which stood in sight of his house. Joshua waved toward the house. "Not a finer place this side of the mountains, except for Haverly's house. But it's too much for me. I like a small place. Easy to build, live in, and keep in good state."

"Aye. The same with me." She was wondering why Joshua had joined her and if there was to be a point to this seemingly idle talk.

"Gabriel has always liked his houses big," Joshua went on. "He had one almost as big back on Hankins Creek."

"I've heard that."

"Speaking of Gabriel," Joshua said at last, "just how is he these days?"

"Oh, I wouldn't know. I've not seen him." Darcy felt self-conscious to be talking of Gabriel, especially with Joshua. "I would think you would know more of him than I do."

"Me? No, no. Gabriel and I haven't had much to say to each other since first we laid eyes on each other. We've been getting on even worse since last week when he accused John Hawk of trying to steal a knife from his blasted store, then preached him a sermon about being a 'cursed heathen.' I would have taken off his head if Israel Coffman had not been there to cool me off. John Hawk took it awfully well, better than I would have."

"I'm sorry you have such trouble with your brother."

"He's not truly my brother, you know. I'm not Alphus's natural-born son."

"Yes, I knew that. Who is your true father?" She asked the question mostly just to perpetuate the conversation, but instantly wondered if it had been too personal a query. She had never heard Joshua mention any of his blood kin, if any such people lived, nor had she heard of him having discussed that matter with anyone else. Not even Gabriel had mentioned it in any of his strained and stiff conversations with her; whenever the subject of Joshua came up, he always quickly changed it.

Joshua didn't answer very quickly, and when he did, his voice was toneless. "It's enough to say my blood father is long gone from me. Maybe dead. As far as I'm concerned, it's Alphus who is my father. And don't worry about Gabriel and me. We're accustomed to disliking each other and have learned to live with it."

They reached the store, and to Darcy's relief, Gabriel was not inside. Tending the store was Jude Breadlow, Gabriel's only full-time employee, and Cooper Haverly, son of Peter. When he saw Joshua, Cooper darted across to greet him. He was all long arms, legs, and feet.

" 'Lo, Joshua—when will you take me hunting again?"

Joshua grinned and stuck out his hand for the boy to shake. "Whenever you want, Cooper. Just give word and we'll go."

"Today, then."

"Well, not today. On Friday, how's that?"

"That's good . . . if Mr. Breadlow will let me go."

"You ask him, then. Where's Gabe today?"

"Out with the packers, I think. He'll be back tomorrow, or perhaps tonight." With that, the boy scrambled over to Breadlow.

"I like that young fellow," Joshua said. "Liked him the first time I laid eyes on him. Must take after his mother, because he's sure not like Haverly in any way I can see."

"I've thought the same thing," Darcy commented.

Joshua accompanied her to the big hewn counter where from Breadlow she made her purchase, which Joshua carried for her.

Cooper approached again, his expression glum. "I can't go with you Friday. Mr. Breadlow says that Gabriel wants me to go with him to the packers that day."

The "packers" were employees of Gabriel and Haverly's newest business venture, a meat-packing operation for which Joshua himself had agreed to work as a hunter, on a part-time independent-contractor basis. In the summer and fall, the hunters would kill what deer they could and render tallow. In the winter, the duties would shift to curing venison and buffalo meat, which would be packed into casks for shipment back east and to New Orleans.

Gabriel and Haverly were not the first to sponsor such work in the Tennessee country. Back in 1768, a man named Joseph Hollingshead, working for Philadelphia's Baynton, Wharton, and Morgan trading house, had supervised two teams of hunters and packers along the Tennessee and Cumberland rivers, and from that enterprise Gabriel had developed his own idea and presented it to Haverly. Haverly had liked the plan so well that he had put Gabriel in charge of it and even listed his name on the business: Haverly and Colter Packers and Shippers. For several weeks now, Gabriel had spent much of his time away from the station, supervising construction of a storage house, barracks, and workyard near Lick Creek.

"Well, there will be another chance soon, Cooper," Joshua said. "Good day to all of you."

As Joshua and Darcy walked back toward the Fiske cabin a mile distant, he asked her, "Is your brother still as restless as ever?"

"He is," she replied. "I don't think he will be staying here long. Ever since the little bit of trouble when we came in, he's been unhappy with the area. He talks now of Kentucky."

"Kentucky? He plans to go there?"

"You know Will—he doesn't plan so much as just act. But yes, I think he will finally go if ever he gets the chance."

Joshua seemed concerned. "And will you go with him?"

"I suppose I will. He is my brother."

"Aye. I had thought, though, that maybe . . . other things might keep you here."

"I don't know what you mean."

In fact, she did. He was subtly sniffing the wind to see if a marriage between her and Gabriel was in it. The very idea of such a thing made her face redden. She hoped Joshua would pursue the issue no further. He did not.

They arrived at the cabin. Joshua and Will talked together, Will doing much of the talking, Joshua most of the listening, casting side-glances at Darcy all the while. The two old parents sat quietly in the corner of the cabin, saying nothing. The woman was whittling out a cedar cane; the old man was simply staring at the far wall, a thin line of rheum trailing from his nose across his whiskered upper lip.

After ten minutes, Joshua said his good-byes and left. Darcy watched his lean form as he strode away and held her withered hand close to her side until he was out of sight.

A week later, another Colter came calling on Darcy, but this time it was Gabriel. He asked her company on an evening walk, and she agreed to go, though without eagerness. Gabriel seemed nervous and would not look directly at her. He wore his finest clothes, including stockings, gaiters, and buckle shoes.

As Darcy expected, the walk took them mostly around the stockade and store. Gabriel seldom ventured far from the settled areas without the company of other men. Often, he kept Patton, his slave, with him, armed with a rifle and pistol. Gabriel seldom carried a rifle himself, though he did sometimes wear a brace of small silver-inlaid flintlock pistols—more for ornamentation than protection was Darcy's guess. He wore them tonight; she had seen the flash of them beneath his coat.

They walked slowly, Gabriel's old limp barely noticeable. In the past year, his old injury either had ceased plaguing him as badly as before or he had learned to compensate for it expertly. Darcy sardonically wondered if he had overcome it because of his driving desire to be like Peter Haverly, who had no limp.

Gabriel began talking as soon as they had left the cabin. As usual, the subject was business, and it was difficult for Darcy to feign interest though she tried. The evening was cool, and she shivered. Gabriel noticed, commented on it, and moved closer to her, slipping his arm stiffly around her waist. It was the first time he had ever made even the subtlest physical advance toward her. At his touch she became taut and tense, then relaxed slightly, for his closeness did at least warm her.

The early-evening sky was beautiful, lit with a score of brilliant surreal colors. Darcy kept her eyes on the horizon, unwilling to look at Gabriel.

Over at McSwain's smithy, a handful of Cherokees were gathered. A hunting party, most likely, come for repairs to their weapons. Gabriel looked toward them and shook his head. "It's a shame that civilized people must deal with such heathens," he commented. "It is my view that our creator intended this land for civilized men, not savages."

Darcy said nothing. She had a great fear of Indians herself but no strong opinions on civilization and savagery or any desire to prompt Gabriel into one of his Haverlyesque sermons.

"The Indians will someday give way—of that I have no doubt," he went on. "And when that day comes, this will be a fine country for a man to live in and raise a family."

She tensed again, fearing that Gabriel's talk was about to move into uncomfortable territory.

He coughed, cleared his throat, and continued. "A good man, fearing God and well settled in commerce, with a fine woman by his side, is a fine thing, don't you think?"

"Yes."

He withdrew his arm from her waist long enough to fetch out a silver snuffbox and draw from it a pinch of powdered tobacco that vanished up each nostril. He blinked in satisfaction, sniffed loudly, sneezed, pocketed the snuffbox, and replaced his arm around Darcy's waist, pulling her a little closer this time.

They continued on, past the smithy to a dirt lane leading into the hills. A man seated on a woodpile beside his nearby farmstead cabin, smoking his pipe and watching two ragged children play with sticks as long Kentucky rifles, waved at them, and Gabriel waved back.

"Darcy," he said, "there is something of importance I wish to discuss with you."

"Oh?" A cool dread crept over her.

"Yes . . . but let's go a little farther. I wish to discuss something with assurance of full privacy."

They kept walking, rounding a curve in the road that put them out of sight of the main part of the settlement. A quarter mile ahead stood another farmstead cabin, but trees obscured it. Gabriel stopped, turned, and faced her. His face looked blanched in the fading evening light, and his eyes were wide. Darcy realized with surprise that he was actually fearful.

"Darcy, I'm a good man—you know that. There are things I have done in my past that have been foolish, perhaps, even wrong—but I am a good man, a civilized man, a religious man. You know that, don't you?"

Darcy did not know what to say.

He seemed dismayed at her silence but went on. "I'm a score and six years old now, Darcy, and as of yet I have never known a woman." He faltered, embarrassed by the connotation of his clumsily chosen words. "What I mean is, I have never had the pleasure . . . of . . . of marriage, of having a partner . . ."

Her eyes were big and bright with apprehension. He saw it and faltered again, turning away.

"Blast it all!" he muttered to himself. Facing her again, he said, "I'm sorry, Darcy—this is difficult for me. Always before, I have centered my life on commerce, lost myself in work, and never had intimacy with women. I do many things well, but not this." He closed his eyes for a moment and swallowed deeply. "What I am trying to say to you, Darcy, is that I admire you. I know my attempts to show it have been feeble and unsure, but I do know my own heart. I have heard rumors that your brother is talking of leaving this place, and it despairs me. I cannot bear to think of you being gone from here. I want you to stay."

Darcy's breath was coming hard; she was shivering again. "I don't understand what you are asking."

Gabriel ran one hand through his hair and fidgeted, scuffing his buckle shoes in the dirt. "I'm asking you to be my wife," he said, then let out a deep, long sigh. "Thank God I've gotten it said. I didn't know if I would have the courage."

Darcy could find nothing to say. A mad impulse to turn and run overwhelmed her, but she did not obey it.

At that moment, something moved at the far end of the road. They turned to see a man approaching on foot, leading a Chickasaw horse that had a noticeably uneven gait. The light was fading, rendering the approaching figure hard to see.

At first, Darcy was glad he was coming, for it gave her reason not to answer Gabriel at once, but as he drew nearer, she began to feel agitated, perhaps by something about the newcomer, her situation, or a combination of both. Gabriel apparently felt some apprehension as well, for she noticed that he pulled back his coat to expose the brace of pistols thrust into his belt and stepped up a little to put himself somewhat between Darcy and the oncoming man.

He was a big fellow, bearded, with a bearskin coat and coonskin hat. He came to within twenty feet of them and stopped. A battered Pennsylvania rifle was gripped in his left hand, swinging horizontally at thigh level. Now that he was close, Darcy felt absolutely frightened, perceiving something familiar about the newcomer.

"Good evening to you both," the man said.

"Good evening, sir," Gabriel answered.

"My horse is in need of a farrier. Is there one here?"

"Just go around the bend. There is a man named McSwain with a smithy near the fort who can help you."

"Thank you, sir, you're most kind," the man said. But he did not go on. He simply stood, looking back and forth from Gabriel to Darcy, a smile on his face. Darcy's nervousness increased, and she stepped closer to Gabriel.

"Fine pistols there," the man said to Gabriel. "I'd like to buy them from you."

"Thank you, but I'm not seeking to sell them," Gabriel answered.

"Why, there's a price for anything," the man answered. "And you needn't worry about me—I'll pay you as soon as I've got money in hand."

At that moment, Darcy knew him. This was the same man who had stopped them on the trace at the first of the year, trying to take Will's horse. "Gabriel," Darcy whispered. "Be careful of this man."

"What's that you're saying?" the man said to her, his smile flickering out.

"Nothing, sir," Gabriel said. "The pistols are not for sale. If you want to find McSwain in, you should hurry, or he'll be closing his doors."

"I want them pistols," the man said.

Gabriel glanced at Darcy. He looked afraid. "I told you, sir, the pistols are not for sale. Now be on with you, or I will be obliged to draw them."

The man's face was cold as chiseled stone. "Is this the way the folk of Haverly Fort welcome a weary pilgrim?" He lifted the rifle and leveled it at Gabriel, who stepped sideways to hide Darcy behind him fully.

"Go away, Darcy," Gabriel said. "Get back to the stockade."

She backed away, started to turn.

The man commanded, "Stay where you are, you sow."

Gabriel drew one of his pistols and leveled it. "How dare you threaten and speak so to this lady?" he bellowed, anger beginning to equal fear.

"Your bleeding mouth galls me, sod," the man said, clicking back his rifle lock.

Gabriel should have fired at once. Instead, he thrust the pistol out straight in front of him and shouted a warning. "I'll kill you, sir!" he shouted.

The man was not so gentlemanly. He fired with no warning. Gabriel doubled over, grunting. He dropped his pistol, held his bent-over pose for a moment, then collapsed. Darcy screamed.

The man with the rifle, upper lip curled into a snarl, glared at her. "He was about to shoot me down! You heard his threat!" He advanced toward the dropped pistol.

Darcy dived for the pistol and got it. She held it up in both hands, pointing it shakily at the oncoming man.

"Give me that pistol, strumpet!" he demanded, reaching out his hand.

Darcy tried to pull the trigger but could not. She was momentarily frozen. The man was upon her in a moment, swinging up his rifle and striking her hard on the side of the head. She fell, landing atop Gabriel and retaining the pistol.

"You give me that pistol!" her attacker roared, raising the butt of his rifle above her head.

From somewhere within, courage and defiance arose. "Take it, then, butcher—the ball first!" she shouted.

She pulled the trigger as the rifle butt descended toward her face. The roar of the shot came simultaneously with the contact of the curved metal butt with her forehead. The sensation was explosively painful, then instantly numbing, and after a moment of hovering in a twilight state of half-consciousness, she slid back into darkness that engulfed her as if she were a stone sinking into deep water.

17

Alphus heard a tumult at the stockade gate and turned, his face set in a grim expression. Joshua was striding through the gate in a cloud of fury that was almost visible. He stopped a moment, looked around until he spotted the cluster of men around the door of one of the largest stockade cabins, and stomped toward them. It was dark, but a large bonfire in the center of the stockade yard sent up huge tongues of flame that writhed and sparked in the wind and with a few torches weakly illuminated the fort's interior. There were many people milling about, the women keeping together, the children running and scampering with at least a dozen hounds at their feet, excited by the tension.

Alphus intervened in Joshua's path, cutting him off with a grip on his shoulder. The younger man jerked to a stop and glared at his foster father.

"Joshua, calm yourself before you go in there," Alphus warned. "Keep your head about you."

Joshua angrily shrugged him off. "Leave me be—it's me who's the under sheriff here."

"That's right—it's you who's under sheriff, and you

mustn't forget it. This is law, not vengeance. Besides, the man's half dead already. He won't live until morning."

"Aye, then there's some justice—though it would suit me far more to see him hang than die on his bed."

"As I said, Joshua, keep your head about you. The people here, they'll be watching to see what you do. You hold an official position and must think of law, not vengeance."

Joshua sidestepped Alphus and continued to the cabin. The crowd of men parted just enough to let him pass, then closed in again. Alphus pivoted and walked out of the stockade, heading for Gabriel's house where Gabriel lay unconscious, a ragged rifle-ball hole in his abdomen, the shadow of death hovering above him, threatening to descend. In another room of the same house, Darcy Fiske also lay, unmoving, her head badly bruised and her skull possibly fractured.

Inside the candle-illuminated cabin he had just entered, Joshua found three men, two of them armed, standing by a cot on which lay a bloodied bearded man. It took Joshua only a moment to recognize him as the man he had bested on behalf of the Fiskes the day he and that family arrived at Haverly Fort. Beside the man's cot knelt Israel Coffman, Bible in hand, and when Joshua entered, the preacher looked up, shook his head, and stood as Joshua leaned his rifle against a wall beside a rifle that was already there.

"Thoroughly unrepentant," he said to Joshua as he stepped toward the door. Pausing as he stooped to duck out the low doorway, he said, "Be careful that you keep control of your fury, Joshua."

Joshua wheeled and faced him, and burst out, "For God's sake, will not everyone leave the doing of my job to me? I'm not a child to be directed!"

Coffman looked at him without expression, turned, and left the cabin. The cluster of men that peered in through the open door parted as before to let him exit, then crowded in again. Joshua slammed the door closed, cutting them off, then went to the cot and looked into the pallid face of the man on it.

"You're going to die—you know that?"

The man grunted, perhaps in response, perhaps in pain.

"What's your name?" Joshua asked.

The man's eyes fluttered shut. "Bugger off, turd," he said tightly.

Joshua struck him in the jaw, making the man's body spasm. The man screamed. The two guards looked at each other uncomfortably and shifted their feet.

"I could find no greater pleasure than pounding your skull like you pounded that of a fine young woman who may or may not survive it or putting a ball into your gut like you did to my own brother. But that would end your life too quickly. Best that you should suffer it out."

The man's breathing became deeper but more difficult. Air wheezed in and out of his mouth.

"Damn you, talk to me!" Joshua bellowed, striking him again.

"I say, now—you'll kill him that way!" one of the guards said.

"Then I'll kill him!" Joshua roared back. "You think he doesn't deserve to die?"

"Of course he does. And he will, soon enough. There's no reason for you to be the one guilty of causing it."

Joshua knew that his anger was dangerously out of control, and with a great forcing of his will, he pushed himself back from the cot and went to the corner of the cabin, letting himself cool down.

"How is Little Pete? . . . pardon me, Joshua. How is Gabriel?" the other guard asked.

"I fear he will die," Joshua said. "Sina is with him, and McSwain has dug out the bullet, but Gabriel is in a bad state."

"And the Fiske girl?"

"Still the same. At least this swine didn't shoot her, too."

"Aye—instead, she shot him," the guard said. "For that, she's earned a star in her crown, in my reckoning."

Joshua went back to the bedside and stared down at the man, who was now almost unconscious. "If you feel no need to mention that I struck him, I would appreciate your silence," he said to the guards.

"We saw nothing," the first one said.

Joshua rubbed the back of his stiff neck. "There's little call for me to be here, I suppose. I just had to look into his face, that's all, and let him know what I think of him. It's clear he's not long for this world, and for that I'm glad. You let me know when he dies."

"We will. Oh—yonder against the wall is his rifle and such, beside yours. You being under sheriff, we figured it should be you who take them."

"Aye, I will." Joshua rolled his shoulders. His head ached terribly. "I'll be back later to see how matters stand." He walked over and picked up the battered rifle and slung the pouches and horn across his shoulder. He hefted his own rifle in his other hand. "I'll put his rifle in my lodgings, then return over to Gabriel's house. You can find me there if you need me."

The man on the cot moaned again and shuddered, and then he was fully unconscious.

"Won't be long now," Joshua said. He opened the door, pushed his way out through the crowd that still lingered there, and walked out of the stockade into the darkness.

Peter Haverly was in the main room of Gabriel's house when Joshua entered. In the yard, a crowd milled, talking over the tragedy, which had stirred the settlement more than any other event in its short history. Haverly offered a pipeful of tobacco, and Joshua laid his rifle across the mantle and accepted.

"How do they fare?" Joshua asked.

"No differently," Haverly replied, his usually booming voice subdued. "Ah, what a terrible thing! And what of the man who did this?"

"He'll not live long."

"If I had my way, he'd be swinging from a limb, shot or not," Haverly said. "He's as good as a murderer, and may yet be one if Gabriel dies."

The two men sat down on stools near the fireplace. Joshua's pipe was a short one, belonging to Gabriel, with a clay bowl and reed stem. Haverly smoked a churchwarden pipe, as pretentious as his personality, with a clay stem that once was a full sixteen inches long but now was down to about twelve. Haverly had broken off the end of the stem several times when it became clogged and toothmarked, as churchwardens were prone to do.

Patton entered the room from Gabriel's chamber, and both Haverly and Joshua stood. "Has he died?" Joshua asked.

"No sir, no, he hasn't," Patton replied. "He's moaning terrible, sir, terrible."

"Moaning is better than lying quiet," Haverly said. "It at least shows there's life in him, fighting to remain."

"What about Darcy?" Joshua asked.

"I don't know, sir. Her I ain't seen for a time, but I'll go look now, sir." Patton went once more into the back rooms. Haverly sat down again. Joshua continued to stand, pacing about.

"Good Negro, that Patton," Haverly said. "He's been much help to Gabriel, but I di miss having him about my own household." He held out his pipe, which had just smoldered out, and frowned at it. "Curse this sotweed— it might as well be a lump of mud, the way it holds fire." Haverly used the smoking tongs Gabriel kept on his hearth to pick up an ember and refire the clay bowl. He puffed quickly, making the tobacco glow red again.

"It's a shame that Mrs. Haverly isn't yet here," Haverly said, resettling his ample body on the stool, which hardly looked adequate to hold him. "She's good with poultices and herbs, and likely could be much help."

"When will she join us?"

"Soon, I hope, Under Sheriff Colter." Haverly had begun calling Joshua by his title right after formation of the Watauga Association. Joshua always detected an undercurrent of derision in Haverly's way of saying it. "She has illness—a foulness of the lungs and pain of the backbone. My last report was that she is much improved. Sometime this summer, or fall at the latest, I will return to North Carolina and fetch her here."

Conversation died at that point, for Joshua could not

sustain interest in any matter other than the welfare of Darcy and Gabriel. He paced about, letting his pipe grow cold.

"I wonder what happened?" he muttered aloud, mostly to himself.

"Eh? What was that?" Haverly asked.

"I was just wondering exactly what happened out there on the road—how the shooting came about, and why Gabriel would have been there alone with Darcy."

Haverly arched one brow. "You aren't implying some impropriety, I hope? Gabriel is a fine, moral man, not one to—"

"I'm saying nothing like that. Just wondering."

"Um. I understand." Haverly took a few more puffs, his plump legs crossed womanishly, his elbow on his knee.

"I might know why they were there," he said at last. "Or at the least be able to take a good guess."

"What do you mean?"

Haverly knocked ashes from the pipe onto the hearth. "I know your relationship with your foster brother is not close, Under Sheriff Colter, but he and I have a close relationship indeed. Almost like father and son. He confides in me often about his plans and hopes. Recently he let me know he was thinking of taking a wife."

"A wife?" It took Joshua a moment to piece together the implication. "Darcy? Gabriel wanted to marry Darcy?"

"He never told me the identity of the young lady upon whom his eye was cast. It is my surmise that it was the unfortunate Miss Fiske. Certainly that is no difficult guess, for the two of them have kept company, to some degree, for a long time now."

Joshua was experiencing some peculiar feelings to hear all of that. What Haverly said was uncomfortably plausible. Gabriel and Darcy, out on a road alone— perhaps they had in fact been discussing marriage. The thought of it carried a great sting.

"I'm going back to see them," Joshua announced, walking to the mantle and placing the pipe on it.

Sina was on a stool at Gabriel's side, leaning across

and holding the wounded young man's limp hand. Alphus, sitting in the corner silently watching the bed, turned a somber face to Joshua as he came in the room. Joshua looked into the white countenance of his foster brother and saw death in it. Gabriel's eyes looked sunken into his skull, and he breathed too slowly, too brokenly.

Placing his hand on Sina's shoulder, Joshua watched Gabriel, feeling surer as he did so that he would not live. Try as he would, he could not keep back the accompanying thought that tragic though Gabriel's death would be, and devastating to Alphus, it at least would eliminate his competition for Darcy's affection—affection that Joshua now wanted at any price.

The thought was terrible, unforgivable. Joshua wondered what sort of man he could be even to think it. He patted Sina's shoulder and walked out of the room, having said not a word.

He went then to the bedroom where Darcy had been placed. Alphus had suggested that she be brought here so that both victims could be watched and tended conveniently. Joshua found Coffman and Patton in Darcy's room, along with Callum McSwain's wife, Jean, who was swabbing Darcy's head with rags that Patton was dampening in a bowl of water and wringing out.

"I'm sorry I ain't come out to tell you about Miss Darcy, Mister Colter," Patton said. "I was put to helping here."

"Fine, Patton. I'd rather see her with my own eyes in any case. How fares she, Israel?"

"I think she will be well, with much rest. She opened her eyes a moment ago, but whether she perceived us I could not say. Be praying for her, Joshua, praying hard, and for Gabriel as well."

"Aye. I fear badly for his life."

There was a sudden ruckus in the front room—the door pounding open, a man talking, Haverly answering. A moment later, Haverly came into the room.

"Under Sheriff Colter, there is a need for you at the stockade," he said.

"What's wrong?"

"Will Fiske—he's down there, trying to get into the

room with the man who did this. Says he's going to kill him with his own hands."

"Oh, my—Will left here some time ago, saying he wanted to walk and clear his mind," Coffman said. "I should have known he would try something like this."

"I'd best be swift from the sound of it," Joshua said. "Though if Will succeeds in killing the devil, 'twould be no more than justice."

The first light of dawn had cast a pale-milk glow across the eastern horizon. Joshua walked slowly, wearily down the dirt pathway that led to his hut. Back in Gabriel's house, matters stood as before, neither Gabriel nor Darcy having changed their status, except for Darcy's having fluttered her eyes open a few more times. Lifting his eyes, Joshua watched the daily display that usually enthralled him: light spilling out of the sky behind the trees atop the ridgeline, so that every distant trunk was clearly delineated and outlined by the backglow. Today Joshua was too weary and worried to notice the beauty of it. Birds heralded the breaking day all around him, but he did not hear them.

He was surprised to find John Hawk, seated cross-legged beside his doorway, apparently waiting for him. The Cherokee had a rifle across his lap and pouches and a powder horn lying on the ground beside him.

Joshua strode up to him and stopped. "You look like you're waiting to shoot someone."

The dark eyes that looked back at him were surprisingly cold. "Is there someone here who deserves to be shot?"

Joshua was too weary for banter, so he ignored the cryptic question, going on past John Hawk and into his cabin.

The Cherokee rose and followed Joshua in. Joshua moved about the cabin, splashing his face with water from a bucket in the corner, drying it on a rag towel. When he was done, he noticed John Hawk's steady stare. In it was no softness or joviality.

"Something eating at you?" Joshua asked gruffly.

"There was trouble, I was told."

"Yes. Who told you?"

"Men from the stockade, passing by as I returned from hunting." John Hawk had been alone in the forest, miles away, when the actual incident had happend. Joshua surmised from his comment that he must have returned sometime in the previous night while the commotion after the shooting was still extensive.

"Will they live?" John Hawk asked.

"Darcy will, thank God. Gabriel . . . I'm not sure. But maybe there's a chance—I thought he would have died by now, but he was alive when I left him. Now I must sleep, or I'll fall where I stand. It's been a hard night. Me and several others had all we could do to keep Darcy's brother away from the prisoner, he wanted so bad to kill him." He peeled off his hunting shirt and hung it on a wall peg.

John Hawk continued to stare at him silently until Joshua became too irritated to stand more of it. "Why are you gawking at me like that?" he asked.

John Hawk's voice was as cold as his eyes. "The coin about my neck—tell me once more how you came to have it again, after I gave it to Awahili."

Joshua became instantly wary, wondering if John Hawk had found some reason to doubt his story about having found the coin by chance. "Why do you ask that? I already told you how I found it."

"You gave me a story. Whether it was the truth—I do not know."

"You're saying I lied to you?"

"It does not matter what I say. There are other things that speak against you."

Joshua pondered the obscure words but could not fathom the meaning. "I'm too weary for this, and have too much weighing on my mind, John Hawk. If we have aught to chew over together, let us wait until I'm rested up and game enough to take a bite."

"I will not wait." John Hawk, who still held the rifle that had been across his lap, now lifted it. "This rifle is yours?"

"No. It belonged to the man who shot Gabriel. It was handed to me last night for safekeeping, since I am the under sheriff. I brought it back here and left it because I didn't want to tote around two rifles all night."

John Hawk heard the answer, but whether he accepted it his unsmiling face would not reveal. "And this powder horn—his as well, or yours?"

Joshua cast up his eyes. "John Hawk, sometimes you're more fretful than a woman. Why are you asking these things? Do you want to have that rifle and horn? If you do, you're welcome to them. I don't want them about my place, and the man they belong to departed this life about two hours ago."

John Hawk said, "The powder horn was not yours, then?"

"That's right."

The Cherokee paused. "I believe you are lying to me, as you have lied before."

Now Joshua was becoming wary indeed of John Hawk's remarks. "I'll thank you to watch what you say to me, John Hawk."

"Why? Are you afraid you will become so angry with me that you will murder me, like you murdered Awahili?"

"Murdered Awahili? I don't know what you mean. Why do you so accuse me?"

John Hawk's answer was to thrust the powder horn into Joshua's hands. He looked at it, confused, then turned it to its other side. What he saw made Joshua's mind flash back to a tavern in Salisbury and Henry Dorey, dying on the floor, his brag about the murder of Awahili, Bloody Eagle of Tikwalitsi, scarcely past his lips. This was the powder horn that Dorey had carried, and on it still was the gruesome little patch of human skin, the patch bearing the devil mark of Bloody Eagle.

"My God," Joshua whispered. "The very powder horn . . ."

"Do you see why I call you a liar and accuse you of killing Awahili?" John Hawk said. "You have not only the coin that Awahili last wore but also a horn bearing his mark. Or will you tell me you found this powder horn by a river, as you say you found the coin?"

Joshua sat down heavily on the edge of his cot, put his hands on his knees, and his head in his hands, wondering how it could be that in one little cluster of hours so much could go so horrifically askew. He looked up again at John Hawk. "You are my friend, John Hawk. And as your friend, I swear to you I did not kill Bloody Eagle. The powder horn was in the possession of the man who shot Gabriel, and I never looked closely at it until this moment."

John Hawk mulled Joshua's words and studied his face. Joshua did not let his gaze falter; to do so would be to assure disbelief in John Hawk.

"And the coin . . . how is it you have it? I want to hear the truth, not another falsehood."

The next moments were ones of rapid thought for Joshua. He could try to perpetuate his lie, possibly—but he no longer wanted to. His deception had weighed heavily on him for months. John Hawk had a right to know the truth of what had happened to Bloody Eagle, the kinsman who had raised him.

"Very well, John Hawk. I will tell you the truth. I confess—I have lied about it to you up until now."

John Hawk said nothing. One side of his lip moved spasmodically, a tiny twitch, his only reaction to Joshua's confession.

Joshua went on. "The man who killed Bloody Eagle was the trader Henry Dorey from Tikwalitsi. I know this because in a tavern in Salisbury, North Carolina, I heard Dorey himself boast of killing Bloody Eagle and saw him try to sell this powder horn and the coin to another man. He said he took the coin and powder horn from Bloody Eagle's body with his own hands."

John Hawk's rage showed in his dark eyes. "I will find Henry Dorey and kill him, or one of his kinsmen," he said.

"Henry Dorey is dead. He was stabbed to death by the man he tried to sell the horn to. I took the coin with me when I left that place. The horn I left behind, and another man took it. It has probably been traded many times since, until it came into the possession of the man who attacked Gabriel and Darcy. There are those who trade in such things. To such men the browmark of Bloody Eagle, the mighty warrior, is a great prize."

"If this is the truth, why did you not speak it to me in Chota, when I first asked you?"

"My companions and I had come on a mission of friendship. We sought the favor of your people, not their anger. I feared that if I told you Bloody Eagle had been murdered by a white man, the Cherokees would not help us and might bring danger to my friends and my people."

"So you lied to me."

"Yes. I lied. But I do not lie now. I did not kill Bloody Eagle. Of that I give my vow."

"The vow of a man who lies. Why should I believe it?"

Joshua had no answer to that.

"You had cause to want to kill Bloody Eagle, did you not, Joshua Colter? Did he not hang the scalp of your father, Byrum, outside his house?"

"He did. And there was a time I did want to kill Bloody Eagle. The day I first gave you the coin, I had come to the house where you lay to take vengeance upon the killer of my father. For a few moments I was ready to kill you in his stead, but it seemed wrong to me, and I didn't do it. That, John Hawk, is the truth, with no clouds hiding it."

The Cherokee reached down, took the powder horn from Joshua's hand, and slung it over his shoulder. From the scarred rifle of Darcy's assailant he loosened and removed the flint, then smashed the rifle against the wall, cracking the stock. He tossed the ruined weapon aside, then walked to the doorway. Joshua watched him.

At the door, John Hawk stopped and turned. "You have been a good host to me for a long time now, Joshua Colter. You have given me friendship and food, and shared my hunts. You have taught me much of the ways of the white men who so want to take our land from us. You have taught me even more of those ways today and shown me that you, like most of your kind, are deceitful and cunning.

"Yet I believe you when you say you did not kill Awahili. Your words have the sound of truth. I will not seek revenge upon you, Joshua Colter. But I will consider whether I will take other lives in vengeance for the life of Awahili."

Joshua, tight with tensions lingering from the night and fresh ones from John Hawk's accusations of the morning, had to respond. "So you will consider killing some white man, or maybe even a woman or a child, in revenge for a thing which they did not do? Is that your way? If it is, then you have no right to scorn me, or my people, for your ways are as foul as any could be, the ways of fools."

John Hawk's eyes flashed. "And are the white men's ways different than ours? I have seen white soldiers destroy the lower towns of the Cherokees in vengeance for what was done by men of the upper towns. I have seen fields of corn burned, and houses destroyed, and women and children of my people driven into the hills in revenge for what they had no hand in. I have seen white men who look on all Indians as the same, seeing no differences, hating them all. I have seen white men wash themselves with sacred water and ask the Great Man Above to cleanse them from their own evil, and then on the next day lie or kill or break their word to my people with no sorrow or sense of wrong. I have read the sacred book of the white men and know its words are good, but I also know the white men do not live by them. They forget the teachings of the book when it is to their advantage and remember them only when they seek to make the Indians into men like they are so that they may more easily control them. But the Indians will not be controlled. They will not listen to the words of white men as long as the white men do not do the things they themselves declare are good."

Joshua did not try to respond to John Hawk's angry oratory. The Cherokee and the long hunter exchanged stares for several seconds. Then John Hawk took the

Roman coin from around his neck. He held it out to Joshua, but Joshua would not accept it. At last, John Hawk let it drop to the dirt floor. He then reached into a deerskin pouch that hung across his shoulder and withdrew the Bible portion that he had carried so long, and this he dropped on the floor as well, beside the coin.

The silence held for several more moments. Then John Hawk said, in the customary Cherokee fashion of ending a visit, "I go."

Joshua knew the custom as well as John Hawk did, and answered accordingly: "You do."

John Hawk turned and walked out of the hut to his own lean-to. It took him only a few moments to gather his few possessions. Joshua watched him carry them to his horse, which grazed a small pasture he and John Hawk had fenced off. Within two minutes, the Cherokee was riding away, not waving, not looking back.

Joshua watched him from the doorway of the hut until he was out of sight, then swept his gaze back up the road to Haverly Fort. Gabriel wounded, perhaps fatally; Darcy beaten; now John Hawk estranged and gone. Life sometimes handed out too many blows to bear.

Weary and sad, Joshua headed for his cot. He stopped long enough to pick up the Roman coin and the Bible fragment. He sat down on the edge of his cot. The Bible he placed on the table, but the coin he held and examined until he dozed where he sat and almost pitched sideways onto the floor. He slipped the thong around his neck and fell asleep, the coin cool against his bare chest.

Joshua was awakened in the early afternoon by Alphus, who had slept only a little that morning himself.

"Alphus, is he—"

"No. They're alive, both of them. And Darcy came awake, though she said little and went to sleep almost right off."

"Thank God."

"Aye, and throw in thanks that Gabriel looks a little better. Nothing much—just not so sunken around the eyes." Alphus gave Joshua an examining look. "You look the worse for last night, Joshua." He noticed the coin and pointed at it. "What's this? I thought you gave that to John Hawk."

"I did. He gave it back."

"Why?"

"It's a long story, one I'm not inclined to tell. You might say we had a disagreement."

"So he's gone?"

"Aye."

"I'll miss him, then. I grew quite fond of that Indian, just like I did Little Carpenter."

Joshua stood and stretched. "I'm hungry, hungry enough to eat my own left leg. You have aught to eat in your cabin?"

"Some salt pork and pone, and cold milk in the springhouse."

"I'll relieve you of some of that if I may, and then I want to see Darcy." He took his hunting shirt from its peg and slipped it on. "Alphus, Haverly speculated upon something last night. He said that Gabriel was thinking of asking Darcy to marry him. He believes that's why he might have had Darcy out on the road like that."

Alphus raised his brows. "If so, that might explain it."

"Explain what?"

"What Darcy said when she last awakened. She and Sina talked, just a little, and the poor girl had trouble making herself understood, but one thing she did say: Tell Gabriel, she said, that her answer to him was yes."

Joshua gazed at his feet a few silent moments. "Come on," he said. "I'm ready for my victuals."

They walked together toward Alphus's cabin.

18

Darcy Fiske walked slowly along the woodland trail, enjoying the splendor of the blossoming dogwoods—or attempting to enjoy them, for her nervous stomach made it difficult to appreciate even the beauty of spring. In three days, she would become Darcy Colter, wife of Gabriel, well-off merchant, landholder, businessman, churchman, community leader, and survivor of an injury that few had believed he could recover from. That recovery had been slow and plagued by occasional setbacks and complications—difficult for Gabriel but helpful for Darcy, for it had given her sufficient time to become accustomed to the proposition she had accepted—becoming Gabriel Colter's wife.

She had consented to his violently interrupted marriage proposal even while he lay nearly dead and for weeks thereafter had wondered if her assent had been given only because she secretly doubted he would live to make her his wife. Others had apparently developed similar thoughts, but with a nastier twist. Her brother Will had gotten himself into trouble by trouncing a man who suggested, with a tongue made too free by rum, that her motivation was to become Gabriel's spouse before he passed on, putting his lands and business holdings into her hands when he died. Darcy was outraged, as was Gabriel, when he grew well enough to be aware of such talk. It was in part to squelch the notion that Gabriel was to be a deathbed groom that he had agreed to postpone the wedding until spring when he would be fully well again and there could be no questioning Darcy's sincerity.

Darcy's consent to marry Gabriel had surprised many people, not least Darcy herself. Her agreement had arisen spontaneously in the emotional aftermath of the attack and now felt as if it had been given by another. Will was supportive of her decision simply because it was hers, though he told her frankly he felt Joshua Colter was a far better man than Gabriel could hope to be. She should have caught him, not Gabriel, in her snare, Will said.

"I've not tried to snare anyone," Darcy replied. "Joshua has never asked me to marry him, Gabriel has. Joshua did not nearly die from a wound received in my protection; Gabriel did. Perhaps I gave my consent overly quick, but give it I did, and there will be no going back on my word."

Will said nothing more about Joshua after that, and she was glad of it, but it made little difference. Forgetting about Joshua was impossible. Only three days remained before he was a hope forever severed, irrevocably cut off from her by the sanctity of marriage to another.

That thought scared her, but there could be no backing away from her engagement now . . . could there? Was it right to marry a man she did not love? Darcy had considered seeking the counsel of Israel Coffman on that question but had never done it. Darcy was shy, not prone to lay her feelings in the open, even before such a wise and understanding man as the Reverend Israel Coffman.

Besides, the preacher had been dealing with enough troubles of his own lately. It had been common knowledge all the past winter that a deep rift had developed between him and Peter Haverly. Gabriel had talked about it some, naturally taking Haverly's side. Coffman, he said, was not being faithful to the sort of teaching Haverly had

recruited him to propagate. The slavery dispute was deep
and bitter between the two men, and there were theological differences as well, centering mostly on Haverly's
insistence that the Indians deserved no morally based
considerations and were not the concern of the church.
Haverly had been developing and honing a thesis that the
Indians were descendants of apostate Jews, and through
a convoluted exposition of supposed history that Gabriel
claimed to understand but Darcy could not, Haverly
concluded that they were under Ham's curse and forever
beyond hope of salvation.

The talk was that Coffman strongly disagreed with
Haverly, his position as preacher and teacher at Haverly
Fort was endangered, and he was certain to leave soon.
Darcy did not welcome the prospect of his departure, for
she admired Coffman much for his willingness to stand
against Haverly. When he was gone, Haverly's hold on
the community would certainly increase, and in Coffman's place he would bring in someone who would parrot
his ideas unquestioningly from the pulpit. Some weaker-
souled man . . . like Gabriel.

Darcy decided that this walk in the woods, undertaken
to calm her and improve her outlook, was not working.
Turning, she walked back down the path until she
reached the edge of the forest. There she stopped, putting a hand on a sapling to steady herself, for she had
made the turn too quickly and it had dizzied her and
brought a sting of pain across her forehead, as sudden
movements often did since the attack last fall. Her cabin
was below; her father sat outside it, his head cocked as
he looked crookedly, mindlessly, at the clouds. Her elderly mother was churning butter. Will was hard at work
shaving a stool leg on the springboard lathe he had set
up beneath an oak tree behind the cabin. With him was
another man—and Darcy's heart skipped when she saw
it was Joshua.

A bolt of concern shot through her. Joshua had been
talking to Will quite often lately, and she knew enough
of Will's current obsession to guess what their subject
must be. Will had it in mind to take their aged parents

and resettle, maybe to Watauga, maybe much farther away. He had never taken much to Haverly Fort; the attack on her and Gabriel had just made it worse. If Joshua was talking often to Will, surely he must be thinking of leaving Haverly Fort as well. That was no happy prospect. The idea of Haverly Fort without her family and without Joshua brought waves of anticipatory loneliness.

She planned to wait until Joshua was gone before coming back into the yard, but her mother spotted her and called to her. Joshua turned and watched Darcy come down toward the cabin, and waved. She gave him a quick smile in return, then went to her mother.

"My arm's done-in for churning," the old woman said. "Could you spell me awhile?"

Darcy took over the job, moving the smooth handle up and down in the thickening cream, the dasher kneading and stirring it continually. Out of the corner of her eye she watched Joshua and Will talking until Well left his lathe behind and Joshua turned. The two men came down together toward her.

"Hello, Darcy," Joshua said.

"Hello."

"Are you afrighted by your big day?"

Darcy did not enjoy hearing Joshua refer to the wedding. "My stomach jumps some when I think of it, but I'll come through it," she said.

"All women feel that way before their weddings, I hear," Joshua replied. "I wish you well, both you and Gabe."

"Thank you, Joshua."

When Joshua was gone, Darcy turned to Will. "What have you men been talking over so much lately?"

"Just some plans, or what might turn into plans, that's all." Will had always given her insubstantial answers, often for no good reason. It was just his habit to keep her uninformed; he did not see the views of women as important, so there was no reason to discuss men's concerns with her.

Darcy kept churning. Her arm grew tired, and she

shifted to the other, which was clumsy because of her withered hand. Her mother had gone inside the cabin after Darcy had taken over the churning and now returned to find Darcy wiping away a tear. Thinking of Joshua's leaving Haverly Fort, combined with the prospect of marriage to Gabriel Colter, had made her cry.

"Why, child, what's wrong with you?"

"The spring trees always make my eyes water," Darcy replied, "that's all." The dasher went up and down more rapidly, making squishing knocking noises in the churn.

Haverly had given public notice that weddings at Haverly Fort were not to be accompanied by the usual frontier frivolities. As soon as the pronouncement was made, Alphus Colter and the other men of the community had promptly overlooked it and set up a huge celebration for the couple.

Joshua Colter stood at the edge of the stockade, outside of which a great crowd of dancers wheeled and spun by torchlight and fiddle jigs were scratched out by Callum McSwain's old violin. Many of the men and some of the women were drunk, or getting close to it. Even the usually sober Alphus had taken several nips too many and was stomping his foot, clapping and hooting loudly in time to the music. Sina, with Zachariah clutched by her side, wriggling in a vain attempt to free himself and join in the fun, sat away from the crowd beneath a tree, watching her husband with disapproval.

Joshua watched the revelry but felt isolated from it. The afternoon's wedding ceremony, conducted in the meetinghouse by Israel Coffman, had gone well, or so Sina told Joshua, for Joshua had declined to attend. Now it was done, and she was gone from him.

Ah, well, he thought. It's my own fault, for letting Gabriel act before I did.

Gabriel . . . Joshua looked at his foster brother and had to smile. Gabriel, he could see, was most discomfited by the wild celebration around him. It trapped him in a position that for him surely was most uncomfortable. On the one hand, the people of Haverly Fort had done him great honor by celebrating his wedding so rambunctiously; on the other hand, the festivities had Peter Haverly's disapproval, and for Gabriel to enjoy them was to act in disaccord with Haverly's expressed views.

Haverly had attended the wedding ceremony but declined to come to the celebration thereafter. His son Cooper, though, must have managed to sneak away from his father, for he was loitering around McSwain's feet, watching him saw at his fiddle, an instrument Peter Haverly declared devilish but Cooper obviously loved.

Joshua took a swallow of rum and walked, cup in hand, over to where Israel Coffman sat talking to Jean McSwain. The woman rose and left, taking a cup of drink to her fiddling husband, as Joshua approached.

The young preacher smiled at his friend and waved for him to sit down in Jean McSwain's place. "Well, it's finally been done," Coffman said.

"Aye. Gabriel and Darcy married . . . I can hardly believe it," Joshua replied.

"What? Oh, yes—but that's not what I'm speaking of. What's done is that Haverly has finally had his fill of me, as you predicted. After the wedding ceremony was done this afternoon, I was told that my services are no longer needed at Haverly Fort."

"Well, I knew it would happen someday," Joshua replied. "What will you do now?"

"Go to Watauga. I've been asked to begin a church there, near Sycamore Shoals."

"I hate to see you go, Israel. And there's probably no need for you leaving, for I don't doubt we could find lots of people willing to join a new church if you wanted to start one on your own."

"It's a thought I've already had, Joshua, but I have no desire to create division in this community. The final end might not be well served by that. I can do the Lord's work just as well at Watauga, and without dividing the people here between churches."

"That's what you should do, then," Joshua said. "Maybe I'll be seeing you there at Watauga."

"You're thinking of moving over that way?"

"Moving somewhere—anywhere. Will Fiske and I have been talking. He's never been happy here, as you know. He's got his finger in the wind to find himself another place. When he goes, I'm going with him. I don't feel much holding me here anymore. And somebody needs to help Will keep an eye on those old parents of his, now that Darcy will be gone from him. Besides, Will can't even keep his own rifle in fix. Some warrior would peel his thatch before he could get off a shot unless he had somebody to guard him."

Coffman smiled at the joke. "When will you go?"

Joshua shrugged. "I don't yet know. The sooner we go, the happier I'll be."

"There's Alphus and Sina to think of. They're both getting older. And you're under sheriff—you have duties here."

"Aye, but Alphus is as strong as a man half his age. And I can come back and see how they fare from time to time, and take them with me if it ever comes to that. As for my duties, somebody else can take over that job."

Coffman looked around, sad-faced in the midst of gaiety. "I'll miss these people when I go. I've got plenty of good friends here, good memories. . . ."

"Don't get weepy-eyed on me, Israel. You know I can't stand that," Joshua said, giving the preacher a friendly pat on the shoulder. He rose and walked off alone, taking his rum with him.

From the darkness he watched the continuing revelry. Darcy was in the midst of it, smiling, receiving all the attention and praise a bride deserved. Tonight, caught up in the excitement of the moment, she seemed happy, but Joshua had to wonder how deeply she felt it and if it would last. He knew Darcy could not really love Gabriel, that she had married him out of a combination of the fear of being forever without a husband and her sense of debt to Gabriel for his efforts to protect her in the attack that nearly cost his life.

Someone cast logs onto the huge bonfire that roared in the midst of the clearing. Sparks and smoke boiled skyward, making the greening tree boughs arching high above the blaze dance in the updraft of heat. Brighter light surrounded Darcy, giving Joshua a clear view of her. She wasn't a beautiful woman by the usual standards, but to him right then, she seemed the most desirable, lovely woman he had ever known, even more so than Tilly had been.

He took a sip of rum. Inside he felt hollow and sad. First Tilly, now Darcy. Two good women, two opportunities for a life of happiness with a loving wife—both now taken from him. Raising his cup, Joshua looked at Darcy. "To you, Darcy Fiske Colter," he said. "May you be happy—if happy anyone could ever be as the bride of a man like Gabriel Colter."

He drained off his cup and wandered back to the table for more rum, staggering a little as he went. Tonight he would drink until he was thoroughly drunk and both old and fresh pains were washed away in rum, and he cared not at all what Sina, Israel, Alphus, or heaven itself thought about it. To the devil with everything and everyone. Darcy was gone from him, Haverly Fort seemed a hateful place, and nothing that mattered before mattered anymore.

Despite a shared eagerness to leave, Joshua and Will Fiske found themselves unable to depart Haverly Fort for two months after the wedding. Will and Darcy's father fell ill right after the celebration and lingered a month before dying, and for a month after that, Will's bereaved mother was ill, primarily with grief. Will encouraged Joshua to go on without him, but Joshua remained to help his crippled friend, knowing he needed it.

The illness of the old man, and then Mary Fiske's, resulted in many visits to the Fiske cabin by Darcy. Joshua was often there as well, and so he saw her much. She was always polite but obviously uncomfortable around him. Joshua himself felt a cruel pleasure in knowing he made her edgy; she had made her choice, and she could live with its consequences. He privately predicted that it would only take a little time for her life with Gabriel Colter to take on a nasty edge.

His prophecy came true quickly, and at the heart of the problem was Darcy's mother. Will told Joshua the details. Darcy wanted to take Mary Fiske in at Gabriel's house to keep her for life, but Gabriel would have none of it. Let Will deal with the old woman, he told Darcy. There was no need for her to trouble herself about such things. Life for Gabriel Colter's wife was to be one without concerns. There was Patton to do much of the work, and soon, Gabriel promised Darcy, there would be a second slave as well, a female to handle what remained of the household chores. Darcy could live a life of ease.

The suggestion horrified her, and she came to Will in tears, unable to believe Gabriel could hold so callous an attitude. Will, true to his nature, grew angry and was ready to confront Gabriel, but Darcy begged him not to. At last the situation was defused. Will decided that the old woman was sufficiently strong to go with him from Haverly Fort. He assured Darcy he would take good care of the aging widow and send word of their location as soon as they found new lands.

Joshua had his own internal battle to fight concerning Gabriel. It galled him to see Darcy walking beside Gabriel on Sunday mornings, heading for the meetinghouse where Haverly himself now preached in the absence of Coffman, who had gone on to Watauga two days after Darcy's wedding. Joshua had attended services often when Coffman was there and had got much benefit from them; now he would not darken the meetinghouse door.

It was not just for dislike of Haverly that he stayed away. Since Darcy's marriage, Joshua had grown cold and uncaring about most things that had been important to him before. He became distant and sometimes rude to friends and neighbors, and drank an uncharacteristically large amount of rum. He grew combative. Callum McSwain was once obliged to throw Joshua out of the smithy when he tried to start a fight with a man who had come for a tooth pulling and had said something that Joshua wrongly took as an insult. Joshua responded by attempting to arrest McSwain under the authority of the Watauga Association, but Alphus intervened and kept the squabble from going further. In disgust, Joshua announced on the spot his resignation as under sheriff and later that day scribbled a resignation letter and conveyed it by courier to Valentine Sevier.

Alphus was worried about Joshua and approached him a few times about the change that had come over him, but Joshua refused to talk to him. In the two months after Darcy's marriage, Joshua's reputation in the community was reversed. Instead of a respected leader, he became known as a rogue, and the reason for the change became a subject of speculation throughout the community.

Some attributed his changed character to a rumored falling-out with the Cherokee John Hawk, whose abrupt and unexplained departure from Haverly Fort and Joshua's company had not gone unnoticed. And in fact Joshua's estrangement from John Hawk contributed to his changed manner. He felt bad about the loss of his Cherokee brother, particularly because his dishonesty about Bloody Eagle's fate had led to it. Others claimed the departure of Israel Coffman had brought about Joshua's transformation, but others more perceptively linked the change to the marriage of Darcy and Gabriel.

In the midst of all this, Joshua got into a quarrel with Gabriel in Gabriel's store. The subject supposedly was the price of a lump of lead, but all who saw it knew from the vigor of Joshua's attack that there was much more to it than that. Because many people had detected Joshua's earlier interest in Darcy, vicious rumors began. Eyebrows were lifted; elbows nudged. "Joshua Colter has been at it with his brother's own wife, and them fresh married," people said. "What do you think of that!"

Alphus and Sina were deeply stung by the rumors, and Gabriel was infuriated. Darcy was hurt by it all and felt staring eyes upon her every time she ventured out. Joshua, preoccupied with himself and his own feelings and cut off from Darcy, did not much consider how the talk was hurting her. He was too morally numbed to care how it affected him. His reputation was all but gone in any case.

By the time he and Will were finally able to leave Haverly Fort, even Alphus was ready to see him go. With only minimal good-byes to his kin—except Gabriel, who received no good-bye at all—Joshua loaded and hitched up his packhorse, then climbed into the saddle of his Chickasaw.

He rode past Gabriel's house one last time, hoping to catch a glimpse of Darcy. He saw no one but Patton, who waved at him from the yard, and Peter Haverly's son, Cooper, who had become Gabriel's unofficial apprentice in the packing business, standing on the porch. He did not return Joshua's wave, and that stung, for one of Joshua's feelings that had not grown cold was his deep instinctive fondness for the boy. As he rode off, Joshua realized that he had never met Cooper's mother, for her ill health had lingered and Haverly had never fetched her to the Overmountain country.

Joshua joined Will Fiske at his cabin. "Old Mother," as Will called Mary Fiske, was already astride her horse when he got there, looking away from the men toward her husband's grave in the stump-filled yard. Will was just finishing strapping the last deerskin pack on one of his two packhorses. The little cabin looked stark and empty, vacant windows shuttered like the closed eyes of a corpse.

Their destination was a settlement to the northwest, in the Clinch River valley, called Castle's Woods. It was one of Will Fiske's old haunts; he had lived with his family there before coming to Sinking Creek. Joshua did not care where they went. One spot was as good as another as long as it was away from Haverly Fort.

They traveled up to an old warrior's path that roughly paralleled Lick Creek. Joshua was familiar with this route, having traveled it many times during his hunts. Often used by Indians and white men alike, this was the pathway along which Cherokee warriors had traveled back in the 1750s on their way to battle the French on behalf of the English. By this route Little Carpenter had spirited John Stuart to safety in Virginia after the fall of Fort Loudoun in 1760. That same year, Standing Turkey had traveled the path on his way to peace talks at Long Island.

Reaching the warpath along the base of a mountain ridge, they went on to the Holston, reaching Long Island, and turned north through a gap in Clinch Mountain. In the Clinch River valley now, they followed a winding creek that ran along the northern base of the Clinch Mountain ridge, then turned north where the ridge to their left declined into a broad low gap. A nearly due-north route took them to Castle's Woods. Here Haverly Fort seemed distant, remote. Joshua liked the feeling, even though the miles had not erased the empty ache inside him when he thought of Darcy.

"Where will we go, now that we're here?" Joshua asked Will. He glanced toward Mary Fiske. "Your mother's tired. She needs a place to rest."

Will had scarcely noticed his mother's weary state, but when he studied her, even his insensitive eye saw the old woman had not traveled well. She needed a good bed beneath a solid roof. Will scratched his chin and thought over the matter. "There's a man here, name of Russell, who I know right well," Will said. "I hadn't wanted to put trouble to him, but maybe he could give lodging to Old Mother for a time."

Joshua had heard of Russell. He was an able old soldier who had fought in the Seven Years War against the French and Indians and had also led in settlement of the Clinch River valley. He was a man with an eye for good land and could probably steer them toward a promising location, Will said.

They found Russell easily enough and were welcomed heartily. Mary Fiske was put to bed, and Russell ordered his two slaves, Adam and Charles, to be ready to provide her anything needed. Russell and his visitors then took pipes and walked the banks of the Clinch River, talking over what news each knew and sharing personal histories and plans. Will told of the death of his father and the marriage of Darcy. Russell seemed quite interested, saying he had heard of Gabriel Colter. A good man of business, folks had reported to him.

Russell also knew Alphus to some degree and had heard of Joshua as well. "You're the lad who traveled alone through the wilds when you were just a sprout, I believe? And, according to the story I've heard, attempted to scalp old Alphus right in his station camp when he found you there?"

Joshua replied, "I didn't try to scalp him. I shot at him with a trade musket."

Russell laughed. "That's sufficient, that's sufficient."

As conversation progressed and Russell discovered that his visitors were searching for new land, he became visibly excited. "You've come at a good time, my friends," he said. "I've got plans afoot with the finest woodsman I know to settle in the Caintuck country before the year is out."

Both Will and Joshua were surprised. Joshua said he had heard rumors that some private attempt might be made in the future to purchase a big part of the Kentucky country from the Indians, but he was unaware any such transaction had actually been completed.

Russell laughed and waved his hand. "There's been no transaction, though there is one planned. This woodsman I mentioned is a man from off the Yadkin River, name of Daniel Boone. You've heard of him, I'm sure, Mr. Colter."

"Call me Joshua—and yes, I'm familiar with Boone. I first met him years ago. And his family has been living down in Sapling Grove for some time now, though Daniel himself has scarce been about."

"Aye. He's been a busy man. He's been traveling on behalf of a man name of Richard Henderson, a circuit judge and lawyer out of North Carolina."

"I recall that name," Joshua said. "Henderson had trouble from the Regulators years ago—driven right off his judging bench by some of them, I believe."

"So I've heard as well," Russell said. "In any case, this Henderson is the man said to have a scheme afoot to buy the Caintuck Valley from the Indians, and Boone's been poking about among them, asking questions and seeing what he can work out for Henderson. He's been exploring Caintuck as well, and the stories he tells of that country will make a man's mouth water. Boone was here not long ago, and we talked of Caintuck until we came to a decision." Russell's eyes sparkled with eagerness. "This very year we'll lead a party of settlers through Cumberland Gap and settle in Caintuck. We're not waiting for Henderson to finish his deal. The land is there—abundant, rich, and going to waste. Virginia has surveyors all over Caintuck, and if we don't settle now, we may miss our chance. Boone is gathering settlers from along the Yadkin to join us; some of his wife's people are also planning to go along. And I'm gathering a party here. Would you gentlemen wish to join it?"

Will looked at Joshua and in his eyes read the answer. Slowly the lame frontiersman's lean face lightened with a grin. "Aye, I think we would like that quite a lot, Mr. Russell," he said.

It was October 1773. The day was cool, the breeze brisk, carrying the rich scents of dying summer and dawning autumn. Joshua shielded his eyes, looked across the rugged russet landscape, and said, "Yonder they come."

"Fine thing, fine thing it is." Russell smiled broadly and rubbed his hands.

Joshua, perched on a high rock to enjoy the breeze while smoking a pipeful of Russell's tobacco, had seen Daniel Boone's party approaching. When they arrived, Boone greeted Russell happily and was pleased to see Joshua again. After asking about Alphus's welfare and noting that he had seen the grave of Levi Hampton at Sapling Grove, Boone talked to Russell about their party.

Boone had brought with him five families from the Yadkin, along with some hired men. Awaiting them in the valley of the Powell River would be some of Rebecca Boone's people, the Bryan clan, and others. Russell's group consisted of about thirty people, including, besides Joshua, such notable frontiersmen as David Gass and Michael Stoner. Boone gave his approval to the group, expressing concern only at the relatively decrepit state of old Mary Fiske. To make this journey, Boone had been forced to part with his own aging mother back in Carolina; he was uncertain that taking along so old and feeble a one as Will's Old Mother was wise. But Will objected with typical vigor, and at last, with Russell's encouragement, Boone relented.

Joshua was glad to see Boone, a man he much respected. Boone, born of Quaker stock in Pennsylvania, had few peers as a scout and woodsman. Fifteen years Joshua's senior, Boone had spent most of his life on the frontier, working as a herdsman at age ten, spending nights in the wilds far from his home. A year after Joshua was born at Charles Town, Boone's father had brought his family to the Yadkin, where the young Daniel grew to full manhood and made himself known as an able frontiersman and soldier. While Joshua was still a child at Fort Loudoun, dreaming of manhood and life as a hunter and fighter, Boone was helping in the Forbes campaign against Fort Duquesne, where Little Carpenter had encountered much trouble.

Joshua had first seen Boone shortly after meeting Alphus and Levi for that first time in 1760; since then Boone was becoming a well-known man. He had traveled as far south as Florida, and had hunted in the richest parts of Kentucky for a full two years before turning his efforts toward negotiations with Indians toward Henderson's proposed purchase of Kentucky. Boone had cause to help out Henderson; the Carolina lawyer had defended Boone in court years in legal wrangles related to Boone's chronic indebtedness.

Once assembled, the party set out from Castle's Woods, snaking across the wilderness. In Powell's Valley they found the Bryan group waiting as planned, and they divided into three groups. Boone, as natural leader, headed the lead party, selecting Joshua to join him since Joshua had also traveled to and through Cumberland Gap. Mary Fiske was taken into the group by Daniel's wife, who seemed to like the old woman and volunteered to care for her. The second was smaller, consisting of

James Boone, son of Daniel, and Henry Russell, son of William. With them was Will Fiske, who volunteered for the job because the second party was to tend the livestock being driven along with the party and he had always fancied himself good with animals. Also in the second party were two of the hired men Boone had brought along, one named Drake, the other Crabtree. Two young brothers named Mendenhall also joined the drovers' band, and Russell instructed his two slaves to stay with them as well. The third group consisted of Russell and a few others.

As the three parties moved along in a narrow line, the distance between them grew. Before long Joshua lost all sight of Will's party, which in turn lost sight of both the first and third groups. The pilgrims plodded along. None of the travelers had brought wagons, for the trail into Kentucky was too narrow for them. Packhorses carried most of their possessions. The men walked; some women did, as well, while others rode on horseback with the young children. A handful of carts were also part of the procession. Much smaller than wagons but big enough to carry churns, pails, and other items difficult to haul by horseback, the carts were pulled by oxen.

The way was difficult and densely overgrown, but on Friday, October 9, the travelers where cheered, for on the next day they would be across Wallen's Ridge and on clearer ground. It was likely that before the next day was through, they would reach Cumberland Gap, even pass through it. When Boone called a halt, the travelers readily bedded down. When Joshua lay down on his deerskin blanket, he was asleep within two minutes.

Back with the livestock, Will Fiske and his companions were having more trouble getting to their rest. The animals were restless and nervous, and something of the same feeling seemed to be affecting the human members of the party. Perhaps it was the howling of wolves in the black forest around them that stirred tension. Will built a huge fire, and the men sat around it after the animals were finally settled. Will spoke reassuring words to the Mendenhall brothers, who were the most nervous. They were trying their best to hide their fright at the howls but doing a bad job of it.

"Don't fret about the wolves," Will said. "I've not seen a wolf yet that will come around a fire."

Isaac Crabtree, the hired hand, laughed. "There's no point in fearing wolf howls, no sir. In Kentucky you'll hear far more fearful things than that."

"What?" one of the Mendenhalls asked.

"Buffalo! Howling up in the treetops! Most fearsome sound ever heard, I'll tell you!"

That brought a laugh, and tension lessened. Blankets were spread, the fire was built up again, and the men lay down to sleep.

Will was the first to awaken the next morning. The sun had just arisen, spilling cool autumn light across the camp. Usually Will awakened in relatively high spirits, but this morning something was different. He felt a sense of caution, maybe some outright fear. Sitting up, he looked around the rim of the clearing and felt his blood chill in his veins.

Looking back at him was a band of Shawnees, standing silently in a line.

19

Will knew two things as soon as he saw the Shawnees, who were watching the camp through a veil of dawn mist rising from the nearby creek: the wolves howling in the forest the previous night had not been wolves, and in a few moments, his life and those of his companions would be over unless they could somehow defend themselves or persuade these Indians not to harm them. There was no question in Will's mind that harm was their intent.

They had positioned themselves adjacent to the camp, awaiting dawn, the customary time of attack. Further, they held bows with arrows already in place.

Will stood, determining to use a ploy that had worked for other frontiersmen in similar situations. Smiling broadly, he put out his hand toward the Shawnees. "My friends—I'm glad to see you!" he said, stepping forward, hoping at least one of them understood English. "Welcome to our camp. Come share what victuals we can offer you."

His voice awakened the others. The two Mendenhall brothers rose up on their elbows, looked blearily around, then froze in fear as they saw their situation. Crabtree leapt to his feet and swore. Drake rose and silently stared. The slaves, Charles and Adam, were equally silent, terror showing in their dark faces. Henry Russell and James Boone were also afraid but reacted more calmly, standing slowly. The seventeen-year-old Boone had his father's deportment and swift mind, and saw at once what Will was attempting. He stepped up to Will's side and also put out his hand.

"Hello, Big Jim," James Boone said to the biggest of the warrior band. "It is fine to see you this morning."

"You know that one?" Will side-whispered.

"Yes. He knows my father and has always been friendly. He's the best hope we have of—"

It took Will a moment to comprehend that what had so suddenly cut off James Boone's words was an arrow that had pierced the middle of the young man's body. Something that felt like the blow of a heavy mallet struck Will in his chest immediately thereafter, and he looked down, gazing unbelievingly at the shaft thrusting out of his breast, a red circle beginning to spread where it entered him.

"Big Jim, no!" James Boone cried out. "I'm James Boone! Don't do this!"

The answer was a rain of arrows. Will felt himself pierced again and again. He and James Boone fell together. Screams rose from the camp. Through a sudden ringing in his ears, Will recognized the cries of the Mendenhall brothers. Their screams came in a sudden burst that ended abruptly, and he knew they were dead. Henry Russell's screams continued; he had survived the first volley. In this situation, survival was no blessing.

Will, on his back, unable to move, twisted his head awkwardly and looked back into the camp, which from this posture he saw upside down. The Mendenhalls were dead. Drake, several arrows sticking out of him like porcupine quills, was on his knees. A warrior came to him and with a savage cry tomahawked him. He slumped to the side, instantly dead. The two slaves were scrambling toward the woods; Charles was brought down by a tomahawk, but Adam disappeared into the undergrowth. Where Crabtree had gone Will could not see.

Suddenly there was a figure above him. Straightening his neck, Will saw Big Jim straddling him, a knife in one hand, a tomahawk in the other. The knife came to his hairline.

"I'm just a poor cripple, and I'd appreciate it a lot if you'd use the other first," Will said. He did not try to fight off the Shawnee, for he could not move.

Big Jim, who had already begun to cut the skin at Will's hairline, paused, then put aside the knife. The tomahawk rose.

"Thank you for your mercy," Will said. He waited until the tomahawk began its downswing, then closed his eyes.

Joshua rose from beside Will Fiske's body and walked to the edge of the stream, down to a tangle of driftwood where he sat down and cried. Such emotional outbursts were not his habit, but the horror he had just seen in the camp clearing was too much for him to take.

Will, at least, had not died nearly as hard as poor James Boone and Henry Russell. His hands, unlike theirs, were not lacerated to ribbons from trying to turn back repeated stabbing from Shawnee knives, and his fingernails had not been torn out or his face sliced. Death for him had come, as best Joshua could determine, from a swift tomahawk blow.

Will's sad old mother, thankfully, would not have to endure knowing what Rebecca Boone would know—that her son had died of slow deliberate torture. Why the Shawnees had spared Will from torture but tormented James Boone and Henry Russell was as much a question to Joshua as the motivation for the attack. Most likely he would never know; sometimes these things simply happened, spurred and guided by irrational whims, fury, or liquor. Knowing the reasons could not bring back the dead or erase pains already endured.

Someone came to Joshua's side. He turned abruptly, startled. It was Isaac Crabtree, the hired hand, who had

escaped by hiding in the very tangle of driftwood where
Joshua now sat. Crabtree's face was ashen.

"In all my days, may I never hear the like of that again.
God! What those poor boys were put through—"

"There's nothing gained by talking of it," Joshua said.

"Aye, aye. But I cannot forget it, cannot get it out of
my head." Crabtree paused, lower lip trembling, eyes red.
"I hate them, hate every damn one of the breed!"

"It was just a small band that did it, judging from the
sign," Joshua said. "What a few Indians do, you cannot
blame them all for."

"So you may look at it. I'll have my own way of looking
at those damned bloody heathens from now on." He
turned and walked down the creek, knelt, and washed
his face.

Joshua pitied Crabtree and understood how he felt,
even though he could not agree with those feelings. He
knew of atrocities similar to this one committed by renegade white men against Indians. He recalled the innocent Cherokees who had been killed and scalped on the
North Carolina frontier years ago during the war so their
scalps could be misrepresented as those of French-supporting Shawnees and turned in for bounty. He recalled
the murder of Bloody Eagle by Henry Dorey. Though he
knew nothing of how Dorey had killed the warrior, there
was no doubt it was treacherously done, simply because
Dorey could never have overcome the powerful Awahili
otherwise.

Atrocities were committed on all sides; they were one
of the most unfortunate parts of living and dying on the
frontier. The moral codes of the times were stern and
prone to emphasize vengeance more than forgiveness, so
one atrocity tended to lead to another. These slayings,
involving the sons of noted frontiersmen, would certainly
generate rage across hundreds of miles. Trouble would
come of them.

Lifting his bullet pouch and drying his tears on the
flap of it, Joshua walked back up into the clearing.
Captain Russell was on his knees weeping as Daniel
Boone wrapped the bodies of his son and Russell's in a

single linen sheet that Rebecca Boone had sent back. "Don't bury my boy in the bare dirt," she had tearfully instructed as Boone had prepared to leave the lead party and come back to the massacre scene. Joshua had found that plea one of the saddest he had ever heard.

Boone's lead party had received word of the massacre from a runner that Russell had sent forward as soon as he learned what had happened. Crabtree was Russell's informant, reaching him shortly after the slayings. Russell was one of the first men to find the scalped bodies. The horrible sight had so overcome him that he collapsed and was unable even to order graves dug, so others had fallen to that task on their own.

Joshua wished he had a linen sheet to wrap Will in, but there was nothing save Will's rumpled old blanket. He dug Will's grave himself, even as Boone was finishing with laying James and Henry to rest in a single shallow hole. Joshua was beginning to cover Will's body with dirt as Boone laid logs and rocks across the boys' grave to keep out wolves. When Will was covered, Joshua piled his grave in the same manner, with Boone's help.

Together, the men buried the Mendenhalls, Drake, and Charles. Adam, who according to Crabtree had fled into the woods, had not yet been found, and it was presumed that he had been run down and killed after the massacre.

The presumption proved wrong. Adam turned up later, after long roaming in the woods, lost and terrified of detection by the Shawnees. He had seen and heard the massacre from his hiding place in the forest, and described in vivid, terrible clarity the gruesome details.

When Boone heard that the Shawnee called Big Jim had been involved, he raged in the sadness and fury of a man betrayed. "I've welcomed that Shawnee into my very home. Why would he do this to my own boy?"

"The Indians are stirred up," Joshua said, wondering if he should be speaking in such a situation. "Surveyors exploring Caintuck, boats coming down the Ohio River— they see their land being taken. This was their way of telling white men to stay out of Caintuck."

"Aye." Boone swallowed and stood straight, breathing

deeply. He was standing beside a small campfire that lit his slender face and wide mouth, his clubbed-up hair, and his black buckskin clothing in a dancing yellow light. "Well, they're right on one score. We will occupy their lands. We cannot let this stop us—we must go on into Caintuck."

Captain Russell, seated on the ground, lifted his eyes to his partner. "Go on? No, Daniel, no. I'll go no farther, and cannot see how you could think of going on yourself."

Boone's eyes narrowed. "Go on we must, William. I've sold most all I own to do this. Without Caintuck, I have nothing left."

"You've got your remaining family," Russell answered. "You've got children still living—that makes you a rich man, Daniel Boone."

"Rich . . . with no roof above my children's heads," the woodsman muttered in sardonic reply.

David Gass, one of Russell's neighbors on the Clinch, said, "There's a cabin on my land not being used. It's yours to use if you've got nothing else to go to, Daniel."

Joshua did not wait to hear the outcome. He rose and went to the makeshift tent he had set up for Mary Fiske. The old woman was lying on her blankets, her feet thrust out of the tent. Joshua knelt beside her, lifted the flap, and looked in.

"Old Mother?" he said, for he had adapted up Will's way of talking to her during their time together. "Are you well?"

The old woman was crying, not loudly and terribly as she had when she first heard Will had been slain, but softly, almost inaudibly. She sat up; in the darkness Joshua could not see her face but felt her looking at him.

"I want to go back to my daughter," she said. "I need to see my Darcy—she's all that's left to me."

Joshua nodded. "Go back we shall, then. Tomorrow we'll set out. I'll take good care of you, Old Mother, just like Will would have wanted. Now, you rest if you can, for we have much traveling before us."

* * *

Joshua learned the next day that Boone had relented at last, partly because Rebecca was appalled at his idea of continuing on to Kentucky. Boone had reluctantly accepted Gass's offer of a cabin on the Clinch.

When Joshua departed the dispirited party, he felt overwhelmed with depression. He was sad at the death of Will and full of pity for the families and friends of those slain by torture. In addition, he dreaded the prospect of seeing Darcy struck with the news of her brother's death.

He was also disappointed at the failure of the settlement expedition. The idea of living in Kentucky, far away from Haverly Fort and the life that had become so difficult, had been appealing. Being near Darcy was a torment, now that she was Gabriel's. Joshua disparaged himself for his chronic slowness when it came to women. He had dallied in uncertainty back in the days of Tilly Hampton, then found her suddenly gone. He had similarly failed to recognize fully and act on his feelings for Darcy, giving Gabriel the opportunity to snatch her from him, even before he had time really to know, until it was too late, that he loved the lady. He still loved her.

The journey back toward Haverly Fort went relatively fast at the beginning, though with much difficulty because of Mary Fiske's feebleness and emotional distress. She cried continually over Will's death, and she became disoriented, grieving as well over her husband's passing, sometimes confusing the details of the two deaths, so that she thought the old man had been killed by Shawnees and Will buried at Haverly Fort. The woman slept poorly, moaning and turning in her sleep, so Joshua got little rest.

Near Reedy Creek, Mary grew suddenly ill and could go no farther. Joshua found a farmstead and went to it, seeking help, which was happily provided by a man and woman in their forties named Kincaid who had settled on Reedy Creek just over a year earlier. Word of the Wallen's Ridge slayings had already begun to spread across the frontier, Joshua found, for the Kincaids were already aware of it and quizzed him closely when they discovered he had been in Boone's party.

Joshua stayed with the Kincaids for two days, waiting for Mary to become stronger, but she made no improvement. At last he realized she might die and that Darcy needed to be here. Bidding goodbye to the Kincaids, who accepted responsibility for Mary without a murmur of complaint, Joshua set off for Haverly Fort, taking two mounts so that he could switch horses when one grew weary.

He had never seen the land more splendid. The rich colors of peak autumn surrounded him with beauty and made him wish he had time to enjoy it all. As he neared Haverly Fort and began to see familiar farmsteads, Joshua received stares and waves from people in fields and about cabins. The closer he drew to the fort, the less enthusiastic the waves became, and he knew then to what extent his reputation had deteriorated in his last days in the region. There were plenty who had welcomed his departure for Kentucky, seeing him as a good man gone bad. Seeing him return would bring them no pleasure.

He thought of going to see Alphus and Sina first but decided to go promptly to Gabriel's house. If Mary Fiske was bound to die, as he feared, there would be no time for personal visits before fetching Darcy to her side. Joshua rode to Gabriel's yard, dismounted, and tied the horses to the paling fence as the front door cracked, then swung open. Patton emerged.

"Mister Joshua?" he said. "Mister Joshua, is that you?"

Joshua stepped over the low fence and walked to the porch, extending his hand. "Who else would it be? Have I changed that much in a few months?"

"No, no sir—I just thought you was gone far away, sir, that's all."

"Well, I'm back, though only for a short time. Is Darcy . . . is Mrs. Colter home?"

Patton seemed very uncomfortable with that question and did not answer. Joshua read his thoughts. "Don't worry, Patton—I'm not here to steal her away, though it likely wouldn't take a lot of argument to make me change my mind about that. I have something important to tell her, about her mother."

"I'll go in and fetch her, Mr. Joshua."

Just as Patton turned to enter, another man came out of the house. It was Peter Haverly, who glared down at Joshua with unconcealed distaste. Joshua wondered why Haverly was at Gabriel's house. "I thought you had left us, Colter," Haverly said.

"You thought wrong, then, as is your habit," Joshua snapped. "I'm here to fetch Darcy."

Haverly's brows raised. He reached out and restrained Patton from entering the house. Haverly was wearing a peruke today, as he sometimes did when dressing up, and looked so haughty in it that Joshua would have liked to peel it from his head and toss it into a tree. Haverly reminded him tremendously of Gabriel right now. There was something funny in that; Gabriel's imitations of his mentor had become so thorough that now Joshua found himself comparing the original to the copy.

"I wonder if your seeing Mrs. Colter would be proper, sir," Haverly said in an icily polite tone.

"The hell with you, and the hell with what's proper." Joshua stepped up on the porch. Haverly stepped forward and blocked him.

"You'll not speak to me in that manner, young man, nor enter this house in such a spirit. Look at you, listen to you—you took our Lord's baptism and profess to follow him, yet you behave like the very heathen!"

Cooper Haverly came out of the door right then, saw Joshua, and lit up with a grin. "Joshua!" he cried out joyfully. "You've come back home!"

"Stay away from here, Cooper!" Haverly ordered. "Get back into the house with your mother!"

"Oh, you've finally fetched her here, then," Joshua said. "Fine life she'll have, living with you. Out of my way, Haverly."

Haverly curled up a fist. Joshua stepped onto the porch, drew back his own fist, and smashed it into Haverly's face, knocking the big man down.

"I've often thought that would be a pleasant undertak-

ing," Joshua said. "I was right. That was given on behalf
of Israel Coffman, a better man than you'll ever be, run
off from a settlement that is far the worse without him."

Haverly sat, sprawl-legged, rubbing his red jaw. "You're
no Christian man, no good man, Joshua Colter. You're a
heathen, like that red demon you used to spend your
time with. I'll have you arrested for this!"

Joshua ignored Haverly, who to him now was no more
than a pest, a gnat in his ear. He said hello to Cooper,
who was wide-eyed at seeing his father knocked down
by a man he had previously idolized, and entered the
house, almost running into the fattest woman he had
ever encountered. So huge was she that Joshua was
startled. Beside her was a girl of about thirteen or four-
teen, greatly resembling her.

"Bet your pardon, Mrs. Haverly," he said. "I didn't see
you . . .". He paused. "Do I know you, ma'am?" There
was something teasingly familiar in her face, though he
could not hope to place what it was.

"I certainly hope not, ruffian! You struck down my
husband!"

"Did you see me do it, or just feel the house shake
when his fat arse hit the porch? Now, where's Darcy?"

"I'm here, Joshua."

He wheeled. She was coming out of the larger of the
two bedrooms. She wore a beautiful dress of fine linen,
the kind Gabriel would dress her in, not the rougher
osnaburg linen more typical of the frontier. She hid her
withered hand, as always, in the folds of her dress. As
soon as he saw her, he knew she had been crying. In the
meantime, the plump Mrs. Haverly and the girl with her
went out the door to comfort her husband.

"Darcy—what's wrong?"

"That's the question I was about to ask you. I heard
what you said to Patton . . . what's happened to mother?"

"She's sick, Darcy. In a cabin up at Reedy Creek, with
a family named Kincaid."

"Is Will with her?"

Joshua closed his eyes, unable to look at her as he

broke the news. "Will is gone, Darcy. He was killed on Wallen's Ridge by Shawnees, just days ago."

No response. He opened his eyes. Darcy had gone white, and as he watched, she fainted to the floor.

"This is a bad mistake and a wrong thing you are doing, Darcy Colter!" Peter Haverly boomed as the young woman mounted Gabriel's best Chickasaw. "When your husband returns, he'll be rightly furious, you running off alone with this scoundrel!"

"Let him be furious, then," Darcy said. Her eyes were red from crying over Will's death, and she was in no mood for Haverly's pompous directives. "My mother is bereaved and ill, and I'll not waste a moment getting to her. If he cannot understand that, then that will have to be his burden."

"You're a married woman, Darcy. You are disgracing your husband's name and character, and feeding hurtful rumors by your carelessness."

"My husband disgraces himself, mostly through his adoration of you," Darcy said. "And it's no disgrace for a woman to go to her mother when she is in need. Good-bye, Mr. Haverly. And good-bye to you, too, Mrs. Haverly; I'm glad to have met you. Cooper, please tell Gabriel that I will return as soon as I can, and Old Mother will be with me. We are going to a cabin on Reedy Creek, belonging to a family named . . ."

"Kincaid," Joshua said.

"Kincaid. You will tell him, Cooper?"

"I'll tell him, Mrs. Colter," the youth said.

She and Joshua rode away together, leaving the Haverlys and Patton staring after them.

As she had rushed about preparing for the journey, Darcy had hurriedly explained her momentary situation to Joshua. Gabriel was gone to the packing works many miles away and would be gone for an indeterminate time. She could not wait for him to return before going to her mother.

Peter Haverly, in the time that Joshua had been gone on the failed Kentucky expedition, had gone away to

Wilmington and returned only a day ago, at last bringing the long-awaited Mrs. Haverly with him. He had driven her over to meet Darcy less than an hour before Joshua had so unexpectedly arrived.

Joshua and Darcy talked little for the first miles. Joshua had replaced one of his mounts with a fresh one out of Gabriel's stock, and the horse traveled well. Darcy's horse kept up easily.

"You had been crying when I first saw you in the house, Darcy, even before you knew about Will," Joshua said at length. "Is there something gone wrong for you?"

"I don't wish to speak of it."

Joshua was overwhelmingly curious but forced himself not to probe. After a few moments, he smiled. "You certainly put paid to Haverly's preachy mouth back there, I must say."

"Aye, and too long I waited to do it," she said with an angry vigor. "I may as well tell you, since you asked: It was Haverly, in large measure, that had me crying when you saw me, if you want to know. Him and his talk of Gabriel needing a son to carry on his name! Heaven help me, but it's all I can do to stand and listen to that man seek to tell me how my life must be lived. He's talked so much of my duty to give Gabriel a son that Gabriel himself now can think of nothing else, and seems to hate me because I have not yet become with child." She paused and looked self-conscious. "I'm sorry, Joshua. 'Tis no sort of thing for me to be talking of to you."

"You needn't fret over anything you tell me. You can say what you wish, and I'll think you none the worse for it."

They rode on, saying nothing more for a while. Finally she asked Joshua to tell her about Will's death, sparing no details, and he did tell her, making sure she knew he had not been tortured. She cried some more, silently, then dried her tears on her sleeve and seemed thoughtful and distant until they stopped to make camp and eat. Joshua asked Darcy about Levi and Sina, and she told him they were well, though they kept to themselves much more than before, ever since Joshua had . . . And there she stopped, not sure what to say.

"Since I became such a shameful soul?" he suggested.

She lowered her head.

"Don't seek to spare my feelings—I've got few left to hurt," he said.

Joshua asked Darcy about general affairs at Haverly Fort.

"Peter Haverly's coming upon bad times, I think," she said. "Many in his church are leaving it; all in all, the people are wearying of his ways, and his notion that because the station bears his name and he is its founder, he is also its ruler."

"So what will happen?"

"I think his influence will drain away, a bit at a time, until he is just one more landholder and man of commerce."

"It could be a time that Gabriel could rise as Haverly sets."

"Yes, if only he could see himself in any terms but as Haverly's reflection. I have always believed Gabriel could be a good man, even a great one . . . perhaps he will be yet."

"Perhaps." Joshua said it out of politeness rather than conviction.

He built up the fire and took a short circular walk around the camp, looking for Indian sign or any other hint of danger. He found none and returned to the fireside. Darcy had spread her blankets and was lying down. Joshua lit a pipe and smoked, keeping watch on the forest around them. At last he spread his own blankets and lay down.

He slept lightly, ever aware of the crucial duty of protecting Darcy, and when the morning came, they ate with little conversation and rode on toward Reedy Creek. As they drew near, Joshua thought about Mrs. Haverly, trying to figure out why she had looked familiar. Certainly he had never known a woman of her girth—he would remember that—but then, it wasn't her size that was familiar but her face.

"Darcy," he asked, "has it ever struck you how different Cooper Haverly is from his father?"

"Yes," she answered. "And different from his mother as well, from what little time I was with her."

"That's what I was about to ask you—if she is like Cooper. There is something in her face that was familiar, and I thought perhaps it was similarity to Cooper, but I don't believe that was it."

"No—they look nothing alike. Did you know, by the way, that Cooper is not his real name? I learned it from Mrs. Haverly only today. It's a name given in jest by Haverly to the boy—something to do with him expressing a desire to become a barrel maker when he grew up."

"So what is his real name?"

"Samuel." Darcy rode on a short distance before she noticed that Joshua had halted his horse. She turned in the saddle. "Is something wrong?"

"Darcy—what is Mrs. Haverly's Christian name?"

"Her name?" She creased her brow, trying to remember. "Haverly did call her by name today . . . a religious-sounding name of some sort, as you might expect for the wife of a man like him."

"Please—you must remember."

Darcy frowned again, digging for the name. "Yes! Now I remember. Her name is Christiana. Christiana Haverly."

20

Darcy's reunion with her mother was a mix of happiness and sorrow. Both women grieved deeply over Will's tragic fate yet were happy to be together again.

Joshua did not pay much attention to them, for he had much to occupy his mind. It was amazing to think he had looked Christiana Cox in the face, had spoken to her—rudely, to be sure, but he had spoken—and had seen Beth, now a plump little girl rather than an infant as she had been when he last saw her. He found it hard to believe. Yet all the pieces fit, right down to Jack Byrum's mention during his streamside encounter with Joshua back in Carolina that he had seen Christiana with a "fat-bottomed husband" in Wilmington.

Most astounding of all was Joshua's abrupt understanding of why young Cooper Haverly had always seemed so different from his father and why Joshua had felt so naturally drawn to him.

Joshua strode around the stump-filled yard outside the Kincaid cabin, marveling again at the unpredictability of his life. At the same time, he wondered if he had the courage yet to reveal who he was to Christiana and

Cooper—or Samuel, as he now had to think of him. How would they respond, particularly Christiana, whom he had so gruffly treated?

But sometime soon she would figure out the truth for herself. Alphus or someone else would mention the story of Joshua's appearance at the station camp in 1760, maybe even note that Joshua's original surname was Byrum. Then Christiana would know. Joshua decided he must return to Haverly Fort and reveal the truth about himself to Christiana. She had probably gone through her life in the same curious, fearful torment that he had during all his years of ignorance about her fate and the babies'. She had a right to be relieved of that burden.

His thoughts were interrupted by the opening of the cabin door. Kincaid came into the yard and joined Joshua. "A lovely lady, that young Mrs. Colter is. Your brother's wife, correct?"

"Aye."

"Her presence is what her mother needed. What a fine woman Mary Fiske is! Reminds me so of my own mother, dead and gone from me for seven years. Tell me, sir, why did Mrs. Colter's husband not come here with her?"

"He wasn't home when I got there. There was no time to wait for him."

Kincaid pursed his lips. "I was hoping to speak with him about a matter—a request somewhat extraordinary that would require his approval."

Joshua wondered what Kincaid meant but did not think it right to ask. The two men walked together about Kincaid's land, talking of other matters and smoking until Kincaid's wife called them in for a meal of venison and corn mush an hour later.

Kincaid unexpectedly got his wish to meet Gabriel Colter, for Gabriel rode up to the house the next morning, along with Alphus. Joshua had slept in a little log shed behind Kincaid's house and after breakfast had returned to it to gather his blankets when he heard the riders come in. He stepped to the shed door and was surprised to see who it was.

He walked out of the shed to meet them. Gabriel quickly dismounted, glowering, and walked toward Joshua. It was a cool morning, slightly damp. Gabriel was limping today, something he rarely did anymore.

Joshua put out his hand. "Gabe. I'm pleased to see—"

Gabriel hit Joshua in the jaw. "Where's Darcy?" he demanded as Joshua staggered backward.

Joshua rubbed his jaw, shook his head, and drew back to give a return blow. Alphus reached him and grasped him arm before he could do it. "Hellfire and damnation!" Alphus bellowed. "The both of you, quit this acting like children!"

Joshua was surprised, for this was a noteworthy moment. Alphus Colter had finally encountered a situation infuriating enough to make him swear.

Kincaid came around from the front of the cabin, rifle in hand. "What the devil's all this?" he asked, raising the flintlock.

It took seven or eight minutes for Joshua to explain the situation, with some help from Alphus and lots of angry interruptions, objections, and clarifications from Gabriel. During that time, Mrs. Kincaid and Darcy emerged from the cabin.

Gabriel went to his wife, rather roughly grabbing her shoulders and talking harshly to her so that Joshua almost intervened. Alphus again held him back. Darcy began crying. Mrs. Kincaid had a horrified look on her face, as if she expected this gaggle of frenzied people to turn on her family at any moment and slay them all like savages.

At length the tumult settled somewhat, and the situation became more clear. Kincaid, who had a smooth, calming voice, proved to be a good diplomat and counselor. Eventually a tense peace reigned, though lightning still flashed between Gabriel and Joshua, and Darcy remained distraught.

Kincaid brought out rum and a loaf. Alphus and Joshua remained outdoors, Alphus's manner with Joshua alternately gentle and scolding. Kincaid, Gabriel, and Darcy conferred privately inside the cabin. Exactly what they were talking of Joshua did not know, but he was sure it was the matter Kincaid had brought up earlier. He suspected it had to do with Mary Fiske, whom Kincaid so adored.

"What's troubling you so these days, Joshua?" Alphus asked. "With all the talk already spread about, you running off alone with Darcy has half the people at Haverly Fort thinking the worst of both you and her. Gabriel was angry as blazes, so much so that I felt I had to come with him. Otherwise he might have tried to kill you. I half hoped we wouldn't be able to find this Kincaid cabin. In truth, Joshua, I don't fully fault Gabriel for his anger. It seems improper that you, of all people, should have fetched Darcy away alone. Do you think nothing of the reputation of your brother and his wife?"

"He's not my brother. And was I to sit about waiting on him to return while Darcy's mother lay ill and wanting her daughter near?"

"By Joseph, don't fret details with me, Joshua! You could at least have brought someone else with you and Darcy—Patton if none other. I know what to think of you no longer, Joshua. I'm told you even struck down Haverly, and were insulting to his wife, which is even worse. You've turned reckless and foolish these many months now, and it's time you straightened yourself."

"To the devil with Haverly and the rest of it," Joshua said, walking away.

Being put off so brought Alphus a volcanic burst of anger. "Maybe your father was right, by Joseph," he called after Joshua. "Maybe the Byrum blood in you really will make you end up no better than he was."

Joshua wheeled and was about to come violently at Alphus, but he caught himself. He was surprised at Alphus for having said such a thing and at himself for the violent way he had been about to respond.

"Don't ever say that to me again, Alphus," Joshua said. "Don't ever let such words cross your lips." He pivoted again and walked back around the cabin.

Joshua remained alone until Gabriel, Darcy, and the Kincaids emerged. Darcy looked grim, but Gabriel seemed unusually happy, as did the Kincaids. Kincaid outlined what had been discussed. He and his wife, he said, had become so enamored of Mary Fiske that they wished to keep her with them permanently, or as long as Darcy and Gabriel would allow. Darcy and Gabriel had agreed.

No doubt Gabriel had agreed very readily, Joshua thought. He had never wanted the feeble old woman about his place, as he had made clear before. Joshua wished he could talk privately to Darcy about the situation, to find out exactly how the decision had been reached, but private talk with her was out of the question now that Gabriel was here.

Alphus, however, was able to talk to Darcy later and conveyed to Joshua what she had said, even though it was clearly difficult for him to talk to Joshua. Their earlier angry exchange remained a fresh wound for both of them. Darcy's initial response to Kincaid's unusual proposal, Alphus said, was a staunch refusal to see her mother placed in the care of others when she felt it was her duty, and Gabriel's, to see to that care herself. But Gabriel had seemed so eager to accept the Kincaids' offer that at last she had relented, realizing that the elderly woman would receive more tenderness and care in this house than in Gabriel's.

"Why is Gabriel so firm against doing his duty by his wife's mother?" Joshua asked.

Alphus lifted a brow. "Can't you see, Joshua? He doesn't like to see feebleness around him. It reminds him that he's mortal and that someday he'll be old. There's two things my son has feared since he was a lad, and the first is being wrong, thinking falsely about something and looking unwise for it. The second is growing old. That's what frightens him worst of all, for at the end of growing old comes dying. And dying, you see, is a thing he cannot control. It comes unbidden, and takes you when you don't want to go. It's my belief that Gabriel will always fear dying, unless there comes a way for him to choose the time and means of it, for then it will be his choice, and not forced upon him."

Joshua smiled skeptically. "I think it's simpler than that. I think he's just a selfish coward."

A vein bulged in Alphus's neck, but he swallowed down an angry retort. He spoke with deliberate softness. "You see nothing good in Gabriel at all, Joshua, but you don't truly know him. Given his chance, he may yet show us good things we don't expect."

"I'll believe that when I see it."

Alphus, Darcy, and Gabriel returned to Haverly Fort two days later when it became evident that Mary Fiske was improving, perhaps because of Darcy's timely visit, and that she also was amenable to the idea of remaining with the Kincaids. Darcy pledged to visit her frequently. Gabriel approved that idea, which cheered Darcy until she found he did not intend to participate in those visits.

"Patton can fetch you to and fro," he said. "He can see well enough to your care."

Joshua left Reedy Creek the day before the others did; remaining in the vicinity with both Gabriel and Darcy was too uncomfortable. He did not head immediately for Haverly Fort but instead went to Watauga, thinking he might look up Israel Coffman and tell him the remarkable news regarding Christiana and Samuel.

When he arrived, he found that Coffman had departed, heading north to claim his engaged bride at last. Joshua was glad to hear such good news regarding his friend but was sorry he had missed him. A good talk with Coffman might have done him some good.

Joshua left Watauga and headed for Haverly Fort. The time had come to make his identity known to Christiana Haverly. The prospect of it made him grow more nervous the closer he came. How would she receive him? Would she be displeased to see a living reminder of hardships long past?

When he reached Haverly's house, now expanded by two rooms, making it by far the largest dwelling within many miles, Haverly met him at the door with a flintlock pistol in hand. "How dare you show your face on my property!" Haverly said. "I'll have you arrested, sir!"

"I hope you won't, Mr. Haverly. You have my apology for the way I treated you before. I've come on an important matter and must speak to your wife."

Haverly looked surprised and cautious. "What business do you have with my wife?" he asked.

Christiana appeared in the doorway behind her husband. When she recognized Joshua as the man who had previously struck her husband, she blanched. A few moments later, however, her expression changed to one of bewildered interest. Joshua could feel her gaze and knew she had detected something familiar in him.

"Hello, Christiana," Joshua said.

"You will not address my wife in so familiar a manner," Haverly said. "And how do you know her name?"

Joshua was not listening. His eyes were locked on Christiana's. He watched her gaze change from fear to question, then awe—and then the tears came.

She bounded out of the door so quickly that she almost knocked down her shocked husband, and she ran to Joshua with arms outstretched, her massive body bouncing with each stride. "Oh, Joshua, oh, my sweet boy, sweet long-lost boy!" she said, throwing her arms around him. Her body shook with great sobs. "My little woodsman, sent off alone, and come back to me at last! Joshua Byrum, do you know I've prayed for you every day of my life? Do you know how I would waken in the night and wonder if you lived? Oh, praise to God, praise to God—my prayer is answered!"

"Christiana," Joshua said, hugging her close, barely finding his voice. "Christiana . . ."

"Here, here—what's this foolishness now?" Haverly said from the porch. "What is . . . why are . . . ." He was utterly bewildered.

Christiana took Joshua's head between her hands and pulled his face close to hers. She looked into his eyes, studied his features. "Joshua, have you been well all these years? Have they been happy years?"

"I've been well. I found a good home, a good man who made himself my father. My name is Joshua Colter now, as you may have heard. I've had many happy times,

Christiana." His eyes warmed with tears. "And of late, some not so happy."

Joshua had not come with the intention of casting his sorrows on Christiana's shoulders, but being with her again and hearing her talk to him as if she saw him not as a man but as the boy she had known broke some wall within him. It was almost as if his own mother was with him again. He could no more control his feelings than he could the day he had futilely lifted a flint knife to kill John Hawk in Awahili's house.

"I'm sorry for the foul way I spoke to you before, Christiana."

"There is no time for sorrow today, my boy. The day we are together again has come. Did I not tell you all those years ago that it finally would?"

"Aye, you did."

She took Joshua's hand and led him toward the house. Haverly, his eyes big with confusion, protested and feebly demanded an explanation, but Christiana and Joshua went past him into the house, leaving him standing alone, his rifle dangling in his hand.

Joshua's reunion with Christiana proved as joyful and healing an event as he had hoped it would. Cooper Haverly at first was taken aback at learning that Joshua was none other than his brother by blood but was thrilled by the idea as soon as he became accustomed to it. For Joshua, the only difficult outcomes of the reunion were that Peter Haverly was far from pleased to learn the link between his wife and the disreputable "former Under Sheriff Colter" and the hostile way Gabriel treated Joshua now that he was back in the settlement.

Even Joshua's relationship to Alphus remained strained. Alphus never apologized for his brutal remark about Jack Byrum's blood legacy living in Joshua, and he and Joshua drifted further apart. Seldom did Joshua visit his foster father's cabin, and the time finally came when Sina turned her head whenever Joshua passed so she would not have to speak to him. Ironically, as Joshua pulled away from Alphus and Sina, Gabriel drew closer to them. For the first time in Joshua's recollection, Alphus and Gabriel seemed to be real friends, not just near strangers who happened to share the same bloodline.

Joshua seldom saw Darcy, who mostly kept to herself in Gabriel's big house. From time to time Joshua heard she was gone, visiting Mary Fiske up on Reedy Creek, and sometimes he considered riding in that direction in hopes of seeing her. But he never did it, despite his feelings.

He wondered if time would take those feelings away and finally concluded it would not. Feelings were stubborn things, and he could not seem to control his where Darcy was concerned. The result was a great deal of frustration, some of which he vented through vigorous hunting and exploration, some of which he relieved through drinking and occasional brawling. His reputation in the community did not improve, nor did his self-respect.

Shining like a beacon in the midst of all this gloom was Christiana Haverly, who proved to be as loving and gentle as she had been in Fort Loudoun days. She rejoiced in Joshua's presence, talking to him sometimes for hours at a time, telling him about her life since their parting.

Only one thing she seemed reluctant to tell Joshua, and that was how she had managed to escape Henry Dorey. The subject seemed to trouble her greatly every time Joshua raised it. Finally she took him aside one evening, walked with him more than a mile to a shady spot near where Sinking Creek spilled into the Nolichucky, and poured out a confession. "I murdered Henry Dorey," she said. "I pushed him over a cliff. Please do not think too harshly of me for it, Joshua. It was the only hope for my dear babies to escape. After you were gone, he turned all his rage on me and even the babies, as tiny as they were."

Joshua laughed aloud. "Christiana, believe me, you did not murder Henry Dorey. I saw him alive in a tavern in Salisbury in 1770."

Christiana was stunned. "But he fell so far, and hit bottom so hard—"

"It wasn't enough to kill him," Joshua said. "He was alive enough when I saw him. But he is dead now. He died in that very tavern. Don't fear—it was not me who killed him."

He told her the story but omitted any reference to Dorey's murder of Bloody Eagle, even though Christiana would have been very interested since she had known Bloody Eagle, at least by sight and reputation, back in Fort Loudoun. The reason for the omission was simple: Joshua did not like talking of the matter that had alienated John Hawk from him.

Neither did he talk of having encountered the scalpless Jack Byrum in the battle in the North Carolina mountains. He saw no reason to tell her about that, for she might let the information slip, and Joshua did not want his kin to know that his father had been among the outlaws who plagued Hankins Creek.

Of all other matters Joshua spoke freely to Christiana. She spoke just as freely to him, confessing that her marriage to Peter Haverly had derived more from her need of a means of survival than from love. She had escaped the wilderness with the babies and made her way into Virginia, arriving in a half-starved condition. "You would never believe it, looking at me now, twice the size I was at Fort Loudoun, but after the wilderness I was nigh thin as a fence post. And the babies were near dead, they were."

She and the babies had been taken in by settlers, nursed back to sufficient health to travel, and then sent to the home of a wealthy and philanthropic family of the surname Plumley in the city of Williamsburg. It was there that Christiana met Peter Haverly, a recent widower. She confided to Joshua that Haverly was distasteful to her from the beginning.

"Only when I compared him to Henry Dorey did he shine with any light at all," she said. "But he did show much concern for me, and great interest in my plans and future, and I responded to him for lack of any other hope.

It was for the babies' sake that I married him, praying that love would follow."

"And has it?"

Christiana smiled. "A little, yes. He is not a bad man, Joshua, not in his heart. He is but a blind one, seeing little but himself. He fancies himself better than other men, and believes they cannot live without his leadership. In fact, it is he who can't live without them, for if they withhold their adoration, he withers like a pumpkin on a severed vine."

Whether Christiana said those words because she foresaw what was coming for Peter Haverly was something Joshua never determined. Through the end of 1773 and into the spring of 1774, however, it became evident that Haverly's influence in the settlement was declining. He had never found a replacement for Israel Coffman in his church's pulpit, and gradually his congregation drifted away until only a handful of people continued to come, chief among them Gabriel, whose adoration for Haverly knew no tempering.

Haverly's declining status resulted not from any one damaging event, such as a revelation of wrongdoing. It seemed, at least from Joshua's perspective, to be the natural result of the man's insufferable vanity, the "blindness" to which Christiana had referred. Joshua considered himself no great student of human nature, but one thing he did know: Men and women of the temperament and skill to carve out a life in the wilderness were not prone to be lorded over by any man. Courtesy and hospitality they would give to all; respect they would give when it was merited; devotion they would give when it was hard-earned—but they gave little honor to those whose authority derived solely from stuffed purses, pretty titles, and unmerited self-pride.

There had been reason for Joshua to think on such matters of late. Though news traveled slowly from seaboard to frontier, what had come in lately had been particularly intriguing. For the past year or more there had been much talk about events in the distant East, events that would affect the frontier settlements, one way or another, depending upon where they led.

Back in the early summer of 1772, the settlers had learned, several boatloads of American colonists had burned a British customs schooner, the *Gaspee*, off the coast of Rhode Island. The mercantile-minded British hated smuggling as much as Americans loved it, for it seemed the only way to circumvent the extensive British trade restrictions that were designed to benefit the mother country primarily, and the colonies only second-arily if at all. The fact that suspects in the *Gaspee* burning were later sent for trial in London rather than tried at home, where the crime occurred outraged the colonists, who saw what meager right to self-rule they possessed being strangled.

Colonial grievances against England were being spo-ken with ever-louder voices and with greater backing of authority. In Virginia, the House of Burgesses created a correspondence committee to coordinate complaints against Britain; before the spring of 1774, most of the other colonies had done the same.

Many of the colonial complaints, as Joshua heard them, centered on trade. In 1773, there had been much ado over the import tax on tea and an act that allowed certain companies' agents to undersell those colonial merchants who were forced to buy their tea through English middle-men.

At the end of 1773, many colonists, including many of the Tennessee frontiersmen, sent up a cheer at news that a group of "Mohawk Indians" had dumped upwards of three hundred casks of tea from an English vessel into Boston Harbor. The story roused much mirth among the Haverly Fort settlers, though Joshua noticed that Peter Haverly did not laugh. One of Haverly's chief financial holdings was a Boston tea dealership that was one of Britain's favored outlets. To Peter Haverly, the rebellion against Britain was a travesty that struck close to his heart and his purse.

*   *   *

Such events as the tea dumping in Boston, as important as they were, nevertheless seemed distant to most frontiersmen. As the spring of 1774 progressed, an event closer to home was to prove traumatic enough to occupy most of their attention and affect Joshua's life as well.

Word reached Haverly Fort in early spring of a celebration scheduled in the Watauga settlement for the Cherokees. A horse race was to be part of the celebration—a race the white participants would surely make sure the Cherokees won, for to best them might do great diplomatic harm. There was good reason for trying to bolster diplomacy between the settlers and the Cherokees at the moment. As more and more white settlers came in and the barking rifles of white hunters echoed ever more through the mountains, a spirit of unrest had been growing among factions of the Cherokees. There was unrest on the white men's side as well, much of it stemming from the massacre in which Will Fiske had died. Many whites tended to make imprecise distinctions between Indians, and the actions of Big Jim and the other Shawnees that morning on Wallen's Ridge were held against Indians as a whole by many.

Joshua rode to Watauga to attend the games and while there sought out Israel Coffman and met Coffman's new bride, the former Virginia Blanton of New Jersey. She was a delightful young lady, though as ill-suited to frontier life as Coffman had been when first he came. Not having seen Coffman for so long, Joshua was able to look at him objectively and see that he had adapted better to his new life than Joshua had anticipated. In his clothing, his bearing, his conversation, and even the way he kept his rifle close at hand, Coffman was growing to be more a frontiersman and less a citified theologian.

Coffman had heard of Joshua's lowered reputation and asked him, frankly but gently, about it. Joshua could give him no answer. He could hardly tell the very man who had baptized him that he was in love with the wife of his foster brother and that because she was now unavailable to him, he could no longer seem to keep control of his own behavior.

Coffman sensed Joshua's reluctance to talk and did not push him further. "I keep you in my prayers always, Joshua," he said. "I want what is best for you and won't rest until I see you have it. You will once again find the right road, with God's help."

"Thank you, Israel," he murmured uncomfortably. Turning to Coffman's wife, he bid her a good-day and wandered off toward a table set in the shade of a spreading maple tree laden with jugs of rum.

There were many Cherokees present, and among them Joshua looked for John Hawk. He did not find him and inquired. John Hawk had not come, he was told. He said there was nothing for the Cherokees to celebrate with the white men at present and he would not be part of it. John Hawk, Joshua was told, was a different man than he had been before when he had listened mostly to Attakullakulla and to Attakullakulla's niece Tsistunagiska. Her name at birth had been Nanye'hi, and she was usually called Nancy Ward by the white men. Joshua had heard of Nancy Ward, who held the powerful rank of *agigaue* in the tribe, giving her a vote in the council of chiefs and leadership of the council of women, represented by each Cherokee clan. Nancy Ward had gained her English last name through her marriage in the 1750s to trader Bryant Ward, and she, like her uncle, had often spoken for peace between the Cherokees and white men.

Now John Hawk heeded Little Carpenter and Nancy Ward no longer but heard instead the voice of Little Carpenter's son, Dragging Canoe, who was militant against the settlers.

Joshua asked when John Hawk had changed his allegiance. It was when he returned from living many months with the white men came the answer. John Hawk returned to the Overhill towns, bearing with him a powder horn marked with the skin of Bloody Eagle, treacherously slain many years ago by a white man. The murder had been hidden from John Hawk while he was among the whites, hidden by a white man John Hawk had thought was his friend. Now John Hawk believed the white men were incapable of truth and could never be true and lasting friends of the Cherokees.

Joshua was greatly disheartened to hear these things. He walked away, musing. Meanwhile, the great horse race that was the highlight of the celebration was taking place. He watched the white riders racing along beside the nearly naked Cherokee horsemen. As the race was nearing its end, he was startled by the sound of a shot. A woman's scream followed. Joshua wheeled and looked for the source of the disturbance. A group of people, Cherokees and whites, began running toward the edge of a large clump of woods across a meadow. He loped off in the same direction.

When he reached the group, which had stopped and circled around something on the ground, Joshua found that what had happened was exactly what he had feared as soon as he heard the shot. A Cherokee, whose name was given by an onlooker as Cherokee Billie, lay dead in the meadow in a circle of blood. He had been shot, someone said, from the forest nearby. That it was murder was obvious; Cherokee Billie, like most of the Cherokees at the celebration, had carried no weapons today.

The Cherokees circled the body of their slain fellow and in threatening silence picked him up and carried him away, disappearing into the forest until the whites were left alone. The silence held for a few moments until it was broken by a child's sob from somewhere across the meadow. After that, a murmur of conversation began to rise among the people.

"There may well come war of this, Joshua Colter," a man said. Joshua, thinking he recognized the voice, turned and saw he was right. It was James Robertson.

"Aye, James. Who did this thing?"

"I'm told it was a man who came here from Wolf Hills. A blasted outsider come in to stir trouble—and the worst of it is, I've already heard three people saying it was a good killing. Served the Indians justice in return for the Wallen's Ridge killings, they say. The killer's gotten clean away, and with some help, I fear."

Joshua suspected the same. "What is the killer's name?" he asked.

"I don't know. But if what I'm hearing is true, he was a witness to the Wallen's Ridge killings. It's said that after he saw that, he swore he would kill any Indian he could kill, upon any chance he received."

"I know the man, then," Joshua said. "His name is Isaac Crabtree."

21

Four horsemen traveled slowly along the Cherokee Road out of Watauga, heading for Chota. The lead rider was James Robertson, followed by Alphus Colter. Behind Alphus rode William Faulin, a man of good reputation with both the Overmountain settlers and the Cherokees, and behind him, Joshua Colter, whose presence was due not to good reputation but to his insistence that his foster father not enter this dangerous country without him along to help protect him.

Alphus had not wanted Joshua on this journey and had made no attempt to hide that fact. At first Joshua was offended, but as he thought it over, he realized that Alphus was simply trying to protect him. This journey would not be the relatively safe venture the 1772 visit to Chota had been. The murder of Cherokee Billie had generated much anger among the Cherokees, particularly since Isaac Crabtree had been allowed to escape without punishment. The purpose of this trip was to make amends with the Cherokees and assure them the murder did not have the support of the Overmountain settlers—though such an assurance would be a half-truth at best.

Though the riders felt unseen eyes studying them as soon as they reached the region of the Overhill towns, they had seen little Cherokee activity. As they approached Chota, however, that changed. Warriors, squaws, and even children watched with open bitterness as they rode in with white beads and other symbolic peace gifts for the headmen openly displayed. As he rode, Alphus sang a Cherokee peace song that he had learned, ironically, from John Hawk during the warrior's extended visit with Joshua.

Some of the warriors brandished weapons at the peace delegation. From somewhere among the children a stone flew, striking Faulin on the shoulder. He did not react but stared straight ahead, a somewhat grim smile etched across his face.

After what seemed half an eternity, the riders came near to the Chota townhouse and were cheered to see the familiar figure of Little Carpenter. The chief had during his journey to London adopted the white man's custom of shaking hands, and now he welcomed the visitors by shaking hands with them all. Joshua he greeted with particular warmth, a broad smile on his thin ornamentally scarred face. Little Carpenter's appearance of exaggerated age was even more apparent now. Even though he was no older than Alphus, he looked at least fifteen years the old long hunter's senior.

"John Hawk spoke to me of your hospitality during his long visit to your fort," Little Carpenter said to Joshua, leaving him wondering how much ironic significance was in those words.

"It was my pleasure to have John Hawk as my guest," Joshua said. "He left in anger, but I hold no anger toward him and hope that I can again be the friend of him and all his people."

Little Carpenter smiled but made no response. He walked away from Joshua to where James Robertson stood.

"Come," he said. "We have much talking to do."

* * *

Alphus looked out the door of the Cherokee house in which Robertson's delegation had been lodged, peering into a darkness broken only by cloud-dimmed moonlight and a flaring fire around which drunken warriors staggered. When he closed the door and turned back to the others, he looked slightly pallid.

"Drunk as Bacchus, and getting more so every minute, by Joseph," he said, walking to the far wall where he sat on the floor, staring at the door.

"What do you think will happen?" Robertson asked.

"If we're of good fortune, nothing more than much drinking of rum and making of threatening noises," Alphus answered. "If we are of bad fortune, our lives might pay for that of the murdered Cherokee."

Joshua, whose usual pipe of clay had been broken earlier in the day, finished gouging the pith from a stub of corncob and rounded out a hole carefully drilled with his knife through the side. "We may need to make a quick run for it if that keeps up," he said, lifting the pipe bowl and squinting at it.

"A run? Through the midst of Chota?" Faulin asked skeptically.

Joshua shrugged, fitting a short reed stem into the hole to complete the pipe. "Either run or fight, and at these odds, a fight makes little sense."

"You think like an Indian," Robertson observed.

"May I have a bit of your sotweed, Alphus?" Joshua asked.

"Aye." Alphus handed his deerskin tobacco pouch to Joshua.

"Thank you." Joshua filled and lit the pipe, sending out rich smoke in the dimly lighted log house.

What nervousness Joshua felt, he hid well; he had learned that skill many years ago, living around Jack Byrum. And he did feel nervous tonight, for good cause; the situation here was volatile.

The day's talks had seemed to proceed smoothly enough. Little Carpenter and the war chief, Oconostota, had seemed receptive to Robertson's assurances that

Crabtree's treachery did not reflect any official hostility
of the Overmountain settlers toward the Cherokees.
Crabtree would be caught and punished. He was a man
of low reputation even before the killing, suspected of
thievery, Robertson said. His actions were deplorable,
and for them the settlers were sorrowful.

The chiefs had listened and on the surface had seemed
to accept Robertson's apologetic words. But trouble
lurked elsewhere in Chota. Indians of Cherokee Billie's
family were still enraged at his murder, and even as the
talks proceeded, Joshua saw dangerous, half-hidden stirrings going on all around him. He kept a placid look on
his face, but his eyes took in much, and his ears picked
up talk. In the midst of all this he kept watch for John
Hawk, who had lived in Chota since the fading away of
Tikwalitsi, but he did not see him.

One thing that he overheard in fragmentary fashion
aroused his concern. One of the warriors mentioned to
another that his brother was among some twoscore Cherokees, led by the swarthy, athletic chief called the Raven,
who apparently were even now in the country of the
Shawnees many miles northward, conferring with the
great chief Cornstalk. "The Raven" was a war title for a
chief known as Savanucah or Coronoh. He was a Cherokee by marriage; by birth he was a Shawnee, and thus
was well-suited to diplomatic missions to that tribe.

The nature of the Raven's current mission Joshua
could easily guess. With the Ohio River country being
surveyed and mapped by Virginia, the Shawnees were
concerned and angry. The Wallen's Ridge killings had
reflected their determination to see Kentucky remain in
Shawnee hands. If the Cherokees were in conference
with the Shawnees, it was surely to discuss the possibility
of a war alliance to deal with their mutual concern of
protecting their lands.

Since the Watauga lease of 1772, the Cherokees had
become embittered by what they perceived—with much
accuracy, in Joshua's view—as a breach of the spirit of
the lease agreements. According to their terms, there
was to be no interference with the Cherokees' right to

hunt on their traditional hunting lands. But in 1772 the Cherokees had not fully foreseen the way the white men's way of life would affect the land around them. Now white hunters flooded in ever-greater numbers into the hills, leading the Indians to complain to the deputy Indian agent Alexander Cameron about the encroachment and its effects on game and Cherokee hunting rights.

The Cherokees were not so much being outright denied access to their hunting lands as they were having those lands made useless to them. Cameron was quick to hear any such complaints; in 1772, he had made his views of the Overmountain men clear when he described them as "absconded debtors, indentured servants, and outlaws."

The Overmountain settlements had in the past two years sent roots deep into the land, roots that many Cherokees were only now beginning to realize could not easily be removed. Further, the existing settlements were growing, spreading out, and this was also against the Cherokees' understanding of the lease agreements, which they saw as limiting the white settlers to the lands already occupied. New cabins were continually being built. More and more fields throughout the Overmountain country were being planted with corn, hemp, flax, turnips, potatoes, pumpkins, melons. Each passing month saw new sections of forest cleared and hogs and cattle turned out to forage and trample the resulting stump-filled rocky barrens.

Further, it was becoming ever easier for new settlers to reach the Overmountain country, particularly the Watauga settlement. The previous year, Virginia's Fincastle County had worked with the Watauga Association to see improvements made on the Watauga Road that led from Wolf Hills, in Virginia, to Watauga. Every new family that came in along that route meant another new cabin and more forests cleared for fields. The Cherokees were resentful, and Joshua, though supportive of the Overmountain settlements through the allegiance of blood and heritage, could hardly blame them.

All these concerns were voiced by Little Carpenter and Oconostota in the day's talks, which Robertson handled skillfully, heightening Joshua's admiration of him. After the talks were completed, Joshua had privately told Robertson what he had overheard concerning the Raven's current visit to the Shawnees in the Ohio country.

"I surmised the same myself, referred to rather slyly by Little Carpenter," Robertson said, his eyes of pale blue narrowing. "Should the Cherokees and Shawnees form an alliance of war, it would be a harsh tune we'd have to dance to. But it's my hope that our talks today have reduced that possibility. I asked Little Carpenter, very carefully, about the Kentucky country, and if he speaks truly, many among the Cherokees are open to the idea of a sale of those lands."

"And why would they not be?" Joshua asked. "The Cherokees have little claim on Kentucky. If someone wishes to give them goods to sell that they scarcely control, why not sell?"

Alphus, who had been posed in a loose slump, staring at the door and listening to the raucous noise of the drunken warriors outside, suddenly sat up straight. "Listen!" he said softly but sharply.

Joshua was already listening; he also had heard the shuffling noise outside the door that had caught Alphus's attention. Every man in the room reached for his rifle. A moment later, the door opened. Joshua was surprised when a familiar Indian figure appeared in the doorway. It was John Hawk.

The Cherokee said, "There is danger here, for rum is flowing. You must go now. Come, all of you, and I will show you the way to safety."

Joshua was uncertain. Could he trust John Hawk, who was now known as a man holding the staunchest sentiments against the Overmountain settlers? Not knowing how to decide, Joshua stood falteringly until Robertson stepped forward and addresssed John Hawk.

"I am the leader of this party," he said. "You are the warrior called John Hawk, I believe?"

"I am."

"If there is danger, why do you seek to save us from it?"

The Cherokee looked directly at Joshua. "Just as there is a warmth that remains for a time, even in a corpse, there also is a bond that can linger between men, even after their friendship has been severed. Come now, and leave quickly, for if the kinsmen of the slain warrior grow more angry, not even the word of Attakullakulla can save you."

John Hawk spun on his heel and stepped back into the darkness. The men in the cabin looked at each other, steeled themselves, and followed.

The Cherokee did not betray them. He took the party along a shadowy hidden route out of Chota and hid them in a remote place in the forest. He told them to stay there and that either he or Little Carpenter would come to them when it was safe to return to Chota for further talks.

John Hawk turned and left, and Joshua followed him some distance. The warrior turned. "Why do you follow me?"

"To thank you. And to ask your forgiveness for having deceived you when you lived at Haverly Fort. Our separation has weighed heavily on me, John Hawk."

The Cherokee held his silence for many moments. At last he said, "We must always be separated, Joshua Colter. I have come to believe that nothing good can come for the Ani-Yunwiya through friendship with the white men, who are liars and encroachers, and who talk of friendship when they really want nothing more than lands and wealth. Friendship between your people and mine is like marriage within a clan. It is against what is good in the great scheme of the world."

Joshua replied, "So you may believe. But I do not believe such feelings rise entirely from the event that divided us. You have heard this sort of talk from others, and these may deceive you and stir you to too much anger."

"It is the deceit of the unakas that stirs my anger. But there are others of my people who believe as I do, yes."

"Who? Dragging Canoe? The Raven?"

John Hawk declined to answer. "Good-bye, Joshua Colter. I have helped you for the sake of our former friendship, as I said. But it is a friendship that is past." He turned and began to walk away. Joshua called his name, and he stopped and looked back, frowning.

"I do not believe our friendship is past. We have been brothers since the day I gave you the coin. That has not changed, and in yourself you know this."

"I gave the coin back to you, and it now means nothing," John Hawk said. "Do not talk so freely of friendship and brotherhood to me, Joshua Colter. We are in peace now, but the day will come when we will meet in battle. Good-bye. I go now."

Joshua waited until John Hawk vanished into the black forest, then returned to the hidden camp and found the others debating whether to remain there or flee back to the settlements. Faulin, and to a lesser degree Alphus, did not trust John Hawk, believing he might have led them out of Chota, a traditional city of refuge, so that they could be killed. But Robertson disagreed, saying his talks with Little Carpenter had given him a feeling of confidence and that fleeing right now would do diplomatic harm. Joshua did not enter the debate, merely observing as Robertson's viewpoint finally won over the others. The group agreed to remain for further talks, though great caution would be maintained.

Little Carpenter came to them a day later and told them the danger was past. The kinsmen of Cherokee Billie had agreed to let the talks proceed. The little band returned to Chota, and Robertson, Little Carpenter, and Oconostota resumed their conferences. Joshua noted that Robertson again cautiously approached the question of a sale of Kentucky lands and again received a veiled but cautiously positive response. Joshua wondered if Robertson had some link to Daniel Boone's employer, Richard Henderson, who was still actively pursuing his plans for a major land purchase, or if he was simply speaking out of his own interest in new lands and settlement.

When July came, the Overmountain emissaries departed Chota, riding back toward Watauga. It had been a successful mission. Robertson was convinced now that no major reprisal for the Cherokee Billie murder would come and that he had subtly wooed the headmen away from support of an alliance with the Shawnees.

The group's arrival in Watauga brought much excitement, for word had come back to the settlements that the entire delegation might have been killed. Fear had seized the settlers; Cherokee raids had been anticipated.

Robertson's news of success cheered the settlers, and word that Joshua's presence and influence upon John Hawk had apparently helped keep the delegation safe bolstered Joshua's stature among his peers. When he and Alphus left Watauga to ride back to Haverly Fort, Joshua felt more cheerful and welcome among his own people than he had in months. Even better, he and Alphus had grown closer through the peace mission, and though no direct apologies had been spoken on either side, their old mutual warmth had substantially returned.

Haverly Fort's people cheered for Alphus and Joshua when they arrived. Sina and Zachariah were ecstatic in their tearful welcome of Joshua and Alphus. Sina seemed happier than she had at any time since Tilly's death and touched Joshua very deeply when she hugged him close and told him she loved him. Her recent coolness toward him was not evident now. Joshua felt as if he had been cleansed.

Gabriel was the only person at Haverly Fort who seemed unsure of how to respond to his father and foster brother. Alphus he greeted joyfully, but toward Joshua he was stiff and ambivalent.

"I reckon you were pleased to hear I had been done in by some of your 'red demons,'" Joshua said to him, prompting a stern reprimand from Alphus that saved Gabriel from having to respond. Joshua assumed that Gabriel's attitude was a simple outgrowth of the previous widespread gossip concerning the supposed adultery between himself and Darcy, but he later received information that further explained matters.

Two events had happened between Gabriel and Darcy

while Joshua and Alphus were in Chota, and both had
put distance between the already unaffectionate pair.
Sina described what had happened to Alphus, who later
passed it on to Joshua.

The first was that Darcy had become pregnant and
then lost the baby in a manner that led Gabriel to hold
her responsible.

According to Sina, Darcy had apparently suspected
she was with child but had not told Gabriel for fear he
would make her cease her journeys to Reedy Creek to
visit her mother. In any case, during one such trip she
was thrown from her horse, resulting in bleeding and
discharge that greatly frightened Patton, who was accompanying her. The slave somehow managed to get Darcy
home where she was put to bed, very pallid and weak,
and examined by Sina and Jean McSwain. Both recognized at once what had happened; Sina sadly reported to
Gabriel that Darcy had miscarried.

Gabriel took the news hard; he assumed that the lost
child was the son he had wanted since his marriage,
though the sex of the baby was not known. Further, he
held the miscarriage against Darcy, blaming her for it.

Then came the second event, a blow that struck Gabriel even harder than the loss of the baby. When the
rumors of the killing of the peace emissaries to Chota
reached Haverly Fort, Darcy went into deep grief, and it
was evident that her grief was deepest not for Alphus but
for Joshua. She wept each time his name was mentioned,
refused Gabriel's very touch, and once called him Joshua.
So vocal was her grief that word of it spread, giving
further support to gossip that Darcy had been improperly
involved with her husband's foster brother. Some even
speculated that the baby lost in the riding accident had
not been Gabriel's but Joshua's and that Darcy might
have intentionally caused the miscarriage to cover her
sin.

"I think you'll not hear that particular rumor repeated
in your presence, Joshua," Alphus said to the enraged
Joshua. "Folks are too fearful of your temper to risk it."

"Any who does dare to repeat it," Joshua said, "will have cause to be fearful."

Alphus smiled, then grew very serious. "We have had differences recently, but I love you no less than ever. I love Gabriel as well, and have come to know him better now as a man than ever I did when he was a boy. I'm growing old now. I hope that before I die, I will see my two sons united—brothers, as they should be."

"For your sake, Alphus, I wish it could be. But Gabriel and I can never be brothers, especially not now. All this talk of adultery between Darcy and me is false. I think you know that. But Gabriel half believes it—that I can tell. He'll always have bitter feelings toward me . . . just as I will always have tender ones toward Darcy."

"A man's feelings are like his beasts. He must guide them, not let them guide him. The marriage of two people is sacred, no matter what feelings come and go. When the pledge is given, it is sealed in the eyes of God himself, and woe be to the outsider who destroys it."

"You need not fret," Joshua said. "I have no plan to destroy Gabriel's marriage. It's my intention to not even lay eyes on Darcy, any more than need be. For when I see her, I can hardly bear the hurting of it."

Joshua tried to keep his pledge, but circumstances made it impossible. He did see Darcy, several times, and could not always determine whether it was by chance or unconscious design. She told him each time of her joy in knowing that he had not been killed in Chota and each time began to say more, then restrained herself. Loving Darcy when she was inaccessible brought pain to Joshua; seeing so clearly that she loved him as well made that pain torturous.

Joshua realized at last that he would have to leave Haverly Fort again. There was more behind the decision than his uncomfortable proximity to Darcy. Financial concern was one factor. Though Gabriel's packing business still thrived, Joshua could not bring himself to work much for either Gabriel or Haverly and thus lost any income he would have received there. Times had changed. A man could not make money in deerskin and furs as easily as just a few years before, partly because of market changes, partly because settlement of the wilderness was driving game farther away. Bit by bit, Joshua was finding he could not make much of a living around Haverly Fort.

A second factor was encouragement by Christiana Cox. She had welcomed Joshua's return from Chota with deep emotion—obviously displeasing Peter Haverly—and Joshua turned to her more than ever as his counselor and friend. Christiana held to as stern a moral code as Alphus's, but she had the sensitivity and wisdom of a gentle mother, and slowly she made Joshua see that his best interests, as well as those of his relations, would be best served if he moved away. "But this time," she warned, "there'll be no waiting another halfscore and three years before you see me again, eh? You will come see your dear Christiana, will you not?"

"Aye, certainly I will," he said.

The third factor leading him away from Haverly Fort was of a more political and practical nature. The Shawnees, despite the decision of the Cherokees not to join them, were bent on war against the Virginia surveyors and woodsmen penetrating into Kentucky. Virginia's Governor Dunmore had ordered an attack on the Ohio River Shawnees, and a plea came south from Evan Shelby for volunteers from Watauga and Haverly Fort. Alphus considered answering the call but at Sina's urging decided not to. He was now sixty-four years old in an era when many men died before their fiftieth birthday. His age beginning to creep up on him, he was too old to be an effective Indian fighter.

Joshua, however, volunteered for service, as did Callum McSwain, James Robertson, and Joshua's former superior in his under sheriff days, Valentine Sevier. From across the region more than forty other men volunteered, though they had plenty of concerns close-by to keep them at home and had few ties to the distant Ohio River region. Such was the way of the Overmountain frontier, and it would not be the last time that frontiersmen from the Tennessee country would rally to the aid of besieged peers in distant areas.

The volunteers met at Shelby's Fort, where Joshua warmly greeted both Evan and Isaac Shelby, and paused briefly to pay his respects at the grave of Levi Hampton. The assembled volunteers promptly traveled northward as a group to join the army of General Andrew Lewis.

On October 10, at Lewis's camp near the place where the Kanawha River flowed into the Ohio, James Robertson and Valentine Sevier left the encampment to hunt and scout, and encountered a huge army of Indians creeping toward the camp. They fired on the Indians, then darted back to camp, shouting the alarm and rousing the large band of colonial troops for what would be the bloodiest battle ever fought on that half of the continent between Indians and whites.

For the whites, the minutes before the battle involved a flurry of desperate, rushed checking of weapons and the inner voicing of several hundred intense prayers. This, Joshua Colter predicted, would be a close-quarters fight, for it was likely to be confined to the triangular spit of land at the confluence of the Ohio and Great Kanawha rivers. Joshua was grateful, as the battle loomed, for Alphus's years of instruction; because of them, his weapons were always in a state of cleanliness and readiness. A final check of his gunflint and horn let him know he was as ready as he could hope to be for the fight to come.

This was a battle being fought against the counsel of the great Shawnee chief, Cornstalk. He had tried to quell his warriors' desire for immediate bloodshed, but had failed. As he had yielded to the inevitable, it had been his choice to attack Lewis's force at this time and place, for delay would have allowed the arrival of more soldiers and provisions. As the first rifles cracked, Cornstalk launched into the battle, urging on the composite force of Shawnees, Mingos, Hurons, Ottawas, and Delawares. Throughout the fight, Joshua would hear Cornstalk's booming battle yells many times.

There were fearsome and prominent warriors among the Indian forces, including the chief Pucksinwah, and his son, Chiksika. These were the father and older brother, respectively, of an Indian named Tecumseh, whose name would one day be listed among the most influential and intelligent of all Indian leaders. Also in the fight on the Indian side were some whites who had been adopted into Indian tribes, and a lone woman, a muscled giantess named Nonhelema.

As Joshua had anticipated, the fight was physically close. The Indians struggled valiantly with muskets, rifles, clubs, knives, and bows-and-arrows. The air grew acrid with gunsmoke so thick that it seared the lungs and stung the eyes to near-blindness. In the thick of the fight, Joshua reloaded and fired off a shot at an approaching Shawnee; the Indian fell, and Joshua ducked behind a tree and scurried to reload, sweat pouring from him and his heart pounding. Another Shawnee drew near, saw him, and with a cry leapt toward him with a club upraised. There was no time to reload. Joshua gave an answering yell, raised his rifle by its barrel, and lunged forward, swinging it like a long hammer at his naked attacker.

Casualties in the day-long fight were great among the whites. As the battle progressed, officers fell, and those under them automatically advanced in authority to fill the gaps. Evan Shelby found himself commanding directly under Lewis himself, and Isaac Shelby replaced his father as commander of the volunteers who had assembled at Shelby's Fort.

When the bloody day was done and the Indians had retreated across the Ohio River, seventy-five white fighters lay dead on the battlefield. Many had been scalped, and some had been so mutilated by the blows of tomahawks that they were unrecognizable. Only thirty-three Indian bodies were found. Among those who had fallen was Pucksinwah. Nevertheless, the battle was interpreted as a victory for the Virginia forces, for the Indians had been forced to retreat, even if they had not surrendered. The exhausted fighters were joyful in the perceived success of what would thereafter be called the Battle of Point Pleasant.

But for Callum McSwain, James Robertson, Valentine Sevier, and the other Shelby's Fort volunteers, the joy was tempered greatly by casualties in their number. Six men had been killed or wounded. As the surviving group assembled, it took only moments to assess the identities of those lost.

One loss in particular weighed heavily on McSwain, Robertson, and Sevier. Robertson, wiping away the trace of a tear, strode up to McSwain and handed him a thong upon which hung an ancient coin bearing strange words.

"Give this to Alphus," Robertson said, "and tell him he fought bravely until the end. I saw him bring down three Shawnees before I lost sight of him."

McSwain took the coin and squeezed it in his fist. "You took this from his body?"

"I found it on the ground where it had come off him— you'll want to wash the blood from it before you give it to his kin. The Shawnees had tormented his corpse considerable." Robertson paused. "If you wish, Callum, I'll ride back to Haverly Fort with you to help give word of his death."

"No, no," McSwain said. There were none of his sweeping gestures or dramatic inflections now. " 'Tis a job I can do alone, and you'll be needed by your own family." McSwain shook his head. "Hard to believe, it is, that he's gone."

"Aye, Callum. That it is."

The volunteers rode back to Shelby's Fort in November and there mustered out to return to their homes. McSwain, wishing solitude to prepare himself for giving the grim news about Joshua Colter, traveled alone after leaving Shelby's. At first he wore the Roman coin about his own neck, but that felt unnatural and somehow inappropriate, so finally he put it in his bullet pouch.

Passing near Reedy Creek, he encountered another traveler and was told that during the absence of Shelby's volunteers, Indian troubles of the most unexpected sort had descended upon the Holston. A Mingo Indian named Logan, whose family had been killed in a brutal and grotesque manner along the Ohio River, had swept down as far as the Tennessee country in a great campaign of vengeance. Logan's warriors struck unsuspecting settlers living along the Clinch and Holston Rivers, and on Reedy Creek, two families were killed. One was the family of a man named John Roberts; the other, a family named Kincaid.

McSwain took the news like a kick in the stomach, for he knew that Darcy Colter's mother had lived with the Kincaids.

"What of an old woman living with the family?" he asked. "Did she die as well?"

"Aye, she did," the man said. "You knew her?"

"Aye, and her kin I know even better. It's some hard blows they have been dealt . . . and I am on my way to deal them yet another."

With the heaviest of hearts, McSwain rode the final distance to Haverly Fort. He did not pause at his house or his smithy before proceeding on to Alphus's cabin. Alphus and Sina were outside stacking firewood when he rode into view. When he saw McSwain was alone, Alphus straightened his shoulders and swallowed deeply.

No words passed, but none were needed. McSwain, his teeth clenched so that his chin would not tremble, reached into his bullet pouch and lifted out the Roman coin. Still in the saddle, he held it out. Alphus walked up and took it, a stunned expression on his face. Sina lowered her head and cried.

Alphus studied the coin for half a minute, then closed his hand around it as he lifted reddened eyes to McSwain. "Did he die bravely?"

"Aye," McSwain replied. "He died bravely."

"Poor Joshua," Alphus said, his voice trembling into feebleness as tears started. "My Joshua . . . by Joseph, I do hate to hear he's gone. I do so hate to hear it."

THE DRAGON
AND
THE HAWK

22

John Hawk looked ahead as
he rode, his eyes sweeping across the forested mountains
watching for any hint of danger, unexpected shifts of the
terrain, or sign of inclement weather. But these things
he did unconsciously; his thoughts were miles away,
back in Chota with Ayasta, his new bride. He had taken
her for his wife only months before, and since then his
mind had seldom strayed from her. Now he had special
reason to think of her, for she had told him, shortly
before he had left with this small delegation accompanying Little Carpenter, that there was new life stirring
within her. Before the next summer came, John Hawk
would be a father.

The thought had overwhelmed John Hawk for a variety
of reasons. It wasn't because he would be intimately
involved in raising the boy. In the matriarchal society of
the Cherokees, his role as father would be of much less
importance than if the Cherokees shared the white
men's paternal culture. Even so, he already felt unusually
close to this unborn child. He had a tremendous curiosity
to know what it would look like, for Ayasta was a beautiful
woman and he was considered a handsome man. If the

child was a son, as he hoped, he certainly would grow up
to be a fine warrior, for Ayasta's only brother was valiant
both as a hunter and fighter. The brother, who had been
stung by a yellow jacket as an infant and thus had been
named Ulagu after a great yellow jacket of Cherokee
legend, would be the boy's chief guide, just as Awahili,
the Bloody Eagle, had been John Hawk's mentor.

John Hawk was deeply curious about what kind of
world his child would grow up in. Only weeks ago he
would have been pessimistic. There would be nothing to
anticipate but a world steadily shrinking under continued
encroachment by the white men. Now he felt differently.
There was suddenly a plausible hope that the trend could
be slowed, perhaps reversed, in the country of the Overhill Cherokees. That hope, one he hardly dared harbor,
was related directly to the mission on which he now
accompanied Little Carpenter.

They had traveled into the mountains, into North Carolina, to meet with a small group of men. One was named
Richard Henderson, a man of some legal authority in
North Carolina. John Hawk did not fully understand
where Henderson fit into the white men's system of law,
which was almost as impenetrable to him as the Cherokee system was to most whites. A second man was
expected to be the well-known woodsman named Boone,
who worked for Henderson. There might be others as
well. At a designated meeting place, Little Carpenter was
to join Henderson and Boone, and examine a large store
of merchandise Henderson was offering in trade to Cherokees for the purchase of a staggering expanse of land.

Initially the idea of such a sale had repelled John Hawk,
who believed it would entrench the white men so deeply
in the Overmountain land that they would never be
driven out. This, he knew, was the view of Dragging
Canoe, whom he had come to admire for his resolute and
clear-minded stand against white encroachment and
who, because of his smallpox scars, reminded him fondly
of Bloody Eagle.

But other things had changed John Hawk's thinking.
The first was the defeat by the Long Knives, along with

their supporters, of the Shawnees along the Ohio River. Though the Raven had conferred with the Shawnees at length concerning a possible war alliance, the Cherokees had declined in the end, largely because of the smooth words of James Robertson during his peace mission to Chota. The Shawnees had fought alone—and failed to drive back the whites. The white men had demonstrated their strength most effectively, giving pause to those Cherokees who had been inclined toward war. Further, the Cherokees continued to face a chronic lack of ammunition. They had suffered this shortage since making war on the Chickasaws almost six years ago.

If driving out the whites by war was not a reasonable option, there remained only one alternative, Little Carpenter had pointed out, and that was to lure the unakas farther away from the Cherokee towns by opening to them the much-desired lands farther north. The white men had always coveted Kentucky, Little Carpenter had explained, so why not let them have it? Then, perhaps, they would vacate their Overmountain settlements, at least partially. The hills of the Cherokee hunting lands would be freer of white hunters, and fields now stripped of trees would grow again into vast forests filled with game.

Such an idea was controversial, but gradually John Hawk had come to accept it above the more warlike notions of Dragging Canoe. John Hawk did not fear war but did believe that when it was waged, it should be in circumstances conducive to victory. It seemed ironic that the easiest way for the Cherokees to lessen the blight of the unakas might be to cooperate with them.

Little Carpenter, riding at the head of the little party, halted, jolting John Hawk out of his reverie. The rest of the party, which included Little Carpenter's soft-spoken little wife, also stopped.

"We have reached our meeting place," Little Carpenter said to his retinue, pointing ahead toward a small cabin, barely visible against its leafless forest backdrop. Smoke belched from the stick chimney, and horses looked back at the Indians from a stock pen built in the snake-and-rider pattern common to unaka farmsteads. They were near the place sometimes called Atahita, sometimes Waya Gap.

The door of the cabin opened, and a distinguished, well-dressed white man with arching eyebrows, a thin line of a mouth, and a flattish nose, emerged and smiled broadly. At the same time, around the cabin walked a tall frontiersman in dark buckskins with a broad mouth and clubbed hair. John Hawk was sure as soon as he saw the pair that the first man was Henderson and the second was Boone.

Little Carpenter rode forward again, and the others followed. Sunlight glinted through the bare treetops, illuminating the path.

John Hawk could scarcely believe what Daniel Boone had told him: Joshua Colter was dead.

He let the thought pass through his mind again but still could not accommodate it. It had the same incongruity as it had hours before when Boone gave him the news. Boone had commanded forts along the Clinch River during Dunmore's War, and from combatants returning from the Point Pleasant battle he had heard that Joshua Colter had fallen. It had obviously saddened Boone, who noted that Joshua had been with him during his recent attempt to settle in Kentucky.

The news saddened John Hawk too, much more than he allowed himself to show, much more than he would have anticipated. John Hawk had worked hard to convince himself that he despised Joshua Colter—but if he despised him, why did word of his death come as such a wrenching shock?

His thoughts occupied, John Hawk did not pay much attention to the large display of stored wares Richard Henderson proudly displayed to Little Carpenter. The diminutive chief and his wife examined the goods carefully, without comment, and when they were finished, Little Carpenter nodded.

Henderson beamed. "Splendid, splendid," he said. "We have an agreement, then?"

"We will talk," Little Carpenter said. "If in these talks you can convince my people that we should sign your papers, then we shall have an agreement."

"I have the greatest confidence, sir, that all will proceed to completion." Henderson was so excited that he looked as if he could scarcely restrain himself from dancing. He brought out food and rum, and heaped lavish praises upon Little Carpenter. John Hawk was secretly offended. Though he held Little Carpenter in high regard, he had always felt that the chief, like so many of the older beloved men of his tribe, was too fond of the white man's praise, and particularly his liquor. John Hawk voiced no protest as Henderson patronized his visitors, but he did refuse his rum.

Little Carpenter and his wife remained with Henderson and Boone, at the home of Nathaniel Hart, another Henderson associate, but John Hawk returned to Chota early. As he journeyed, he felt a strange mix of emotions. He thought alternately of his beautiful Ayasta and the unknown child within her and of his old friend-turned-enemy, Joshua Colter. The former thoughts made him happy; the latter, sad.

Back in the Overhill towns, word of Little Carpenter's mission was eagerly awaited. John Hawk's news that Henderson's offered provisions were satisfactory to the old chief brought cheer to many of the Cherokee people, including John Hawk's Ayasta, who had a way of being easily lured by the promise of baubles and finery.

But to one Cherokee chieftain the news was not welcome. That was Dragging Canoe. Now in his midthirties, he was head warrior of the town of Malaquo and already showing evidence of military genius beyond that of most men, including, in John Hawk's opinion, the aging war chief Oconostota. There seemed to be nothing that could rouse fear in Dragging Canoe, but rousing fear in others Dragging Canoe could do with hardly more than a glance and dark expression. Having suffered through and survived smallpox in the 1760s, he was scarred and pitted, which only added to his ability to terrify. John Hawk had seen Dragging Canoe in battle and was glad to be his ally and not his foe. He was a fierce fighter.

Dragging Canoe was not without influence in important places. He was respected by his own people and had taken the Indian agent Alexander Cameron as his adopted brother, so that anyone who dared harm Cameron would have to anticipate Dragging Canoe's vengeance. Beyond that, it meant that Cameron and Dragging Canoe could influence each other.

Yet John Hawk had to wonder who, if anyone, could exercise any ultimate influence over the fierce Dragging Canoe. The warrior of Malaquo, more than any man John Hawk had ever known, embodied the Cherokee spirit of individualism that allowed a man to follow his own conscience when it came to making war or living in peace. Dragging Canoe had chosen peace for now, but the day might come when he would turn to war, and if that happened, John Hawk was sure, the influence of Alexander Cameron and all the elder beloved men would not restrain him.

Weeks passed, and the year of 1774 ended. Scarcely had the new year begun before hundreds of Cherokees began a slow migration toward Watauga. Though Henderson and Little Carpenter had set March as the time of the massive meeting and transaction period, no one wanted to risk missing a moment of the event. Besides, there was good food to be had, even in advance of the real meeting, and a prime opportunity for visiting between friends from the various towns. Gradually the ancient Sycamore Shoals meeting ground filled with quickly erected Indian huts, and hunters from the Overmountain settlements trekked the mountains to bring in game to feed the Cherokee visitors. All this had been contracted in advance by Henderson, who also had arranged for an abundance of corn to be available.

John Hawk brought his pregnant wife with him, built her a sturdy little lodge near a trickling creek at Sycamore Shoals, and settled back to observe the unprecedented event.

In addition to the Indian visitors, the Wataugans were also besieged by white newcomers, who vacated their own homes in the other settlements and came to Watauga to see the spectacle. As January passed and February rolled on, scores upon scores of people filled the region, new ones coming daily, ignoring the winter cold for the sake of the grandest and most flamboyant event in the history of the Overmountain settlements. By the end of the month, there were six hundred white visitors to Watauga and twice that many Indians. John Hawk wondered if the Wataugans Henderson had hired could possibly keep so many people fed, but the food never ran short. There was no rum, though; that was to be held until after the transaction.

The most influential of the Cherokee headmen came to the treaty grounds, for this massive a transaction would require much talk and ceremony. Little Carpenter was there, colorfully dressed in a matchcoat, his lobes hung with silver. Oconostota, Willanaugh, and Onistositah were also there, along with others. The white settlers were greatly taken with looking at their Indian visitors, who in such sheer numbers were indeed a colorful and impressive sight.

In early March, preliminary talks began, mostly involving much gift giving, compliment sharing, oratory, and general strutting on all sides, with little substance behind it all. During this time Henderson made sure the Cherokees had opportunities to examine the six wagonloads of goods he had brought across the mountains and displayed in specially built huts on the treaty grounds.

It was the middle of the month before serious negotiations began. These involved alternate talks by the Cherokee representatives with Henderson and his agents, followed by more private sessions in which the Cherokees debated among themselves what Henderson offered.

Though not an active participant in the debate, John Hawk did hear much of it. Henderson, he surmised, was offering a total settlement of ten thousand English pounds—eight thousand of it in merchandise, the rest in cash—in exchange for the Cumberland Valley and a big portion of the Kentucky Valley. As he listened, John Hawk began to realize fully what a vast area Henderson wished to call his own and to question whether such a sale would be wise after all, despite his earlier favoring of the idea.

Some of the headmen, clearly, had doubts as well, but just as clearly most seemed to be steadily inclining toward approving the sale. The more he watched, the more concerned John Hawk became. He had moved for several days among the Wataugans and their neighbors, asking questions, and from the answers, he detected no hints that many Overmountain settlers were planning to vacate this region in favor of Kentucky. In fact, many even talked of negotiating a second purchase after Henderson completed his, this one on behalf of themselves, taking in the very lands John Hawk had hoped they would vacate.

The warrior was disturbed by such talk, though he didn't know how seriously to take it. "If the unakas buy this land, they will never be driven out, short of war waged by all the Indians together," he said to Ayasta as she lay beside him in their hut near the Watauga River. "I hope this talk is nothing but sound in the wind. I will keep a close watch to see what comes of this."

Little Carpenter spoke much at the treaty sessions, and in his longest and most significant talk, in which he gave his backing of the proposed sale, he spoke of his long history of representing his people. As he was so fond of doing, he related his journey across the great water to represent his people to the king over all the British. He spoke as well of the help he gave the British during the Seven Years War against the French and their Indian allies. Though sometimes he had been ill-treated by the white men, Little Carpenter said, still he stood in good favor with them and with his own people. He had been treated many times with honor by the white men, and he now was ready to repay that honor and put his mark on Henderson's papers.

Other chiefs stood and spoke similar words. Henderson could scarcely restrain himself from bursting into chuckles of joy as his transaction became all but final. He was confident his offer would be accepted, for he had already sent Daniel Boone to the Long Island to begin carving out a road to Kentucky.

But all feelings about the purchase were not the same. Throughout all the speeches, John Hawk kept his eye on Dragging Canoe, who sat in the councils with a dark expression on his pox-pitted face. As the talk of the headmen turned more and more in favor of Henderson's plea, that expression became only darker.

At last Dragging Canoe broke his silence. He stood before the council and began an oration John Hawk would never forget. The young warrior could not know how often Dragging Canoe's words would come to his mind in days ahead and give a final shape to what was at that time a still pliable view of the world.

In a deep voice that all could hear, Dragging Canoe began describing the great nation the Ani-Yunwiya had once been. He recounted how the white men had first come and how over the years they had encroached farther and farther into lands of the Indians. Always they came asking a little land, only a little land, upon which to make homes and live in quiet harmony with the natives around them. But always the little land became more land, then more, and more again, and harmony became dissonance. Only when it was too late had other Indian nations seen the true nature of the white men.

What had happened to those nations? Dragging Canoe waved toward the north as he asked that question and let his eyes meet those of the older beloved men, one by one. Had not entire nations of Indians melted away like snowballs under the sun? Where now were the Delawares, the "grandfathers" of the Cherokees? Would not the Cherokees find the same fate if they followed a compliant course and did not resist the usurpation of their lands?

The whites, he said, had long ago passed over the mountains to place their homes on lands forbidden to them, even by their own king. Now they wished such illegal settlement to receive the official approval of the Cherokee people. But this, if given, still would not be enough for them. Later they would seek more lands, even what meager grounds had been left to the Cherokees, and when at last there were no places left into which the Cherokees could be driven, they would declare that the world had no place for them and wipe out the Ani-Yunwiya.

Why should warriors stand by and let this be done? Is it not worth all risks, Dragging Canoe asked, to stop this carving-up of Cherokee lands? Will old men who are too old to fight or even to hunt put marks on paper and give away that which so long has belonged to the Ani-Yunwiya?

Perhaps they will, he said—but Dragging Canoe will not. Dragging Canoe and his young warriors will never willingly yield their lands. Henderson's purchase will never receive the support of brave warriors who are willing to fight for their ancestral lands.

So stirring was Dragging Canoe's speech that a near frenzy erupted on both sides. Henderson, seeing his long-desired transaction about to be snatched from him, called an immediate recess and urged all the chiefs to come feast again. In the meantime, Henderson's agents began talking to individual chiefs, trying to persuade them away from Dragging Canoe's viewpoint.

When the meeting resumed, it was evident to John Hawk that Dragging Canoe's words had been nothing more than momentary turbulence in a stream that had already cut its course. The headmen were determined to see the sale through. As Dragging Canoe watched in sullen silence, Henderson's offer gained the acceptance of the tribe's chief dignitaries, until at last it was complete and the Cherokee hunting lands were sold.

Dragging Canoe stood when it was over, and all eyes turned to him. His pitted face was as dark as a thundercloud as he waved his hand north. "You have bought a fair land," he said. "But over it hangs a dark cloud. You will find that land to be a dark and bloody ground."

He turned and stalked away. A large band of younger warriors rose and followed him—and for a moment, John Hawk was tempted to follow too. But Ayasta was back in their hut, having felt ill today. John Hawk would not leave her.

When the transaction papers were signed by the headmen, a great celebration was held. John Hawk did not participate, seeing nothing to celebrate. Dragging Canoe's words rang in his memory, and he pondered them. As he wandered in the midst of the revelry, he felt cut off from it all. At last, standing alone beside the Watauga River, he heard the approach of someone and turned, expecting to see Ayasta.

It was not Ayasta but Little Carpenter. "You seem lost in your own mind, John Hawk," the great chief said. "I saw you standing alone. Tell me—what do you think of all of this?"

John Hawk looked into the lean dark face marked by scars—some ornamental, some deriving from long-ago battles—and buffeted to a deep bronze by weather and age. "Before I give my answer, I ask that you give me one first: Will there be another sale, giving to the white men of these settlements the lands they leased from us?"

Little Carpenter said, "Yes. I believe this will happen."

"Then all your talk of luring away the white men closest to our towns and on our hunting grounds—this will come to nothing?"

"I fear it is so. It was my hope that most would go, but as we talked, I saw that this will not be. I see now that the unakas are determined to keep their homes."

"Then why did you yet favor this sale?"

"I am old, John Hawk. I have learned many things through my years, and among them is that our people must live with the world as it is and draw the best they can for themselves from it. The white men are far more numerous than we, and their tide cannot be stopped. If we do not sell them the land, then they will take it from us. Our loss will be the same, but without profit. Have we not suffered much from the white men already? Should we not take from them what goods they offer, so that our women and children have something in return for what they have lost, and yet will lose?"

John Hawk felt deep frustration. He understood Little Carpenter's points, but was loath to accept them. "Is there nothing to be done but watch our life vanish like fog in a wind?" he asked.

"There is nothing to do, John Hawk, but live in the world as it is given to us by the Great Man Above, and gain from it when we can."

John Hawk thought over those words as the talks proceeded to their second phase. Word came that Boone and a band of thirty axmen, armed and mounted, were proceeding speedily and were already well away from the Long Island, chopping out a wilderness road into Kentucky. To allow for this, Henderson had purchased a right-of-way that included a route to and through Cumberland Gap, and it was this route, an ancient warrior's path, that Boone's axmen would follow. John Hawk found it galling that work on the route had begun even before Henderson had broached the idea of a right-of-way purchase. Did the white men have no limit to their arrogance?

Dragging Canoe had returned to the talks by the time Henderson asked to purchase the right-of-way. The Carolina speculator said he did not wish to tread over the grounds of his brothers.

The right-of-way request renewed Dragging Canoe's fury. He rose once more and in an angry voice asked, "We have given you a great land—now do you ask yet more?" When he stalked away this time, he returned no more, vowing never again to sit in council with the white men.

When all of Henderson's transactions were done, the Overmountain settlers made good their talk of further purchases from the Cherokees. The lands that had been leased before they now bought, along with new tracts, after two more days of negotiation.

John Hawk recognized many of the white men involved in these negotiations and transactions: Jacob Brown from the Nolichucky, Charles Robertson, James Robertson. There was also a recent newcomer, striking in appearance, named John Sevier. And there was the very unstriking Peter Haverly. The latter, he noticed, did not treat directly with the Indians but only with Jacob Brown. John

Hawk did not understand the reason for this until he learned later that Haverly apparently was unable to pay the price for full purchase and that Brown had stepped in to purchase the land in his place, then lease it to him.

None of those details mattered much to John Hawk. The final result was the same, no matter how it was framed: The white men now owned the Overmountain lands. These were the lands of the Cherokees no longer. After the final transactions were done, John Hawk returned to his hut. Ayasta was lying on a blanket, sleeping, but she awakened when he entered, rose on one elbow, and smiled at him. He did not return the smile as he lay down beside her.

"Go back to sleep," he said. "Tomorrow we return to our home. And then I must find Dragging Canoe."

"What has happened?" Ayasta asked.

"The old men have betrayed us," John Hawk said. "For tables full of trinkets they have sold our lands to those who will drive us away. Only Dragging Canoe had the courage to stand against their betrayal." He put his arm around Ayasta and touched her belly as if to feel the life within. "From now on," he said, "Dragging Canoe will not stand alone. I will stand with him. If he makes peace, so will I. If he goes to war against the white men, then I will go to war, too."

Darcy Colter jerked awake at the sound of the closing front door. She was seated at a small spinning wheel in her bedroom, spinning flax. The hypnotizing job, combined with the lazy afternoon atmosphere, had lulled her into a doze; she had slumped back in her chair, dreaming images that vanished, unremembered, upon awakening.

She began spinning again as Gabriel passed her closed door and went into the main bedroom—his room now, for she no longer shared it with him. Not since her miscarriage had she shared his bed. Not by her choice but by his. Darcy had never come to love Gabriel as she had hoped she would. She knew now how bad a mistake her marriage had been.

For a long time, despite the difficulty of their relation-

ship, Darcy had determined to make the best of her
loveless union. Such had proven all but impossible. Gabriel not only did not love her but now seemed to despise
her most of the time. It was hard not to feel the same
toward him.

Joshua Colter's death at Point Pleasant had dealt almost as great a blow to the marriage as the miscarriage.
Darcy had been unable to conceal her grief, and Gabriel
had resented it. She suspected now that he believed the
lies told about her and Joshua; for whatever reason, he
treated her now as if she were foul.

She had once in a burst of anger brought up the
subject of divorce, but Gabriel had laughed in her face.
"Divorce? So you can find you some other tick-scratching
woodsman, like our departed Joshua, to give yourself to?
No, my dear. I'll not free you so easy as that."

Dislike it though she might, Darcy could make sense
of Gabriel's reluctance to divorce her. Divorce would be a
blight upon his name. It might affect his precious business interests. It would give further vindication to the
existing image of himself as a pitiful betrayed husband
and of her as an adulterous shrew. That latter part hardly
mattered to her now; her reputation had been so damaged by rumors that she had no good name to save.

Darcy well knew Gabriel's dedication to maintaining
his public image. He strived to mask their troubled marriage every time they were seen together in public, calling her sweet names and taking her hand as he had in
the days when he loved her. He publicly declared that his
wife was his faithful loving companion and that anyone
who spread stories besmirching her reputation would
find himself in mortal peril—even though, in Darcy's
opinion, he would probably never have the courage to
pick up a dueling pistol and face any man.

What Darcy couldn't understand about Gabriel's feelings was the depth of his vindictiveness toward her when
they were alone. That vindictiveness was what had finally
convinced her that he believed the adultery rumors. At
least he had not struck her with his fists. Twice he had
felled her with flat slaps. The first time he had apolo-

gized; the second, he had seemed to derive some bitter satisfaction from her tears. Gabriel had never been a pleasant man, even when he held her in high regard and wanted to be a true husband to her. Now he was insufferable. Darcy knew there were reasons for his deterioration going beyond the miscarriage and the rumors. Gabriel's decline was linked with that of Peter Haverly.

As sentiments against the British increased in the East, businesses of merchants favored for British trade—men such as Haverly—had suffered. The tea disputes and embargoes had severely damaged Haverly's financial situation even as his personal influence declined in the frontier community he had hoped would be his perfect society: a community built upon his highly personalized concept of Calvinist religion, with himself at the apex of control and adulation. Haverly Fort had hardly turned out that way. The name of Big Pete Haverly was used mostly in jest these days, and his church was scarcely visited by anyone.

Darcy knew the details of Haverly's troubles better than many because Christiana Haverly confided in her in the same way she confided in Christiana. The marriage of the Haverlys, though not troubled in the way Darcy and Gabriel's was, was still a cold affair, especially since Haverly's financial distress.

Darcy felt a certain pity for Haverly, though she had never liked him. Back during the big land transaction at Sycamore Shoals some weeks back, Haverly had been greatly shamed by his inability to make his own land purchase. He had been forced to go begging to Jacob Brown, who now was the rightful holder of the land beneath and surrounding Haverly Fort. Only by Brown's good graces and extension of credit was Haverly able even to hold a lease.

Christiana's description of her husband's plight roused Darcy's sympathy, but other things she said roused fear. Haverly, Christiana said, was a staunch loyalist to the king. As American sentiment turned toward independence, Haverly remained true to his old allegiances. There would be trouble from this, she predicted.

Darcy did not doubt it. A month after the land purchases at Sycamore Shoals, the Overmountain settlers had recently learned, a battle had occurred far away, at Lexington and Concord, between colonists and British soldiers. This, the general feeling went, was simply the first rumblings of a major fight that would finally come to the doorstep of the Overmountain settlements. Though Lexington and Concord were distant and the mountains buffered the revolutionary activity along the seaboard, the settlers had the Indians to consider. Would the British stir them against the Overmountain settlements if the settlers joined the rebellion?

These questions were much discussed all across the frontier. Darcy was cut off from most news because of the relatively isolated life Gabriel had imposed upon her, but even she picked up enough to know that views on the rebellion question were still quite mixed. Along the Nolichucky lived many loyalists. Their numbers and their involvement if open war should break out were open questions.

Most of the Overmountain settlers, as best Darcy could speculate, seemed likely to join the revolution. The idea of freedom was harmonious with their independent spirit, but there was more to it than that. Erasing British rule would mean erasing the hated proclamation of 1763, whose edicts against transmountain settlement were still in force despite all leases and purchases from the Indians. Darcy had overheard Haverly confiding to Gabriel that Henderson's purchase of Transylvania, as he called his proposed new colony in Kentucky, was illegal. Henderson had dug up some legal document saying that the British government would not interfere with land purchases from the Indians, but the crucial point was that the Indians referred to were not American Indians but those of India.

Even Christiana did not fully know her husband's attitude toward the land purchases from the Cherokees and the official British stance against them. That he had himself violated the edict of 1763 in establishing Haverly Fort showed he was not above bending or breaking troublesome British laws, yet there remained a basic unyielding loyalty to the Crown. Christiana was worried. What would happen to Haverly, she asked Darcy, if he should remain loyalist while his neighbors joined the rebellion? What would happen to her and her children?

And to me, Darcy mentally added. Whatever course Haverly took Gabriel would surely take as well. After all his success in business, all his developed skill in commerce between the frontier and seaboard, Gabriel remained subservient to and adoring of Peter Haverly. He was still Little Pete and ever would be, it appeared.

Darcy put the thoughts aside and concentrated on her spinning. Worries enough she had without adding new ones based on speculation beyond her ken. Outside, Gabriel passed her door again, not pausing to speak or even knock. The front door opened and closed. She peeked out of her window and saw him walking toward the stockade, Patton at his side.

Once again she was alone. She breathed a deep sigh and began spinning again.

23

$\diamond$

$\mathbf{A}$s 1775 passed, Darcy Colter found reason to become ever more disturbed, by events in her life and in the world around her.

Darcy's expectation that most of the Overmountain settlers would join the growing rebellion against Britain was proving accurate. The clearest evidence of this, apart from some violence done to local loyalists who spoke too openly in favor of the Crown, came initially from the North of Holston settlement, which because of its link to Virginia was more immediately responsive to colonial political developments than the other settlements. In North of Holston a "Committee of Safety" was formed, and Evan Shelby was appointed a leader of the body. The committee was formed under the jurisdiction of Fincastle County, Virginia, and by declaration was loyal to the Second Continental Congress in Philadelphia.

Formation of that committee set in motion similar plans in the other settlements. In the fall, a meeting was held in which representatives of the Overmountain settlements also officially cast their support to the American cause. Conspicuously absent from the meeting were Peter Haverly and Gabriel. Alphus Colter represented the

Haverly Fort district. The settlers declared themselves the Washington District, named in honor of George Washington, the new commander of the American army, and created a Committee of Safety similar to that from Fincastle County. John Carter chaired the committee, the membership of which included Alphus, John Sevier, James Robertson, Jacob Brown, William Bean, and many other settlement leaders.

Gabriel was deeply affected by the revolutionary action; Darcy could see it clearly, despite the fact that he seldom talked to her anymore in anything but an abrupt, cursory way. At the same time, Darcy noticed that the house seemed to be under constant watch. Whenever she glanced out the window, there was always someone about, usually involved in some activity—but watching, always watching. Patton noticed it as well and seemed frightened. Christiana confirmed that the same phenomenon was happening at the Haverly house. Surely it was because of Haverly's and Gabriel's loyalist leanings. Both women were deeply frightened.

There was another factor that concerned them. Christiana told Darcy that there had been secret visitors three times now in the Haverly house. Peter Haverly had sent her to bed and then stayed up long hours, talking in a hushed voice to men she was not allowed to see. Christiana had tried to hear what was said, but could not, though she did detect that Gabriel was present at one meeting and that at two of them at least one participant was an Indian.

Darcy, knowing Haverly's attitude toward Indians, was surprised by that information and horrified by it, for her fear of Indians was overwhelming now that her brother had died at the hands of Shawnees and her mother at the hands of Mingos. If Haverly was talking secretly with Indians, then something significant was going on. Haverly dealt with Indians only when there was some advantage to be gained from them, as when he had originally leased the Haverly Fort area.

In the volatile revolutionary context of the moment, anyone dealing closely and secretively with Indians was treading dangerous ground. Indications were strong that the Cherokees would ally themselves with Britain. Dragging Canoe's antagonisms toward the settlers were well-known, as was his declared brotherhood with Alexander Cameron. Already many Cherokees were bitter about the earlier land sales to Henderson and the Overmountain settlers; once distributed, the payments had amounted to very little individually. The British had officially condemned the land sales as illegal, so the sullen Cherokees might see an alliance with the British as a way of getting back their land.

Darcy and Christiana decided to learn what they could of their husbands' activities. At the back of both women's minds was the terrible possibility that their menfolk might be plotting to help the British and Indians in any attack that might come should the course toward massive war continue unabated.

Darcy's attention, however, was not primarily focused on such broad matters as revolutions and Indian worries. Gabriel had found a new way to make her life hellish. He had recently resumed his physical attentions but in a way that was brutal and fierce. Though they still slept apart, Gabriel would sometimes appear at her bed late at night, smelling of rum, and force himself upon her wordlessly. Of all the humiliations she had endured in life, this seemed the worst. He made her feel like a common whore whose only purpose was to give him physical gratification. She suffered his assaults, biting her lip with tears in her eyes, because she sensed that to resist him would result only in worse abuse. Gabriel's molestations were a secret she kept even from Christiana; they shamed her too much to allow her to speak of them, even to one so close.

Darcy sometimes felt as if nothing but loss would ever be her lot. To death she had lost her father, her mother, her brother, her baby, and Joshua Colter, the only man she had ever really cared for. Through marriage to Gabriel she had lost the chance for a normal and happy life. She had lost even her good name in the community because of the abundant rumors about her purported adultery. More than once Darcy had thought of taking her own life—thought of it, but no more than that.

One thing that living with a withered hand had taught her was that nothing good is gained without perseverance and struggle. Disadvantages could never be allowed a victory; if so, they destroyed like parasites. Darcy was determined to endure until from somewhere new hope and new life could come to her. What that hope could be in her situation Darcy could not imagine, but she refused to give up her faith that it could come to be.

She thought about such things often when she walked alone at night. One advantage of sleeping in her own room was her freedom to slip away when Gabriel was asleep and roam in the darkness with no company but Gabriel's dogs and her thoughts. Patton, who lived in a small cabin on the edge of Gabriel's lot, knew Darcy took such secret walks, but he had pledged to her that Gabriel would never know of them from him, and Darcy trusted his word. Patton was a good man, faithful, far better than his master.

Now that Gabriel had begun coming to Darcy by night, she worried more when she left the house for her nocturnal strolls. One night, surely, Gabriel would discover her gone and would then try to find a way to stop her from leaving again. She did not doubt that he would go so far as to bar her door and window at night. So now she had something new to worry about. It hardly mattered; Darcy was used to living with worry. Worry and loneliness, she sometimes joked darkly to Christiana, were her ever-present, ever-troublesome sisters, so much a part of her life now that she might not know how to live without them.

The new year came, bringing with it cold winds and snowfall, but still Darcy continued her nighttime walks, bundling herself against the cold. Gabriel had so far not detected what she was about, and gradually she had begun roaming farther and farther, walking on the roads like a lonely robed phantom in the darkness. She learned the routes that would avoid baying hounds, staying in areas where her scent was familiar to the dogs.

One of those areas was the vicinity of Alphus and Sina's cabin. On a cold Friday night, January 5, Darcy was walking just after midnight within view of their cabin. Gabriel had been with her earlier in the night; the ache of his abuse lingered both in mind and body. Tonight was one of the nights when Darcy could not keep the tears away, and she sat down on a stump, her back to the cabin, and cried silently, wrapping her cloak closely around her against the cold. Lost in her unhappiness and hovering on the edge of a doze, she did not hear the approach of Sina Colter until the aging woman was at her side.

"Darcy?"

The young woman jerked upright in surprise but did not shout. As a daughter of the frontier, she had learned not to cry out in moments of surprise; sometimes that surprise might be a lurking Indian who could be avoided by silence.

"Darcy—it is you! Praise be! God must have sent you here tonight."

"Sina, I'm sorry. I didn't mean to awaken anyone—"

"He's alive, Darcy! I just saw him!"

Darcy noticed that Sina had a most unusual expression on her face—it might have been awe. "Who is alive, Sina?"

"Joshua! I just saw Joshua, clearer there in the dark even than you are to me now!"

Darcy suspected that Sina was sleepwalking, talking in a dream. Nevertheless, the words set off an explosion of emotion. "Oh, Sina, you mustn't say what cannot be true!"

"Ah, Darcy, but it is true, it is! Throughout my life I've dreamed and seen the dreams come to pass. I knew of my first husband's death in the wilderness through a dream, even before he was dead. This dream was so much the same—but it was a living dream, not a dying dream. Joshua's alive and well, Darcy. I know it to be true."

Sina spoke with such an intense assurance that Darcy was half convinced. She had heard the story of how Sina had seen Levi Hampton in a dream and known intuitively that he was doomed. Maybe Sina really did have a way of knowing the unknowable.

Darcy looked down and was shocked to see that Sina was barefoot. Now Darcy was sure Sina was sleepwalking; she would never come outside barefoot on so cold a night if her wits were about her. "You must go back to your bed, Sina," Darcy said. "You're not dressed to be out in this cold."

"Yes, yes, back to bed," Sina repeated, smiling. She turned. "Alive!" she said as she walked away. "Alive, before my eyes!"

Darcy next saw Sina two days later, perched on the seat of a wagon Alphus had just built and was trying out. Darcy was walking toward Gabriel's store as they passed, and they stopped to chat. Sina said nothing about her dream or having met Darcy in the night. When Alphus made a passing reference to Joshua, speaking of him as one dead, Sina showed no reaction and said nothing.

Darcy knew then that Sina did not remember her dream. The realization depressed her. The ghost of a hope that Sina's dream had really meant something faded like mist. If the dream had been so insignificant that Sina herself could not recall it, then there was no real hope hidden in it.

Darcy turned back, not even completing her errand to the store, and hoped she could make it home before anyone noticed how hard she was fighting not to cry.

John Hawk heard a chorus of joyous cries from the throats of some eighty warriors and knew that the long-awaited packtrain of British-supplied ammunition had arrived. Dragging Canoe stood close by, a look of unmistakable eagerness on his usually unreadable face on this early spring day. The warrior had a way of making even that expression seem fierce. John Hawk could understand why so many of the unakas had begun calling Dragging Canoe by the name Dragon. The white men had always freely given titles and nicknames to Indians.

John Hawk, since allying with Dragging Canoe, was often referred to as the Hawk, or simply Hawk.

Leading the packtrain, which had originated at Pensacola, were Alexander Cameron and Henry Stuart, younger brother of Indian Superintendent John Stuart, who had sent the ammunition upon request of a delegation of Cherokees who had journeyed all the way to Florida to pledge loyalty to the Crown in the American-British conflict and urgently to request lead and powder from British supplies.

It had been a busy and turbulent year for John Hawk and the Cherokees in general since the Transylvania Purchase of 1775. News of the growing squabble between the Americans and British had come to the Cherokees almost as soon as the transactions were completed. In the beginning they had not known what to make of it, but as time passed, it became clear that this was no minor argument. John Hawk was fascinated by these remarkable developments among the unakas and watched them closely. One important intervening development in his personal life distracted his attention from such matters for a while: the birth of his son.

After hard labor, Ayasta delivered the boy one beautiful morning. Even as a newborn, he looked much like his father. They named him Wasi—Moses, in the white men's tongue. During his time with Joshua Colter at Haverly Fort, John Hawk had learned about the biblical Moses from Israel Coffman. He wanted his son, like the biblical character, to grow to be a leader devoted to the good of his people.

As the infant Wasi began to thrive and grow, so did the rebellion of the Americans. When the rebels drove John Stuart out of Charleston down to the loyal region of Florida, the Cherokees realized that the rebellion would mean hardship for them. With Stuart now far away, trade connections were severed. Powder and lead, always in short supply, began to dwindle to critical levels. It was this shortage that had prompted the visit of the Cherokees to Florida.

John Hawk was glad the Cherokees were ready to

support the British, though it remained unclear for some time just what that support would be. Dragging Canoe was ready to launch a major campaign against the settlements, but the British were hesitant about such a drastic course. Though the British general named Gage had advocated using the Indians as fighters on the frontier front, John Stuart had instructed his brother to encourage no sweeping attacks, for there were among the Overmountain settlers many who were loyal to the Crown. Further, others might be persuaded to choose the loyalist side, or at least vacate the region. All these things Henry Stuart had explained carefully to Dragging Canoe.

Even so, the warrior of Malaquo made no attempt to hide his eagerness to use the ammunition to rid his home region of white intruders. "Our people are almost surrounded, having now only a little spot of ground to stand upon," he told Henry Stuart shortly after greeting the packtrain. "The unakas want to destroy us as a nation."

Henry Stuart chose his next words carefully. "I understand you, brother. But was it not the Cherokees themselves who sold land to the unakas?"

Dragging Canoe violently waved off the assertion. "With that I had nothing to do. That was the work of old men without teeth, too old to fight. I and my warriors are young, and we will stand our ground."

The Cherokee band, joined by the loyalist trader Nathaniel Gist, escorted the packtrain to the Overhill towns, arriving there in late April. Through the rest of the month Henry Stuart had some difficulty restraining Dragging Canoe, who began acting the role of war chief, even without the official designation as such.

Early in May, a great council meeting was held at Chota, attended by seven hundred Indians and several presumably loyalist whites. Henry Stuart found that his brother's legacy of friendship and mutual respect with the Cherokees served a good purpose for him as younger brother. The great townhouse of Chota was marked with five colors, and in Stuart's and Cameron's honor a party of naked painted warriors met the British agents at the end of the town square with twelve tails of eagles and two drums, and there danced for them and described their war exploits before escorting them with honor to the townhouse.

John Hawk played his usual role of quiet observer and learned three things from the meeting. First, the British favored seeking voluntary removal rather than launching an offensive against the settlements. Second, whenever the time for such an offensive came, the Cherokees would be ready; Dragging Canoe had fanned the smoldering sparks of bitterness against the unakas into flame.

John Hawk's third observation was the most intriguing to him: Many unakas were not supportive of the rebellion against Britain. Nathaniel Gist was a prime example; he was ready to serve the Crown in any way he could, and virtually all the white men among the Cherokees swore oaths of loyalty to the British cause. There were whispers of planned cooperation against the rebels by loyalists along the Nolichucky and Sinking Creek. John Hawk heard the name of Peter Haverly mentioned in this connection several times.

Despite the younger Cherokees' eagerness to fight, Stuart successfully pleaded a case for restraint. Many of the settlers, he said, were ignorant people, understanding nothing of laws and having been told that the Cherokees had no objection to white settlement on their lands. To attack such souls without prior attempts to remove them peaceably would bring down harsh feelings upon the Cherokees from all quarters.

On May 7, a few days after the meeting, Stuart and Cameron sent correspondence, by way of trader Isaac Thomas, to the Watauga and Nolichucky settlements. The letter demanded that the settlements be vacated within twenty days. The results were mixed. Some settlers, alarmed at the prospect of war, fled the region, the Cherokees subsequently learned, but many chose to remain and hold their lands.

John Carter, writing as a spokesman for the Wataugans, sent back a letter dated May 13 in which he stated that the settlers were surprised to hear the Cherokees would consider moving against them and confirmed, in carefully chosen words, the presence of many loyalists in the settlements, asking for an extension of time before the settlements had to be abandoned. John Hawk did not believe Carter's letter was sincere. Later he would learn his perception was correct, for at the same time Carter was writing in conciliatory fashion to the Cherokees, the Wataugans were appealing to Virginia for military protection.

Not content to await word of developments from second- or thirdhand sources, John Hawk ventured toward the settlements on his own, wanting to see if there were signs of war preparations. Moving unseen through the forests, he found many. On the Nolichucky River, along Great Limestone Creek, a stockade was under construction. Near Sycamore Shoals a stockade was being built a half mile northeast of the mouth of Gap Creek. For the most part, John Hawk saw little sign that many settlers had left or intended to leave.

Heading back to the Cherokee towns to deliver this intelligence, John Hawk passed by the site of old Fort Loudoun, the ruins of which were now mostly gone. Most of what remained after the burning of the palisades and buildings a decade and a half ago had long since rotted into dust. But as he looked across the overgrown expanse where red-coated British regulars had once drilled and marched, something new caught his eye. A less observant man might have missed the little stone marker that stood on a recently cleared spot surrounded by thickets. John Hawk had not noticed this when he passed on his way toward the settlements. Whatever it was, it had been placed there by someone between the time he had left and now. Curious, the Cherokee dismounted and walked over to the little clearing. The day was waning, sunset just about an hour away, clouds rising on a stormy wind.

The marker was a slab of flat stone, apparently taken from the river. Onto it words had been laboriously chipped: *Hester Byrum, b. 1736, d. 1760 in Loudoun Fort—a Beloved mother.*

John Hawk stood, a ripple of chills going from his neck all the way down his spine. Hester Byrum—the squaw of the old trader Jack Byrum, blood father of Joshua Colter. Joshua himself had told John Hawk of Hester Byrum's death and burial within the fort even as it fell and had mentioned his sadness that she had been buried with no lasting marker in soil she had never wanted to tread upon.

The wind wrapped itself around the young Cherokee as he stood, trying to fathom what this could mean. He knelt, examining the piles of brush and weeds that had been cleared from the grave and tossed aside. They had been cut raggedly, as if by a knife, not more than hours before. Dirt had been piled upon the grave—so fresh, it had hardly settled.

His heart beginning to pound, the Cherokee began examining the land all about the tiny clearing. Yes, there was sign, just hours old, already beginning to fade and hard to see in the dimming light, but still there. He followed it.

The sign led him on a winding path that was often broken. Whoever had left these marks—surely the same person who had marked and cleaned the grave—had walked along rocks and logs where possible. Feeling unusually anxious, John Hawk scoured the dark land repeatedly, losing and finding the trail again. He followed it as rapidly as he could.

Then the trail was gone. Before him stretched a field of stones upon which no sign could be found. Dismayed, John Hawk stopped, looking around. Perhaps he was foolish to expose himself to view by a white man, for whoever had worked at the grave had been white, that he knew. No Cherokee would so mark the long-forgotten grave of a trader's wife, dead for sixteen years. Only a unaka would do that, and any unaka who could achieve it without detection so close to a Cherokee town would have to be skilled and cunning.

John Hawk had known several white men who had such skills, but only one who would have reason to mark the grave of Hester Byrum. But it was impossible. He could not be here. He had died at Point Pleasant.

For a long time, the young Cherokee remained where he was as the sun lowered westward and the light faded. Just when he was about to turn away, convinced that he was looking for phantoms, he saw the figure of a man, far away and barely discernible in the twilight. Whether the man was Indian or white was hard to tell, but he wore more clothing than most Indian men usually did and seemed to have a beard. Whoever or whatever he was, he was tall and lean, looking back at John Hawk, standing in an easy slightly slumped stance that stirred a great sense of familiarity in the young warrior.

For several moments the two men looked at each other in the darkening twilight. Then the distant figure raised his right hand to the sky.

John Hawk did the same, his sense of awe heightening. What was happening could not be truly happening, and what he saw he could not be really seeing—unless this was a phantom, from Tsusgina-i, the ghost country in the distant west, come to mark the resting place of a woman beloved to him in life. But did phantoms leave sign when they walked? Did they wear moccasins and the clothing of frontiersmen? Did their beards grow long?

Yet if this had not been a phantom, then who had it been? Could the man who had turned from John Hawk's friend to his enemy, and yet somehow remained tied to him with an unseverable bond, be living after all?

The warrior, overwhelmed with questions he could not answer, turned and walked back through the forest, across the place where Fort Loudoun had once stood to his horse. As night slid in, he mounted and rode away, toward Chota.

Darcy Colter heard that subtle shaking of the door that always preceded its opening. She squeezed her eyes shut, praying that Gabriel would think her asleep and not plague her this time. The idea of his heavy body crushing her, his rum-reeking breath against her face, was more than she could endure tonight.

She heard him walk in, felt him standing beside the bed, looking at her. Through the slits of her closed eyes she saw a faint flicker of light. She smelled burning tallow. She waited, dreading, for his touch. It did not come. Instead he spoke to her, surprising her, for usually he said nothing during these trying conjugal visits. His voice sounded strained and quivered. She opened her eyes.

"Darcy." Gabriel said her name wearily. He was directly beside her, looking at her in the light of a tallow lamp he held. "Darcy." He sat down heavily on the side of the bed, his shoulders rounded over, his face turned toward the puncheon floor. The smell of rum rose from him.

She did not speak to him, just stared and waited for him to say or do whatever he had come for. As she watched him, she realized he was distraught, almost in tears.

"Darcy, you must help me. Never before have I faced anything like this. Never have I so badly needed someone to tell me what to do."

The words were mystifying, but she said nothing. She seldom spoke to Gabriel unless words were essential. Feigned acts of affection were reserved for strolls across the settlement for Sunday morning worship services in Peter Haverly's nearly empty church. She saw no need for such deceptions when she and Gabriel were alone.

Gabriel did not seem to notice her silence and continued talking, bringing to Darcy the surprising realization that he was coming to her this time not out of lust but out of a need to make some type of confession. She was not sure she really wanted to hear it.

"Peter Haverly weighs on my mind," Gabriel said. "Peter Haverly. I'm becoming . . . frightened of the things he talks of. He's different than he used to be . . . changed, somehow."

No, Darcy said mentally to her husband. It's just that he's just showing his true nature all the more, so much so that even a blind follower like you can at last see it.

"This rebellion against the Crown is a disgraceful thing, Darcy. I am appalled by it, just as Peter is. But my own father is part of the rebellion, and most of the people I know, and who work for me. I want no harm to come to them. I care about their welfare. I consider myself a loyalist, just like Peter . . . but no, not really. I'm not like he is, and that's the point. I fear he's actually willing to turn on his own people, to see evil come to them."

Darcy dared to venture an observation, for she could tell now that his attitude toward her was not his usual icy one. She found it ironic that only at a time of distress did he treat her as a person worthy of hearing his thoughts.

"Perhaps he's as he is because his own people have turned on him," she said. "Few have anything good to say of him anymore."

"Aye, aye. That I've seen."

Darcy asked him what he meant when he said Haverly was willing to see "evil" come to those around him, for the words put her in mind of the fears she and Christiana had shared in secret.

Gabriel turned and looked at her. For a second she believed he was wondering why he was in this room, of all places, and talking to her, of all people, about his worries. She expected that he would rise, turn his back on her, walk out of the room. . . .

He did not. Instead he reached out and touched her hand, her good hand, for he had never touched the withered one or allowed her to touch him with it. "Haverly is part of a plot of some sort. That much I know. He's both hosted and visited secret gatherings, with British agents, Indians . . . and once with me as part of it, at the very beginning. But when I was there, all the talk was unclear, obscure, like perhaps they did not fully trust me and were not sure they wanted me to be part of it."

"Part of what, Gabriel?"

"Of whatever it is they are planning, and what that is I cannot truly say. But it's bad; I know that. I'm cut off from the details of it now. Peter doesn't trust me, perhaps because my father is so supportive of the rebellion. Peter has said little to me now for days, and whenever I'm near him, looks at me as if he doesn't want me about."

Gabriel's hand was still on hers. For the first time in months, Darcy felt the slightest twinge of an old forgotten tenderness, a ghost-remnant of the feeble warmth that she had once hoped could develop into actual love for this man, before abuse and bitterness and blame had made the warmth fade to coldness.

"Did you hear what Isaac Thomas, the trader, said when he brought the warning letter from the British agents, Darcy? He said that no matter what the British or the old Cherokee headmen say or do, eventually the Dragon will lead his warriors against the settlements. War with the Cherokees will come, no matter what hopes some may harbor. And when it does, I think that Haverly and other loyalists might be part of it, actually cooperate with—" He stopped suddenly.

"Go on, Gabriel," Darcy encouraged.

"No," he said, removing his hand from hers. "No—I've said too much, and speculated on matters I really cannot know." As he looked at her now, it was as if she could actually see him withdrawing, growing distant and cold again. The familiar harsh Gabriel was overcoming the gentler one she had just seen. He stood and walked to the door, still holding the tallow lamp.

He paused there, looking at her again, and for the briefest of moments smiled—an uncomfortable smile and so quick that Darcy could almost have thought it was a trick of the shadows that the flickering lamp made across his face.

"Good night, Darcy. Thank you for listening to me, but forget what I've said. That's the best thing—just forget it all."

"Good night, Gabriel."

He walked out and closed the door behind him.

24

The frontiersman crouched, as still as if he were carved from wood, his rifle held tightly, cocked. He was hidden at the edge of a canebrake, his eyes scanning, constantly scanning, the enclosing landscape. All was incongruously silent; there was no noise but the chirps and whistles of the forest birds, the rustling of the cane in the breeze, and the occasional faint patter of a sweat drop falling from the frontiersman's rough beard to the ground between his moccasined feet.

Then came a movement, a crackling in the brake that was not caused by wind. The frontiersman took a deep breath, tensed, waited, then lunged outward when his instincts told him to.

His rifle blasted, sending an echoing roar through the canelands around him and forest beyond. Birds screeched and flew from their perches. The frontiersman was already reloading even as the Cherokee, who had taken the rifle ball squarely through the chest, made a final writhe and died amid canestalks stained with fresh wet crimson.

The frontiersman was running as he ramrodded the

patch and ball atop the powder charge, then put the hickory ramrod back into his slides. Dodging about to avoid the frequent sharp upthrusts of broken canestalks, he left the brake, crossed the marshy somnolent creek, and entered the forest.

Four Cherokees there had been; now there were but two. The frontiersman realized how fortunate he had been. Had they surprised him when his rifle was empty or he was asleep, he would now be minus both his life and his scalp.

The first Indian he had shot at the edge of his camp. He had used his fleetness and a conveniently located laurel thicket to escape the others, who had been slow to fire upon him. Cherokees had no powder to waste, and these had not been willing to risk emptying their weapons at a furtive figure barely visible on the other side of a tangle of laurel. The frontiersman had run like a deer, reaching the creek, then the canebrake, and there he had hidden until a second warrior had tracked him down.

Would the remaining two pursue him? Perhaps not, now that two of their fellows had lost their lives to him. But he could afford no assumptions. The best option for him was to gain distance as quickly as possible.

The trees near the creek had been scrubby and undergrown. Now he reached the deeper forest where virgin timber towered, branches interlocking above so that the sun was nearly blocked and the space beneath the overspreading boughs was like the interior of a vast cathedral with a green, luminescent arched ceiling. The frontiersman traveled by stepping from rock to rock when he could or running across deadfalls, but he knew that in his haste he would leave at least some sign, no matter how hard he tried to avoid it.

Looking back occasionally and keeping watch around and ahead of him to avoid any new dangers, he put a half mile, then a mile, between himself and the canebrake he had just left.

He stopped shortly after that, dropping behind a massive limestone boulder of the sort so frequent in this landscape. He panted for breath and winced as he gripped his side. This was the first time in two weeks that the wound he had received at the Ohio River had given him any pain. Though it was now healed, sometimes he still felt a dull ache at the place where the rifle ball had dug into him.

As he caught his breath, he checked his rifle to make sure his hasty loading had not been faulty and continued to listen and watch all around. The forest was deep and dark, even by day, the kind of ominous woodlands that brought awe and fear to many who saw them for the first time. Forests like these had often led westbound travelers to frontier settlements to turn back and go home to more familiar and settled areas on the eastern slopes of the mountains. These forests brought no such fear to this man. He often felt more at home alone in them than in the company of human beings. In the forests, life was dangerous, but it was also straightforward, uncomplicated by human entanglements. The frontiersman had only months ago decided that such a life was to be the only one he would live for the rest of his days.

But that had changed, just as the times were changing. There was trouble in the wind, stirred by political fires in the East and recent rekindling of smoldering old resentments among the Indians. The frontiersman could no longer hide away; he had to return to the settlements and give his help to those he cared about. He smiled wryly to himself. Quite a surprise he would bring them, walking in alive when they believed him dead.

He remained where he was another hour, then quietly slipped away. The Cherokees had not followed him. By now, they had probably gathered the bodies of their dead, cleaned out what goods he had been forced to leave behind in his camp, and taken his two horses. He shook his head when he thought of the loss but did not grieve much over it. Such losses came with the life he had chosen, and he could accept them.

He still had his rifle, shot, powder, and a good supply of dried beef and pone tucked into his hunting shirt. And soon he would be back among the settlements where food was plentiful and served in steaming heaps on wooden trenchers behind thick safe log walls. The settlements had their good aspects, even if he had never found much happiness in them.

He continued through the shady forests until the evening fell, the air grew cool and sparkled with fireflies, and it became too dark to travel.

Alphus Colter, standing before the stockade gate of Haverly Fort, stepped forward as the band of riders drew near. He knew who they were even before he saw them, for he had heard of what they were doing down on the Nolichucky and had sent a rider to intercept them and bring them up to Haverly Fort.

The lead rider was Captain James Robertson. He dismounted and walked up to Alphus, his hand thrust out.

"Hello, Alphus. Good to see you again."

"And the same at seeing you, James. How did you fare down on the Chucky?"

Robertson smiled, his blue eyes crinkling at the corners beneath the dark hair overhanging his brow. "Quite well, I think, though it's hard to know whether a forced oath of loyalty will hold much influence. In any case, we've run some out of the settlement who I really believe might have lent a hand to the Cherokees. That blasted Nathaniel Gist has been poking about among them of late, stirring up loyalist blood. He may well have come up this far, Alphus."

"I believe he has, or sent someone of his ilk. It's because of such matters I sent for you."

"Aye? Well, then, we'll talk, as soon as we've put these horses out for some rest."

Alphus watched as Robertson and his riders hobbled their horses in the grassy area around the fort. He hid his feelings behind a friendly half-smile.

Calling Robertson to come here had been a difficult decision for Alphus, but with what Christiana Cox and Darcy had told him recently, he felt he had no choice. Robertson, after all, was one of two men the Wataugans had put to the vital task of cleaning out the loyalists, who were congregated most thickly along the Nolichucky.

Robertson and Captain John Shelby, brother of Evan Shelby, had been patrolling the entire region with their armed horsemen, rounding up suspected loyalists and forcing them to take an oath of allegiance to the revolution or leave the country in disgrace.

What made Alphus's call difficult was the fact that his son was among those declaring themselves loyal to the Crown, though the declaration had been secret in Gabriel's case. Alphus had long suspected that Gabriel was loyalist, as Peter Haverly was, but had not asked him to confirm it until recently, for he was reluctant to know the truth. Alphus had firmly aligned himself with the revolution and expected the entire affair to come to battle sooner or later. That Gabriel might wind up on the opposite side troubled him.

The news related by Darcy and Christiana had made it impossible for Alphus to hang fire any longer. Obviously the two women had been in close contact for some time, talking about their husbands' ways and activities. Christiana had confirmed that Peter Haverly was involved in some sort of loyalist conspiracy.

She had overheard talk of Indian attack and secret markers to distinguish loyalist houses from those of rebels, and of loyalists' taking up arms with the British-backed Cherokees to battle and kill their rebel neighbors. Christiana had been so distraught upon learning this that she initially did not know what to do, until she and Darcy talked and decided to bring what they had learned to Alphus.

"But please, please," Darcy pleaded, "don't let Gabe know I came to you. He'll hurt me if he knows I talked, for he was drunk when he told me of it, and may not have told me at all if he had been sober."

That plea disturbed Alphus. He knew, despite his son's attempts to hide it, that Gabriel and Darcy had a troubled marriage. But he had never dreamed Darcy was afraid of physical harm from Gabriel. What had Gabriel done to her already?

Alphus asked Darcy about it as delicately as he could, but she refused to answer him. "Very well, then," Alphus

told her. "Suffice it to say that if Gabriel ever gives you
hardship, you may come to my cabin and be safe from
him."

Saying such a thing regarding his own son gave Alphus
an uncomfortable feeling. He had grown closer to Gabriel
in past months, and the idea that there could be a dark
aspect to that brightening picture was distressing, especially since Gabriel was now the only son left to him.

Alphus reached beneath his hunting shirt and fingered Joshua's old Roman coin. Since Callum McSwain
had brought the coin back from Point Pleasant, Alphus
had worn it to remind him of Joshua. The pain of his
loss had not faded.

Alphus had brooded over the information Darcy and
Christiana brought to him for half a day before deciding
to send down to the Nolichucky for Robertson. Now that
Robertson was here, Alphus knew his decision had been
right, but being right didn't make it any easier.

Robertson walked up to him, slapping dust from his
hands. "Have you some good cold water about this place,
Alphus? I'm so dry, my marrow's gone to powder on me."

"This way," Alphus said. "There's a cold well within
the stockade."

Robertson and his men drank deeply of the cool water,
and Alphus welcomed Robertson's praise of Alphus's
foresight in making sure there was a well within the
stockade. Often the people of the frontier were either too
busy, too optimistic, or just too careless to make sure
they provided adequate water supplies for their stockades
and thus suffered in time of siege.

Alphus took Robertson into the forest to ensure privacy
and there spilled out what the women had told him.

Robertson took it all calmly but seriously. "I've had
suspicions about Big Pete Haverly for quite some time.
My men and I will have to pay him a visit."

"And Gabriel?"

Robertson said: "Him too, sorry to say. But cheer
yourself, Alphus. If what Gabriel's wife had to say was
correct, then he's not truly involved in Haverly's plotting.
The main wrong he's done is suspecting that Haverly

was involved in a loyalist plot, then keeping his mouth closed about it."

"You have to understand Gabriel's loyalty to Haverly," Alphus said. "It's far too firm. It's the kind that can make him stand by and see much wrong done and not act against it."

"Aye, and in the worst case could make him even join with it. That's what we must seek to avert. Do you wish to come with me when we make our visits?"

Alphus considered. Arriving with Robertson would make it evident to Gabriel that his father had reported him as a loyalist. What new affection they had gained would probably be lost. But to not go along would be to hide like a coward.

"I'll go with you."

"We'll be stern with Gabriel, but also fair," Robertson said. "I pledge you that. You were right to call on me, Alphus."

"I hope so," Alphus said.

The hours passed, the visits to Haverly and Gabriel were made, and an eventful day faded into night.

In Gabriel's shuttered house, Darcy backed up against the wall, so afraid she trembled, as Gabriel leaned toward her in deep anger. Gabriel's fury had not subsided since the afternoon, when Alphus, James Robertson, and Robertson's men had left, having nudged out of the stunned Gabriel a reluctant path of loyalty to the Continental Congress, the Committee of Safety, and the American Revolution. Peter Haverly, they told him, had refused such an oath and also declined to leave the settlements, so now he was locked up in one of the cabins in the stockade. Peter Haverly had made his final fall from grace and was now a prisoner of the very people he had once sought to lead.

Nothing had been said by Robertson or any other to implicate Darcy as the one who had informed on Gabriel's loyalty to the Crown, but Gabriel had blamed her right away, had turned on her as soon as Robertson's band was gone. Since then he had stormed first about

Darcy's disloyalty to him, then about Alphus's. He had stopped a few times to drink some rum, then gone back to his pacing and raging.

At the moment, he was in the midst of raging against Darcy again, repeating the same bitter assertions and questions he had fired at her since the afternoon: "So that is how you repay my confidences with you, is it? Running off and spewing my name as some sort of traitor to my people? God, woman! Do you know what you've done to me?"

He paced the room three times, rubbing the back of his neck and running his hand through his hair. Gabriel, at thirty, was quickly going bald and from the exertion of pacing and the heat of anger, was sweating now, big droplets riding on his scalp among the thinning hairs. He wheeled and stopped so quickly that a few went flying and sizzled in the flame of the lamp on the mantel. Gabriel aimed a long finger at Darcy's face. "What else have you been declaring to Christiana Cox and God knows who else? Have you talked of our intimate affairs?"

Darcy was still afraid but also angry. "What affairs do you mean? The deceptions we put on together in public, walking side by side with lying smiles on our faces? Or our true affairs, in which you insult and degrade me and believe all manner of lies told about me?"

"Lies, eh? Lies?" He scowled. "Sometimes I wonder what's lies and what's not. Perhaps the time has come to test the iron in the fire. Tell me true, woman. Did you commit adultery with Joshua?"

Darcy's eyes flashed. "As I have told you often enough already, I have been true to you from the day I married you."

He studied her sullenly. "That's a damned lie. I can see it in your deceiving eyes, Darcy Colter."

"You drunken scoundrel, how dare you—"

"No, my dear, how dare you! The rumors were all true, weren't they! Even about the baby you lost—it really was his, wasn't it?"

"You're mad. And you're dangerous. I'll not stay another night in the house of a man who could think so little of his wife. I fear for my safety with you."

"And well you might, strumpet! If I beat you into your grave, I'd be within my rights!" He waved at her in disgust and turned his back. "You're no better than some rutting Cherokee squaw, giving herself to any savage she pleases."

Darcy's temper flared. "Aye, and any savage would be a better man than you, Gabriel Colter! There was a time I thought I could learn to care for you, but I see now what a fool I was. There's nothing in you but emptiness. You're hollow, vacant . . . and I hate you. God help me, but tonight I can no longer deny that I hate you."

He stared coldly at her. "If you hate me, why did you marry me, woman?"

"Because I felt a debt to you for standing up to that ruffian who attacked us on the road, and because I once thought there was greatness buried somewhere in you." She paused. "And because the man I should have married never asked me. Heaven knows, I wish I had given him more of a chance."

"This man—"

"You well know who I mean. Joshua, your despised Joshua . . . fifty times and a score a better man than you will ever be."

Gabriel's face went red. He came at her abruptly, and the next thing she knew, she was lying on the floor, looking up at the ceiling and trying to focus her vision. She had the impression that several minutes had passed when she was senseless.

Gabriel was crouched beside her, stroking her forehead and weeping. "I'm sorry, Darcy, I'm sorry. I never meant to strike you so hard. Please forgive me."

She rolled away from him and rose, pulling herself up against the wall. The room spun for a few moments. Her head throbbed. Gabriel's blow had sent pain spasming through the old injury received in the accident that had taken her unborn baby. He touched her shoulder.

"No," she said, and shrugged him off.

"Darcy, please, let me get you to your bed."

"Don't touch me."

She stumbled back toward her room, and there put a couple of garments into a cloth pouch. Gabriel came to the door, still weeping. Darcy did not weep. She was determined not to let Gabriel Colter bring the tears from her eyes ever again.

"What are you doing, Darcy? Where are you going?"

"Go away, Gabriel. Leave me be."

"Darcy, you must tell me!"

She closed the pouch and turned toward him. "Get out of my way."

He obeyed. She brushed past him and went back into the main room, heading for the door.

"Darcy . . ."

She opened the door and walked into the darkness.

He went after her. "Darcy, please . . ."

Darcy did not stop or look back at him. He went no farther than the edge of the porch where he clung to one of the cedar roof supports as if his legs could no longer hold him up. "Darcy!" he shouted into the darkness. "Come back, Darcy!"

She did not come back.

Darcy did not go at once to Alphus's cabin, for now that she was away from Gabriel, the tears did come. Very well, she decided. I will let him make me cry one time more, just one. But after that I am through with him, and with Haverly Fort, where my name has been ruined and my life destroyed.

Out in the familiar darkness again, away from the house, Darcy soon began to feel more at ease, and her weeping stopped. Her head did not hurt so badly now. Gabriel had not really injured her when he struck her down, but he had, to use a phrase of Alphus's, knocked some good sense into the space beneath her topknot. Life under Gabriel's oppressive hand was hopeless. She had tried first to improve it, then simply to endure it, and now there was no point in trying any longer. She would not let him beat her again.

She roamed in the darkness, letting the cool air and

concealing night heal her spirit. In the forests, owls hooted mysteriously, cattle moved quietly, their bells making a dull jangle, and hogs rooted at rotting stumps. The cabins of Haverly Fort were dark and silent, the stockade a black monolith against a backdrop of even darker treetops that moved in the breeze of a new summer.

Darcy wondered how Alphus and Sina would react to her appearance at their cabin in the middle of the night. Despite Alphus's invitation, she felt hesitant to go there at once. With all the worries about Indians, a tap on a door in the middle of the night might be misconstrued as a warning of attack. Darcy did not want to rouse unwarranted panic. At the very least, going to Alphus's cabin would disturb the family's rest. Darcy decided to wait out the night and go in the morning.

She walked about an hour more, following her usual private path, then drew close to Alphus's cabin and sat down against a massive oak tree. She leaned her head back against the bark and closed her eyes. She felt peaceful now; Gabriel would not find her here. In a few moments she went to sleep.

What made her awaken she did not know, but when she did, it was with a keen sense of excitement. She knew at once that she was not alone. Standing, she looked around, expectant but for some reason not afraid.

"Hello?"

There was a moment's pause; then a figure stepped from the darkness. "Darcy?"

She closed her eyes and opened them again, just to make sure this was not a dream. It was not.

"Joshua?"

"Aye, it's me."

A pause, then, "Oh, Joshua, we were told you were dead."

"I know, I know. But dead I'm not, and I'm back here now. I'll tell you all about it soon enough. I was waiting until morning to go down and show myself to Alphus and Sina—and then I saw you. Why aren't you at home?"

"It's not my home any longer, not after tonight. Don't

talk of that place anymore." Gazing in awe at his shadowed form, she said, "This can only be a dream—but it's the most wonderful dream. I've missed you so, Joshua." She went to him and put her arms around him.

"Darcy," he said. He wrapped his arms around her and drew her close, and in a moment he was overwhelmed by her presence, lost in her, and it was, as Darcy had said, as if it were all a dream.

Israel Coffman heard the amazing story from another rider he encountered two miles from Haverly Fort. Coffman was riding in; the other, riding out. "Joshua Colter's back," the man told him. "He wasn't killed at Point Pleasant after all, just wounded, and now he's back."

Coffman accepted the news with a nod but did not really believe it. He knew from experience that there were those who thought it terribly funny to give a wild tale to a preacher, particularly one with a reputation for being a little gullible.

When he reached Haverly Fort, to which he had been called to conduct a wedding, Coffman discovered that it was no joke. Joshua Colter had really returned, showing up that very morning on Alphus's doorstep. He had told his story to the family, and by way of young Zachariah Colter, it had quickly gotten out and was making the rounds of the community.

The young frontiersman, the story went, had been badly wounded at Point Pleasant and had crawled off to nurse his wounds. He had passed out, then been found, nearly dead, by some passersby and taken to the nearest station and gradually nursed back to health. The only part that was not clear to people was why he had not returned home or at least sent word he was well. It was almost as if he wanted people to believe he was dead, one man commented to Haverly.

Others had speculations along the line of the rumors that had circulated earlier about Joshua, reaching even Coffman's ears all the way over in Watauga. "Who do you suppose has also showed up at Alphus Colter's cabin, the very morning Joshua came home?" they asked. "That's right—Darcy Colter. Gone away from her own home and husband, and now living in the house of her own father-in-law, with the foster brother of the man she deserted. Terrible thing, Preacher. It's a shame folks won't follow the Christian road better than they do."

"That's true," Coffman responded. "If they did, they wouldn't be nearly so prone to gossip." With that, he walked away to do the marrying job he had come to do.

When the wedding ceremony was done, Coffman heard even more speculations about the relationship of Darcy and Joshua, and he headed for Alphus's cabin to see Joshua.

He found a cabin occupied by people struggling with an oil-and-water mix of emotions that could not come together. Sina was joyful, as was Zachariah, but Alphus's happiness seemed mixed with some sadness. Joshua, long-haired and bearded now after months in the wilderness, was obviously happy to see his kin again, but there was something uncomfortable in his manner that Coffman could see as soon as he looked at him. As for Darcy, she was the most unreadable of all—happy, sad, carefree, troubled. Gabriel Colter was not present, Coffman noted. That made him suspect that it was true that Darcy had left Gabriel.

"Why did you not let us know you were alive, Joshua?" Coffman asked when he and Joshua were alone.

Joshua managed an uncomfortable smile. "There were reasons."

"But your body was found . . ."

"They found a bloodied-up body and the coin that I wear on the ground beside it." Joshua lifted the Roman coin, which Alphus had ceremoniously placed back around his foster son's neck that very morning. "I lost the coin during the fight, I suppose. It took me weeks to get back on my feet—at the station, they had to dig a rifle ball that had near killed me out of my side—and when at last I got down along the Clinch River, I heard people talking about all who had been killed fighting the Shawnees and that Joshua Colter was among them.

"When I heard that, it gave me a mighty strange

feeling of freedom. Life has taken some bad turns for me, you know, and I wasn't happy around Haverly Fort anymore. So when I found out I was thought dead, I just said my good-byes in my mind and headed into the wilderness. Roamed, hunted. I went west, out along the Cumberland River, and on up into Kentucky a little, keeping hid all the way. Then I headed back down and a few days ago went near the Cherokee towns to put a stone on my mother's grave where Fort Loudoun used to be. I had been wanting to do that for her for years.

"By then, I knew I had to come back. It wasn't right to leave those who cared for me thinking I was dead and gone when I wasn't. And I had been close enough to the Cherokee towns to smell the trouble beginning to boil. There'll be fighting soon, Israel. I had quite a little fight with some Cherokees on my own, and they nigh got my scalp. The Indians have the British behind them now. It's going to be bloody, I fear."

"So you came back to join the defense?"

"I did."

"You did the right thing, Joshua, and I admire you for it. It's hard, after all, to return to a place where so many lies have been told about you." He looked at his old friend piercingly. "And they are lies, are they not?"

Joshua looked very uncomfortable. "I don't know what you mean." He quickly walked away.

Coffman did not immediately return to Watauga as he had planned. Several people of Haverly Fort asked him to remain for a time so they could discuss with him the possibility of beginning a new church and school that could operate at least part of the time if Coffman was willing to travel between Watauga and Sinking Creek. Coffman agreed to stay around long enough to talk out the proposal. There was nothing compelling him to rush back to Watauga other than lending a hand in war preparations there, but that he could do right here at Haverly Fort where the stockade was being strengthened daily and siege provisions made.

Coffman had already sent his wife to safety in Virginia,

in the company of some of those who had fled the Tennessee country at Alexander Cameron's behest. Virginia Coffman had developed a deep fear of Indians from all the war talk. She had wanted her husband to flee with her, but Coffman had declined, telling her it was part of his duty to remain with his people in time of trouble. He would do his duty and trust to the Lord to keep him safe if that was the Lord's plan.

Coffman kept temporary quarters at Haverly Fort in the same stockade cabin he had once shared with Joshua. He was stunned to learn that Peter Haverly had been locked up in a cabin farther down the row as an unrepentant loyalist. Two armed men guarded Haverly's prison cabin. Coffman walked over and talked to them one evening, hoping they would let him visit with Haverly. The preacher had no great liking for Haverly but felt obliged to offer him what comfort he could.

The men declined to let Coffman see the prisoner, saying they had been told by James Robertson to leave him in isolation to persuade him to become talkative about whatever plots he might have made with the British and Cherokees.

"Haverly's done himself in as far as ever again having the regard of the people. He's lost for good any respect he ever had," one of the guards told Coffman. "As of today, we don't even call this Haverly Fort no more, for there's not a man here willing to fight off Indians in a stockade named for a man who was ready to help those very savages."

"What is the fort's name, then?" Coffman asked.

"Colter's Station. Named after Mr. Alphus Colter, the man who built it. A good name, eh?"

"A good name indeed," said Coffman.

With that, the man leaned over and gave Coffman a private wink. "Speaking of the Colter family, tell us, Preacher, is it true that Joshua Colter and Gabriel's wife have been . . . well, you know what I'm talking about."

"I do indeed, gentlemen," Coffman said. "And all I can say to you in answer is have a pleasant evening, and raise a shout if the Cherokees attack. Good night."

He turned and headed back toward his cabin.

25

Israel Coffman walked through the stockade gate. The afternoon was hot and dry; a whirlwind blew a cloud of gritty dust up from the battered yard and into his eyes. He stopped and rubbed his eyes, blinked, and looked around at the dozen or so men busy replacing weak palisades with strong ones and putting an extra support under one of the weaker block-houses. Then his gaze drifted over toward the little cabin where he had been staying.

He was surprised to see Darcy Colter standing there looking back at him shyly, as if she were waiting for him. Darcy was a woman he had never known particularly well; she had always seemed shy and withdrawn around him. Dusting off his shirt, Coffman put on a smile and went toward her, not letting a certain discomfort that her presence brought him show on his face. He had heard the rumors about this woman's purported infidelity. He would have to be careful about his associations with her, so that his own reputation would not be endangered.

"Good day to you, Mrs. Colter."

"Good day, Reverend Coffman. I hope you don't mind that I waited for you to return."

"Not at all, not at all."

He invited her inside, making sure to leave the cabin door standing open after they entered, for he had felt the eyes of the workmen upon them as they walked inside. Coffman secretly studied Darcy. Despite the continuous puckish talk circulating about her, something about it struck Coffman as incongruous. Darcy Colter simply didn't look like his idea of an adulteress, though he realized what an illogical notion that was. He knew from experience that sinners came in all sizes, shapes, and sexes.

Since his marriage, Coffman had become a wiser and more discerning man where females were concerned. He promptly sensed today what might have gone past him some months ago: Beneath a carefully maintained veneer of calm, Darcy was agitated and upset about something.

"I have springwater in this bucket, pure and fresh though no longer cool. May I offer you some?"

"Yes, please. Thank you, Reverend."

She drank the water slowly, out of the gourd dipper, for Coffman had no cup to offer, and stared all the while into the corner. Coffman suspected she was trying to collect herself to present some question or revelation that was important to her. He waited patiently.

She abruptly put down the dipper and looked up at Coffman. "I've abandoned my husband, you know."

"Yes, I heard about it."

"He's been cruel to me for a long time. He struck me."

Coffman nodded.

Darcy's lip began to tremble. "I'm a sinful woman, Reverend."

"We are all sinners, Mrs. Colter, are we not?"

"Yes . . . but not all are guilty of what I've done."

Coffman cleared his throat; giving counsel in such situations was not something he had often done, and it sat uncomfortably with him. "If it's leaving your husband's house that concerns you, I must say I see no sin in you protecting yourself, if it's fear of harm that led you to leave. I'm not one of the opinion that a woman must submit to being beaten, even by a husband."

"It's not just leaving my husband that I speak of, Reverend. I've done a far worse sin than that."

Coffman suddenly felt a sick little twinge inside. Obviously she was about to confirm the rumors about herself and Joshua that he had hoped were false.

"There has been much talk about me and Joshua since the very day of my marriage. Lies, hurtful lies." She paused, and her gaze fell. "Lies they were, at least, until two nights ago. When Joshua came home, we met in the night, by accident, outside Alphus's cabin. It was the same night I left Gabriel. I was so amazed to see Joshua alive, so happy, and feeling so empty at the same time for what had happened, that I, that we—" She stopped, then began speaking more intensely, looking into his eyes. "We did not mean to do wrong, Reverend, neither of us. We did not intend to commit any sin . . . but we did sin. I made myself an adulterer with him. I made myself the very thing all those rumors said I was. I am bitterly ashamed."

A tear rolled down her face. "I need help, Reverend. And I need to get away from Haverly Fort, from both Gabriel and Joshua and all the wagging tongues. I'm so weary of it all. God help me, I don't think I can bear to be here another day!"

Coffman mentally voiced a quick prayer for wisdom; he had not dealt with a situation just like this one before. He took a deep breath. "Let me begin by assuring you that all you say to me will be held in confidence," he said. "I will be honest in what I say to you, and I hope you will be equally so with me . . . and if leave here you must, there may be a place I can take you. I have friends down on the Chucky—good people who will be glad to take you in for a time."

He smiled to put her at ease. "But first, my dear, I believe we have much talking to do."

John Hawk felt a stirring in his fighting spirit unlike anything he had known before. Since the recent arrival in Chota of a delegation of northern Indians, the sacred town and all the Overhill towns around it had been in an uproar.

The fourteen-member delegation, consisting of representatives of the Shawnees, Mohawks, Nancutas, Ottawas, and the Delawares, the "grandfathers" of the Cherokees, had arrived in the Cherokee capital wearing the black paint of war, which made their mission's intent clear even before they spoke the first word. It was not only the Cherokees, they said, who were offended by the encroaching white men. The northern Indians also wished to see them punished and halted from their reported warlike plans against the Indians.

The fiery talk of these visitors had fanned and spread war flames throughout the Overhill towns, and now John Hawk, like almost all the young warriors, eagerly awaited the appointed day for the visitors' official Grand Talk to the entire Cherokee nation. Dragging Canoe in particular was eager for the talk; he saw the arrival of the Indian deputation as the most fortuitous event that had yet happened.

John Hawk was prone to agree. Prior to the visitors' arrival, matters had been proceeding too slowly and uncertainly to suit him. Henry Stuart and Alexander Cameron, still among the Overhills, had been ambivalent about launching a campaign against the whites. So far, their activity had consisted mostly of counseling patience on the part of Dragging Canoe and other firebrands, and sending letters and messages, via trader Isaac Thomas, back and forth between the Overhill towns and the unaka settlements.

Now the influence of the British agents was being overshadowed by that of the visiting deputation. Many of the young Cherokee warriors were already painting their faces black, readying for war. The talk already spread informally by the visiting deputation was being repeated everywhere: The white men were taking over Indian lands from south to north, building forts and gathering armies. The British agents in the North were encouraging solidarity among the Indians, who were usually divided and fighting among themselves. Through Indian cooperation, the white men could be overcome and the lands west of the mountains kept in the hands of those to whom it had been given by the Great Man Above.

John Hawk observed Henry Stuart and Alexander Cameron during this period, trying to determine their true attitudes toward war against the whites. They declared a reluctance to favor full warfare, yet they had delivered ammunition to the Cherokees. Additionally, according to rumor, the settlers were circulating a letter, supposedly from Henry Stuart, declaring a strong intention to wage Indian war against the Overmountain settlements. Stuart reportedly claimed the letter was a forgery, designed by conspiring settlers to bolster the spirit of rebellion against Britain. The truth about that letter John Hawk did not know; what was significant was the fact that unaka settlements were not being substantially vacated because of the threats it contained. Clearly the settlers were preparing to make war, not flee.

The day for the Grand Talk came at last. Chota was filled to overflowing with Cherokees from all the towns and clans. War spirits were high among the young, but the old men such as Little Carpenter seemed glum and hopeless. It seemed to John Hawk that Nancy Ward was unhappy as well, but that was to be expected, for she and Little Carpenter spoke with the same tongue and saw with the same eyes.

It was strange to John Hawk to see the Shawnees and others who had traditionally been the enemies of the Cherokees counseling here in Chota. Principal among them was the well-known Shawnee chief Cornstalk, who sat in silence throughout the preliminary talks.

And fascinating talks they were. According to the Northern visitors, the white men, principally Virginians, were overtaking the frontier at an alarming pace. Some of the claims John Hawk had difficulty believing and later discounted as exaggeration: for example, that in two forts in Kentucky alone, two thousand Long Knives were assembled, ready to drive out the Indians.

As the talks progressed, Dragging Canoe became ever

more agitated. By the time Cornstalk rose for the final talk, it appeared to be all Dragging Canoe could do to restrain himself from leaping up to strike the warpole.

Cornstalk, who had made peace after "losing" the Point Pleasant battle, was now ready again for war. There was no time to delay preparation for this, he said. As the white men carried on their own internal squabbles and the king's enemies on the other side of the mountains were put down by the British, the Indians could strike a fatal blow against the whites on the western side. Cornstalk declared that he and his fellows intended to carry such war talks throughout the entire western country and bring the Indians together as one force—and those Indians who declined to join the effort would find themselves enemies of all who did.

Stuart and Cameron made efforts, perhaps just token ones, to overcome the effect of Cornstalk's talk, but without much success. They declined to accept the vermillion-stained, nine-foot-by-six-inch warbelt Cornstalk offered, saying that without the express consent of John Stuart, still in Florida, and coordination with regular British troops, no war effort should be launched.

The Grand Talk stretched on for days, the war issue remaining undecided. Then trader Isaac Thomas, who had been sent out many days before with messages to the settlements, returned, bringing with him a written "talk" from Virginia's Fincastle Committee, whom the Overmountain settlers had contacted for aid.

The written talk was stern in tone, having been written in response to the controversial, possibly forged, warlike letter that had been written over Stuart's name and circulated among the settlements. The talk from Virginia warned the Cherokees not to be swayed by those who wished them to fight on behalf of the British. Dragging Canoe should be restrained and the British agents ignored, or the Cherokees could look forward to nothing but destruction.

Thomas added his own verbal note, which struck John Hawk as a likely exaggeration designed to dampen the Cherokees' war spirits. He reported that a full six thousand men who had been prepared to battle the king's troops in the East had instead decided to turn westward to fight the Cherokees.

If Thomas, who clearly had little stomach for the proposed attack, thought such a tale would avert war, he thought incorrectly. After the talk was read and Thomas's claims of massive unaka military strength presented, the younger Cherokees only solidified their warlike position. Dragging Canoe rose and covered himself with black paint, then with a hatchet ceremoniously struck the warpole.

John Hawk was among the braves who cheered the dramatic action. The visit of the Northern Indians had done its persuasive work on all except the old leaders.

Stuart, maintaining the official British position, warned that an indiscriminate attack upon the settlers would likely result in harm to innocent people, including women, children, and loyalists. The king himself would be displeased by such things.

Stuart's urgings were to no avail. After all, had not a plan already been developed, by Gist and others, to protect the loyalists? By the simple expedient of raising a white flag, the loyalists could mark their dwellings and be spared. Those who would do so could even join the Cherokees and march against the rebellious unakas.

Whether Stuart's and Cameron's advocacies of peace were sincere or simply an expediency to allow them to claim innocence for any massacres that might follow John Hawk could not guess and did not care. The point was that ammunition was at hand, the warpole had been struck, and the unakas could at last be driven out.

Stuart and Cameron departed the Overhill towns shortly afterward, giving a final urging to avoid killing loyalists, women, and children. Gist offered to ensure the safety of loyalists further by taking four white traders with him, including Thomas, and privately visiting loyalist homes to reiterate the word that a white flag above the door would bring protection. Stuart and Cameron agreed.

John Hawk, his face now painted for war, watched

them leave. He was glad of their departure; now Dragging Canoe could lead the war preparations uninterrupted. The letters and messages sent by the British agents to the settlements had done no more than give some forewarning of attack and allow the unakas to build and strengthen forts. Key strategies of Cherokee warfare were swiftness and surprise; an enemy forewarned was an enemy harder to defeat.

With that thought still going through his mind, John Hawk watched Alexander Cameron and his retinue disappear down the trail toward the Lower Cherokee towns. Stuart had already left, heading back to Florida to report to his brother. When Cameron was out of sight, John Hawk turned toward his house and saw Nancy Ward, the Beloved Woman, or War Woman as she was also called, standing nearby. She had been watching the departure of the British agent, the ceremonial swan's wing, symbol of her rank, in her hand. On her face was a look of sadness. John Hawk knew why: The Beloved Woman had no spirit for this war.

Nevertheless, she would participate in the preparations for it. It would be her task to prepare the purging, emetic "black drink" brewed from holly leaves, that the warriors would imbibe repeatedly and vomit as part of their ceremonial battle preparations. It did not matter now if she stood against warfare; the course was already set. Soon, very soon, blood would flow in the Overmountain country.

Alphus Colter did not like to admit it, but he was beginning to feel his age these days. A mere walk from the stockade to Gabriel's house had left him winded. He supposed that at age sixty-six when many men of his day were long gone from this world, he should be glad to be alive and walking about at all. Still, it was distressing to see himself declining. It did not seem that long ago he could walk five miles across rugged country on a hot day and hardly break a sweat, all this while toting a heavy rifle, with pouches hanging all around him and a nicely wrapped tenderloin for his supper riding next to his belly beneath his hunting shirt.

He knocked on Gabriel's door. He had kept in frequent contact with his son since Darcy had left him. Gabriel had initially refused even to open the door to his father. Talking through the closed door, he had accused Alphus of treating him wrongly in reporting him as a loyalist to James Robertson's band. Alphus defended himself by pointing out that such an action might have saved Gabriel's life. When the actual fighting came, spirits might become so enraged that loyalists who had not recanted might suffer harm from rebel neighbors.

On the third visit, Gabriel had allowed Alphus to come in. Gabriel looked terrible—pale, unshaven, haggard, his usual haughty manner gone. He had been examining his life and heart, he told Alphus, and had at last seen himself for what he really was. Darcy had been right to leave him, and Alphus had been right to call down James Robertson upon him. All his life he had been blind to his true nature, thinking himself a good man when really he was bad.

Alphus had been alarmed by such words. This seemed the talk of a man set upon punishing himself. Fearing Gabriel might be thinking of taking his own life, he had asked Gabriel to come live at his cabin for a time or to allow him and Sina to move in here—just to help out now that Darcy was gone, he had explained, covering his real concern.

Gabriel had declined. Patton could take care of his needs, he said; he did not need any resident helpers. And certainly he could not go live with Alphus. Darcy was there, was she not?

Alphus had dreaded giving the answer. She had been there, he told Gabriel, but now she was gone. She had talked privately to the Reverend Coffman, who had now left the fort with her, escorting her toward the Noli-chucky, for Darcy had expressed a desire to leave the area. Alphus had advised against it, feeling it would be safer to avoid such travel at the moment, but both Coffman and Darcy had held firm. Coffman said he knew a gentle, friendly family down near Great Limestone Creek with whom Darcy could stay for a time and rest until she felt ready to come home.

Gabriel had seemed quite disturbed to hear that Darcy was gone. "Why didn't you force them to stay?" he asked Alphus.

"They're both grown people," Alphus replied. "I couldn't force them to do anything."

That was where the last visit had ended a few hours ago. Now Alphus was back, praying he would find Gabriel safe and sound. He had privately alerted Patton to keep a close watch on Gabriel and to report immediately if Gabriel seemed to be acting peculiarly or talking in any way implying suicide. Patton had not come to him, so Alphus was optimistic.

Alphus knocked again, and again. There was no answer. A great burst of worry began to overcome his optimism. "Gabriel!" he yelled through the door. "Are you in there?"

As he pounded again, thinking of forcing open a shutter to enter through a window, Patton came around the house. "Mr. Colter, sir?"

"Patton—where is Gabriel?"

"He's gone, sir, gone now for three hour."

"Gone! Where?"

"I don't know, sir. He just saddled up a horse and rode off. He told me firm not to say a word of it to nobody, and I didn't."

"You should have come to me, Patton. He might be going off to do harm to himself."

"I hope you won't mind me saying it, but no, sir, I don't think he was. If it had been that, I would have fetched you. He was fretting over Miz Darcy. I think he's just gone off to find her. Said we wanted to tell her he was sorry and all."

"God help us," Alphus said. "I surely wish you had come to me."

"I'm sorry, Mr. Colter. I was just trying to do what Mr. Gabriel said."

Alphus walked back toward the stockade, wondering

what he should do. He had much work to do right here
at the fort, preparing for the possibility of siege, but he
felt an impulse to try to overtake Gabriel. Gabriel was an
adult, but he was an even more amateurish woodsman,
after all his years on the frontier, than Israel Coffman. If
he was forced off the trace, he would likely become lost—
no small concern, particularly in a time of Indian unrest.

Alphus was still debating what to do when he reached
the gate. Callum McSwain, who had shortly before finished adding a second bar to the gate, approached him
rapidly. With him was another man, covered with grime
and sweat, obviously having just finished a long ride.

"Alphus, this man has come as a messenger from John
Sevier, down at Fort Lee. The Cherokees are on the
move."

"What? Already?"

"Aye," the messenger said, stepping forward. "You are
Captain Alphus Colter, leader of this fort's defense?"

"I am."

"My name is Stokely. I've come straight from Fort Lee.
The entire countryside all along the Nolichucky is being
abandoned. There's a bloody six hundred Cherokee warriors on the march, aiming to plunder all the way to the
New River, from the word we received."

Joshua had walked up in time to hear what was said.
His eyes narrowed at the news. "How do you know this?"
he asked, taking the question right off Alphus's tongue.

"Issac Thomas showed up, along with three other
traders. They had just left the Overhill towns—escaped
is more the way to say it, for they had been supposed to
go with that devil Nathaniel Gist and warn the loyalists
along the Nolichucky about the attack and tell them to
mark their houses for safety and join in fighting against
the rest of us."

"Aye—we know well enough of that damnable plot,"
Alphus said, looking toward the cabin where Haverly was
locked up.

The messenger continued. "The War Woman, Nancy
Ward, came to the traders on the sneak, fresh from
making the black drink, and sent them off to warn us all

of the attacks. She helped the traders get away, and they got to the Chucky three days later. They say the Indians plan to divide and strike several forts at once, including this one. Lieutenant Sevier was the first to get word, and he sent out messengers to all the forts right off. People are leaving the Nolichucky like they were shooed flies, heading for Watauga, or east across the mountains. There's scarce any time left to get ready, so you'd best call in your people."

Joshua turned to Alphus. "Darcy and Israel were headed for the Nolichucky when they left here."

"Aye, and now Gabriel's out there, too."

"Gabe?"

"He went after Darcy—I learned it from Patton not ten minutes ago."

"Went after Darcy? What does that fool think he can do for her?"

Alphus ignored the question and turned back to Stokely. "Did you encounter any travelers along your way here?"

"Nary a soul, but I traveled off the trace much of the way. Thought I saw Indian sign, you know."

"God, I hope you were wrong about that," Alphus said. "We have some folk from our fort here traveling toward the Chucky. I fear for them, but with any good fortune, they'll make Fort Lee."

Stokely shook his head. "'Twill do them little good if they do, I suspect. Even as I was being sent off, Sevier's men were beginning to abandon him and head for the new fort at Sycamore Shoals. Fort Lee is unfinished, you see, and now I feel certain Sevier is left with insufficient men to garrison it. Likely as not, your friends will reach Fort Lee and find it abandoned."

Word of the impending attack spread across the countryside like a dry autumn fire. Standing atop one of the rifle platforms, Alphus could look in any direction and see riders and pedestrians approaching in what he could think of only as a slow rush, most of them driving livestock and carrying bundles of their most precious items.

Already the stockade was nearly full of people. The little stockade cabins were occupied by the very old, very young, and ill; newcomers were having to pitch crude tents or build rough shelters wherever they could around the stockade yard.

Peter Haverly had been freed from his cabin; there was not enough available space to justify devoting one entire shelter to a prison. Now he was tied to a wagon wheel and receiving many bitter looks. Christiana, Beth, and Samuel stayed close-by him, looking sad, and for them Alphus felt pity, though for Haverly himself he felt none.

The fattest livestock had been led inside the stockade and penned. Other hogs and cattle were being grazed outside the fort but close to the walls. If the anticipated siege grew very long, some of those animals might have to be gathered by brave volunteers and driven into the fort to supplement what was already there. Alphus did not expect matters would come to anything that drastic, but he had to be prepared. He was glad for all the work that had been done on the stockade over the past weeks, glad for the extensive riflery and ammunition stocked inside the walls, and glad in particular for the good well. A fort without a well became a living hell in a long siege.

Alphus saw Joshua returning from scouting, striding across the clearing in front of the fort, and descended from the rifle platform to meet him at the gate.

"Find anything?"

"No Indian sign yet. No Gabriel, either, though I did find what I think are his tracks. Then I lost them. So many have started traveling over the trails, coming to the fort, that what sign is out there is pretty much beaten away before long."

Alphus felt an aching dread. "I hope to heaven that Gabe comes back on his own soon," he said. He paused, wondering if he should say the other part of his thought, then went ahead. "In truth, Joshua, I'm not sure we will see Gabriel again, Cherokees or no Cherokees."

"What do you mean?"

"I fear he might take his own life out there."

Joshua looked surprised. "Because of Darcy?"

"Aye. He told Patton he was leaving to find her—but if he does, what will come of it? She'll never go back to him." Alphus shook his head. "I fear for what will happen to him, no matter how this Indian scare ends."

Joshua looked a little ashen. "I'll go out for another scout. If I can bring Gabriel in safe, Alphus, I pledge to you before almighty God that I'll do it."

26

From the beginning of his journey toward the Great Limestone with Darcy Colter, Israel Coffman had felt ill at ease. This resulted partially from Alphus Colter's warning to him about traveling when Indian attack threatened, but mostly he worried over appearances. Here he was, not only a married man but also a minister, traveling in lone company with a woman who had already confessed to marital infidelity. The situation could rouse lots of harmful talk.

Well, he thought, if it does, then it does. He believed that a minister's primary duty was to the need of whatever individual he was trying to serve at the given moment; in this case, that person was Darcy Colter, and her need was to be away from Haverly Fort, now Colter's Station. So here they were, an odd pair of travelers indeed, riding through the wilderness.

As they neared the juncture of the Nolichucky and Great Limestone, Coffman found reasons for concern that made mere worries over his reputation seem insubstantial. He had noted several empty farmsteads and seen evidence that livestock had been driven hurriedly along

404

the roads and trails. Coffman noted these things but said nothing of them to Darcy.

What could have so emptied the countryside? Coffman could think of only one thing: an Indian alarm. The Nolichucky region was one of the farthest outposts of settlement, and relatively close to the Overhill towns. Word of advancing Indians would probably reach here before it reached other regions. The farther the pair traveled, the surer Coffman became that such an alarm had come, probably since the time they had departed Colter's Station. When the travelers reached the farmstead they had been seeking and found it abandoned, the last doubt that something was amiss was erased.

"We must make for Fort Lee, Darcy," Coffman said. "We are in danger here."

"Aye," she said. "I know."

They traveled faster and more silently, eyes always searching, ears listening closely, for any hint of danger. They passed two cabins; both were empty. They were up Great Limestone Creek from Fort Lee, so now they were traveling southwest toward the fort along the creek. As they drew closer to the mouth of the creek, Coffman's tension lessened. Soon they would be at Fort Lee, protected by stockade walls.

Coffman hailed the fort as soon as he saw it, waving his hand above his head and shouting his identity. No answer came back. He hailed again and again. Still there was only silence.

"Heaven help us—abandoned!" he said.

The silence of the forest became ominous. All was still, yet Coffman was aware of every moving leaf and wind-stirred branch. The creek's noise seemed amplified.

"We must go to Fort Caswell," Darcy said.

"No," Coffman replied tensely. "It's too far." Fort Caswell, the new fort built at Sycamore Shoals and named in honor of Richard Caswell, governor-elect of North Carolina, was twenty or more miles away as the crow flies and even farther, given the necessary turns and twists of land travel. At that moment, from Coffman's viewpoint, the distance might as well have been five hundred miles.

"We must return to Colter's," he said.

Darcy shook her head. "If you return there, you return alone."

Coffman felt a burst of exasperation. "Don't be foolish, Darcy. Personal feelings are not important now. We must go to the closest station."

"I see no Indians about. Look at the sign—it's fresh. In the time since we left the station, we met no one traveling from here to Colter's, even though it is closer than Fort Caswell. That can only mean Fort Lee had received no warning so urgent that the people here believed they had no time to reach Sycamore Shoals. If we go now, we can reach Fort Caswell long before there is any danger."

Coffman still refused. Darcy glared coldly at him. "Very well, then, go back to the station. I'm going on to Fort Caswell. I would rather face a few more miles of Indian danger than return to where Gabriel is. I cannot bear the idea of being locked in the same stockade with him for an entire Indian siege."

"You're being both foolish and stubborn, Darcy—I can't allow you to do that."

"You can't stop me, Reverend."

Coffman was stunned. Never had he met so headstrong a woman. He didn't know what to do. Obviously, Darcy meant it when she said she would go on alone. He saw no option but to relent.

"Very well," he said. "To Fort Caswell we will go. But let's set off at once, and keep our wits about us and our prayers rising for providence to be with us, for if we encounter Indians, we will have quite a row to hoe—and I'll hold it to your fault."

Joshua Colter heard motion beyond the briar thicket and froze in place. His rifle was half raised, his thumb on the lock. Barely breathing, he listened and watched, his nostrils flaring slightly, sniffing the air. Movement again, and then a voice—a familiar voice, moaning and complaining about some sort of pain. Joshua straightened.

"Gabe!" he said. "It's me, Joshua! I'm coming to you!"

He rounded the thicket, which was heavy with ripe blackberries, and found Gabriel seated on the ground, his hand on the back of his head. There was dried blood caking one ear. Gabriel's horse was nowhere about, and his rifle and pistols were gone.

"What happened to you, Gabriel?" Joshua asked, kneeling before him with his rifle cradled.

Gabriel looked at his despised foster brother with distaste, still gingerly touching his head. "I was attacked," he said.

"Indians?"

"No."

"I didn't think so—you've still got your scalp. Who, then?"

"A white man. I didn't see much of him. He was fleeing toward the fort and must have liked the look of what I had. He came out from beside the trail and struck me from behind."

"He took your fixings?"

Gabriel apparently didn't see the need to answer so obvious a question. He fired a silent glum look at Joshua.

"Listen, Gabe, I know you've got no cause to be happy to see me, but I am glad I found you."

Gabriel laughed sarcastically, though the spasms made his skull throb and he quickly stopped.

Joshua chose to ignore the laughter. "Alphus has worried himself sick over you."

"Aye, so he sent his beloved woodsman son to fetch his roaming simpleton—is that it?"

Joshua was beginning to see the depth of bitterness in his foster brother. He also realized the time had come to do something he had felt compelled toward since his nighttime encounter with Darcy. He cleared his throat and shifted uncomfortably.

"There is something I must confess to you, Gabriel."

Gabriel chuckled icily. "What—that you've been an adulterer with my wife? That's nothing I need told to me. I've known that almost since the day I married her."

"You've only thought you knew it. I never put a hand

on Darcy in all the months that talk was raging so fierce, Gabriel. I swear that to you before God himself." He paused. "But that changed lately. I'm not an innocent man anymore. The night I returned, the night that Darcy left your house . . . that night I became guilty. 'Twas not intended, and 'twas not right, and I confess it to you. I think I owe you that."

Gabriel studied his foster brother. He was still seated on the ground, blackberry briars clinging to his clothing. "I should hate you for that, I suppose. But what does it matter now? She's gone. I'm already humiliated before all my neighbors. My good name is ruined."

Something about that angered Joshua. "Your good name—that's all you ever cared about, isn't it? About Darcy herself you've never cared at all."

He expected Gabriel to react sharply to that, but he didn't. Instead he seemed to deflate, as if the spirit were draining from him. "When I married Darcy, I had convinced myself that I cared. The truth is, I'm not sure now I've ever really known how to care about anyone . . . except Father."

Old frustrations were beginning to flare in Joshua. "If you didn't care for Darcy, why did you choose her? Why marry her, of all people?"

Gabriel smiled, but without warmth. "I've asked myself that same question quite often. I think I finally have the answer."

"Tell me, then."

"Revenge."

" 'Revenge'?"

"Aye—revenge against you. Against the foul little trader's brood that came crawling out of the forest sixteen years ago and took my father away from me. I knew you loved Darcy—I could see it when you looked at her. By taking her away from you, I could bring you pain. Of course, I didn't think of it exactly that way at the time; sometimes our own motivations become clear to us only after time has passed. As I said, I did convince myself that I cared for Darcy."

Joshua could have spat into Gabriel's face. "You're a foul and damnable scoundrel."

"I've reached much the some conclusion of late. And don't think such a realization makes me happy, Joshua. You may not believe it, but the fact is that I despise myself far more than you could ever despise me. I always have, since I was young. I have never wanted to be as I am."

"I don't understand what you're saying."

Gabriel stood, pulling clinging briars from himself and dusting off his clothing. He winced and staggered as his rising brought pain to his bruised skull, then walked over to lean against a young maple until more of his strength returned.

"Of course you don't understand—how could you? Look at you: strong, skilled, a fine woodsman, hunter, fighter—and a handsome man. Everything Alphus Colter ever wanted in a son. Everything I am not. God knows I wanted to please him. I spent my whole childhood trying to, not by being what I couldn't but by trying to be the best at what I could—my business, commerce, even my religion. I thought I was doing it for myself, for my community, for God, but really it was for Father. All for Father. I thought if I could be a leader, a wealthy man, like Peter Haverly, then Alphus would care for me like I wanted him to. But you were ever in the way. No matter what I did, there was always you in the center of his eye. He always cared for you more."

Gabriel stopped for a moment. "And I could never rid myself of you. Twice I thought you were dead, and you came back both times. Back from the grave to fill my father's eye again so there was no room for me."

Joshua had never heard Gabriel talk like this and hardly knew how to take it. He felt compelled to try to comfort Gabriel. "Alphus cares for you more than you think. Right now he's fierce worried about your safety. I was too. That's why I came after you."

Gabriel smiled again and shook his head. "No, Joshua. You came for Father's sake, and your own, not for mine. You had to find me to ease Alphus's mind. And you had to find me to give your confession, to cleanse your soul for what you did with my wife. Well, you've confessed now, and you've found me safe as you hoped to do, and now you can take me back and receive Alphus's adoration."

Joshua saw no reason to carry the conversation any further. "Come on, Gabriel. This is no time or place to be standing about and flapping jaws. Let's get back to the fort before the Dragon comes to take our scalps."

More than seven hundred warriors—Cherokees with a handful of Creeks and a few whites—moved in remarkable silence through the wilderness. They spoke few words, communicating mostly through hand signals. These warriors had readied themselves for battle in isolation, fasting, abstaining from the pleasures of their wives, and keeping watch for signs that would tell them if war should be engaged or delayed. No discouraging signs had come, and the warriors had departed, covered with paint; laden with bows, arrows, and rifles; and filled with the thrill of coming battle.

John Hawk traveled close to Dragging Canoe, for with him he would fight. Plans had been carefully laid for the attack: After the entire group struck Fort Lee, the Raven of Chota would depart the main body with a small band of warriors and strike the isolated farmstead cabins in Carter's Valley. Old Abram, of Chilhowee, with a force of three hundred warriors, would advance to Sycamore Shoals and attack Fort Caswell. A body of more than one hundred, under Tsula, the Red Fox, would strike the stockade still known to the Cherokees as Haverly Fort, and some two hundred warriors, including John Hawk, would go with Dragging Canoe to the Long Island country and devastate the forts and settlements there. It would be a major undertaking, but spirits were high. The Cherokees would not fail.

Only two aspects of the venture worried John Hawk. The first was the abrupt disappearance of Isaac Thomas and the other traders from the Overhill towns, just after the black-drink ceremony. Why, and how, had they vanished? John Hawk had heard it rumored that Nancy Ward, aided by women of her clan, had helped them get away so that they could give the war alarm to the unakas.

The second bothersome matter was the vision of Joshua Colter that John Hawk had seen near the old Fort Loudoun site. Surely it had been a vision . . . and if so, it might have meant something. Was it a sign that he should not go to war against Joshua's people? If it was, he wished the meaning had been clearer.

Both of these concerns mattered less and less as the war party moved toward the settlements. Just ahead lay Fort Lee, where the first blood would be drawn and a siege undertaken in earnest. John Hawk could hardly wait to begin the battle. He was disheartened when the warriors found Fort Lee abandoned. Not only did this delay battle, but it indicated that the unakas had, as John Hawk had feared, received warning.

The warriors put the torch to the empty stockade. John Hawk watched with some satisfaction as flames leapt and smoke rose into the sky. Before this campaign was done, he hoped, he would see many settler cabins, barns, and stockades similarly destroyed. Let the white men be stricken with terror and loss; perhaps then they would see that this country had best be left to the Cherokees.

The huge Indian force divided soon after the stockade was destroyed. The Raven departed toward Carter's Valley, and Tsula began the trek toward Haverly Fort. Because of its proximity, a strike against Haverly could be accomplished almost at once. The other bands had much farther to travel before they could do battle.

Departing with Dragging Canoe and his warriors, John Hawk's mind was filled with the songs of war. Though the lack of a fight at Fort Lee had been a disappointment, there would be many opportunities for battle soon, and he would be all the hungrier for them.

Joshua and Gabriel, upon returning to Colter's Station, found the stockade packed with people in a great state of excitement over an unusual incident that had just occurred. A man had arrived at the fort, riding Gabriel's

horse and bearing his weapons. The man claimed he had
found the horse and guns near the trail, which threw
Alphus into despair, for he was convinced that Gabriel
had gone off in shame and sorrow over his personal
affairs and killed himself in the forest.

The lie was given to that idea when sentinels on the
rifle platform saw Joshua and Gabriel emerge from the
forest and approach the stockade. The news was shouted
down to Alphus, who realized at once that the newcomer
had not found Gabriel's goods but stolen them. A mad
scramble to put the man under arrest ensued, but the
fellow was fortunate; he was among those who had taken
to the rifle platform to watch for Indians and was able to
vault the wall and escape into the forest before Gabriel
and Joshua were through the gate.

"Let him go," Alphus directed. "It's not worth the risk
to send someone after him. Let the Cherokees take care
of him for us."

Alphus's welcoming of Gabriel was somewhat emotional; he had not really expected to see his son alive
again. Peter Haverly, still chained to his wagon wheel,
watched the scene with a glum face. Meanwhile, the fort
was busier than it ever had been, and an atmosphere of
tension overhung the whole scene. That evening, when
the last of the scouts returned and reported that they had
seen smoke rising to the sky from the direction of Fort
Lee, grim expectation was in every mind. The attack
would come soon.

And it did. The Indians struck the first blow against
Colter's Station the next morning, and the battle almost
cost Joshua Colter his life hardly before it had begun.

He, Callum McSwain, and two relative newcomers to
the station, Benjamin and Preston Halliforth, brothers
with fair freckled skin and flaming red hair, scouted the
forests around the stockade shortly after dawn, looking
for Indian sign. Nothing was seen initially, though both
McSwain and Joshua, who scouted close together, felt a
prickling sense of danger. The Halliforths, good woodsmen who had scouted extensively during the Dunmore
campaign, were more confident than their companions.

"There's not a savage within twenty miles—on that I'll wager my scalp," Preston Halliforth said when he joined Joshua and McSwain.

"Wagering your scalp is exactly what you're doing when you draw such a conclusion," McSwain commented.

At precisely that moment, a horrible scream was heard, coming from deeper in the forest. More screams quickly followed, coming ever closer.

"Benjamin!" Preston Halliforth shouted.

As if answering his brother's call, the screaming Benjamin Halliforth appeared, his hands atop his head. Blood poured between his fingers and down his face. Part of his scalp was gone, and it looked to Joshua as if the left side of his skull were partially caved in. How the man had managed to live, much less run, in such a condition Joshua could not imagine.

"Benjamin!" the other Halliforth called again, heading toward his brother.

Benjamin Halliforth did not seem to see his sibling. He was running in stark terror, his mind blank, every move driven by pure survival instinct. He swept past Preston Halliforth and made for the stockade, just visible from where they were out beyond the edge of the forest.

"I think poor Benjamin's got the best idea of the day," Joshua commented rather wryly.

He fell in behind the injured runner, knowing that the Indians who had hatcheted and partially scalped him would not be far behind. He wondered if Benjamin would live to tell how he had managed to escape them. He hoped so; that story would be worth hearing.

The first Indians came into view just as the scouts began to run. Joshua glanced over his shoulder in time to see the closest of them launch an arrow in his direction. The flighttime of an arrow shot from a Cherokee bow—a type of bow typically so strong that many white men could not bend it—did not provide opportunity for planned reaction, but fate or providence stepped in to save Joshua's life, ironically ending that of Preston Halliforth.

Just as Joshua had glanced back over his shoulder, his foot caught on the root of a stout vine, and he sprawled flat on his face—just quickly enough to allow the arrow to fly above him. It thunked squarely into the spine of the fleeing Preston Halliforth, turning the man's legs to limp rag-doll limbs that collapsed beneath him.

Joshua came out much better; his fall did no more than knock the wind from him. Still, when he came to his feet again, the Indians were almost upon him. He had not lost his rifle, but leveling and firing it in such a short time seemed preposterous and would do him no service but felling one of several potential slayers, leaving him unarmed against the others.

It made him heartsick to see the fallen Preston Halliforth, who stretched out a hand toward him as he ran toward him. All the others were far ahead, halfway across the clearing to the stockade by now. There was none other to try to save the fallen woodsman; the others had not even seen what had happened. Joshua performed the most intricate spin of his life. Had he tried to plan and practice such a move, he could never have done it. His rifle swung down and fired even as it moved, the ball spitting out through the air and into the heart of the same Indian who had fired the arrow that dropped Preston Halliforth. The timing was fortuitous; the Indian had just fitted another arrow to his bowstring when the ball pierced him.

"I'll carry you to the stockade, Preston!" Joshua declared as he shifted his spent rifle to the other hand and stooped. A glance showed at least fifteen Indians visible in the forest behind him now, coming at him on a run—fifteen painted naked Indians who at that moment looked like five hundred.

Joshua hefted Preston Halliforth. The wounded man was tensed to the rigidity of a post from the waist up, but his legs hung loosely. Joshua handled him as if he were no more than a cloth bag stuffed with down. He turned to begin his run as a rifle cracked behind him. Preston grunted; his stiffened torso suddenly felt like a bag of warm loose mud. Joshua knew then that Preston had absorbed the ball; a glance revealed blood pouring out a fatal entry wound in the back of his skull.

Looking behind, Joshua saw a warrior with livid eyes and an upraised battle-ax bearing down upon him. With a shout and heave, he tossed Preston's dead body at the Indian and knocked him down. Up went Joshua's rifle, then down; the buttplate caved in the fallen Cherokee's forehead. The Indian jerked and died.

The edge of the forest was just ahead, and Joshua ran for it with such determination that Callum McSwain, now panting but safe inside the stockade and watching the entire incident from the rifle platform, would later tell Joshua that when he came out of the forest, he was leaning almost level with the earth, flying like an arrow toward the stockade. Joshua did not feel like a flying arrow—more like a terrified rabbit with a hundred hounds nipping its tail. The stockade gate was closing, closing before his eyes, even as he made for it, the other scouts inside. Surely they would not shut him out, leave him to be hatcheted and scalped before the line of riflemen watching over the pointed palisade tops down the barrels of their long rifles.

Twenty weapons fired as one, Joshua could almost feel the spinning spheres of lead hurtling above his head. Screeches close behind him, too close, let him know that at least some of the balls were lethal. Puffing, straining as hard as he could, he dove toward the stockade gate, which did not seem to be closing now. Through the opening he saw the white face of Alphus Colter, his arm beckoning . . .

And then he was inside. The big log doors swung shut, and the two hewn bars fell into place with a comforting double thud. Joshua fell to his knees, gasping. Above, on the rifle platform, another fusillade sounded; there were more screeches from the other side of the wall, followed by answering gunfire. A rain of arrows sailed over the wall and thudded into the roofs of the cabins on the far wall and the dirt of the stockade yard.

People screamed and scrambled for shelter. Peter Haverly let out a whoop and slid beneath the wagon to which he was tied, going as far under as his bonds would allow.

Cooper Haverly strode up to Alphus, his face set in stern determination. "I'm going to cut my father free," he said. "He has the same right to shelter as any other man."

"Aye, I think he has suffered enough shame on his wheel," Alphus said. "Go free him, Cooper. He'll run nowhere now."

"My father is not a man who will run from anyone."

Cooper obviously resented the treatment Haverly had received from Alphus and apparently blamed Joshua as well, for he gave a hateful look to his brother-by-blood. It stung, but Joshua had no time to worry about it now.

He reloaded his rifle and climbed atop the platform, joining the other fighters. A brigade of women stood below the rifle platform, reloading for the men, so that a steady stream of rearmed rifles went continually up to the riflemen as the spent ones came down.

After mounting the platform, Joshua quickly inspected the scene outside the fort. The Indians had retreated from the clearing immediately around the fort and were firing from the edge of the forest. They had at much risk dragged off their handful of dead and wounded, but this did not surprise Joshua, who well knew the Indian conviction that mutilation after death was a great humiliation that they would never allow to befall their people if it could be avoided. The morning air was hazy and blue with rising powder smoke. Judging from the number of blasts and powder bursts, there were plenty of armed Indians in the forest.

"Thanks be to providence that the Cherokees have mostly muskets and we have mostly rifles," Joshua said.

"Aye, Joshua," came the answer from the man beside him. "And thanks be to providence that you are a swift runner—though anyone runs swift with an army of red buggers on his heels."

"Callum! I didn't even notice it was you! Tell me, did Ben Halliforth make it in?"

"He did—just in time to die," McSwain answered as he

peered down the length of his rifle and paused to squeeze off a shot.

Joshua fired a shot and handed down his rifle to Jean McSwain for reloading as she handed him a fresh one. He scanned the treeline, looking for a target.

"Did you see who's fighting on the west palisade, Joshua?" McSwain asked.

Joshua ducked and peered across. Gabriel was there, aiming and firing. His slave, Patton, was at his side, giving him assistance. Joshua was honestly surprised.

"Well, I'll be! I thought certain that he would sit it out at best."

"There may be more to Gabriel Colter than we've given credit for, eh?" McSwain said. "When it comes to the squeeze, he does what he should."

The battle continued in its initial pattern for no more than fifteen minutes. The Indians suffered no more casualties that Joshua could see, and the fort's defenders lost only one man, a lad of about sixteen who apparently received a spent ball in the forehead, its force so weakened that the ball bounced off his skull and was caught bare-handed by the man beside him. What brought about the lad's death, as McSwain later put it, was "not ball, but fall." When the missile struck him, he stepped back off the platform, and in the resulting tumble struck his head on the edge of the same wagon to which Peter Haverly had been lashed earlier. He died instantly.

Shortly after that, the gunfire began to slow significantly. It was evident that the range was too far for the Cherokees' Brown Bess muskets to be accurate. The worst threat the defenders faced was the random arrows that fell into the stockade, fired in an arc from the forest. At the beginning, the Indians tended to under- or overshoot the stockade, but with practice some of them became quite adept at landing the arrows within the walls.

"Makes a man long for a lead bonnet, eh?" McSwain commented.

An hour later, there was no gunfire from the forest. Alphus called down most of the riflemen from the walls, and from the cabins and half-faced shelters all about the stockade, the women, children, and elderly began to emerge.

"We've come through the first of it and have lost three, but it could have been worse," Alphus announced. "But we must be ready for more, for this, I believe, is far from the last. The Indians have more to gain by patience than by wasting ammunition. So prepare yourselves for living in close quarters for a long time. Before this is done, we will all know each other quite well."

That brought a murmur of good-humored chuckling, but Joshua did not join in. He was remembering a previous time, sixteen years before, when he was a ten-year-old boy trapped inside a besieged fort. The circumstances here reminded him much of the last days of Fort Loudoun.

Before the siege of Colter's Station was done, he would have yet other reminders of Fort Loudoun, but of those he knew nothing yet. He hunkered down on his haunches, supporting his weight on the stock of his rifle. "At least we have a good well for to have a drink and a swill from time to time," he said to Callum McSwain.

"What I want to know is, is there a place here where a man can make his water without all God's saints watching him?" McSwain whispered.

Joshua rose and gently patted McSwain's shoulder. "It isn't just for shooting that Alphus built these rifle platforms, Callum," he said in mock seriousness. "Though I advise you to hold such use of them for after dark, for otherwise you make quite a tempting target for the Cherokees."

McSwain nodded; having never been through a siege before, he took Joshua's playful advice very seriously. "Aye, aye. I'll take that for a good warning, and thank you for it, Joshua."

The young frontiersman grinned, patted McSwain's shoulder again, and walked off toward the well for a drink. It was a trip he would make many times before the day was done, for there was no hotter place than the inside of an unshaded stockade where thick walls blocked the breeze and held the heat generated by the sun, milling livestock, and two hundred cramped sweating human bodies.

Joshua knew that before long, finding a private spot to relieve himself would soon be the least of the worries of Callum McSwain or anyone else.

27

Life at Colter's Station quickly settled into the steady, tense drudgery of a besieged fortress. Lingering fear permeated every activity, hiding behind forced smiles and artificial cheerfulness, occasionally breaking through in squabbles and curses. Children cried much more than usual, and neighbors who were friendly during normal times found cause to dislike each other.

The stockade, which had always seemed large to Joshua in peaceful times, now seemed tiny. People accustomed to open space and neighbors beyond shouting distance were now forced to live side by side, smelling each others' stench, sharing each others' lice, and enduring each others' irritating habits. And it was interesting, Joshua noted, how in this situation almost any habit had a way of irritating at least someone.

Joshua dealt with the unpleasant circumstances by staying on the rifle platform most of the time, keeping watch on the forest beyond the clearing. Tsula's Cherokees remained there, occasionally sending a rifle ball toward the stockade just to make sure unaka nerves remained tightly strung. Most of the Cherokees' efforts were directed toward simply ridiculing the stockade's inhabitants. They made deliberate shows of burning every building within view of the fort, and plumes of rising smoke across the woodlands revealed that they were putting the torch to the more distant farmsteads as well. As the fires ate up the fruit of the settlers' labors, the Indians would shout mockeries toward the stockade in clumsy English, employing obscenities learned from the British to add spice to their ridicule. Sometimes the more brash warriors would dance out of the forest, waggle bare buttocks toward the stockade, then dart back into the trees as the riflemen fired hurried and ineffective shots at the fleeting targets.

"Just once I'd like to plug one of them heathens right in the backside and teach 'em a new kind of dance," Callum McSwain said.

Such teasings by the Indians did not much bother Joshua. Words and gestures alone could not harm him, and he owned almost nothing, so there was little for him to lose to them. Many families suffered deeply under the assault, however, Gabriel among them. He stood on the rifle platform and sadly watched the Indians destroy his store after hauling off almost everything inside it. Then his house was burned to the ground. He voiced no complaint, to Joshua's surprise, and Joshua grudgingly admired him for it.

Joshua's attitude about Gabriel had undergone a quiet but significant shift since the beginning of the siege. Despite his earlier flirtations with loyalism and his continuing expressions of doubt about the wisdom of the Revolution, Gabriel manned his rifleman's station readily. His quiet perseverance in defense of his neighbors was beginning to regain the respect of his peers. Perhaps, Joshua thought, the experience of losing Darcy, his public status, and his life's labors was going to make Gabriel a stronger and better man, not so wrapped up in himself.

Peter Haverly, unlike Gabriel, did not seem at all strengthened by his situation. Even though he was no longer locked up or tied and roamed the stockade freely with his peruke cocked crazily on his round head, he was suffering quite a lot of abuse from those around him. He was loudly unrepentant of his loyalty to Britain and sometimes, when his temper got the best of him, raged that the American rebellion was history's most treacherous betrayal since Judas Iscariot's.

His tirades brought him nothing but ridicule and occasional dollops of spittle launched from the rifle platform. When the missiles struck home, loud laughter erupted from the riflemen, along with invitations for Haverly to walk out of the fort and join the only other British supporters around, the Cherokees. "See how they receive you if you dislike us so much," the riflemen challenged.

Haverly's eyes flashed. "I may do that very thing," he said. "I would suffer no harm for it, for I am known as a man loyal to my king."

Joshua did not join in the ridiculing of Haverly, not out of respect for him but Christiana. He was worried about her. She did not seem physically well anymore. Further, she was deeply humiliated by the ridicule heaped upon her husband and withdrew from everyone, including Joshua. That hurt him, as did the icy stares of Cooper. Joshua hoped that when all this was over, he could regain the affection of his brother and Christiana.

When he wasn't lambasting the fort's defenders, Haverly spent much of his time talking quietly to Gabriel, who seemed uncomfortable conversing publicly with his old mentor. Alphus told Joshua that Gabriel had come to him privately and complained that Haverly was giving him trouble, seeking his support and friendship in light of all his past favors.

"I told Gabe that it fell to him to decide how to deal with Haverly," Alphus said to Joshua. "But I warned him off the man. Haverly is a snake, in my estimation, and if you get too close to him, he bites."

The third night of the siege, as Joshua dozed beneath his little tent in a corner of the stockade, someone touched his ankle and stirred him awake. He was surprised to see Cooper. "What is it, Cooper?"

"It's mother—she's bad sick and calling for you." Cooper looked scared.

Joshua felt a rush of dread. He rose, and in bare feet padded across the moonlit stockade, stepping between the tents and shelters throughout the yard.

The Haverly family was living in a crude tent on the opposite corner of the station, almost beneath one of the blockhouses. Christiana was stretched out on a blanket; Haverly's slave had just finished bathing her brow. As Joshua approached, Peter Haverly turned his broad expressionless face up at him, his thick lips clamped tightly shut. "She's dying," he said flatly. "She asked to see you."

God above, no—not Christiana. Joshua began to shake. The idea of losing the woman who had become his mother was intolerable. Joshua's mind was swept back to Fort Loudoun and the bedside of Hester Byrum, dying as she expelled a baby into a world in turmoil.

"Christiana?" he softly said.

Her big eyes fluttered open; Christiana smiled feebly at Joshua. "Oh, my dear boy is here," she said. Her voice sounded weak and weary. "Joshua, I fear I'm soon to die. My heart—it has long been weak, and I can feel it failing me more and more. But I could not die without seeing your face again and putting away the bad feelings of these unhappy days."

"Don't talk of dying, Christiana. You will live . . . you must live."

"I have lived, and have had many good things in my life. Now I go to the best . . . do not ask me to stay behind, in all this suffering, Joshua. I have heard my call."

Joshua's chin trembled, and tears began. He felt like a boy again, about to be left alone. "I need you, Christiana," he said.

"No, Joshua. You only think you do. I told you years ago that I saw unseen hands upon you. I see them still. It's those hands you need and must learn to trust. And now, talk to me of the old days. I want to live my life again before it is through."

He stayed by Christiana's side for another hour, talking

to her of the past they had shared and hearing her speak of her life beyond his experience with her until she grew so tired, she could scarcely keep open her eyes.

Peter Haverly touched Joshua's arm. "Please . . . I need to be with her, alone." His face was puffy, and his eyes were reddening.

At that moment, personalities, pride, and bitter feelings seemed insignificant to Joshua; even national loyalties and revolutions seemed puny, meaningless affairs. He patted Haverly's shoulder. "Yes, you do," he said. "Thank you for giving me time with her."

Haverly sniffed and nodded. "She has cared for you deeply, you know." He paused. "You and I—we've had our differences, but perhaps I should say . . . I . . ."

"You needn't say anything," Joshua said. "Be with Christiana now. With any good fortune, she will live."

He kissed Christiana before he left, then went across the stockade and sat awake the rest of the night. An hour before dawn, Peter Haverly strode up to him, looked down sadly at him, shook his head, and walked away.

In the midst of the crowded stockade, Joshua suddenly felt more alone than ever before.

They buried Christiana just after dawn in the corner of the stockade. Patton dug the grave. Her death placed a pall of silence over the people of Colter's Station. Haverly seemed deflated and old, his booming, critical voice silent now. Those who had harassed him now left him alone.

He spent the morning seated in his tent, staring straight ahead. Cooper sat with him, crying silently. Joshua wanted to say something to Cooper, but the feeling of acceptance that he had felt the previous night he did not feel now. And there was really nothing to be said.

In the afternoon, Joshua saw Haverly rise and go to Gabriel. The two talked together in hushed voices, Cooper close-by. Joshua wondered what they were talking about.

By the next morning, he and everyone else knew. Haverly, Gabriel, and Cooper were gone. They had slipped out of the stockade in the night. Haverly had made good his hints of leaving the stockade and had apparently cajoled Gabriel, through the latter's long-felt loyalties, into going with him. Patton also had gone, along with Haverly's slave.

Alphus was heartsick. "Does the fool believe the Indians will let him pass because he is loyal to the king? They'll have him killed and scalped before he can even make his declaration. And how could Gabriel have been so foolish?"

"Because he felt he owed Haverly, no doubt," Joshua replied, noticing that he had spoken in past tense. He regretted it, for Alphus had noticed it too.

Dragging Canoe and his warriors had no knowledge of the status of the siege of Colter's Station as they approached the flats around Long Island. Hopes for successful overthrow of that stockade by Tsula and his warriors were high. Tsula was a patient besieger, which was what was needed when the stockade to be taken was strong and high-walled.

Dragging Canoe's target, Eaton's Station, was not so good a stockade as that at Colter's Station, but even it would provide its challenges. It was never easy to defeat fighters protected by even a crude fortress. If the white residents of the Long Island region had been forewarned in some way of the attack, the challenge would be even greater. The Indians had been careful to conceal their advance, even passing up the chance to capture two white women they had seen bathing in the river. Still, John Hawk would not be surprised if they found the settlers knowledgeable of their coming and waiting for them, rifles ready, behind stockade walls.

As matters turned out, the battle waged by Dragging Canoe's warriors would not be a stockade siege at all. Only well after the battle was over would John Hawk piece together the full details of what had happened, based on what he witnessed and what others told him:

Dragging Canoe sent an advance party of about twenty warriors ahead of the main body, and near the Long Island Flats that party encountered a similar but smaller advance guard of unakas. The white men, about a dozen in number, opened fire upon the Indians and scattered them. A few Indians were wounded, and several bundles of battle gear were lost to the whites.

That skirmish between scouting parties was only a prelude to the remarkable battle to come. The body of Indians discovered that rather than fight from behind stockade walls, the forewarned unakas had opted to go out into the countryside to find and surprise the Indian force. John Hawk would later theorize that this had been done in fear that the warriors might simply bypass Eaton's Station, which was about five miles east of the Island Flats and the other stockades in the area, and proceed on to destroy without resistance the cabins, barns, and fields beyond.

The Cherokees soon discovered the white war party, placed its size at about equal to its own, and attacked from the rear. John Hawk was among the first warriors to make violent contact with the frontiersmen, entering a fierce battle waged at such close quarters that much of it was fought with fists and knives as well as rifles and bows.

The whites, who had been moving in two lines, swung both flanks around to form a battle line about a quarter-mile long as Dragging Canoe's warriors closed in. Some of the frontiersmen ran, however, and Dragging Canoe, encouraged, waved his arm and shouted, "The unakas are running—come and scalp them!"

The Cherokees attempted to outflank the frontiersmen, moving in a line with a conical center and crescent-shaped ends, but the whites lengthened their own line and overcame the ploy. As the Indians came into range, a volley of rifle fire greeted them, and several warriors fell. The unakas had taken refuge behind trees and fired with lethal accuracy. John Hawk was grazed, though so lightly that the wound scarcely bled.

The combatants soon closed in upon each other, struggling hand-to-hand when weapons were emptied. The battle lasted about an hour, and for half of it John Hawk struggled mostly with a burly frontiersman who had obviously picked him out for particular punishment.

"You are the Hawk!" the frontiersman called to him, gazing intently at him.

"Yes—come feel my talons," John Hawk challenged.

"It's your hair I'll have, you hell-devil," the man yelled back. He fired at John Hawk but missed. John Hawk fired, with equal ineffectiveness. Knives were drawn, and the two men began a fierce, exhausting struggle. At times the big frontiersman would almost prevail, then the sinewy Indian would gain the upper hand, but not until the battle was half done did either gravely hurt the other.

It was endurance that helped John Hawk in the end. The frontiersman began weakening from exertion, and finally he was unable to keep John Hawk's knife from slicing his abdomen. Entrails emerged; the white man fell back, fear on his face, and tried to drag himself away. John Hawk charged at him, but a rifle ball struck him in the shoulder and knocked him down. The white man managed to crawl away and hide in a gully.

John Hawk picked up his fallen rifle and found safety behind a tree. Binding up his bleeding shoulder, he reloaded and rejoined the fight, firing from cover. As he did so, he tried to ascertain the progress of the battle, for he had been too busy to assess the overall situation. What he saw dismayed him. He saw several wounded frontiersmen but not a single dead one anywhere on the battlefield. Dead Indians, however, lay here and there, along with many more wounded. John Hawk squeezed off another shot and tried to fight despair. Where was Dragging Canoe? He looked for him but could not find him.

The battle went on until it became even more evident the Cherokees were losing. Warriors began dragging the bodies of the fallen Cherokees from the field. John Hawk counted a full ten Indians assuredly dead, another two or three who appeared to be so, and still more badly wounded. Among the dead he recognized Dragging Canoe's brother, Little Owl, who early in the fight had rallied his companions. Now he was still and silent, almost a dozen bullet holes in his body.

And then John Hawk saw Dragging Canoe. The pitted warrior was down, his leg covered with blood. He appeared to have been shot in the bone of the thigh. Now despair overwhelmed John Hawk, and he knew the battle was over. With Dragging Canoe wounded, the warriors could not sustain their spirit. Within minutes, the warriors had withdrawn from the bloody field, leaving behind much plunder that the frontiersmen quickly seized.

Dragging Canoe's thigh was shattered, and he had to be carried away from the scene. John Hawk had never felt so thoroughly beaten. His shoulder wound, though not severe, ached badly, but the pain in his spirit was worse. He had believed that Dragging Canoe could not be overcome, that a concerted effort against the unakas would drive them away. He had been proven badly wrong.

The unakas would not forget this victory. It would bolster their spirit and determination just as it had drained that of the Cherokees. Further, the Cherokees had been turned back. They would not be able to pillage the settlements beyond or proceed into Virginia as had been hoped.

John Hawk thought of Ayasta, anxiously awaiting him back in Chota, and of his little son, Wasi. He was glad the child was still too young to understand the meaning of war—and of defeat.

Since arriving safely at Fort Caswell on the Watauga with Darcy Colter, Israel Coffman had felt tremendously grateful for that blessing. It was now daybreak on Sunday, July 21, and Coffman had it in mind to spend this traditional day of worship giving thanks for the safety in which he and Darcy had traveled to this stockade.

He and the other inhabitants of Fort Caswell knew nothing of the defeat of Dragging Canoe on the previous day, or of the continuing siege of Colter's Station. Life at Sycamore Shoals had consisted mostly of waiting—waiting, in Coffman's opinion, without quite the degree of caution that was needed. Frontier folk could sometimes be reckless and overly optimistic, he had discovered long ago.

Besides many women, children, and animals, Fort Caswell was occupied by about seventy-five riflemen, who would provide the defense when the Indians finally came. Among their number was the former Fort Lee garrison, under the dashing Lieutenant John Sevier. Colonel John Carter had overall command of the fort, and James Robertson served as his captain.

Coffman himself would be a rifleman when the attack came. He anticipated the inevitable battle with both dread and eagerness, eagerness mostly to have it done and behind him. He had never fought before and could not imagine taking the life of another man, even an attacking Indian. Nevertheless, duty was duty, and he would do his, whatever it might be, whatever it might cost. Every man in Fort Caswell capable of holding a rifle was expected to join in the defense.

Coffman had arisen early this morning, earlier than most of the others in the fort. Examination of the land beyond the stockade had revealed no sign of immediate Indian presence, though smoke in the distance betrayed the location of abandoned cabins put to fire. Coffman stood in the open stockade gate, rifle in hand, and watched the distant rising smoke as the morning light spilled in. He smiled in greeting when a cluster of women emerged from the cabins and passed out of the gate to do the milking. Darcy was one of them.

Ten minutes passed. Coffman strolled back into the stockade, wondering rather doubtfully if he could stir up any interest in a Sunday morning worship service today, when a piercing scream rose outside the fort. The voice sounded like Darcy's. More screams followed, and from everywhere around the stockade people emerged. John Sevier appeared from somewhere, wrapping his hunting shirt around himself with one hand and gripping his rifle with the other as he darted toward the open gate.

"Indians!" someone yelled from the rifleman's platform. "The damned sods are after the women!"

Darcy . . .

Coffman ran to the gate and was horrified to see the women racing back toward the stockade, some with milk buckets still in hand. He looked for Darcy but could not see her.

Some of the women reached the stockade and made it in. Meanwhile, the riflemen in the fort began firing upon the Indians, who about the same time began their own volley, with rifles and bows. Coffman watched as one of the women, Catherine Sherrell, ran for the stockade gate but was cut off by the advancing warriors. She veered to the side and ran around to the other side of the fort.

"Blast and blazes!" John Sevier shouted.

He leapt from his perch on the platform, ran across the stockade yard, and scrambled up on the other side. He reached down over the palisades as arrows and bullets peppered around him, then heaved up, Catherine Sherrell clinging to his arm.

A moment later she was across the wall and safe inside—the last of the women to come in. It had been a dramatic and daring rescue, and would ingrain itself into the folklore of the Tennessee frontier. Four years later, when John Sevier took the lean tall "Bonnie Kate" Sherrell as his second wife, the story would take on an even more romantic aspect.

Coffman sent up a prayer of thanks for the safety of all the women who had made it inside, but his stomach was wrenching itself into knots all the while, for he did not yet see Darcy.

"Darcy Colter! Where is Darcy Colter?" he shouted into the tumult of excited people.

Catherine Sherrell turned and answered him. "They seized her," she said, eyes wet with tears. "They came from the forest and pulled her away, and there was naught any of us could do."

Coffman stood for a full minute, unmoving in the middle of the stockade yard, stunned and nauseous. Darcy Colter, taken by the Cherokees. What would they do to her? He had heard stories of Indian torture so horrible that it strained his belief—and such tortures were not always reserved for men. Women and even children sometimes also suffered them.

A hand roughly grasped his shoulder and spun him

around. "Preacher!" James Robertson all but shouted into his face. "Onto the platform with you—there's a battle to be fought here!"

"Darcy Colter's taken prisoner," Coffman said, as if he had not heard Robertson. "They've taken her prisoner."

Robertson gave him another yank, and that was enough to snap him out of his stupor. Hefting his rifle, he headed for his assigned station. He would have to trust Darcy to the care of his God, for at the moment there was nothing else he could do for her. And there was, as Robertson said, a battle to be fought.

The course of affairs at Fort Caswell closely followed that at Colter's Station: The siege began with a vigorous, fire-heavy onslaught that quickly faltered, with some losses to the Indians, and a long wearying siege began.

The next two weeks were torment for Israel Coffman, who rather irrationally felt responsible for Darcy's capture. It was he who had taken her away from Colter's, he who had refused to follow Alphus's advice and remain where they would probably have been safe.

Yet he could not really know that, he reminded himself. Probably Colter's Station had been besieged even before Fort Caswell. Darcy could have come to a similar end there. What had happened had happened; there was nothing he could do about it now. It was no use. Coffman found that his counsel, which often seemed to help others, was of little help to himself. He prayed vigorously for Darcy's safety and yearned for the end of this long siege.

Other times of excitement, and tragedy, came in the two weeks after the initial onslaught. As the siege dragged on, some of the fort's people became irresponsible and careless, despite Coffman's pleadings for caution, and began taking unreasonable chances. The saddest to Coffman was an incident involving a man named James Cooper and a boy named Samuel Moore. The two, apparently believing the Indians had withdrawn, left the stockade to search for wood to repair one of the cabins, and were attacked. The man was killed and scalped, and the boy was taken captive to the Cherokees' camp on the Nolichucky.

Sometime later, the Indians launched another assault upon the stockade, this time intent upon setting the walls ablaze. Because of the several-sided knoll-top design, there was one wall that could not be swept by rifle fire from any angle, and the Cherokees, apparently having observed this, made for that wall, torches in hand.

James Robertson's sister Ann and other women of the fort who followed her lead were the ones who saved the stockade from destruction. A huge kettle of water was boiling in the center of the fort when the Cherokees attacked, for the women were preparing to do washing, and the quick-thinking Ann Robertson dipped out a bucketful of the bubbling water and dashed onto the rifle platform. She dumped the water over the palisades, directly on the attacking Cherokees; their screeches resounded loudly.

The other women quickly fell in line and began a brigade, passing steaming bucketloads of water to the brave woman. A rifle ball nicked Ann Robertson at one point, but she ignored the wound and kept up her scalding defense until the frustrated Indians retreated back to the forest, many of them nursing terrible burns. Ann Robertson was declared a heroine for her action, her brother visibly proud of her.

Carter and Sevier conferred often throughout the long siege, and at last the decision was made to send a courier northward to petition for a relief force. The courier's job would be difficult and dangerous, but despite this, several men volunteered for the task, Coffman among them.

His application was denied. There were better woodsmen than he to attempt the task. By night, the chosen envoy was sent out of the stockade, and into the darkness he vanished.

Coffman gripped his rifle tightly and waited to hear the telltale scream that would surely come, indicating the courier had been caught and killed. Minutes passed, and the cry never came. The preacher smiled. The courier had made it through.

That night, Coffman dreamed it was he out there in the forest, running beneath trees that seemed to have eyes. He sensed danger everywhere, saw lurking painted figures in the gloom, heard whispers of coming death. Then he came upon a clearing where there was light. He was drawn into it, and there before him stood a tall pole, with wood circling its base and a woman standing, bound. Flames began to rise as she looked at him, and he saw it was Darcy.

He awakened just in time to squelch a shout. The night was hot, and he was drenched in sweat, yet shaking as if he were cold. He rose and walked to the gate, peering out through a crack into the night, praying again that Darcy Colter would be protected from harm—if it was not too late.

28

T hree days now, and not a sign of Indians outside Colter's Station. A sense of hope was rising in the dispirited people; perhaps the Cherokees had finally withdrawn. Even Joshua was beginning to believe it. An envoy from Eaton's Station had made it into the fort safely, reporting that he had not seen a single Indian in the forests during his journey.

That was not all the welcome news he brought. Dragging Canoe, he said, had been defeated at Island Flats. Furthermore, the Raven, in striking Carter's Valley, had found little there to destroy, for most of the settlers had fled to the forts farther east. And an extended siege of Fort Caswell appeared to be ending as well. A messenger from that fort had safely made it through, and a hundred mounted men from Shelby's Fort, along with a band of Virginia rangers, were on their way to relieve Fort Caswell. The Cherokees, it appeared, had failed in their bid to drive the white men from their settlements.

Many of the long-confined people in the Colter's Station stockade were ready to leave the fort at once and return to their homes to assess their damages, but Alphus would not allow the gate to be opened. "We'll send

434

scouts out to see what we find," he said. "There may yet be some Cherokees lingering."

Joshua and Callum McSwain volunteered immediately for the task, and Alphus nodded acceptance, then announced that he too would go.

"No, Alphus," Joshua said. "Leave it to us—you are too important to be risked."

"By Joseph, I'll not send men out to do so dangerous a job unless I go too," Alphus stubbornly replied. Since Gabriel's disappearance with Haverly, Alphus had been short of temper and very obstinate in all he did and said.

Sina, standing nearby, blanched. "Alphus, you must not go."

He turned to her. "I'll be well and safe, my dear. I've dealt with such dangers before. It's a thing I must do."

Before leaving the stockade, Joshua approached the newly arrived messenger and asked if he had heard word of any particular captures or slayings.

The man scratched his head. "Well . . . there was a preacher who showed up at Eaton's Station after nearly losing his scalp to the Indians . . ."

"A preacher? Was his name Coffman?"

"No—Mulkey, I think. From Carter's Valley. He and a friend were attacked on the way in; he swam across the river and got away safe. The friend made it to the station too, but without his scalp."

"Oh." Joshua didn't know whether to be relieved or disappointed that the preacher had not been Coffman.

As concerned as he was to know what had become of Darcy and Coffman, it was for Gabriel, Cooper, and Peter Haverly that he feared the most. Darcy and Coffman could reasonably have been expected to make it safely to one of the other frontier stations, but Gabriel and the others almost certainly had been taken prisoner, or killed, unless Haverly's optimistic expectation of being recognized and welcomed as a loyalist proved valid. The odds were certainly against that, in Joshua's estimation.

He, Alphus, and McSwain slipped into the forest at the closest place. All was silent. They saw no Indians, sensed no other presence. At length, they worked around to the area of the forest from which most of the Cherokee gunfire had come. They found abundant sign left by the Indians during the weeks of siege but no evidence any had been about for the last two or three days.

Alphus stopped abruptly, sniffing the air. "Smell it?" he asked.

Joshua did—a distant but distinct odor of death. His stomach gnarled.

"God, I hope, I hope to heaven, that it's not Gabe," Alphus said.

The scouts advanced, following their increasingly offended noses. Before they finally reached the little woodland ravine where the body lay, they had clapped handfuls of dried leaves across their noses and mouths to filter the sickening stench.

Peter Haverly was bloated in death, his white belly turned up to the sun. He had been tomahawked repeatedly, scalped, and otherwise mutilated. Beside him lay Patton and the other slave, similarly butchered. The three men looked at the pitiful corpses for only a few moments before moving quickly away so they would not retch.

Silently they searched about, dreadfully anticipating the discovery of Gabriel's and Cooper's bodies as well, but they did not find them.

"Taken prisoner, then?" Joshua asked Alphus.

"That's my thought."

"God help them," McSwain murmured. "Let's pray the Cherokees are merciful."

The scouts headed back toward the fort. Alphus led the way several yards ahead, filled with sickening thoughts of his only natural son slowly dying at the hands of torturing Indians in some Overhill town. Perhaps it was such distracting worries that kept him from detecting the two warriors before they descended upon him, dropping out of a hillside thicket with tomahawks upraised. One of them struck him a grazing blow down the side of the head before he could react.

Joshua saw the attack from a distance and sent up a shout as he lifted his rifle and fired. He missed his target, but McSwain, following up with his own shot, put a ball through the head of the Cherokee who had struck Alphus. The Indian pitched over, dead.

The other Cherokee raised his bow and sent an arrow hurtling toward McSwain. It passed into McSwain's shoulder and lodged, making him scream and drop his rifle. Joshua—anticipating that the Indian would now quickly finish off Alphus, who was trying to crawl away as blood poured profusely from his wounded head—let out a shout and ran as hard as he could toward the warrior, ready to strike him with the heavy barrel of his rifle.

He saw that his effort was doomed to fail, for already the warrior had strung another arrow and would surely fire before Joshua could reach him. "No!" Joshua screamed in frustration and fear.

And then a most remarkable thing happened.

From a tangle of bushes behind the warrior, another man appeared, a white man, staggering weakly forward with a knife in his hand. The knife flashed forward, and the Cherokee lurched and spun to face the unexpected phantom who had just sunk a knife into his back. The warrior's quick turn wrenched the knife from the white man's hand, and it now rode in the Indians's olive-copper flesh, blood running out around it. The Indian lifted a foot and kicked the man back. With his arrow already strung, it took the Indian only a moment to send the shaft into the heart of his foe.

But the distraction and delay had given Joshua an advantage. A half second after the Indian killed the knife wielder, Joshua was upon him, his rifle swinging, and the warrior fell after the heavy barrel crashed against the side of his shaven head. Two more quick blows ensured his death.

Alphus, wincing and covered with blood, had dragged himself to the side and collapsed. Now he sat up. "Who is he?" he asked urgently. "Who is he?"

Joshua ignored the question, a more important one in mind. "How bad hurt are you, Alphus?"

"I'm fine, fine—it's nothing—but I want to know who saved my life, by Joseph!"

Joshua went to the side of the dead man, who looked with blank eyes toward the sky. A very white-faced Callum McSwain, the arrow still sticking out of his shoulder like a quill, came up and joined Joshua in looking down into the dead man's face.

In a pain-tightened voice, McSwain said, "Why, that's the very same bugger who ran from the station when you tried to have him caught, Alphus! You remember—the one who had come riding in with Gabriel's guns and such."

Alphus, still gripping his bleeding head, teeteringly rose to his feet and walked over clumsily to investigate, dripping crimson drops the size of rifle balls all the way. "So it is," he said. "Now, I wonder why he would do what he did for me just now?"

"The poor devil's been wounded earlier on—see the dried blood on him there?" McSwain said. "The Indians must have gotten to him shortly after he got away, wounded him. I suppose he was too weak to run far, so he just hid out here in the woods."

"Have mercy—hid out, wounded, all that time, with the woods full of Cherokees? Quite a hell for any man to suffer," Alphus said. "He must have seen us for white men and come out of hiding." Alphus shuddered, knowing what fate he had escaped because of the valor of the stranger. "I'm thankful he came when he did."

Joshua, who had been very silent, took a deep breath and began to heft the body of the dead stranger onto his shoulder.

"No need for that, Joshua. We can come back and get him easier with a sledge a bit later," McSwain said. "We'll have to come for Haverly and the Negroes in any case."

"No," Joshua said. "No. I'm carrying this one in myself."

"Quite a load to haul all the way to the stockade."

"I don't mind it," Joshua replied in a noticeably clipped voice.

He picked up the dead man and shifted him onto his right shoulder. The head and arms of the corpse dangled down, and the woven cap on the head fell off. McSwain, grimacing at the pain any motion brought to his pierced shoulder, crouched and scooped up the cap. As he did so, he glanced again at the dead man.

"Alphus—take a look at that!" he said.

"By Joseph!" Alphus declared. "This man's been scalped, years and years ago, from the look of that scar."

"So that's why he wore such a warm cap in July," McSwain observed. "It was to hide the scar."

The three made a strange sight as they walked back into the clearing around the stockade—Alphus with his bleeding head, McSwain with the arrow poking out of him, and Joshua with a corpse across his shoulder. The gates swung open and let them in. The news that the Indians were gone, except for some possible lingering recalcitrants such as the pair that had attacked the scouts, was heralded with joy that was tempered only by the report of the slaying of Haverly and the slaves, and the apparent capture of Gabriel Colter and Cooper Haverly.

But it was the story of the attack upon Alphus, and the way this mysterious unknown man had emerged from the bushes to slay the attacker, that was received with the most interest, for it was an unusual tale. Only Joshua, who was atypically emotional, had little to say about it.

As the wounds of Alphus and McSwain were tended, the people of Colter's Station buried the dead scalpless stranger outside the stockade. They marked the grave with a stone upon which no words were written, for no one knew his name—no one but Joshua, and he had already decided not to reveal it. It would be his knowledge alone that the man who had given up his life to save that of Alphus was the same man who had given him his own life many years before. It was hard to know just how to feel, realizing that it was Jack Byrum himself who had done so heroic a thing.

Joshua had long been ashamed that Jack Byrum's blood ran in his veins. Knowing he was the offspring of a cold and heartless man had often made him feel polluted and destined for wrong. No longer did that notion make much sense to him.

Byrum had just taught his son, in the final act of his life, a most important lesson that Joshua would not forget: It is not a man's bloodline but his own free choices that determine what kind of man he will be, from one moment to the next.

Only one thing had kept Darcy from total despair since she had been snatched by Cherokee warriors outside Fort Caswell—the kindly encouraging woman who shared her captivity.

The woman was Lydia Bean, wife of William, and she told Darcy she had been captured while riding pell-mell on horseback toward Fort Caswell at the very outset of the Cherokee siege. She, like Darcy, had been carried back to the Cherokee camp on the Nolichucky, and there had been questioned extensively about the strength of the Overmountain forts, the amount of powder and lead in them, and their susceptibility to starvation. Lydia confided to Darcy that she had lied extensively, exaggerating the strength of the stations.

Held now with Darcy in the Cherokee town of Togue in the aftermath of the failed Indian military campaign, Lydia Bean was beginning to show signs of breaking under the stress of her situation. Darcy did not welcome that. Lydia's strength had become hers, and if Lydia gave up hope, Darcy did not believe she would be able to sustain her own.

"Are there other prisoners?" Darcy asked Lydia.

"I do not know." The woman's face showed her fear. "If there are, there is probably nothing for them to look forward to but the fate that awaits us."

"What is that?" Darcy asked.

"The stake and the fire."

That night, Darcy did not sleep at all.

Ever since they had been brought to Togue, life for the two women had been a continual hellish uncertainty. At times they were taunted by warriors who told them they would certainly be killed by torture, but others, particularly the women, often sounded as if they were trying to present veiled hope.

"There is one who can save you," one Indian woman told them furtively as she brought them food. "She is in Chota, and my sister has gone to tell her of you."

Darcy clung to that word of hope in the midst of her despair, though she could not imagine what it all meant or who this mysterious savior, obviously a female, might be.

A day came when warriors dragged Darcy and Lydia from the house where they were held and took them toward the center of town where stood a pile of wood and a tall pole.

Darcy sank to her knees, weeping, for she knew what this meant. She and Lydia were to be burned to death as sport for their captors. Darcy saw Lydia dragged first toward the pole. Her clothes were shredded from her, she was painted and mocked, her hair covered with clay, then she was taken to the pole and tied. Darcy felt the world starting to spin beneath her feet. She was about to pass out, but that merciful escape never came. The Indians holding her pulled her to her feet and slapped her back to awareness so she could watch Lydia Bean put to the torment that would shortly come to her as well.

Darcy's last hope vanished when the fire was brought out. In only a moment, the final torment of Lydia Bean would begin.

And then Nancy Ward, the Beloved Woman, was abruptly, amazingly, there, having arrived from Chota at the last possible moment. She strode resolutely into the square, her face locked in fury. Darcy did not know her, but something in her manner and strong bearing generated a burst of hope within her.

The Beloved Woman, bearing her swan's wing, walked up to the stake and kicked away the brands that had already been set ablaze. The angry warriors watched, but there was nothing they could do; the power of the Beloved Woman to pardon prisoners was absolute.

She put out the fire and turned a bitter gaze on the assembled warriors. "I am revolted," she said in the Overhill Cherokee dialect, "that warriors can fall so low as to revel in the torture of a squaw."

And with that, she walked up to the stake, freed Lydia Bean, and led her down. Lydia, knowing how close she had come to a horrible death, could hardly keep from crying. Nancy Ward was leading her away when Lydia stopped and pointed at Darcy. "Please, save my friend, too."

Darcy, to the end of her days, would never see a face that looked more beautiful to her than that of the Beloved Woman at that moment. Nancy Ward looked at Darcy, smiled, and gestured for Darcy to join her and Lydia. The warriors holding her let her go grumblingly, and Darcy ran to the Beloved Woman and fell at her feet.

"Thank you, thank you," she said, kissing Nancy Ward's hands.

Nancy Ward's English was better than that of any Cherokee Darcy had ever heard, save Joshua Colter's old friend John Hawk. "You will live with me now," the woman said. "None will harm you, now that you are pardoned by me. I have helped you, and now you may help me."

"We will do whatever you wish," Lydia Bean said.

"I wish to learn to use the milk of the white man's buffalo"—it took Darcy a moment to realize this was a reference to a cow—"to make butter and cheese. My people must know how to do these things, for our world is changing and we must learn to live in it. Come with me, and be my teachers."

Ahead, a little delegation of attendants waited for Nancy Ward. There were extra horses. Darcy climbed quickly onto one offered to her. She was eager to put Togue behind her—and the memory of the stake where she had almost ended her life.

John Hawk rode into Tuskegee bearing two rifles, some pelts, and various other goods, and all the while he wondered if he was losing his good sense in even bothering to do what he was doing. Whatever the case, he would now see his mission through, for since hearing that among the prisoners taken in the just-completed campaign against the unakas was a man named Colter, now being held in Tuskegee, John Hawk had felt compelled to know just which Colter it was. Alphus Colter, possibly, or Joshua's foster brother, Gabriel . . . or even Joshua himself, if he still actually lived.

John Hawk had learned through inquiry that the Colter prisoner had been claimed, along with another, by a warrior named Fire Carrier. John Hawk had set out at once for Tuskegee to find this Fire Carrier and—if the prisoner turned out to be Joshua Colter—to attempt to purchase him from his captor with the goods he had brought, just as Little Carpenter had purchased John Stuart years ago after the fall of Fort Loudoun. John Hawk could not stand by and let Joshua Colter be taken to the stake. His pretenses that he cared nothing for his old friend were gone now, even though his resentment of white men in general was all the stronger now that the Cherokee campaign had failed.

In Tuskegee John Hawk found Fire Carrier and asked if he might see the prisoner named Colter. Fire Carrier, seeing the goods John Hawk had brought and smelling the possibility of easy gain, gladly complied with the request. He took John Hawk to where his two prisoners were confined in separate small huts. A third prisoner, the boy Samuel Moore from Fort Caswell, had already been burned to death at the stake.

Fire Carrier waved toward the prison huts. "One holds the Colter you ask about; the other holds a boy whose name is Haverly. They will both go to the stake soon."

The door opened, and John Hawk stepped in. A pallid face, pasty and pleading, looked back at him. It was Gabriel Colter, the same Gabriel Colter John Hawk had learned to despise during his stay at Haverly Fort. John Hawk felt disappointed; he had hoped to find Joshua here.

Gabriel, his eyes intense with the anticipation of a fiery fate, stood and approached John Hawk with his hands outstretched. "John Hawk . . . it is good to see you! Please, you must help me."

John Hawk looked at him coldly. "I came to see if it was Joshua Colter who was held captive here. I see now it is only you and there was no reason for me to have come. Joshua Colter is surely dead, as I had heard."

"No—he is alive!" Gabriel said intensely. He paused, his mind working with the cunning of one fighting for survival. "And he will be very sorry if his old friend John Hawk lets his brother die."

John Hawk asked, "Is this the truth? Joshua Colter lives?"

"Yes. He was wounded at Point Pleasant and wandered a long time before coming home. . . . I'll tell you all that happened if you wish to hear it."

John Hawk did wish to hear it and listened with interest to the story of Joshua's return—a story much embellished by Gabriel with talk of how he and Joshua were now very close and affectionate, truly brothers again, and how Joshua would surely seek revenge upon anyone who let harm come to his kinsman Gabriel.

John Hawk doubted much of what he heard, for Gabriel was obviously terrified and desperate for his freedom. Nevertheless, John Hawk was in a merciful spirit. "I will seek to save your life—not for your own sake but for that of your brother. By the standards of the unakas, I know you are counted as his kinsman, even if you do not share his blood."

"Oh, thank you, John Hawk! Thank you for your mercy!" Tears came to Gabriel's eyes.

"Who is the prisoner in the other hut?" John Hawk asked him.

"A boy, a young boy, the son of Peter Haverly. Joshua would like to see him made safe as well. You see, though his name is Cooper Haverly, by blood he really is—" He stopped abruptly.

What had come into Gabriel's mind was a disturbing realization. If he told John Hawk that Cooper Haverly was really Joshua's brother by blood, then he, a mere foster brother, would have less right to ransom than Cooper. John Hawk would assume—rightly, Gabriel was sure—that Joshua would prefer the freedom of his natural brother to that of his foster brother. If John Hawk was inclined to save only one life or did not have enough goods to purchase both prisoners from Fire Carrier, that would mean the stake and fire for Gabriel Colter.

Even as he thought all this, Gabriel was panged with overwhelming guilt. How could he be so selfish as to stand by and seek to save himself, leaving a mere boy, with more right to rescue than he, to die a horrible death by fire? Surely he could not. He would have to tell John Hawk that Cooper Haverly was far more Joshua's brother than he and for that reason as well as his youth was more deserving of rescue.

But his impulse for personal survival reasserted itself. Gabriel could not risk losing this chance to escape the stake. Let Cooper seek to save his own life, however he might. Gabriel's concern must be first and foremost for Gabriel Colter.

John Hawk went back to Fire Carrier and talked to him. Gabriel watched intently, hoping, hoping . . .

John Hawk turned and came to him. He looked into his face. "Fire Carrier has agreed to my offer," John Hawk said. "You are my prisoner now and will come with me."

Gabriel had to fight to restrain himself from bursting into joyful laughter. Then his feeling of guilt rose again, compelling him to ask, "And what of Cooper Haverly?"

"He must remain here and face his fate," John Hawk said. "Fire Carrier has lost kinsman, and demands blood vengeance. Because I do this for Joshua Colter, I must choose you, his kinsman, instead of the boy."

Gabriel's face drained of color. He looked toward the hut where Cooper was imprisoned. God in heaven, could he really hold his silence? Could he really let a mere youth die and himself go free?

Right then, he almost spoke, almost told the truth to John Hawk. But as the words were about to come, he bit them off. He turned away and would look no more at the hut where Cooper Haverly waited for death.

Gabriel hoped that John Hawk would take him away from Tuskegee at once, but he did not, for it was nearly night. John Hawk slept in the home of acquaintances, Gabriel tied to a tree outside. If he had thought being

John Hawk's prisoner would be the equivalent of being John Hawk's guest, he was quickly relieved of the notion.

Soft rain fell on him that night, and Gabriel did not sleep. Not that he would have slept anyway. He could not forget the terrible thing he was doing—a far worse thing than he had thought he was capable of. Every time he closed his eyes, he saw the face of Cooper Haverly looking accusingly back at him, and then he imagined Cooper as he would be after the flames finished with him. . . .

God forgive me, God forgive me, Gabriel prayed over and over. It was futile, and he knew it. How could he be forgiven when he even now perpetuated his sin by his silence?

John Hawk emerged from the cabin the following morning and walked past Gabriel without even glancing at him. He went to the river and took his usual morning plunge. When he came back, Gabriel, still tied, was standing, waiting. His face was so ashen that his lips looked blue.

It had been a hard battle that Gabriel had fought with himself all through the night. Only before dawn had he made his decision, the most difficult of his life. "John Hawk, there is something you must know," he said.

And then Gabriel spilled out the truth, even though it would be a costly truth, the price being his own pain and death. But when he was through, he felt clean, purged, and stronger than he had ever felt in his life. He had done what was right.

John Hawk looked at him and nodded. "Come," he said. "We must return to Fire Carrier. You have done a brave thing, Gabriel Colter."

Cooper Haverly rode out of Tuskegee with John Hawk later that day. Even as they passed the chunkey-game yard, the stake was being readied for Gabriel Colter's execution. Of the three prisoners who had been brought back to Tuskegee, only Cooper would escape a fiery death.

He had been allowed to see Gabriel before he left, and it had been a wrenching but remarkable experience.

Cooper had expected to find Gabriel full of fear, as Cooper had been, but it had not been that way. Gabriel, though frightened, had also seemed surprisingly at peace.

"Go back to Alphus and tell him all was well with me at the end," Gabriel said. "Tell him that I was like Samson—my strength came back to me when I needed it. Tell him I love him and that I hope he will remember me with pride and happiness."

"No, Gabriel, don't talk so," Cooper replied. "I can't bear to hear it."

"We bear what we must, Cooper. There is nothing to be done for me now. I can blame no one but myself for my situation. I was a fool to listen to your father and leave the fort, but leave it I did, and now I will pay the price for foolishness, as Peter himself did, there in the forest."

"I love you, Gabriel," Cooper said, choked with rising emotion.

"I love you too, Cooper, and I do not want you to be here when the time of my death comes."

"He will not be," John Hawk said. "Come—we will go."

Cooper threw his arms around Gabriel's neck and cried bitterly.

Gabriel squeezed him close. "Pray for me, Cooper. I do not do this in my own strength, you know. I need the hand of God strong upon me right now."

Cooper pulled away and looked into Gabriel's face. "Everyone will know of this—I'll make sure that they know. They'll know that of all the men who ever came into this wilderness, there was none braver or better than Gabriel Colter."

"Come," John Hawk said again, reaching out to Cooper.

"Wait, Cooper," Gabriel said. "One more message you must give, this one to Joshua. Tell him to find Darcy, for I believe she is alive, and when he finds her, tell her that I hold no grudge against her, or him, for what happened between them. It was me who drove them to it. And tell them both they are free to marry if they want . . . and that I'm sorry they knew only the worst of me during my life. I was a hard man, and too often harsh, and for that I'm sorry. Now, Cooper, good-bye to you, and remember me often. I am ready to die, and soon I will be where there is no more suffering and death, so do not cry too much for me."

John Hawk and Cooper Haverly rode away shortly afterward. When they had gone to the point where they were about to lose sight of the town, Cooper was about to turn and take a final look. John Hawk sharply ordered him not to do so. He had already seen the rising smoke from the chunkey yard and knew what it meant for Gabriel Colter, who in his death had become a far grander man than he had ever been in life.

In silence the two riders proceeded. They reached the Cherokee Road and proceeded toward the Overmountain settlements, and then Cooper knew beyond question that John Hawk was taking him home. Through the intervention of this warrior and the nearly inconceivable personal sacrifice of Gabriel, the youth was being given back not only his life but his freedom.

They rode for a full day, camped, and the next day rode again until noon, at which time John Hawk halted his mount.

"You will go alone from here," he said. "There are things you must tell Joshua Colter for me. Tell him that I am happy to learn that he did not die fighting the Shawnees. Tell him that it is for his sake that I have bought your freedom. But tell him as well that this is the final mercy John Hawk will ever give to any unaka, except those who honor the British king. Like Dragging Canoe, I will ever be the enemy of the white landtakers.

"The war between our peoples has not ended. The days of blood are only beginning. I will give the unakas much reason to shudder at the name of the Hawk, as they do at the name of the Dragon. Tell Joshua Colter these things for me."

"I will," Cooper said.

John Hawk turned and rode slowly back down the trail toward the Overhill towns. Cooper watched him until he was out of sight, then turned his own horse toward the settlements.

29

It was not long before the Cherokees found themselves paying a heavy price for their alliance with Britain.

Colonel William Russell built a three-sided fort at the Long Island of the Holston River in September of 1776 and named it Fort Patrick Henry, after the governor of Virginia. To that bastioned structure marched Colonel William Christian, leading a force of Virginians, and along the way he found the frontier in continued distress. Many of its people still lived much of the time in confined forts and suffered for it. Cherokee war parties still ranged throughout the countryside, striking swift blows against the war-wearied settlers.

Captain William Witcher was left to garrison Fort Patrick Henry as the offensive forces marched out toward the Cherokee towns. Near the base of Chimney Top Mountain, the troops paused to rest at what Christian dubbed Six Mile Camp and were joined there by militiamen off the Nolichucky and Holston, led by Captains John Sevier and James Robertson. Among their number was Joshua Colter. Israel Coffman was there too as one of three chaplains who would accompany the force.

449

Joshua had two deeply personal reasons for participating in this campaign. The first was to gain the freedom of Darcy. One of the goals of Christian's campaign was to obtain the release of all captives taken during the summer attacks. It was Joshua's intention to return from this effort with Darcy safe at his side—and then, at last, he would make her his wife if she would agree to it. The second was to strike a hard blow against the Cherokees who had slain Gabriel. Cooper had come home bearing the story of Gabriel's heroic death, and now the name of Gabriel Colter was often on every tongue.

Joshua could not think of what had happened without a rise of emotion. To realize that Gabriel, of all men, had carried within him the potential for such unselfish sacrifice astounded and moved Joshua. No more did his past differences with his late foster brother matter. He was proud to share Gabriel's surname and claim his kinship.

Alphus had suffered greatly from the news of Gabriel's agonizing death. In one night he had aged a decade. Joshua was thankful that Sina, already tested so much in life by loss and suffering, was there to support Alphus and help him through his grief. Another source of support for Alphus was Cooper, who had moved into the senior Colter's home now that both Peter and Christiana Haverly were gone.

Through the wilderness slowly moved the army of some eighteen hundred men, hacking a crude road through groves and canebrakes so that the wagons at the rear could pass. They met no real resistance. Reaching the towns, they found that the Cherokees had largely abandoned them and fled into the hills. Christian burned the towns that had been loyal to Dragging Canoe and in which prisoners had been executed. Chota was spared at the pleading of Nathaniel Gist, who was sent to Christian as a spokesman for the Raven of Chota.

The older Cheorkee leaders, seeing little hope of overcoming so massive a force, were quickly ready to come to terms with the invaders. Even before Christian's forces had set out, the Lower and Middle Cherokee towns had been struck by Georgian and Carolinian forces. The headmen wanted no such devastation in the Overhill towns. A truce was established, and prisoners were turned over, among them Lydia Bean and Darcy, both of whom had been kept safely by Nancy Ward.

Joshua found upon his joyful reunion with Darcy that she had already learned from the Cherokees of what had happened to Gabriel. "I always knew there was something grand hidden in him," she said. "I even told him that. Sad it is that it showed itself only at his end."

After setting plans for peace talks to be held on the Long Island early in 1777, Christian's forces returned to Fort Patrick Henry, and from there Joshua and the others of Sevier's command returned home.

By the time they reached Colter's Station, Darcy had revealed to Joshua some startling news: She was pregnant, whether by Gabriel or her one union with Joshua she did not know.

"It makes no difference to me," Joshua said. "I would be as proud to raise Gabriel's son as I would a son of my own blood."

"Is that your way of asking me, then, to marry you, Joshua Colter?"

"Aye, Darcy, it is—if you will have me."

Have him she gladly did, and just after Christmas, Joshua made Darcy his wife, Israel Coffman conducting the ceremony, a private affair at Alphus's home—a new, larger cabin than before, for his old cabin had fallen victim to Tsula's torch.

Coffman had at first been reluctant to conduct the marriage ceremony of a couple whom he knew to have been guilty of an adulterous union; he wondered if he was violating principles he had been ordained to uphold. It was Alphus who finally convinced him that he should have no qualms.

"What's past cannot be changed," he said to the preacher. "Joshua and Darcy did wrong, no denying, but there is naught that can be done to change it now. Life must go on, and we must learn to salvage what right we can out of the wrong. There is no reason I can see that Darcy should be forced to bring her child into the world without a man to raise it—or even worse, that she should marry someone else she cares nothing for, just so her child can have a father. Gabriel himself gave his blessing on this union, and you would be wrong to deny it to them."

Coffman had thought it over. "You are a wise man, Alphus Colter."

"Not wise, by Joseph," the old long hunter replied. "Just experienced."

In the early spring of 1777, Joshua Colter, helped by the now slow-moving Alphus, young Zachariah, and Cooper Haverly, built a cabin on Gone to God Creek near the place Levi Hampton had died, and there Joshua welcomed into the world a newborn son he named William.

"After poor Will Fiske," he explained. "Will never had much and was never well known, and it seems fitting that at least his name should live on after him."

Joshua's life was happier now than it had ever been before, but the times remained difficult. From across the region came continuing reports of raids by Dragging Canoe and his followers. James Robertson and John Sevier were kept busy, leading armed bands down the trail of first one raider, then another. Of particular interest to Joshua were the swift Indian raids that were specially marked by a singular item left conspicuously at the scene—the feather of a hawk.

As spring became summer in the "year of the three sevens," Joshua journeyed to the Long Island to observe a portion of the peace talks the Cherokees had promised to Christian. Among those present were Oconostota and Little Carpenter, the latter now very slow and much quieter than before. When he saw Joshua, he rose, smiled, and came to him.

"Hello, my friend Ayunini. Are you well?"

"Very well, sir. And you?"

Little Carpenter looked sad. "These are difficult times for my people, and for me," he said. "My sons have brought me sorrow. Little Owl is dead, killed by the unakas on the flats at Long Island. And Dragging Canoe still makes war and will not know peace."

Joshua felt a sincere pity for the tired old chief. He waved his hand sweepingly, indicating the treaty ground. "Will you speak for your people here?"

"I am too old now to speak. Old Tassel will be our spokesman now."

Joshua studied the aging face he had first seen almost twenty years before. Little Carpenter was declining, both physically and politically. There was something very sad in that. Joshua was glad he had known Little Carpenter in the days when he was vigorous and swift of mind, and wielded power among the Overhills when they had yet composed a stronger nation, living their lives with pride.

Joshua remained at the talks long enough to hear Old Tassel speak, and he was glad he had. The Cherokees had been asked to cede a tremendous portion of their remaining lands, and the stout broad-faced Old Tassel's oration was a strong rejection of it, full of bite, yet also pathos.

It was no surprise, Old Tassel declared, that each time the Cherokees and white men came together to treat, the unakas' cry was ever for more land. But on what basis could the unakas claim these lands they now wanted? Not by conquest, for even now young Cherokee warriors continued to fight on those very lands and march across them, driving the whites repeatedly into their stockades. The unakas could hardly claim the land simply by merit of having marched across it, driving women and children from their houses and towns, burning fields and cabins.

Nor could the white men claim the lands by merit of law, for the white men's law was not that of the Cherokees and did not bind them. Neither had the white men always acted toward the Indians in accord with the laws they themselves recognized.

Always the whites talked of the lack of civilization among the Indians, Old Tassel continued. They pressed always for the Indians to adopt the white men's laws, customs, manners, and religion. But how could the Indians be expected to find any reason to do this while the white men themselves ignored their own doctrines and did not do that which they declared godly?

The whites, Old Tassel said, ever asked why the Indians did not till the ground and live as white men lived. Could not the Indians ask, with equal propriety, why the white men did not live as the Indians? The white men, he said, thought it no wrong to kill the deer and buffalo that were the Indians' natural cattle, but they condemned and punished any young Indian hunter who happened to kill a free-roaming hog or cow belonging to a white man.

The Indians wished no more than to be treated as the white men would themselves wish to be treated, Old Tassel declared. Pausing and looking around at the assembly, he concluded his speech with words that rang. "The great God of Nature has placed our peoples in differing circumstances," he said. "He has given you many superior advantages over us—but he has not made us to be your slaves. We are a separate people!"

Old Tassel sat down. For several moments, there was silence. Joshua looked at Little Carpenter and saw tears on his face. Ever after, this image of Little Carpenter would be the one he would most clearly remember: a lean scarred face, full of grace, even a rough, weathered beauty, lined with tears.

Joshua would hear news of Little Carpenter only once more, when the old chief would appear at Long Island later in the year with a band of young Cherokees ready to recant their British allegiance and fight on behalf of the Americans. Then, within a year or two, Little Carpenter would be dead. His status would by then be so fallen, and his nation in such disarray, that no one would even remember to record the date of the passing of the man who for much of his life had been the most influential of all the Cherokee headmen.

By the time of the peace talks on the Long Island, Dragging Canoe, John Hawk, and the peoples of the towns burned by Colonel Christian no longer numbered themselves among the Cherokees. Dragging Canoe, long recovered from the wound received at Island Flats and as vigorous as ever before, led his ragtag refugees down to ancient town sites on Chickamauga Creek where they were joined by renegade Creek Indians and even a few embittered whites, to become, in effect, a new tribe. The Chickamaugas, they were called, and they quickly came to be feared throughout the settlements.

After his secession from the Cherokee nation, John Hawk became far more vicious in his strikes against the whites. The Hawk, as most now called him, ranged for hundreds of miles in many directions, striking isolated cabins and leaving his victims scalped and marked with his identifying hawk feather, sometimes thrust into their dead hands.

Darcy Colter watched her husband brood over every new report of John Hawk's brutalities and wondered how he was feeling, knowing that the man who did these things had once been his close friend. At times she would watch in silent worry as Joshua brooded, sitting in the cabin door and staring out across the creek, fingering the Roman coin that still hung around his neck.

In October, John Hawk began striking closer to the Colters' home. Reports came that he and his warriors had been sighted along the Nolichucky, and a family on Camp Creek gave a terrifying story of having their cabin besieged by a small band of Indians whom they managed to hold off with gunfire. When the frightened family at last emerged from their cabin, they found their hounds and cattle slain and a hawk's feather thrust into the nostril of each dead animal.

Then, two days later, Callum McSwain was attacked while hunting on the Nolichucky. Though badly wounded, he managed to escape by hiding himself beneath a small waterfall, then made his way to the closest cabin, whence he sent for Joshua.

"It was John Hawk," he said. "I saw him with my own eyes. He was painted for war and had rung his belt with scalps."

Joshua felt a grim anger rising within. "I'm going after him, Callum."

"With a big militia, I hope."

"No. No militia this time. I'm going alone."

"God save us, Joshua, you canna think of doin' that!" Callum sounded very Scottish when he was agitated. "Your scalp will be the next to hang on his belt!"

"I'm not like any other white man to John Hawk. We once declared ourselves brothers. I don't believe he will have forgotten that, even yet. That's why it must be me alone who goes to him."

Joshua returned to the cabin on Gone to God Creek and gathered his rifle. He held the infant Will for a long time, hugging him close to his face and rocking him slowly from side to side. Darcy stood weeping all the while, for she feared she would see her husband no more. Joshua put the baby back into his crib, wrapped his arms around Darcy and kissed her, told her he would be gone for many days, then walked out to the log barn where his horses waited, already saddled.

Few white men had the skill to achieve what Joshua Colter did in that autumn of 1777 when he rode undetected to Chickamauga Creek and observed, from hiding, the town where John Hawk was reputed to live. He watched the Chickamaugas for three days, vainly looking for John Hawk in their number. When he was about to decide that his intelligence was wrong and John Hawk resided elsewhere, he saw the warrior come riding in, trailed by a motley but fierce-looking band of warriors.

That evening, close to sunset, Joshua captured a young Chickmauga boy who had come into the forest hunting squirrels. With the boy's throat constricted in one big hand so that he could not yell an alarm, Joshua bent close to him, and in the Cherokee language said, "Go tell John Hawk that Ayunini has wishes to talk to him. Tell him to meet me, alone, within six days, at the place where once stood the house of Awahili. And so he will be sure there is no treachery, give him this." And into the boy's hands he placed the Roman coin, hanging on its thong.

"I will take my hand from your throat now, and if you

shout, I will cut the heart out of your chest," Joshua said. "Do you understand me?"

The boy, eyes shining with fright, nodded. Joshua released him; the boy started to run away.

"Wait," Joshua said. "Sit on this log until you have counted seven hundred of your heartbeats, and then go to John Hawk. If you move before then, I will know, for I have eyes that see everywhere."

He hiked back to the place his horses were hobbled. When he was about to go out of sight of the boy, he looked back. The youth was seated on his log, hand on his heart. Joshua knew then that the boy would not run and betray him. He mounted his Chickasaw and rode, heading northeast.

The place where Tikwalitsi had once stood was now overgrown with saplings and underbrush. Joshua came to it and made his camp where Awahili's house had once been; on the earth, beneath a crust of several years of decayed leaves, he could still find the marks of its corners. It was difficult now to imagine this dismal place as the busy village it had been back in 1760.

Joshua was patient as he waited for John Hawk. He never doubted he would come. As the time for his arrival drew nearer, Joshua began spending much of his time scanning the landscape toward the southwest, from which direction he expected John Hawk to approach.

He was involved in just that activity on the brisk blue autumn day that John Hawk did arrive, but not from the southwest. He had left his horse some distance back in the forest, circled around on foot, and came in through the underbrush from the north, so that Joshua did not see him.

Joshua simply turned, and there he was, looking back at him, the Roman coin glinting against his chest.

"I could have cut your throat, Joshua Colter, before you knew the knife had touched you."

"Yes, you could have—but you would not have done it. You would not be able to bear coming this far, only to silence me and leave, never knowing what it was I wished to say to you."

John Hawk gave the faintest trace of a smile. Joshua studied his old companion with an up-and-down sweep of his eyes. John Hawk, like Joshua himself, was still a young man, not yet to his thirtieth year, but the harsh life he led was beginning to leave its marks on him. He was weathered and scarred; the wind and sun had left deep crow's-foot crevices around the corners of his dark eyes. He wore his hair in the defiant style of many warriors—shaven all around, with an enemy-taunting scalp lock at the top, well greased. On his chest were many tattoos, added since Joshua had last seen him. His muscles were leaner, more sinewy and taut, for life was harder now for Indians than in the old days.

"I was glad to learn you did not die at the hands of the Shawnees," John Hawk said.

"No Shawnee could ever best me," Joshua boasted. "I am a greater fighter than the strongest Shawnee."

Again the flicker of a smile, perhaps a little warmer this time. Nevertheless, John Hawk's eyes remained cold and remote. "You talk big talk, Ayunini." His use of "Indian" English was more than a little mocking.

"Yes. That is why I have called you here—to talk a big talk with you."

"What is this talk?"

"I have come to ask you to make peace with my people, to stop making war on us. The women and children live in terror of you."

"Not just the women and children—the men as well," John Hawk said haughtily. "Many is the unaka man who puts on a show of courage before his own but inwardly trembles at the thought of being found with his scalp and life gone, and a hawk feather in his hand."

"Are you proud of this?" Joshua asked.

"I am proud to do war against the unakas. I am proud to stand for my people when the old men have all lay down and rolled themselves over like frightened dogs."

"You talk of standing for your people. What people? You have left the Cherokees; there is bitterness between the Cherokees and the Chickamaugas."

"It isn't the Chickamaugas who have left the Cherokees, Joshua—it is in the Chickamaugas that the spirit that was once that of the Cherokees still lives. The Cherokees are like men who still walk and talk, but with their spirits gone."

"I saw Little Carpenter shed tears on Long Island as he thought of what has befallen his people. I do not believe his spirit has gone."

"Little Carpenter has spent his life trying to make peace with the destroyers. He has never learned that there can be no such peace. We must fight, or we will lose all we have, and then finally lose ourselves, as Dragging Canoe said at the Sycamore Shoals. I will fight until I am dead, and when I am dead, my son after me will fight in my place."

"You have a son, John Hawk?"

"Yes. He is the finest gift yet given to me by my wife, Ayasta."

"I did not know. I am pleased for you. I also have a wife now, and a son. I do not want my son to have to grow up fearing every sound in the forest, every whisper in the night. He has done nothing to you or your people. Why should he suffer so?"

There was no warmth in John Hawk's expression now. "When your soldiers and militiamen burned our towns and destroyed our crops, do you not believe our children, as innocent as your own son, went without food and shelter?"

Joshua began to feel frustrated. This exchange reminded him of times he had tried to argue with John Hawk, on matters both mundane and serious, back in the time of their friendship. The warrior's swift mind seemed to operate on a different basis than his; he saw the world through different eyes.

There was no point in trying further persuasion. Joshua had hoped he might be able to talk John Hawk into giving up his warfare against the settlers, but clearly this was not going to happen.

"John Hawk, if you are not willing to make peace, then let us make war, you and I, against each other."

"I am already at war against you, and all your kind."

"No, you're not," Joshua countered. "Ever since you gave me back the amulet coin and left my home, you have talked as if we were enemies, but you have given the lie to your own words by what you have done. You led me and my companions to safety that night in Chota when the kinsman of Billie were ready to kill us. You ransomed my brother from death by fire. You have never been at war against me, John Hawk—but if you try to walk away from here today to go back to butchering and scalping my people, then I will consider myself at war with you. Not with the Cherokees, not with the Chicamaugas . . . just with you. And I will show no mercy."

John Hawk's eyes flashed cold lightning. "Then it is war. I must be true to my people."

"And I must be true to mine."

John Hawk looked around him and waved his arm. "This was once a good place to live. Let us now see if it is a good place to die, Joshua Colter."

Silently, they stripped off their clothing until John Hawk wore only a breechcloth and leggins and Joshua wore only his trousers. They put aside their rifles and drew knives. Then they closed upon each other.

The fight was eerie in its silence. There were no onlookers, no one to shout or cheer or cry out in horror. There were no rules of warfare, no codes of battle— nothing but two battling men, each knowing and understanding the world of the other, and knowing equally well that those two worlds would never be joined. Like themselves, one would ultimately be overcome by the other.

For an hour they grappled, drenched first in sweat, then also in blood. The battle went on, brutally, until at last came the final mortal thrust, and the eyes of John Hawk locked with those of Joshua Colter and held. Slowly a smile spread across the warrior's face.

"So, Ayunini, it is again the unaka who prevails," he said, then collapsed, fresh blood gushing from a deep wound between his ribs.

Joshua, panting, emptied, tossed down his knife and knelt beside the bleeding warrior. "John Hawk, God help me, I don't want to see you die." Tears came. He could no

more restrain them now than he had seventeen years
before when he had knelt beside this same Cherokee on
almost this same spot of ground.

John Hawk's eyes closed, and he winced spasmodically. Joshua thought for a moment that he had suddenly
died, but then the warrior's hand raised, and so did his
head; and from around his neck he took the Roman coin.
Weakly he held it up to Joshua, and Joshua accepted it,
closing his hand around it.

"Do not leave my body to be eaten by the birds and
wolves," John Hawk said, his voice barely more than a
whisper.

"I will take your body back to Chickamauga Creek and
send it with your horse into the town. I promise you
that."

John Hawk's eyes closed more tightly; his body grew
stiff for a few moments, then relaxed. He whispered once
to himself, "Ayasta . . ." Then to Joshua, "I go."

"Yes," Joshua replied through his tears. "You do."

When the Cherokee's breath was gone and his bloodied chest was still, Joshua slipped the thong holding the
Roman coin around his own neck and walked slowly
down to the river. He felt a deep overwhelming sadness,
but even so, he knew that what had happened had been
inevitable, a turn in the river of his and John Hawk's life
that had been carved out for them long before Joshua
first gave the old Roman coin to Awahili's ailing nephew.

Or maybe there was no destiny guiding this at all, just
a series of millions of individual choices, good and bad,
that led wherever they led. Joshua did not know. Such
questions were beyond him.

Whatever the case, he found it remarkable that when
he glanced down at the Roman coin hanging against his
chest, his eyes were drawn to something that lay on the
ground before his feet. He reached down and picked it
up.

It was the wing feather of a hawk, a feather identical
to the one that John Hawk had held on that October
morning in 1760. Joshua looked at it as the breeze tried

to tug it from his hand, just as it had seventeen years ago.

He held it high above his head, and opened his fingers. The feather caught, rose, danced on the wind.

Joshua watched it until it was gone, and then he turned his back to the river. He walked slowly back to the place where Tikwalitsi had stood.

AFTERWORD

THE OVERMOUNTAIN MEN is a novel written with two goals in mind. The first and most important is to present readers an entertaining story; the second is to provide an overview, through interweaving the story's fictional aspects with abundant history, of the thrust of Tennessee's frontier development during the period depicted. History provided the framework for this novel. Where I have presented facts, I have tried to be accurate; where I have presented fiction, I have tried to be plausible, to tell a story that really could have happened within the historical framework of the time and place.

As a native Tennessean who is proud of his home region, I hope that THE OVERMOUNTAIN MEN will help spur interest in an area that is too little-known by many Americans and under-exploited by writers of both history and historical fiction. Tennessee's frontier days gave a foretaste of the subsequent frontier history of our entire nation. The drama and violence of Fort Loudoun, the early infiltrations of the traders and hunters, the continual migration westward, the individualism and sense of self-reliance exemplified in the Watauga Association, the determined and often ruthless wresting of the land itself from its native inhabitants—all these things and others anticipated the flow of our nation's settlement and development for more than a century thereafter.

For the sake of readers who like to know what is historical and what is fictional in the novels they read, some explanations are needed. Most of the central characters—such as the Byrum, Cox, Colter, Hampton, and Fiske families, Israel Coffman, John Hawk, Bloody Eagle, Henry Dorey, and Callum McSwain—are fictional, though many of the situations in which they find themselves actually occurred or are based on events that actually occurred, and many of the characters with whom they interact really existed in the roles and contexts described. Further, some of the story's fictitious characters play roles partially borrowed from other, historic figures. The Jack Byrum character, for example, is partly based on a Carolina trader, named Elliott, who conveyed cannon from Fort Prince George to Fort Loudoun in the manner described. Israel Coffman has a background (though not, I believe, a personality) closely paralleling that of the historic Tennessee frontier preacher-educator Samuel Doak. Peter Haverly, in one of his several aspects, is representative of several throughout the frontier who viewed native Americans as beings to be despised and overcome at any cost.

Other characters, major and minor, have been extrapolated and interpreted directly from history. These include Little Carpenter, Nancy Ward, Dragging Canoe, Oconostota, John and Henry Stuart, Daniel Boone and family, James and Charles Robertson, the Shelbys, Jacob Brown, William and Lydia Bean, the Seviers, Richard Henderson, Alexander Cameron, Nathaniel Gist, Isaac Crabtree, William Russell and sons, plus many others

who make brief appearances throughout the story. As
the saga that begins in THE OVERMOUNTAIN MEN
continues in future books, several of those named above
will continue to be important characters, and some of
those who play minor roles here will play more major
ones.

The waterways, mountains, valleys, gaps, towns, and
settlements named in the book are historical, with four
exceptions, each of which were made so as not to allow
the necessities of plot development to lead to the over-
fictionalizing of actual locales. Though there were at
various times at least three towns or villages called Tikwalitsi in the Cherokee country, none of them should be
identified with the Tikwalitsi of my story, a fictional
village which I have placed near the sites of the historic
Fort Loudoun and nearby Tuskegee, in what is today
Monroe County, Tennessee. Hankins Creek is a fictional
rill that I have placed along North Carolina's South Fork
Yadkin River; the residences associated with it, and the
Thomas Colter trading post, are also fictional. Gone to
God Creek, similarly, is a created stream that I have
placed in the area between Camp Creek and Horse Creek
in what is now Greene County, Tennessee. The settlement area leased in the story by Peter Haverly and called
first Haverly Fort, then Colter's Fort, was in actuality a
section of the lands Jacob Brown purchased from the
Cherokees. Brown became an important vendor of lands
to early settlers. Haverly Fort itself I have placed in the
vicinity of a site upon which an actual frontier fort,
Henderson's Station, was built along Sinking Creek in
the late 1770s. The area is now part of the Afton community in modern-day Greene County.

Other locales mentioned in the book are authentic,
and beyond involving my fictitious characters in their
history, I have tried to remain as true to their facts as
possible. In a few necessary cases I have taken liberties
with progressions and timing of events (as in the time of
arrival of the cannon at Fort Loudoun, and some of the
developments of 1772), but this has been minimal.

Some explanation of the novel's device of the Roman

coin may be of interest. Such a coin was actually found on the Elk River in 1818, where Fayetteville, Tennessee, is now located. Other similar coins have also been found in Tennessee. According to Tennessee historian Samuel Cole Williams, the Elk River coin was probably issued in A.D. 140, in Roman-invaded Wales. Williams speculates that the coin might have been lost by one of the followers of Spanish explorer Hernando De Soto in his journeys through the region in the 16th century. But he also notes references made in ancient Welsh ballads to a Prince Madoc ap Owen Guyneth who, according to tradition, sailed west from Wales and discovered an unknown land sometime after the year 1190. Williams speculates that Madoc's men might have brought the coin with them to ancient America.

Particularly intriguing in this context is an old Cherokee tradition, also cited by Williams, of white-skinned residents who reportedly already resided in what is now the lower portion East Tennessee when the Cherokees came to the region. Also of interest is a letter written by John Sevier in 1810 to a Major Amos Stoddard, in which Sevier recounts a 1782 conversation he held with the Cherokee war chief Oconostota. In that discussion, prompted by Sevier's observance of ancient fortifications, the then-aged chief described legends, handed down to him by his own father and grandfather, of an ancient white regional populace, called the Welsh, who were said to have "crossed the Great Water" and settled in the Indian country. Oconostota also told Sevier of an ancient and tattered book he said had been given to an old Cherokee woman by an Indian purportedly of the "Welsh tribe," which was said to live at that time "high up the Missouri." A fire that burned the woman's house and possessions robbed Sevier of the chance to examine the book for himself and possibly determine its origin.

In the same letter, Sevier recalled a conversation with a French trader who had lived among the Cherokees and who claimed to have personally traded with the "Welsh tribe." This "tribe," he declared, still spoke in a Welsh dialect, claimed descent from white forebears, included many "fair and white" females in its number, and possessed "small scraps of old books" that were too tattered to be legible.

I possess no authority to evaluate such questions as the authenticity of the "Welsh tribe," and I am aware of those historians who deride the idea. Nonetheless, I am enough of a romantic to find the possibility intriguing and appealing. The past hides many mysteries; we should not be too adamant in saying what could and could not have occurred.

I cannot close this afterword without expressing thanks to some who have contributed to this novel in various ways. First thanks go to Gregory Tobin, senior editor at Bantam Books. It's my hope that THE OVER-MOUNTAIN MEN provides Greg a sense of tangible justification for the tremendous faith he has repeatedly invested in me over the past dozen years. Appreciation also goes to the ever-helpful Meg McNally of Bantam's editorial staff, and to all those at Bantam who are involved in editing, producing, promoting, and selling my books.

Thanks are due to Richard Curtis for being a fine literary agent, teacher, counselor, and encourager—not to mention an enthusiastic Manhattan tour guide. Associating with Richard's agency is one of the many strokes of good fortune that have come my way professionally.

Special thanks go to my friend Jim Brown, of the U.S. Forest Service, for providing helpful information on the East Tennessee forests of two centuries ago.

I also express appreciation for those descendants of the original Overmountain people who have preserved and shared family stories and traditions that have bolstered this novel and will continue to be of value in similar books yet to come, and to all who have supported or encouraged this effort in any way.

Lastly, I especially thank my wife, Rhonda. She has been remarkably patient with me as I have piled up the house with books, maps, papers, and stacks of manuscript, and as I have interrupted many conversations in the car to excitedly point out sites where long hunters once camped, or forts once stood. She and the children are the ones who make all my work worthwhile.

CAMERON JUDD
Greene County, Tennessee
August, 1990

CAMERON JUDD

Writing with power, authority, and respect for America's frontier traditions, Cameron Judd captures the spirit of adventure and promise of the wild frontier in his fast-paced, exciting novels. In the tradition of Max Brand and Luke Short, Cameron Judd is a new voice of the Old West.

☐	27897-5	**TIMBER CREEK**	$3.50
☐	27405-8	**BITTERROOT**	$2.95
☐	28149-6	**JERUSALEM CAMP**	$3.50
☐	28204-2	**CORRIGAN**	$2.95
☐	28244-1	**CAINE'S TRIAL**	$3.50
☐	28258-1	**BAD NIGHT AT DRY CREEK**	$3.50
☐	28341-3	**THE TREASURE OF JERICHO MOUNTAIN**	$2.95
☐	28476-2	**MR. LITTLEJOHN**	$3.50
☐	28591-2	**BEGGAR'S GULCH**	$2.95
☐	28800-8	**SNOW SKY**	$3.50

Bantam Books, Dept. CJ, 414 East Golf Road, Des Plaines, IL 60016

Please send me the items I have checked above. I am enclosing $_____ (please add $2.50 to cover postage and handling). Send check or money order, no cash or C.O.D.s please.

Mr/Ms _____

Address _____

City/State_____ Zip_____

CJ—7/91

Please allow four to six weeks for delivery.
Prices and availability subject to change without notice.

A Proud People In a Harsh Land

THE SPANISH BIT SAGA

Set on the Great Plains of America in the early 16th century, Don Coldsmith's acclaimed series recreates a time, a place and a people that have been nearly lost to history. With the advent of the Spaniards, the horse culture came to the people of the Plains. Here is history in the making through the eyes of the proud Native Americans who lived it.

☐	BOOK 1: TRAIL OF THE SPANISH BIT	26397-8	$3.50
☐	BOOK 2: THE ELK-DOG HERITAGE	26412-5	$3.50
☐	BOOK 3: FOLLOW THE WIND	26806-6	$3.50
☐	BOOK 4: BUFFALO MEDICINE	26938-0	$3.50
☐	BOOK 5: MAN OF THE SHADOWS	27067-2	$3.50
☐	BOOK 6: DAUGHTER OF THE EAGLE	27209-8	$3.50
☐	BOOK 7: MOON OF THE THUNDER	27344-2	$3.50
☐	BOOK 8: SACRED HILLS	27460-0	$3.50
☐	BOOK 9: PALE STAR	27604-2	$3.50
☐	BOOK 10: RIVER OF SWANS	27708-1	$3.50
☐	BOOK 11: RETURN TO THE RIVER	28163-1	$3.50
☐	BOOK 12: THE MEDICINE KNIFE	28318-9	$3.50
☐	BOOK 13: THE FLOWER IN THE MOUNTAINS	28538-6	$3.50
☐	BOOK 14: TRAIL FROM TAOS	28760-5	$3.50
☐	SUPER: THE CHANGING WIND	28334-0	$3.95

Bantam Books, Dept. LE10, 414 East Golf Road, Des Plaines, IL 60016

Please send me the items I have checked above. I am enclosing $_____ (please add $2.50 to cover postage and handling). Send check or money order, no cash or C.O.D.s please.

Mr/Ms _____

Address _____

City/State _____ Zip _____

LE10-7/91

Please allow four to six weeks for delivery.
Prices and availability subject to change without notice.

In The Tradition of *Wagons West* and *The Spanish Bit Saga* Comes:

RIVERS WEST

☐ 27401-5 **The Yellowstone #1**
Winfred Blevins $4.50

☐ 28012-0 **Smokey Hill #2**
Don Coldsmith $4.50

☐ 28451-7 **The Colorado #3**
Gary McCarthy $4.50

☐ 28538-1 **The Powder River #4**
Winfred Blevins $4.50

☐ 28844-X **The Russian River #5**
Gary McCarthy $4.50

Buy them at your local bookstore or use this handy page for ordering:

Bantam Books, Dept. RW, 414 East Golf Road, Des Plaines, IL 60016

Please send me the items I have checked above. I am enclosing $_____
(please add $2.50 to cover postage and handling). Send check or money
order, no cash or C.O.D.s please.

Mr/Ms _____

Address _____

City/State _____ Zip _____

RW–6/91

Please allow four to six weeks for delivery.
Prices and availability subject to change without notice.